DREAD THE FED
A NOVEL

*To Lee,
Beware the tentacles
of the Fed!
Salt & Light
Frank Amoroso*

FRANK AMOROSO

simply francis publishing company
North Carolina

Dread the Fed
Copyright © 2015 by Frank Amoroso. All Rights Reserved.
No part of this publication may be reproduced, stored in a retrieval system or transmitted, in any form or by any means – electronic, mechanical, photocopying, recording or otherwise – without prior written permission from the publisher, except for the inclusion of brief quotations in a review.

All brand, product and place names used in this book that are trademarks, service marks, registered trademarks, or trade names are the exclusive intellectual property of their respective holders and are mentioned here as a matter of fair and nominative use. To avoid confusion, simply francis publishing, inc. publishes books solely and is not affiliated with the holder of any mark mentioned in this book.

This book is historical fiction. Any references to historical events, real people or real places are used fictitiously or metaphorically. Other names, characters, places, and events are products of the author's imagination, and any resemblance to actual events or places or persons, living or dead, is entirely coincidental.

For information about this title or to order other books and/or electronic media, contact the publisher:

simply francis publishing company
P.O. Box 329, Wrightsville Beach, NC 28480
www.simplyfrancispublishingcompany.com
simplyfrancispublishing@gmail.com

Library of Congress Control Number: 2015917394
ISBN: 978-1-63062-004-2 (paperback)
ISBN: 978-1-63062-005-9 (e-book)
Printed in the United States of America
Cover and Interior design: Christy King Meares

Publisher's Cataloging-in-Publication

Amoroso, Frank L., author.
   Dread the Fed : a novel / Frank Amoroso.
   pages cm
   ISBN 978-1-63062-004-2 (paperback)
   ISBN 978-1-63062-005-9 (ebook)

   1. Federal Reserve banks--Fiction. 2. Financial crises--History--20th century--Fiction. 3. Depressions--1907--Fiction. 4. Lindbergh, Charles A. (Charles August), 1859-1924--Fiction--Fiction. 5. Aldrich, Nelson W. (Nelson Wilmarth), 1841-1915--Fiction. 6. Warburg, Paul M. (Paul Moritz), 1868-1932--Fiction. 7. Historical fiction. 8. Thrillers (Fiction)
   I. Prequel to: Amoroso, Frank L. Behind every great fortune. II. Title.

PS3601.M668D74 2015   813'.6
                          QBI15-600202

Dedication

To my mother Rose whose boundless love
and belief in me helped
make me the person that I am

Dread the Fed is a prequel to **Behind Every Great Fortune®,** another book written by Frank Amoroso that delves into the human passions, fervor and frailties involved in the accumulation of great fortunes.

Excerpts from reviews of Mr. Amoroso's prior historical novel:
Behind Every Fortune® . . . captures in exquisite detail the political intrigue of the early 20th century. . . . Incorporating glimpses into Kahn's opulent and secretively hedonistic lifestyle, Amoroso brings to life the "monopoly man" through his well written prose and extensive historical research.

$ $ $

Behind Every Great Fortune® is an entertaining story which successfully and seamlessly interweaves fact and fiction. The action passages are exciting and believable. . . .

$ $ $

The characters in *Behind Every Great Fortune®* include Otto Kahn, the main character, Czar Nicholas and his family, Teddy Roosevelt, Margaret Sanger, Trotsky, Lenin and others. Mr. Amoroso mixes fact with fiction in this very interesting saga . . . . There is intrigue and plots and sub-plots all expertly interwoven into one fascinating story. And let's not forget the sex scenes which also add to the enjoyment of the characters.

$ $ $

Readers who enjoy sumptuously detailed, intricately plotted historical novels will find much to enjoy in this meticulously researched and boldly imaginative novel. *Behind Every Great Fortune®* takes the reader on a wild ride through board rooms, throne rooms and bedrooms of a large cast of intriguing characters from the early 20th Century.

Top 7 Reasons to Dread the Fed

It is comprised of privately-owned, locally-controlled corporations and has the power to print money from nothing.

It controls the money supply and interest rates.

Its Federal Reserve Notes are legal tender for 'all debts, public charges, taxes, and dues,' and are obligations of the U.S. taxpayer.

It is exempt from Federal, State, and local taxation, except for real estate taxes.

It is the fiscal agent of the U.S. Treasury and the Nation's banks, and receives interest on the national debt which is used, *inter alia*, to pay all its expenses.

It guarantees member banks a dividend of 6% on stock investments in the Fed and the payment of interest on required reserves.

It has its own police force with the same police authority as federal law enforcement agencies and has access to the Nation's crime databases.

CAST OF CHARACTERS

(in order of appearance)

C. A. Lindbergh, Sr. – five time Minnesota Congressman and crusader against the Money Trust. Father of the famous aviator, Charles A. Lindbergh, Jr.

August Lindbergh - born Ola Mansson in Sweden. A member of the Swedish *Riksdag*, legislature, for twelve years until he was accused of scandal and immigrated to Minnesota with his mistress and infant son.

Samuel Wurthels – real estate developer and business partner of C.A. Lindbergh.

Jockety "Jock" Pierz, a farmer and client of C.A. Lindbergh. Nephew of Father Francis Pierz who helped save Little Falls from the rampaging renegade tribe led by Chief Hole-in-the-Day during the Dakota Wars in '62.

Evangeline Land Lindbergh – second wife of C.A. Lindbergh, mother of Charles A. Lindbergh, Jr.

Mary Lafond Lindbergh – first wife of C.A. Lindbergh, mother of his daughters, Lillian and Eva.

Charles "Big Charley" Weyerhaeuser – son of Friedrich Weyerhaeuser. The Weyerhaeusers owned forests, saw mills, dams, boom areas, sorting facilities, mills factories, water power structures, warehouses, and storage areas.

Hiram Walker – Canadian whisky distilled in wood barrels to "create colour" and a smooth taste.

Blake – C.A. Lindbergh's Labrador Retreiver named after English poet, William Blake who wrote *Songs of Innocence & Experience*.

Norbert Hyatt – Commander of the veterans who served in Company D of the First Minnesota Infantry of the Union Army and original Clearwater Guard.

Clarence Bennett Buckman – Congressman for Minnesota's 6th District.

Carrie Jorgens Fosseen – wife of Manley Lewis Fosseen, member, Executive

Committee of the Hennepin County Republican Party.

Elisha Sharlette – consort of disgraced mayor of Minneapolis, Dr. Alonso Ames.

Otto Hermann Kahn - partner in the banking house of Kuhn Loeb & Company and chairman of the Metropolitan Opera.

J. Pierpont Morgan - the fabled head of J.P. Morgan & Company, known as the Zeus of Wall Street.

Paul Warburg – partner in the banking house of Kuhn Loeb & Co.

Elisabeth "Bessy" Marbury - literary and theatrical agent.

Elsie de Wolfe- former actress who made her mark as a pioneer in interior design.

L. Frank Baum – writer of *The Wonderful Wizard of Oz*.

Joeseph "Uncle Joe" Cannon – legendary Speaker of the U.S. House of Representatives.

Senator Nelson W. Aldrich - Republican, chairman of the Senate Banking and Currency committee.

Anne Tracy – New York City socialite, philanthropist, and intellectual.

James E. Watson – four-term representative from Indiana, the Republican Whip under Speaker Cannon.

Charles T. Barney –president of the Knickerbocker Trust whose attempt to corner the market of United Copper helped precipitate the Panic of 1907.

President Theodore Roosevelt - the 26th and youngest Presidentin the Nation's history. He was an avid hunter and conservationist. Roosevelt was known as the Trust Buster on account of his challenge to the Northern Securities Company, a railroad holding company organized by financier J.P. Morgan and his actions to dissolve other business monopolies.

Mammon Mob – a.k.a. the First-Name Club, for their secretive use of first names only to avoid detection. A group of bankers and public officials who, under the pretense of duck hunting, participated in a secret conference on Jekyll Island, Georgia in November, 1910 to draft the Federal Reserve Act. Despite extraordinary secrecy, the following men may have been involved: Nelson Aldrich, Senator from Rhode Island and chairman of the Senate Banking and Currency committee and the National Monetary Commission; Abram Piatt Andrew, Assistant Secretary of the Treasury after a stint as Director of the U.S. Mint; Henry "Harry" Pomeroy Davison, a J.P. Morgan & Co. partner; Otto Hermann Kahn, Kuhn Loeb partner and chairman of the Metropolitan Opera; Benjamin Strong, Jr., a vice president at the Bankers Trust Company and future governor of the Federal Reserve Bank; Frank Vanderlip, president of the National City Bank of New York; Paul Warburg, Kuhn Loeb partner and future governor of the Federal Reserve Bank.

David Graham Phillips – muckraking journalist and novelist, who published a scathing exposè, entitled *The Treason of the Senate*, which attacked the corrupt practices of Senator Nelson Aldrich and provided the impetus for the 17th Amendment.

Prince Felix Yusopov - Heir to the largest fortune in Russia.

Glossary

Mammon – greed or debasing wealth, the devil of avarice, one of the seven princes of hell. "You cannot serve God and Mammon." Matt: 6:24

Money Trust - concentration and control of money in the hands of a few influential financial leaders who exerted powerful control over the nation's finances.

National Citizens' League for the Promotion of a Sound Banking System – organization conceived by Paul Warburg, to promote banking and monetary reform. Headquartered in Chicago to avoid stigma of New York banking interests.

National Monetary Commission – legislative commission established in the wake of the Panic of 1907 to study the banking laws of the United States, and the leading countries of Europe under the leadership of Republican Senator Nelson W. Aldrich.

Pujo Committee - a special subcommittee of the House Banking and Currency Committee led by Arsene P. Pujo to investigate the Money Trust.

Rennen von Blut, the 'Race of Blood,' is a high-stakes gambling match, based on the French card game called *Trente et Quarante*, Thirty and Forty, basically, a combination of Black Jack and roulette.

Glossary

Mammon – greed or debasing wealth, the devil of avarice, one of the seven princes of hell. "You cannot serve God and Mammon." Matt: 6:24

Money Trust - concentration and control of money in the hands of a few influential financial leaders who exerted powerful control over the nation's finances.

National Citizens' League for the Promotion of a Sound Banking System – organization conceived by Paul Warburg, to promote banking and monetary reform. Headquartered in Chicago to avoid stigma of New York banking interests.

National Monetary Commission – legislative commission established in the wake of the Panic of 1907 to study the banking laws of the United States, and the leading countries of Europe under the leadership of Republican Senator Nelson W. Aldrich.

Pujo Committee - a special subcommittee of the House Banking and Currency Committee led by Arsene P. Pujo to investigate the Money Trust.

Rennen von Blut, the 'Race of Blood,' is a high-stakes gambling match, based on the French card game called *Trente et Quarante*, Thirty and Forty, basically, a combination of Black Jack and roulette.

Foreword

It is well enough that the people of this nation do not understand our banking and monetary system, for if they did, I believe there would be a revolution before tomorrow morning.
~ Henry Ford

Contrary to widespread belief, the Federal Reserve Bank is not an agency of the government. The Federal Reserve Bank is a cartel of private banks that creates money out of nothing and profits obscenely at the expense of the taxpayer. For more than a century, the Federal Reserve Bank has successfully engaged in the most astounding sleight of hand and kept this simple truth concealed. *Dread the Fed* is a book that novelizes how the Federal Reserve was conceived in iniquity and born in sin.

In the early 20th century, there was an epic battle for control over the money of the United States. This struggle was, for the most part, clandestine and cleverly disguised by the Money Trust so that the people would not know that their sovereign power over the monetary system was being stolen.

One man, C. A. Lindbergh, Sr., recognized the true nature of the Federal Reserve Bank and sacrificed everything a man holds dear, to oppose the brazen effort by the Money Trust. Although the name Charles Lindbergh evokes images of the intrepid aviator who revolutionized flight, this book is about his father, Charles Lindbergh, Sr., a five-term Congressman from Minnesota.

Dread the Fed chronicles his quest to save the dollar from the diabolical clutches of the Money Trust. Much like Don Quixote, Lindbergh fights the unbeatable foe with an indomitable spirit and similar results.

Although Lindbergh believed that the economy was controlled by a small group known as the Money Trust who manipulated monetary system, others denied the existence of the Money Trust. At great personal risk, Representative Lindbergh proved that the Money Trust existed. Due to his insistence, Congress declared that there was ". . . *a vast and growing concentration of control of money and credit in the hands of comparatively few men . . . .¹*"

However, that was just the beginning.

In perhaps the most lopsided conflict since David took on Goliath, Lindbergh opposes the most powerful men on earth as they attempt to commit the perfect crime. The small town lawyer from rural Minnesota, combats powerful men like J. Pierpont Morgan, President Theodore Roosevelt, Otto Hermann Kahn, Senator Nelson Aldrich, Paul Warburg, and a mysterious stranger nicknamed Nitro. Their weapons of choice are fire, bribery, bullets, propaganda and poison. Despite a tumultuous marriage and an enigmatic relationship with a New York socialite, Lindbergh perserveres against treachery, deceit, suicide and secret meetings.

For more than a hundred years, the Fed has kept its true nature hidden in plain view. It has used the complexity of the monetary system to disguise or obfuscate the truth. Revelatory of the sleight of hand performed by the Fed is a statement made by then-chairman Alan Greenspan during testimony to the U.S. Congress. When one of the legislators remarked that he understood Greenspan's testimony, the inscrutable Greenspan famously replied, "If you understood what I said, then I must have misspoken."

Dread the Fed attempts to lift the shroud of secrecy by using the drama of story-telling and the tools of historical fiction. The basic facts related in *Dread the Fed* are historically accurate. The issues of a century ago should resonate with protestors today who complain about the inordinate power of the 1%. Not much has changed in the last hundred years.

Before entering the labyrinth of our protagonist's life, the reader should know that prior to writing this book, I received a literary license to imagine, speculate, and create scenarios that may or may not have occurred, but that are within the realm of possibility. Many of the characters are based on real persons. Some of the characters are fictitious; others are used fictitiously. There are relationships, conversations and timing that have been created or connected for dramatic effect to enhance the impact of the story. None of these artifacts negate the essence of the drama surrounding the origins of the Federal Reserve Bank. When the actual words of an historical figure appear, they are italicized and referenced in the endnotes.

It is my sincere hope that *Dread the Fed* will teach valuable historic information, provide insight into the unique stranglehold the Fed has on the economy, and will inspire readers to delve more deeply into the complex nature of money and who controls the dollar.

To those who would say that the Fed has evolved to become a benign, indispensable part of the 21st century global economy, I would suggest that, at the very least, the Fed is an opaque enigma. Whether the Fed today is a government/private hybrid or mutant is for the people to decide.

I leave you to enjoy *Dread the Fed* with the words of the Apostle Luke:

> There is nothing concealed that will not be revealed, nor secret that will not be known. Therefore whatever you have said in darkness will be heard in the light, and what you have whispered behind closed doors will be proclaimed on the housetops.
> Luke 12: 2-3

Happy reading,
Frank Amoroso,
Wilmington, North Carolina
2015

Opening
NYC 1910

It's amazing how much you can learn about a person when you follow them around for a week. She had been assigned to tail the Congressman from Minnesota during his stay in New York City. Her mistress, Lady Anne, as she called her, had instructed her to learn if he had any unsavory habits. "This man is a great danger to my father. I need to know where he goes and what his weaknesses are. You are my little street urchin. You are street smart; you know how to handle yourself."

He was a tall fellow in his forties whose lean build was, no doubt, the result of his penchant for walking. Much to the dismay of her tender feet, she learned of his fondness for walking on the first day of her assignment. He rode the City's splendid underground train system only as a last resort. He favored Manhattan's filthy streets, often tramping through mud or slush or worse. By the end of the day her dogs were barking. From that day forward, she wore sturdy boots.

Even though he rarely did the same thing two days in a row, he did have a routine. He left the Waldorf Astoria Hotel every morning at 7:30 A. M. and walked to Grand Central Station where he ordered a bagel and a cup of coffee, no cream, no sugar. He ate standing up while he watched the crowds stream into Manhattan like so many ants. He would then do his research, alternating between the Astor in lower Manhattan or the Lenox library on the Upper East Side.

When Lady Anne gave her this task, the girl had imagined daring adventures; trailing the mark from a dangerous rendezvous on the waterfront, to a soiree at a private club in the Silk Stocking District, to an illegitimate gambling parlor in Greenwich Village. The reality was quite the opposite. On most days, she was so bored that she would have traded places with prisoners in solitary confinement. On more than one occasion, she fell asleep within eyesight of him while she pretended to read a tome that was the size of a breadbox. All that was about to change.

The day was bitter cold. She loitered in the lobby of the Waldorf and overheard the Congressman asking the clerk to arrange for transportation that evening. He advised him that he would be spending the day at the New York Clearing House. With this advance knowledge of his destination, she lingered behind more than usual as she followed him to the Association's building on Cedar Street between Broadway and Nassau Street.

At first, she thought nothing of a man in a black Stetson who walked twenty yards behind the Congressman. But the seeming coincidence continued into Grand Central Station, paused during the coffee and bagel break and recommenced when the Congressman boarded the IRT line heading downtown. After the Congressman exited the subway, the man in the Stetson repeated every move the Congressman made as he weaved through traffic and dodged trolley cars.

Having followed the Congressman for about a week, she had developed a proprietary interest in him. She resented the stranger's intrusion into her domain. Her mood darkened with each passing block. The Congressman was oblivious to the drama forming behind him. He walked in his brisk fashion, his leather briefcase swinging in cadence with his gait.

The Congressman consulted a paper from his coat pocket and walked directly to the New York Clearing House on Cedar Street. It was the oldest and largest bank clearing house in the country. This temple of commerce had been completed a decade earlier. When the cornerstone was laid in 1894, the *New York Times* reported, *"The new building will be four stories high, 96 feet long and of substantial and attractive architecture. It will have a marble front and a sweeping dome. Strongly built vaults will occupy the basement.*²*"* The elaborate Renaissance Revival building was truly a temple to Mammon, the devil of covetousness, greed, and money.

She slowed and blended into a vestibule of the building opposite the Clearing House. She figured that he would be inside for several hours if her quarry's past behavior was predictive. As an un-credentialed woman, she was unable to follow the Congressman into the building. She stationed herself in a coffee shop across the street where she viewed the entrance.

From a table by the window she sipped her coffee and watched with interest as the man in the black Stetson spoke with some workmen who were working on the building. They were assembling scaffolding in the front of the building, adjacent to the entranceway. The man in the black Stetson gestured toward the coffee shop and walked to it. She averted her gaze, pretending to fuss with the contents of her purse. He sat at the counter and ordered breakfast.

She loosened her coat and settled in for what might be a long wait. She pretended to read a newspaper while she puzzled over the black Stetson. What might he mean to her assignment? After an hour or so, the cups of coffee she had consumed had their natural effect. When she returned from the ladies room, the black Stetson was gone. Panicked, her eyes swept across the coffee shop. Nothing.

She stared through the front glass. Through the condensation, she watched the figures of the men now working on the scaffolding. One scraped around the edges of the window frames on the second floor adjacent to the entrance. The other was on the ground securing a large, thin flat object that was wrapped in some kind of cloth. He loaded the object onto a sling and hoisted it up the scaffold where he unwrapped it. The large pane of glass caught the sun, sending a ray of light that nearly blinded her. Her hand reflexively shielded her eyes.

She started at the noise of a door closing behind her. She was so engrossed in watching the workmen that she had forgotten the black Stetson. He emerged from the men's lavatory adjusting his trousers. Straining to see him from the corner of her eye, she saw him pay his bill and gather his belongings. A small notebook fell from his coat pocket. Olivia turned to see him bend to pick it up. Something dark and black swung from under his armpit. She brought the tips of her fingers to her lips to stifle a gasp. He was armed.

When her gaze lifted, she saw him looking at her. With her loveliest ingénue smile, she returned his look. A look of wariness flickered behind his eyes, he shook his head and his clean shaven face turned into a placid mask. He nodded to her and touched the brim of the black Stetson. She would report to Lady Anne later that his eyes were cold, silent, and deadly like predators she had seen at the aquarium. She watched him check his watch and talk to the workmen again.

It was nearly noon. If she knew anything about the Congressman, she knew that he was punctual and would be emerging from the building shortly. A moment of panic gripped her as she searched for the black Stetson. Then, she saw him stationed within eyesight of the workmen and the entranceway. There was a flash of steel. One of the workmen wielded a knife. The Congressman would soon be walking directly under the heavy glass poised over the entrance.

She told herself to be calm. She knew what she had to do. She raced out of the coffee shop, reaching into her blue winter coat. Behind her she heard the shopkeeper shouting, "Miss, Miss, your bill!"

The black Stetson looked at her with a perplexed expression, then, at the man with the knife. He was reaching toward the rope above the glass. She fingered a smooth round marble and loaded her weapon. She watched as the Congressman emerged and the black Stetson signaled to the man on the scaffold. Fighting the urge to scream a warning, she set her feet and aimed her slingshot. A slight gust of wind twisted the glass flush toward her. She pulled back as far as she could and unleashed the marble.

A sharp reflection of light glinted off the catseye as it raced across the street at the exact instant the workman cut the rope that released the glass. The heavy pane fell toward the Congressman. The sound of glass hitting glass was followed by a shattering sound. The pane exploded into a rain of pieces. At the sound the Congressman covered his head with his briefcase. The shattered glass fell harmlessly on to the sidewalk.

The black Stetson glared at her with a look that could best be described as astonished hatred. The workman, a sheepish look on his face, held his hands out palms up in a gesture of embarrassed apology. With an unfocused gaze, the Congressman looked toward her, then up toward the workman, then to his feet. He was surrounded by broken glass. His eyes fixed on something. He bent and picked up a catseye marble and put it into his pocket. When he straightened and looked across the street, the girl in the blue coat was gone. He was not quite sure what had just happened, but he knew that his young son would love the marble.

PART ONE
Start

June 1906 Little Falls, MN

**The world is not charitable. It is unjustly critical,
and we have to take notice of things as they are
and not assume that it is sufficient to be right alone.**
~ C.A. Lindbergh

A glimmer of pre-dawn light flickered off the black surface of the water. With his shotgun broken and cradled in his elbow, C.A. squinted through the steam rising from his tin cup. He had no idea that the events of the day would change his life forever.

His thoughts drifted to a time long ago in 1871. He was traveling in an ox-drawn wagon with his father heading toward Little Falls, Minnesota to buy supplies for the upcoming harvest.

"Why America?" asked the 10 year old boy.

"What?" said the father, looking into the blue eyes of his son.

"Papa, you left Sweden when you were fifty-one years old. Why did you choose America?"

"In Sweden, everywhere there were limits. There were always limits from the government, from the church, from family – limits on what a man could do or say; limits on what a man could earn. And, if you questioned those limits, or if you tried to go beyond them, they pulled you back. They stopped you. But, here in America, there are no limits," said August Lindbergh.

The sun barely shone through the thick, pine forest on a long, low ridge overlooking the Mississippi River. The boy inhaled the fragrant smell of pine coming from a nearby logging camp. They could hear the occasional cry of "Timm-berrr," followed by a crashing thud. The sound of axes felling and limbing trees reverberated through the forest.

"I don't understand. How can the government tell you what to do?"

"Well, son, that's a very interesting question." With his strong right arm he pulled the reins and the wagon stopped.

Pointing toward a stretch of pineries and waterways that extended as far as they could see, August Lindbergh said, "C.A., just take in this view. When we are in town, or on the farm working, it's easy to forget that God created all this wonder and beauty. Out here, it's easy to believe that God is in control; that man is puny with his hopes and dreams. Just think of the last time you were in a thunderstorm. Did you think that the government could stop it? God laughs at man and his government."

August leaned back in his seat and pulled out a pipe, and, while balancing it in his lap, stuffed it with some "tobakky" as he liked to call it in his mock American accent. With practiced ease, he struck a match and puffed rapidly on the pipe.

C.A. looked up at his father. The left sleeve of his shirt was pinned to the shoulder. The boy could barely make out the outline of the stump that was what remained of his father's left arm.

August drew on his pipe and continued, "But that does not stop the government from trying. Oh, no. They want to tell you how you should do things because they think they are smarter than folks. Well, let me tell you, the average person is smarter than a whole passel of them government men. Part of the problem is that people are too busy working for their daily bread to know all about the mischief that the government is up to. But, do you know what the real problem is?"

Of course, the question was rhetorical, but C.A. struggled for an answer. After a pause, his father answered his own question. "The real problem is man himself. Man is by nature flawed and fallen. Never underestimate man's capacity for greed, deceit, and evil."

"Are you with us, C.A.? You sure seem far away," chided Sam Wurthels.

"I was just thinking of my father and how he struggled after the accident. But, he never gave up. He was determined to carry his weight, regardless of the odds. And, he did. He managed to run that farm and support his family 'til the day he died. That spirit of independence and self-reliance is what makes this country great, don't you think?"

Sam greatly admired his partner. He was a brilliant lawyer and astute businessman. Yet, Sam wished that Lindbergh would turn off his mind every once in a while and enjoy the experience. The two men sat in a camouflaged blind, along the Crow Wing River, a tributary of the Mississippi bordered by a marsh. It was a perfect feeding area for the wild ducks that were heading down from Canada.

"I'll tell you what I think. I think that our buddy Jock sure knows how to build a duck blind. When those greenheads come flying across this marsh, we'll have some real, nice sightlines," said Sam.

Sam Wurthels sipped his coffee and glanced at his friend. C.A. Lindbergh was a trim, athletic man in his forties. He had a full head of light brown hair. With his glacier blue eyes and fair complexion, he was the model son of the Swedes who immigrated in the last century to the Upper Midwest. The two men had been friends and business associates for over a dozen years. They were as close as brothers and, if it weren't for their obvious physical disparities, would have been taken as brothers. Indeed, such was their affinity for each other that many who spent time with them thought that they were actual brothers.

Their collaborations on real estate deals and construction projects had made them both wealthy. C.A. provided the legal expertise and Sam provided the business acumen. Lindbergh's intimates called him Ridge or Ridgy. Sam was not sure where the nickname originated. It was either because C.A. was rigid in his approach, or, it came from Ridgy-Didge, Australian slang for authentic, honest, upright. Regardless of the origins of the name, both fit C.A. Lindbergh to a Tee.

A flutter of wings stopped their ruminations. It was time to knock down some ducks.

BAM, splash, BAM, splash, BAM, splash.

For the next two hours, they fired at flocks of mallards. Jock's black lab, Binny, splashed into the chilly water joyfully after each kill. Jock bagged the ducks that she retrieved and encouraged Binny to get the next round. He placed the gunny sack on a small raft tied to a pine tree on the shore. Jock was Jockety Pierz, a farmer and client of C.A. Lindbergh. Jock had a well-deserved reputation as the best duck-hunting guide in Morrison County, Minnesota.

"As soon as I rearrange that string a' decoys, I'm going to rustle up some breakfast. You fellas keep at it. Binny will handle whatever you kill, eh."

Jock waded along the shore, trailing decoys behind him. The river and forest were dead silent when he was done. C.A. thought, if I were a duck, this would surely look like an enticing place to land and feed. Sam broke the silence with a duck call. And they waited.

Suddenly, the sky was filled with flapping, quacking greenheads.

"Fire at will, Ridgy," smiled Sam, reverting to military jargon. Both men scored repeatedly and Binny dutifully kept up with the braces. She was working so fast and furious that the raft rocked each time she deposited a duck. Gradually, the line holding the raft loosened.

When the barrage of shotgun fire subsided, Sam noticed that the raft was floating away from the shore. He tapped C.A. on the shoulder and gestured toward the raft that was gaining speed as it headed toward a series of rapids. If it tipped over in the rapids, all their efforts would be lost. Without a word, C.A. stripped to the waist and jumped into the frigid water. He ran knees high, through the marsh grass and then dove into the deeper water. He swam with a determined stroke until he reached the rope that trailed the raft just before it was about to tumble into the rapids.

With the rope in his mouth C.A. dog-paddled toward the shore. Binny thought it was a lovely game and swam alongside him, splashing merrily. Sam stood on the shore, laughing at the sight a retriever imitating his dignified lawyer friend. Or, was it the other way around?

Suddenly, there was a backwash of water that pushed the raft toward C.A. It struck him behind the ear and he sank beneath the water stunned. Sam watched in helpless disbelief; frozen, immobilized by the tragedy unfolding. The roar of the rapids downstream dominated the landscape. His friend was drifting toward the swifter water and the devil's tongue.

Binny, sensing C.A.'s distress, swam to him and dived. Sam found his voice and started croaking, "Help, help," as he raced along the shore. He cursed himself for never learning how to swim.

Then, he saw Binny surface with her head under C.A.'s armpit. She lifted him so that his head was above the surface. She got her bearings and swam toward the bank. They drifted toward the rapids. Sam gauged their trajectory and feared that they would be swept into the current in the middle of the river. Binny redoubled her efforts; her eyes wide and primordial.

The powerful dog surged toward the shore in a desperate effort to break free of the river. The chalky water churned white in the fury of her strokes. Sam stared incredulously. The only sound he could hear above the loudening roar of the approaching rapids was the thumping of his heart in his chest. After what felt like an eternity, Binny's legs gained purchase on the rocky bottom.

She steadied herself and dragged her charge to safety. For an interminable moment Sam watched his partner. Lindbergh's torso was ashen and, worse, immobile. A cold terror gripped Sam. He stared in disbelief, his legs trembling. Tears filled his eyes.

Binny nudged the body, whining piteously. With one last frantic push, she flipped C.A. on to his back. His hair, dark and wet, outlined his pale skin. Seeing a bluish pallor around his friend's lips made Sam turn away, his hands covering his eyes as if to erase the scene before him. How could this be? Sam staggered back toward the trees.

By this time, Jock had returned to the blind, only to find his clients missing. A surge of panic raced through him as he tried to conjure how he would explain the disappearance of two prominent businessmen on a duck hunting trip. He raced downstream shouting. He heard nothing over the din of the rushing water. Through a thicket he saw movement. It was Sam, bumbling in circles through the underbrush. Jock searched for Binny. He saw her standing over something. My God, it was Lindbergh, motionless at the river's edge.

Like a newborn experiencing his first breath, C.A. revived, snorting and shaking his head from side to side. Binny mimicked C.A., sending a shower of spray at no one and every one. Lindbergh gathered his legs under him and tottered toward Sam. As the water lapped against their feet, the color returned to both their faces. Firmly on the shore, C.A. raised the rope in mock triumph and roared. Both men laughed out of relief until they could no longer breathe.

Jock rushed to C.A., covering him with his coat.

"Let's get you men dried off, then. My cabin's not far. You can warm up in front of the fire there. Follow this path a ways and I'll get the equipment from the blind and bring the greenheads along. You dry off. There's coffee, eggs and cornbread n' budder for you, eh." Jock retreated toward the blind with exaggerated urgency.

Later that afternoon, C.A. and Sam sat in the billiard room of Lindbergh's home enjoying the warm fire and a whisky. Ever the stoic, C.A. demurred when Sam tried to discuss the events at the river.

"I'm fine, Sam" was all he would say on the subject. There was something that disturbed him more.

"Sam, were you as shocked as I was when we went into Jock's

house? *Why, Sam, you can see daylight between the cracks in those floors and boards. There's ten little youngsters, and most of 'em barefoot and nearly naked. There's next to nothing on their beds, and probably the same is true of their cupboard. . . . We've got to do something, Sam. We've surely got to do something about it.³"*

"It's hard for me to comprehend how a farmer like Jock can live in such squalor. His family has farmed that land for three generations. My grandfather sold his grandfather farm equipment back when this county was first settled. Why his great-uncle, Father Francis Pierz helped save Little Falls from the rampaging renegade tribe led by Chief Hole-in-the-Day during the Dakota Wars in '62. To see how low their fortunes have sunk breaks my heart."

"I know. I could almost count the ribs on his little daughter Belinda; she's so skinny. Since the Panic of '93, our farming community has suffered. They are trapped in an endless spiral of debt because the prices they can get for the goods they produce are manipulated by the Money Trust. There are insidious forces of greed that stack the deck against the farmers. Through their control of the currency and credit, these forces siphon off the farmers' gains into their own coffers. These forces work under cover of darkness," said C.A.

"I agree," said Sam. "The farmer is helpless in this system. Because we don't live off the land, we don't see it every day."

"That's true. The prosperity of the lumber industry in Minnesota has masked the plight of the farmer. Sam, we must help our friend Jock. Tomorrow is Saturday. I will meet you first thing in the morning and we will go to everyone we know and gather up coats, dresses, shoes, bedding for Jock's family."

"On our way out to Jock's, we can stop at Engstrom's grocery and get supplies to fill his larder," added Sam.

"Splendid," said C.A. "I'll pick you up at seven."

"C.A., the Pine Tree Bachelors are here," announced his wife, Evangeline.

"Send them up, Evy,"

When Charley Weyerhaeuser and Drew Musser came to Little Falls fifteen years earlier, the title "Pine Tree Bachelors" was bestowed on them by the local society who knew eligible bachelors when they saw them. Reportedly, the men embraced the title and used it on invitations to wild parties they threw at the Antler Hotel. Though no longer the term of hope it had been before the men found wives, the moniker had stuck.

"How are you, Big Charley?" C.A. asked the first man up the stairs.

"Good to see you, Ridge," said Charley Weyerhaeuser, clapping C.A. a bit too hard on the shoulder.

Known as "Big Charley," Weyerhaeuser was a tall, powerfully built man as befit the operations manager of the Pine Tree Lumber Company. His thick head of brown hair defied grooming and stood haphazardly atop his head like an unruly porcupine. He wore a plaid flannel shirt that was flicked with splinters, a testament to his hands-on management of the saw mill.

He was the son of Friedrich Weyerhaeuser, one of the richest men in Minnesota. When Friedrich arrived in America from Germany thirty years earlier, he had sensed the unbounded potential of the American continent. With great foresight, he purchased tracts of virgin forests that he would turn into lumber to meet a seemingly insatiable demand for wood to build the American frontier after the Civil War. One thing led to another and, soon, the Weyerhaeusers owned forests, saw mills, dams, boom areas, sorting facilities, mills, factories, water power structures, warehouses, and storage areas.

"Afternoon, C.A.," muttered the second man up the stairs.

"Hello there, Drew," said C.A. Drew nodded curtly.

Richard "Drew" Musser was the polar opposite of his partner Big Charley. Short, slight of build, he had lacked Charley's lumberman's exuberance. He was quiet and deliberative in his movements and speech. Drew handled the finance side of the Weyerhaeuser lumber interests. His dark eyes flitted around the room. His father, Peter Musser, had joined forces with Friedrich Weyerhaeuser decades ago to build a formidable business empire. It was Peter's genius that supplied the detailed implementation of Friedrich's vision to create an enterprise that controlled every aspect of the industry.

"Would you care for some whisky, then?" asked Sam who was already pouring the caramel-tinted liquor into four tumblers.

"Here's to our good buddy, Hiram Walker, eh," joked Big Charley.

While Sam regaled their guests with stories of their hunting prowess and C.A's heroic rescue of the raft, C.A. stared out the window, thinking about Jock's plight while half-listening. His hand went to the lump on the back of his head where the raft had struck him. It was tender.

When the stories subsided, C.A. asked, "So, what brings my two favorite clients here?"

"There are a couple of things. I'll let Drew take the lead. Go on, then," Big Charley said.

"As you know, the upgrades to the Westside mill are complete. We now have the best saw mill in the world. We are running double shifts with 800 men. Last year was our best year ever. We cut more board feet of lumber than the rest of the mills in the state. As a result of our success, Little Falls is growing exponentially." He paused.

"That's wonderful. What could be the problem?" interjected Sam.

"Our success is the problem. The railroads have increased their shipping rates and our customers are further west as the country grows. We believe that there is an opportunity right under our noses that we should be exploiting," said Drew. C.A. waited for Drew to continue.

Not getting the question he anticipated, Drew spat out, "Retail."

"We see an opportunity in retail lumber right here in Morrison County to start and then, following the railroad lines. We'd like you to set up the legal structure for us and maybe, you, Sam, can help us with the design of the physical yards," said Drew.

"Sounds like a winning idea. But you don't need me to tell you that. You will need a separate corporation – keep the enterprises separate. Do you have a name?"

"How about the Morrison County Lumber Company?" offered Drew.

"You know," said Sam, "with all the greenhorns heading west, you could also sell pre-cut homes and architectural components."

"If you did that, you might want to trademark your brand name," C.A. added.

"That's why ya fellas are the best!" said Big Charley. "I think we deserve another round of old Hiram's medicine, eh."

Sam obliged, refilling the tumblers.

"And what was the other business you wanted to discuss?" asked C.A.

"C.A., you know that I don't mince words. I'm as subtle as a stamp hammer. We think you need to run for Congress. That damn fool Buckman who's in there now has misrepresented the district. He works hand in glove with the 'money interests' and contrary to the needs of our district. Little Falls needs someone with some common sense to stop those fools in Washington.

"That damn fool Roosevelt is riling up the country against honest businessmen. It's wrong, I tell you. We need you to bring some sanity back to our guvmint. I know that you Pa was a member of Parliament in Sweden. You got it in your blood. The 6th Congressional District needs you. Whatcha think?"

Before C.A. could respond, Drew said, "Listen, you don't have to worry about providing for a campaign, not a bit. We'll take care of your expenses."

C.A. stood, speechless, his expression blank. His father had taught him to temper his reactions. His first thought was how he could work in Washington to protect the farmers and tradesmen. They were being ruined by some insidious force behind the government itself that manipulated currency and credit without regard to the common good. Could he make a difference, he wondered? Could he expose the wizard behind the curtain?

At that moment, a picture of the barefoot, emaciated Belinda, Jock's daughter, entered his mind and he knew that this was a call he had to answer. Then, in a disembodied voice, he heard himself say, "That's very kind of you. I will think it over. I will need to discuss it with Evy and I'll let you know.... Thanks."

As was his habit when preparing a legal presentation, C.A. paced across the bed chamber marshaling his points. His lips moved silently. He strode to the nightstand and bent to scribble on his legal pad. He had already divided his thoughts into pros, cons, campaign projections and proposed legislation. The top pages were flipped back and he wrote the words "stop the Money Trust from seizing control over the currency." But how?

He shuffled back and forth across the ring rug as if in a trance.

Evy stood in the doorway watching. She had just put Charles, Jr. to bed. The moon was beginning its ascent. This was her favorite time of the day. She would have C.A. to herself, without the demands of children or clients. Or would she? A sense of dread overcame her. They had been married for about five years and she had seen him consumed like this only a few times, but they were the loneliest times of her life.

Evangeline Land Lindbergh was an attractive young woman who had left her comfortable home in Detroit to become, as she liked to think of it, a "frontier educator." She had mixed feelings about her life on the rough edge of civilization where men battled daily against danger and the elements, not to mention the Indians who not infrequently resisted the incursion into their way of life. She taught elementary school to the children of the farmers and loggers – that is, when they could be spared from family chores. During harvest season her classes shrunk to a bare few. To her, this was the best time because she could provide concentrated learning without distraction from the older more boisterous pupils.

She was Lindbergh's second wife and seventeen years his junior. His first wife, Mary Lafond Lindbergh had died at the age of thirty-one from surgical complications, leaving C.A. with two young daughters, Lillian and Eva. After Mary's funeral, C.A.'s family rallied around him and his daughters. His mother, his sister Linda, and his brother Frank embraced C.A. and the girls in their close-knit family. They became a fixture at the homes of the Frank Lindberghs, the homes of his brothers-in-law, the Butlers and the Seals.

Lillian and Eva recalled in later life that the family holidays were joyous events. They were too young to see through the stoic fortitude of their father. He followed the example of his own deceased father who never allowed his pain to show. So, C.A. Lindbergh grieved inwardly for his deceased wife Mary. He threw himself into his work and career. Yet, every triumph and success was empty.

He was devoted to his daughters. With the help of his elderly mother and the other women in the family, C.A. made sure that his daughters knew how much he loved them. He would leave them notes of scribbled doggerel in their school books, or, bring them little trinkets, a doll or bonnet, whenever he traveled. Yet, his heart ached. He had just turned forty and was alone.

His family worried about him and tried to bring him out of his grief. Their efforts, though well-meaning, were abject disasters of such monumental dimensions that they became family lore for generations.

His sister Linda tried to get him involved in the church choir. C.A. truly loved music and in the privacy of his study he sang along with the Enrico Caruso records that he had purchased from the Victor Recording Company. Linda convinced Ridgy that the choir might be the perfect hobby. When the choirmaster convened the chorus, Bertha Magnuson sidled up to C.A.. Her nickname was Bertha the buxom and she had the voice of an angel. She knew that this was her chance to snare the widower. It was not to be.

Despite being classically trained, the choirmaster had the disposition of a turkey buzzard and was called "Beakface" behind his back. On the evening C.A. attended his first choir practice, the choirmaster was in a particularly foul mood because he had received a rejection notice for a libretto he had submitted to the Metropolitan Opera. The letter, signed by one Otto Kahn, suggested that the choirmaster might be prudent to consider another occupation.

So when C.A. began to sing, the choirmaster unleashed the most vile, acerbic diatribe upon Lindbergh that any choirmaster had ever unleashed upon any singer in the history of choirmastering. In C.A.'s defense, had his effort been rewarded with results, he might have endured. Had volume counted over being harmonious, he might have endured. Had being off-key been a minor transgression, he might have endured. Unfortunately, the sounds he produced could be called a lot of things, but singing was not one of them.

Even without Beakface's vitriol, Lindbergh realized that he had the tonal talent of a bullfrog. Nor could he deny Bertha's grimaces. She looked like she had eaten one of her Aunt Burka's sour, garlic pickles. Lindbergh never returned after that one practice.

On another occasion, his brother Frank brought him to a venison roast with his hunting buddies and their wives in the hope that C.A. might connect with a recent arrival to Little Falls. While the hunters went to play horseshoes, C.A. was left alone to tend to the venison chops with Inga, the attractive sister of Martin Engstrom.

The well-intentioned ploy turned into a disaster when Inga slashed her palm while Lindbergh was trying to show her how to whittle with his pocket knife. In his urgency to bandage the wound, C.A. forgot the meat. It burned to a carbonized crisp. The ensuing derision and catcalls from the hungry and, slightly tipsy, horse-shoe players drove C.A. away in embarrassment.

During this dark period of his life, he lived at the Antler Hotel in Little Falls which was within walking distance of his law office. Nothing like a brisk walk to get the brain working, he told himself. And then it happened. The shroud of grief lifted.

Whether by chance or design, C.A. met Evangeline Land while he walked to his law office and she to her teaching post. She was tall and thin. She wore her hair in a bun atop her head in a manner that accentuated her high forehead. When he described his encounter with her to his sister, he remarked that his overriding impression was one of softness – in her eyes, her skin, her lips.

"Mind if I walk with you?" she said.

"Of course, of course. Excuse me. My name is C.A. Lindbergh," he said, doffing his hat. She smiled the smile of a dentist's daughter.

"And, I am Evangeline Land, my friends call me Evy."

"My friends call me Ridgy."

"What an unusual name. How did you get it?"

"I usually don't . . ."

There was something in her expressive, brown eyes that engendered trust. Before he could divert the subject, he was telling her about how his brother and he got into a squabble over the rules of some game they were playing and he had insisted that they abide by the rules.

"In frustration, my younger brother said, 'You and your silly rules. You are always so rigid. I'm going to call you Ridgy from now on.' Wasn't he the silly one? How can you have a game without rules? Well, anyway, the name stuck."

"I think it's a wonderful name. I always tell my students that a man has to stand for principle after all," she said, swinging her fist across her body for emphasis and laughing in a high, infectious giggle. He surprised himself when an exuberant laugh emerged from his belly. He could not remember the last time he had felt joy. As he approached his office, he found himself slowing in order to extend his time with her.

Before he knew it, the walks were a daily occurrence. He eagerly anticipated them and they were the highlight of his day. Their conversations were never dull or forced. They talked about science and religion, hunting and world affairs. She impressed C.A. with her depth of knowledge. Three years after his first wife's death, Evangeline's quick wit and sensitive spirit released something in Lindbergh's heart. Romance between the two walking friends blossomed. They were married in the spring of 1901 and the next February, she gave birth to Charles A. Lindbergh, Jr.

In short order, the Charles A. Lindberghs moved into a three-story home that had been designed and built by his partner Sam Wurthels. C.A. referred to it as the Pike Creek house because it was built on a bluff overlooking the confluence of Pike Creek with the Mississippi. The house was an exemplar of rustic elegance, with red oak paneling and large fireplaces to give it a comfortable ambiance. In a few years, Lindbergh would make a decision that would turn this joyful home into a scene of tragedy.

Once they were married, Evy struggled to cope with two teenage stepdaughters, an aging mother-in-law, and an energetic young son. She often thought longingly about her life growing up in Detroit where her father was a wealthy dentist, having invented the revolutionary porcelain jacket crown. The contrast between her privileged life in sophisticated Detroit and her demanding life in the relatively primitive Little Falls, left her despondent. This was not the life she had envisioned when she fell in love with the successful, older lawyer.

When she articulated her disappointment, C.A. would quote his father. *Massor av vintern , massor av sommaren*, which translated to English means "Lots of winter, lots of summer." C.A. explained that life is full of good and bad, then, shrugged. It did not help.

C.A. had been thrust into responsibility early in life. He was not quite four when his father suffered the horrible accident that resulted in the loss of his left arm. Their family lived a pioneer existence on the edge of civilization. They fought and scraped for the bare necessities. Food came from C.A.'s prowess as a hunter and fisherman. On most days, he packed his rifle and fishing gear and tracked off into the woods intent on returning with enough food to feed the family.

As he grew to manhood, Lindbergh was single-minded in his determination to succeed. Whenever he felt like slowing the pace, the image of his father splitting logs with one arm propelled him to push harder. Immediately after the accident, August Lindbergh convalesced, unable to leave his bed for more than a year.

During that time he spoke to his son about the trials of life and the need to be self-reliant. The most profound lesson he passed on to his son came not through words, but through his spirit and actions. August Lindbergh taught his son that *no degree of adversity can conquer the unconquerable.*[4]

Lindbergh and Wurthels complemented each other perfectly. Both were energized by the burgeoning growth of America and blessed with the talent and work ethic to achieve greatness. Ridge had a tendency to pursue grand schemes, while Sam was the ultimate pragmatist who kept their ventures focused. The prospect of this balance being tipped by a run for Congress weighed on C.A. His thoughts were so centered on his relationship with Sam and the possible ramifications on their business that he never saw the tornado brewing right under his own roof.

"Honey, it's getting late . . ."

C.A. looked up, his deep, blue eyes re-focusing as if he had just walked inside from the blinding whiteness of a Minnesota snow storm.

"Yes, yes, of course. You know that Big Charley and Drew want me to throw my hat in the ring for Congress? I'm just evaluating the options," he replied, waving the errant yellow pages of his pad toward her. The flapping pages and his intense expression struck her as comical.

"Oh, do sit down, you're liable to slash yourself to death with paper cuts, the way you are wielding that pad."

C.A. caught a glimpse of himself in the vanity mirror and paused.

"I guess I do look a little ridiculous standing here in my underwear, robe flying open and the pages on this darn pad flapping like a skittered greenhead."

Evy laughed the strained laugh of a wife preparing for battle.

"So, tell me about your meeting."

"There's not much to tell. They want me to run for Congress and will bankroll my campaign completely."

"I hope you told them it was out of the question."

C.A. gave her a quizzical look as if that never occurred to him. Why would I do that, he thought. If I get to Congress, maybe I can make a difference. He did not want to end up like his father, crippled, spent, and discarded. He pictured his father's shriveled body just before they had closed the casket and how C.A. felt like life had maliciously consumed his father. From the charges of bribery and embezzlement in Sweden, to the dreadful accident, August Lindbergh had fought until the last ounce of vitality left him.

Evy hesitated, a tight knot rose between her eyebrows.

"Surely, Sam is against your running, what with your plans to operate the cold storage facility to benefit the farmers."

"At first, yes, he saw it as a disruption to our business. But, when I explained that there were more important things than making money and that I felt empty for quite some time, he understood. I told him that this might be my chance to make a real difference in the lives of our neighbors. Ever the pragmatist, Sam analyzed this as a business opportunity to promote the idea of a cold storage co-operative on a national scale. We talked about farmers across the land banding together to take control of their own produce without the bloodsucking finance men in the middle of their business."

"Stop," cried Evy, "You sound like a politician – nothing but empty promises."

C.A. sat on the bed as if thrust down by her verbal intensity. "Evy..."

"Don't you 'Evy' me. I can't believe you decided to uproot our lives without even consulting me!"

She rebuffed C.A.'s attempt to move closer to her. Wiping her eyes, she lowered her voice, "And, have you spoken to your brother Frank? I'm sure your law partner can't afford to lose you; you run the practice. He would be lost...."

From his blank expression, she knew this tack was not persuasive.

"I'm afraid that it will be dangerous," said Evangeline.

"Don't be foolish, Evy," C.A. scoffed. His wife recoiled as if he had struck her.

"You always belittle my worries. But they are real. My God, have you forgotten how they murdered President McKinley? The news made us cancel our honeymoon; there was so much turmoil."

C.A. embraced her and said, "Don't you worry. If I do God's bidding, He will protect us."

"I wish I had your faith," Evangeline whispered, half to herself.

"What about little Charley? He's only four. He needs his father. If you go to Washington, what about him?"

"I've considered that. By the time I take office he will be five and he can travel with me for some of the sessions," said C.A.

"Do you really think that is wise? Dragging a five year old to a strange city is the height of foolishness. And, what about me? Are you going to leave me behind to raise your daughters alone?"

"My mother is here to help." He realized his mistake as soon as the words left his lips.

Evy cast him a withering look. She had lost the argument about bringing his mother into their new home when they had completed construction. The woman spewed an effusion of bitterness and reproof in a stream of pigeon Swedish that irritated Evy to no end.

"Evy, please..."

His words were drowned out by the sound of a slamming door. Standing with his arms slightly reaching toward her, all he could hear were the sounds of sobbing and gasping for breath in the locked bathroom.

Summer 1906 Morrison County, MN

**An honest man in politics shines more
there than he would elsewhere.**
~ Mark Twain

He often reflected on the events of that June day as being among the most momentous of his life. From the near death experience on the river while saving the little raft carrying the ducks, to the invitation to run for Congress to the knock-down-drag-out argument with his wife, he mused that it was unlikely that he would have a day like that anytime soon. He was not entirely correct. There were many more eventful days in his future.

The real question was how to weather them. Right now, he had to focus on his election. The entire process was new and unfamiliar. In many ways, the quest for office was exhilarating, sort of like mastering the plow behind old Jenny, the family mule. There were lots of rocks and bumps along the way and you had to sidestep a lot of manure, but you hoped that the end result would be fruitful.

The headlamps of the Clarkmobile barely lit the road. As he rounded the bend by Jameson's farm, a flash of lightning illuminated the figure of a man in a saturated slicker. C.A. pulled alongside the man and opened the passenger door. A burst of wind snapped the door back. A felt hat drooped in rain covered the man's eyes.

"Howdy, neighbor. Get in before you wash away in this here duck-drownder," said C.A.

"Thank you, Mr. Charles," replied the man as he hefted himself into the cab. He was hunched forward and when he settled into the springy seat, C.A. saw two eyes and a soft black nose poking out at him through the thick black beard of his passenger. The creature whimpered.

"What you got there, Jock?"

"Mr. Charles, I was on my way to your place when this godforsaken storm bust open. I got somethin' for you." A small head wriggled further out from Jock's mackinaw. The halting of the pelting rain, combined with the comfort of the cab, incited the pup's curiosity. He wriggled out further.

"My goodness, just look at that – a carbon copy of Binny. That baby's gonna catch his death of cold out here."

"No, sir, he won't 'cause he's on his way to his new home," said Jock. He unbuttoned his slicker and pulled out a squirmy pup. His big hands enveloped the dog's ribcage. Jock passed the retriever onto C.A.'s lap. The car swerved as C.A. tried to steer and balance the puppy who was intent on exploring the steering wheel.

"Whoa! Take it easy little guy," said C.A. as he pulled off the road.

"Will you look as that. He is one handsome animal. Look he's shaking. Here, Jock, you take him."

"Mr. Charles, I want you to have him. You've done so much for us. I want you to have him. He'll guard you with all his might. Lord knows you is gonna need it, what with all you 'paining."

C.A. grinned at the way Jock mangled the word campaigning. "No Jock, I couldn't take him. He's part of your breeding business. You need him . . . ."

"I insist. He's yourn. Yessir, he's yourn. Looky, he knows it, too, the way he's lickin' at you."

The lawyer held the pup to his face and reveled in the shower of affection that bubbled out of his new friend. "I guess you are right. He sure knows how to catch a man. Look at those eyes, and what beautiful markings. He'll make a wonderful companion on those back roads I've been hitting. How did you know?"

"Missy Evy. She say that you been traveling alone all over the state, 'painin', so's I figured you needed some company."

"Thanks, Jock," said C.A. Nuzzling the pup's neck, he said, "Now, what shall we call this bloke?"

"I've got it," exclaimed C.A., "we'll call him, Blake. What do you say, Blakey?" A rush of feathery licks was all the answer C.A. needed.

$ $ $

"It's that simple, boys. It surely is," said the wiry fellow in the suit.

He stood on a bale of hay before a group of about twenty men dressed in denim overalls and rough work clothes. A few women folk hung back at the edge of the gathering, just listening. Although they could not vote, they often bore the brunt of economic downturns. A faded red barn was at his back. It was a utilitarian place, sparse. The barnyard smelled of moist earth and dairy cows. The early fall sunlight suffused the land with a contented orange glow as if blessing the days' hard, harvest labor.

"Now, C.A., I knowed you since you was knee-high to a grasshopper and I knew your Pappy. You's good, honest folk. Why you became a fancy ahturney, I'll never know? But I still like you, eh," remarked Caleb Swanson. He waited for the chuckle and snorts from his fellow farmers.

C.A. basked in the familiarity. These were his folk, the farmers of Morrison County. They were the ones who worked the farms that raised the food that fed the country. Their existence was tough and getting tougher because the Money Trust was siphoning the cream from their earnings. That was what compelled him to declare for Congress. He wanted to represent them in Washington so that they could get a square deal – not the piddling crumbs that they've been getting for the last fifty years since the Civil War. The way he saw it, the bankers had replaced chattel slavery with industrial slavery. Someone had to sound the alarm. That someone would be C.A. Lindbergh, or he would die trying.

"Let me get this right. You's tellin' us that the more dairy I produce and the more wheat Jackson here grows, the less we gonna get?" asked Caleb who gestured incredulously, shaking his head.

"I jest don't get it."

"Look at it this way, Caleb. You see that sow over yonder, Daisy's her name, right?" said C.A. pointing to an enormous pig. She was the pride of Swanson's farm. She won blue ribbons at the last three county fairs. Caleb's chest swelled.

"How many piglets did she farrow last spring? Sixteen, eighteen? Now let's suppose that Mr. Banker comes along with forty-seven piglets. What is that going to do to the price you're gonna fetch for each of Daisy's piglets?"

"Drive it right through the floor," commented Jeb Anderson bitterly.

"Exactly," replied C.A. "Well, my friends, Mr. Banker can't create piglets out of thin air, but he can do it with dollars. That is what the Money Trust is doing with our dollars. The dollars that you work so hard for. They are creating dollars out of nothing and that makes your dollars worth a whole lot less." He paused to let his words sink in.

"The more dollars out there, the less each one is worth. And the less you get for each of your dollars."

"How can they do that?" someone in the back asked.

"They do it by controlling the supply of money. *The money that we deposit forms the basis for an amount of credit many times greater than the amount of actual money. The bankers have the advantage of all that, and it is pyramided and sold and resold many times.*[5]

"The banks are specialists in the manipulation of that credit to enrich themselves and impoverish the tradesman and the farmer. This election is about removing the ridiculous system we currently have and replacing it with a system that helps the working man.

"You might ask, why do we stay with a system that is ridiculous and unfair? The answer is simple. The Money Trust likes to keep it shrouded in mystery, make it more complicated than it needs to be. We need to unravel it, make it simple – reduce it to its parts. Some say that it is too complicated to fix. Why even bother?

"To those I say, *but even if no remedy were possible we should still seek to know about the game that is being played by the speculating interests. We certainly do not wish the financially fat fellows to be able to look beguilingly into our eyes, and with the concealment of their innermost amusement and delighted at our stupidity in permitting ourselves to be so bamboozled, talk brazenly about the game that they are playing, knowing all the time that we do not understand it.*[6]"

$ $ $

In short order, his campaign took him out of Morrison County and into the other counties in the district. He no longer had the security that came from familiarity. Any hesitation he might have felt when addressing a crowd populated by unfamiliar faces was overcome by his earnestness. Yet, as the crowds got larger C.A. faltered. Connection with his listeners was elusive. After one particularly lackluster event where much of the crowd drifted off before he was finished, C.A. slumped into the car. His normally tidy hair was tousled and his tie was askew.

"What's the matter?" asked Sam.

C.A. was silent, his chin lowered into his chest and his eyes vacant.

This behavior was unlike his buddy. Usually he was animated and talkative after a campaign appearance, often remarking about the expressions on faces in the crowd. But, on this occasion Sam sensed that C.A. was struggling with something.

Sam replayed the appearance in his mind. Ridgy's speech had the usual crisp, lawyerly delivery, if anything C.A. had it down perfectly. So what was troubling him? C.A. turned his face to Sam and shook his head slowly, almost mournfully.

"There was no connection. I don't know these people. There was no connection," Lindbergh said, the last few words almost a whisper. Sam saw that his usually confident partner had been shaken and was wracked by doubt.

The next day, they attended church services in St. Cloud. Afterwards, while eating lunch at the Stearns House, a Gothic Revival Style hotel, neither man could recall the substance of the sermon. However, they left the church energized.

"I think I have the answer," said Lindbergh.

Sam's response was muffled by a mouthful of steak and eggs. Before he could wash down the food with a gulp of coffee, C.A. continued.

"Two words. My speeches need two words." A puzzled look draped Sam's face as if his friend was speaking Swahili. He would have thrown up his hands in a questioning gesture had he not been so busy devouring lunch.

Back in their rooms, Sam could hear Lindbergh in the adjoining room practicing the speech he was scheduled to give later that afternoon at the Masonic Lodge.

If Lindbergh was nervous as he approached the rostrum, he did not show it. He took a deep breath, head held high and launched into his presentation. Once again, he dissected the relationship between the farmers and working men and the Money Trust. But this time it was different. Instead of using the Money Trust, he referred to it as Mammon, the god of greed. He was more animated. A light shone from his eyes as he explained that during the Middle Ages Mammon was commonly regarded as an evil deity who corrupts and seduces with earthly treasure. At times he gestured so vigorously that his normally neatly-laid hair became wild, giving him a slightly unglued look. The crowd was rapt.

"*. . . All of these things were scientifically figured out, then commercialized, then specularized, and finally gamblerized both as to* *the present and the future. All have been overdone and all pulled as a common charge against the products accruing from the expenditure of our life's energy.* [7] And that is how the Money Trust is destroying your life. Join with me to slay the beast. We can do it together if you wield the mightiest weapon you have – your vote!"

The crowd rose to their feet and roared approval. Even staid, old John Zapp, founder of Zapp's Abstract and Loan Bank, cheered Lindbergh. By golly, Sam thought, he has incorporated 'fire and brimstone' into his speeches.

As the campaign progressed, Lindbergh received more and more attention. His speeches were reproduced verbatim in the *Little Falls Daily Transcript* and other newspapers throughout the district. A candidate from an obscure congressional district challenging Mammon made good press. Soon, his speeches garnered national coverage.

There was no direct response to C.A's questions and accusations against the Money Trust. None of the other candidates wanted to be seen as defending the Money Trust because no one was willing to admit that it even existed.

This phenomenon was captured in a political cartoon depicting the Money Trust as a globe with stick arms and legs, with a sign under his nose declaring "I Don't Exist." C.A. seized on the notoriety created by his attacks on the Money Trust by publicizing a debate against the Money Trust.

Flyers promoting the debate were posted in almost every store window in the District. Almost a thousand voters turned out to watch C.A. debate an empty chair at the Grange Hall in St. Cloud. C.A. mocked and derided his non-existent opponent with questions that began with, "If you don't exist, Mr. Money Trust . . ." and ended with some grievance of the rural voter.

For example, "If you don't exist, Mr. Money Trust, then, why do I pay a higher interest rate than my cousins in the city back east? If you don't exist, Mr. Money Trust, then, why do I pay more for my farm machinery than my neighbors up north in Canada?"

Candidate Lindbergh had tapped into the frustrations of the farmers and they loved him for expressing their grievances so plainly. After the debate concluded, Lindbergh was surrounded by well-wishers and even autograph-seekers. The debate was so successful that they repeated it in every county. On several occasions, he noticed a man wearing a black Stetson hat, loitering on the periphery of the crowd.

His icy demeanor exuded menace. Whenever Lindbergh asked local law enforcement about the man, they either did not recognize him, or, he had vanished like a wraith into the night.

C.A.'s campaigning led him farther afield into reaches of the district that were unknown to him, and vice versa. He was tireless and accepted every invitation to speak, regardless of how distant. Days shortened and he often found himself driving large distances on lonely back roads in the dark to another library or grange hall where he would deliver his stump speech and answer questions from voters. Lindbergh would hit the campaign trail with only his briefcase and his faithful sidekick, Blakey.

The problem with this arrangement became apparent quickly. The plain fact of it was that Lindbergh was a notoriously poor driver. He did not quite grasp the foot work required. He preferred the tug of the reins to pressure of foot pedals. Consequently, his car had to be pulled out of a ditch by some farmer with a tractor on more than one occasion when he mistook the accelerator for the brake. C.A's driving was so bad that his wife feared for his life. Finally, Evy insisted that Sam, his campaign manager, become his driver.

Sam was perfect to drive C.A. around on the campaign trail. He was good company and C.A. was relieved that he could concentrate on his campaign instead of pesky details like directions.

"I think those Presbyterian ladies loved your speech, Ridgy," said Sam. "Why don't you rest while I drive to your next appearance?"

"No, I'll study my notes."

Within a few minutes, Sam heard a gentle snoring from his passenger. He turned his head to see C.A. asleep with Blakey cuddled on his lap. It took them about an hour to drive north to Brainerd. It was after dark when they arrived. There were only a few vehicles outside the local schoolhouse where C.A. was scheduled to address the Crow Wing County Veterans of the Civil War.

"Ridgy, I can see that you are dead on your feet what with all the speeches you've been making. I've listened to everyone and I think that I know it by heart. I know it so well that I can present it. Let me give it a try. They don't know you here and we kind of have the same build. You can sit in the back and cue me if I start to mess up."

C.A. was bone weary. "OK, but don't try to get fancy." Sam's eyes danced as his expression changed to a mixture of solemnity and giddiness. C.A. sighed and followed a respectful distance behind Sam who strode into the building with his shoulders back and head held high. C.A. chuckled inwardly, at his failure to realize just how much ham resided in his partner's body. C.A. glanced back at Blake who was on his hind legs, whining softly for his master.

"We'll be right back, Blakey. You be a good boy."

Inside the schoolhouse, a white-haired woman carrying a tray of "*småkakor*" (little cookies) approached Sam.

"You must be our speaker. I'm Victoria Hyatt. My husband is the Commander here. Several of our members served in the original Clearwater Guard, militia that was organized to defend us against the Indians. Welcome."

Sam nodded and gave her his best serious smile. He followed her into the gymnasium where a group of men wearing various hats, tunics and medals from Company D of the First Minnesota Infantry of the Union Army. Sam took the tray from Mrs. Hyatt and began serving the cookies, all the while chitchatting with the grizzled veterans. One man spilled coffee on Sam's shoes. He smiled, bowed and sopped up the tawny liquid with as much grace as he could muster.

Commander Hyatt walked over and introduced himself. He guided Sam off to the side and engaged him in earnest conversation. C.A. watched tall, old gentleman bend toward Sam, hovering over him like a father eagle instructing his offspring. From Sam's solemn nodding, it seemed as if Hyatt were extracting some kind of promise.

After a gracious introduction in which Commander Norbert Hyatt exhorted his comrades to welcome candidate Lindbergh with a "Clearwater Guard huzzah," there was a blood-curdling war cry that would have made their Viking ancestors proud. C.A. smiled at the vitality of these comrades-in-arms.

Buoyed by the rousing welcome, Sam delivered the stump speech without a hitch.

".... *It is not the bankers who have primarily fastened upon us this system of capitalizing our life energies for their own selfish use. It is the banking and currency system, which we have allowed to remain in operation.... The people alone have the power to amend or change it. Therefore we and not the bankers are responsible for the existence of the present system.*[8]"

"Can we stop it, Mr. Lindbergh?" questioned Ellet Perkins, puffing on his corncob pipe.

"Absolutely, you, the voters, have the power. The frightening thing is that they are fixing to make it even worse. That's why I'm running for Congress - to help expose the Money Trust and put a stop to their stealing the fruits of your labor with their fancy money schemes. If we don't put a stop to this legalized thievery, you just might as well be slaves. I for one won't allow that. So, I'm asking for your vote.

"Thank you," said Sam to polite applause. "Are there any questions?"

Commander Hyatt searched the room for a hand. Not seeing one, he decided to assist the speaker by posing a question.

"Will the aftermath of the earthquake in San Francisco last year and expansion of the authority of the Interstate Commerce Commission to control maximum railroad shipping rates put so much pressure on the money supply to cause England to raise interest rates?"

As the Commander articulated his question, Sam slumped his shoulders and pleaded visually with C.A. for a rescue. Standing against the back wall, C.A. enjoyed watching his partner squirm. There was a long silence as Sam gazed at the back wall. Then, a light of revelation sparked on Sam's face. He pulled himself up to his full height and in a slightly bored tone said, "That question is so simple that even my driver in the back there can answer it."

All eyes shifted toward C.A. who regretted the charade that threatened to turn this engagement into a disaster. He answered the question in a clear, direct manner.

The group warmed up and asked more mundane questions that Sam handled with aplomb. Commander Hyatt led the group in a round of polite applause for Sam. The crowd mingled for a while and then dispersed. C.A. searched the hospitality table for treats for Blakey. He looked up just in time to see Sam disappear with Hyatt through a door off the vestibule.

After a few minutes Sam emerged with a leather satchel slung over his shoulder. On the way back out to the car, C.A. whispered to Sam, "Well played in there."

As they approached the car, it rocked with the force of Blakey rushing from one window to the other, whining impatiently. When Sam opened the door, Blakey bounded out with such force and exuberance that C.A. thought that his hindquarters might wag off. Lindbergh dropped to a knee and nuzzled the pup. Wild face-licking and wagging earned Blakey a fistful of Mrs. Hyatt's cookies. C.A. gave the pup some water and they were ready to depart.

Back in the car, C.A. asked, "What was all the hush-hush conversation with Hyatt?"

"What a nice old codger. He just wanted to share some war stories. He was attached to the Treasury under Secretary Chase. Oh, I almost forgot. You are not going to believe this, Ridgy. He said that his father knew your father . . . from Sweden. Did business with him, seemed like they were in Parliament together. Old man Hyatt admired Gussie, that's what he called him. Said he got a raw deal all around. Said, he deserved better."

"What's in the satchel?"

"A Bible. I didn't quite get what he was saying. You know, how old folks can get. He kept talking about the Bible and how it binds us together and how he wanted to make it up to your father. That I, I mean you, should have this Bible because it binds us. I don't know. He spoke in Swedish some."

"Sure sounds unusual," Ridge said. "After the way you delivered that speech tonight, maybe I'll use that Bible to take the oath of office when I win. Put it in the office safe with the campaign money when we get home. Let's hurry, that bed of mine is calling me."

1906 Minneapolis, MN

**The rich rule over the poor, and
the borrower is slave to the lender.**
~ Proverbs 22:7

After many months on the campaign trail, the rigors of the campaign wore on him. He insisted on visiting as many gatherings as possible. If he had to travel twenty miles to explain his policies to a handful of people, he was willing to make the effort.

"I could never forgive myself if I lost by one vote. Today's meeting might just provide our margin of victory."

While C.A. valued the face-to-face campaigning of rural politics, he had trouble tolerating some of the other aspects of campaigning that distracted him from meeting his constituents. Near the end of the Republican primary campaign, his manager insisted that they attend a dinner in Minneapolis which was not even in their district.

"Sam, I know that you are the campaign manager and all, but are you sure it makes sense to travel to Minneapolis to speak so close to primary day? Minneapolis is way outside our district. I don't get it."

Sam, who had been pressed into chauffeur duty, kept his eyes on the road.

"Good Lord, Ridgy, we've been over this how many times? You sure can be one stubborn Swede. I told you that we must look past the primary. These folks in Minneapolis can help you once you win the primary."

"But what if we don't win the primary because we're here in Minneapolis, while ole' Buckman is campaigning in the district?"

"Trust me, the press coverage that you will get for this speech in Minneapolis will overshadow anything old Clarence is doing back in Little Falls. Plus, this is an opportunity for you to meet Manley Fosseen. He is a member of the Executive Committee of the Hennepin County Republican Party and is a powerhouse in state politics. He has a wide circle of friends, and he enjoys the respect and confidence of the citizens of Minnesota. His friendship would be helpful in the future."

C.A. was staring at the beautiful scenery outside the car window. Sam sighed. He knew that his friend was easily bored with the mundane process of relationship building that was critical in politics.

"Are you going to include your new proposition in your speech?"

"Do you think I should?"

Sam hesitated. "It could be risky."

"I know, that's what you told me when I showed it to you last week. I just feel that if someone does not step forward and start the push for it, then, we shame ourselves as a society."

"As if you weren't already upsetting enough apple carts. Well, you are intent on going there. All I can say is be careful." Sam shook his head from side to side, he looked at his friend in the same way that C.A. looked at little Charley when he was standing on the arm of the sofa ready to fly onto Blakey. The look a parent gives when they want to stop a little one from venturing too far, but are resigned to let the learning experiment proceed.

C.A. lapsed into silence. What was he doing if he did not speak the truth? He wondered how his father would react to his radical stance. C.A. knew that he must be true to himself, or he would die. He thought ruefully that sticking to the truth might also result in his death. Maybe he was stubborn, but he came from a long line of mules. He chuckled to himself at the memory of his mother admonishing his father for cursing the family mule. "Don't you see that 'that stupid mule' is exactly like you?"

"We're here. Now, remember you will be sitting next to Manley Lewis Fosseen and his wife Carrie. Don't be grumpy."

"Yes sir," said C. A., giving Sam a snappy salute.

Once they were in the ballroom of the Nicollet Hotel, C.A. followed Sam through the obligatory introductions.

"C.A., this is Manley Fosseen, our host. He is a member of the Hennepin County Republican Central committee and is running for state senate."

"A pleasure, sir," said C.A., holding out his hand.

"Likewise I'm sure, C.A. You are raising quite a stir in your congressional race," said Manley, "It's always a joy to welcome bold, new thinkers into the fold."

C.A. reddened and shrugged. They continued along the reception line. After numerous, names, faces, hands and pleasantries, C.A. made his way to the dais where he found himself standing between two young women. The contrast between the women was dramatic. The one directly before him was plain, wore little make-up and was dressed modestly. The other, to his right, was a stunner. She carried herself like a courtesan of the French *Belle Epoque*. She wore a fashionable lace ensemble in blue with opera gloves snaking up her arms. Little did C.A. realize that one of these women would have a monumental effect on his life.

Bowing slightly to the woman before him, Lindbergh extended his hand, "C.A. Lindbergh, ma'am."

"Carrie Fosseen. Nice to meet you, Mr. Lindbergh."

Carrie Jorgens Fosseen was a short woman with a piercing stare that she developed in the classroom to cow her grade school students. Beneath a bun of honey-gold hair, she exuded wholesomeness. Notwithstanding her school marm demeanor, she had a calculating mind that was subtle and nuanced. Carrie was the mastermind behind her husband's political career. Looking over her spectacles, she measured Lindbergh.

"Please, call me C.A."

"Yes, of course. C.A. it is." Carrie's hand lingered on his for a second too long.

C.A. turned to his right and introduced himself to the other woman.

"I'm Elisha Sharlette, a guest of the former mayor. He is out of prison while his appeal is being processed," she said, gesturing toward a tall, tired-looking man. Alonso "Doc" Ames puffed furiously on a cigar while he listened to a man in a police officer's uniform who, behind a cupped hand, was whispering into the ear of the former mayor. The police chief bore a familial resemblance to Doc Ames. In actuality, it was his younger brother, Fred, who according to court testimony, had implemented Doc's reign of crime. Lindbergh's mind snapped to the scandalous tale of corruption, deceit and avarice that was exposed by Lincoln Steffens in his award-winning article entitled *"The Shame of Minneapolis."* The resultant public outcry led to indictments, trials, convictions and appeals.

"Good evening, Miss Elisha," C.A. nodded.

"Oh, my, what a cute accent you have there." C.A. raised his eyebrows and tilted his head. Elisha waggled an index finger at him like she was correcting a schoolboy.

"Sir, I must correct you," she admonished. "It's not Eleesha. It's pronounced E-**lish**-sha, like de-lish-us."

Those in the immediate vicinity laughed at her bawdy pronunciation. No one laughed harder than Sam who was transfixed. Elisha Sharlette was the daughter of a Parisian chanteuse who married an American inventor from Minnesota. Unfortunately, when Elisha was very young, her father, Emmet Sharlette, was killed in a logging accident while demonstrating his idea for a mechanized saw using a chain as a blade. The chain snapped and decapitated him.

Raised alone by her mother who struggled to make ends meet, Elisha spent her adolescence deprived and dreaming of one day becoming a rich entertainer. As she grew into womanhood, Elisha blossomed. With honey-blonde tresses and a flawless complexion, she became an object of desire sought by all the boys in school. Her large expressive eyes flashed hazel-green when she focused. Her eyes like her dreams were starting to fade; she knew that if she did not escape from Minnesota she would perish from blandness.

At fifteen, she took up with a neighborhood tough who had aspirations as a prizefighter. Starting in local clubs, he built a reputation as a powerful puncher who refused to back down. She followed him, nursing his wounds and supporting his dreams. When in training before a bout, he was celibate. He did not want to sap his strength. After a victory, they joined in wild love-making that lasted until he started training for the next fight. One night, they were in Minneapolis for a fight against the state boxing champ. It was not pretty and her man was pummeled so badly that he was carted away to the hospital. Elisha, barely out of her teens, was alone and vulnerable.

As the arena emptied, she wept until someone took pity on her. With all the compassion of a tiger shark sensing blood on the water, the fight doctor offered to take her home.

That night she and the doctor joined in wild love-making in his mansion on Lowry Hill. His name was Dr. Alonso Ames and he treated her well. He encouraged her to improve herself and she flourished. Doc's recent entanglements with the criminal justice system led her to conclude that it was time to find another sugar daddy.

She had trained as a dancer and moved with lynx-like grace. For a split second, the way she looked at him, reminded C.A. of the barn cats on his father's farm toying with their vermin prey. As quick as a lightning bolt, the look morphed into one of charm and grace. A bejeweled cigarette holder emerged. With a graceful flourish, Elisha thrust her unlit cigarette toward Lindbergh flashing an irresistible look that screamed, light me up, big boy.

He turned toward Sam and gestured for him to accommodate the lady. Sam jumped to the task. Lindbergh exhaled audibly and nodded his appreciation to Sam.

"I must say that I've been reading your speeches with great interest," said Carrie, interrupting his thoughts.

"Why, why, yes, thank you," said C.A.. "That is good to hear. Sometimes I feel like my message is not reaching the folks."

Elisha took a swig of her drink and addressed C.A. with venom.

"Oh, quite the contrary. Many of the ladies in my circle agree with you wholeheartedly. We have seen it ourselves. The Hebrew bankers have controlled things for centuries. We won't abide that here in Minneapolis. We are careful to keep the stinking Jews away from the levers of power. We won't even let them into our good neighborhoods. Just last month, Solomon Wittenberg tried to buy a house in the Red Wing neighborhood. Can you imagine? The gall of the man!"

There were nods and murmurs of concurrence, as an unseemly side of Minneapolis seeped to the surface. Her vehemence and the bystanders' reaction caught him off guard. C.A. had encountered anti-semitism before, but usually it was subtle, like the time the German American Bank in Little Falls denied a loan to farmer Jacob Mickle. It cited poor water table levels as a potential detriment to his plan to build hothouses to grow tomatoes and cucumbers. The reality of the denial was quite otherwise.

The emcee rescued C.A. with a request that the guests find their seats. They complied after a fashion. Lindbergh settled into his chair on the dais and turned to the podium where the master of ceremonies was introducing the Right Reverend Ezekial Smithson to say grace.

C.A's face bore the campaign smile that Sam had coached him to exhibit when he was bored or threatened. After an interminable hour of announcements, small talk and insipid fare, C.A.'s smile muscles felt like *rigor mortis* had set in. When his turn to speak finally arrived, C.A. patted the speech in his jacket pocket for the twentieth time to make sure it was still there. He scanned the audience of several hundred and saw a figure in the back waving vigorously at him. It was Sam. He pantomimed that he was leaving with Elisha. Lindbergh smiled amiably. A momentary flash of worry crossed his consciousness before he heard, ". . . Please welcome our keynote speaker, the next congressman from District 6, Charles August Lindbergh."

Putting Sam and the floozy out of his mind, C.A. launched into his speech, excoriating the Money Trust with anecdotes of the deleterious impact of the Money Trust on Minnesota's workers.

"*. . . The people's money placed in the banks is principally used as a basis for credit and on that credit the banks collect the interest which operates to reduce the prices of what we sell and increase the prices of what we buy. The banks use the clever device of requiring only a small amount of the people's money deposited be retained as reserves. They can satisfy this by depositing the people's money in reserve banks or central reserve banks.*

"*To those not knowing the tricks of the business, the practice of keeping reserves in other banks may seem harmless. But upon examination, we find it to be a most clever device and operated in order that the banks generally shall supply the financial speculators and gamblers with the people's money.*"

Through the low light of the flickering incandescent bulbs, he could see that the audience was engaged. Faces were upturned. There was no whispered buzz. Even the wait staff had refrained from jostling plates and silverware.

"*. . . In our studies this will become as plain as the noon day sun on a clear day.*"[9]

"Ladies and gentlemen, I stand before you asking for your support so that we can strike at the heart of Mammon, the parasitic Money Trust that is draining away our lifeblood."

Manley Fosseen started to rise to lead a round of applause. However, he froze between sitting and standing and the applause dwindled to silence because Lindbergh's palm out hands indicated that he had more to say. Feeling the benevolence of the crowd, Lindbergh's sense of purpose overcame Sam's admonition to use caution. Lindbergh enveloped himself in the attitude of Admiral David Farragut who famously commanded, *"Damn the torpedoes, Full speed ahead!"* C.A. decided to announce the new initiative that he would pursue if elected.

"I would be remiss if I did not address another despicable evil that pervades our political system."

Using his growing skill as an orator, he paused. A mood of excited expectation grew like an approaching thunderhead over parched farmland.

"While on the campaign trail, I have spoken with many veterans of the Civil War. These brave men sacrificed much to eradicate the scourge of slavery. The right of human beings to be free and participate in life is fundamental. Hundreds of thousands of American boys died at Gettysburg, Antietum and Chancellorsville for the principle that all Americans are created equal before God. I know that you share this principle that is enshrined in our Declaration of Independence - all men are created equal."

He had their attention, where was he going with this?

"Yet, here we stand at the dawn of a new century and deny basic citizenship rights to fully one half of our society."

Another pause . . . quizzical looks were exchanged throughout the crowd. He can't be.

"Yes, my friends, I believe that *there is an absolute fundamental right in the women to vote.*[10] As a lawyer, a sworn officer of the court, I find the denial of suffrage to women unconscionable."

Despite a grumbling undercurrent, he forged ahead.

"As a son, brother, husband and father of two bright and beautiful daughters, I am perplexed that we deny them the right to vote. I would venture to say that *'the politics of this country would be very much improved and purified'*[11] if women were permitted to vote. I ask you all to examine your consciences on this issue. If I may paraphrase the Declaration, I believe that once you do examine your consciences, you will conclude that it is self-evident that women should be entitled to vote.

"I ask for your support to send me to Congress to fight these battles. Thank you."

He smiled and turned toward his seat. After a pregnant silence, a loud, feminine voice shouted, "Hip, hip, hooray for Lindbergh!" With that the hall erupted into raucous applause. C.A. waved his campaign wave, smiling broadly.

Suddenly, he felt a sharp pain in his torso. Had he been shot? No, his ribs were crushed by a grinning Carrie Fosseen who grabbed him in a bear hug.

"C.A. you are an inspiration. You are my hero!" she shrieked.

June 26, 1906 New York City, NY

... the passionate idealism of the young democracy had also become covered with rust, like the bronze statue, eating away the soul with the corrosive of commercialism.
~ Maxim Gorky

Otto Kahn read the news with stunned horror. Kahn was a partner in the venerable banking house of Kuhn Loeb & Company, New York City. At 39, Kahn was a rising star in the firmament of New York society. Not only was his banking career rocketing, he was a fixture on the society pages on account of his involvement with the Metropolitan Opera and many of the most notable charities in the City. So, it was with shock and sorrow that he read about the demise of his friend, one of New York's most engaging personalities. The headline of the *New York Journal American* blared:

HARRY THAW KILLS STANFORD WHITE ON ROOF GARDEN![12]

Kahn could not believe that his friend Stanford White had been murdered the previous evening at the Madison Square Roof Garden theater. White was in the audience watching the musical comedy *"Mamzelle Champagne,"* when Harry K. Thaw fired three pistol shots into the face of Stanford White, killing him instantly. The report stated that Thaw murdered the famous society architect and renowned womanizer in order to avenge White's seduction and ruination of a Broadway chorus girl named Evelyn Nesbitt. Sensitive to the irony of the moment, the newspaper reported that the shooting occurred during the rendition of *I Could Love a Million Girls,* an allusion to

White's decadent promiscuity.

Otto and Sandy had spent many an evening of revelry with beautiful chorus girls at White's opulently appointed love nest at 22 W. 24th Street. It was a two story space that featured a red velvet swing that was rendered legendary in the lurid press. What sort of debauchery occurred on that red velvet swing was left to the reader's imagination. When Otto read that the murderer was Harry Thaw, a wealthy businessman whose wife had been seduced by Sandy, Otto thought morosely that his ginger friend had finally reaped what he had sown. Otto had frequently chided his friend to stay away from the married ones. Kahn vowed to adhere strictly to his own advice in the future.

As he exited the red-and green-paneled taxicab at the new Tiffany building on Fifth Avenue between 36th and 37th Streets, Otto welled up. This building was one of Stanford White's crowning architectural achievements. After the President of Tiffany & Company had directed the architect to "Build me a palace," Stanford complied, delivering a masterpiece. He had modeled the building after the 16th-century Palazzo Grimani in Venice. Otto found himself gazing at the marble, Corinthian columns that Henry James had described as "a great nobleness of white marble." Stanford White's genius, not to mention his flamboyant personality, would be sorely missed.

Otto stood at the entrance with mixed feelings of mourning and anticipation. White's death was a shocking loss that would probably reverberate through New York society for years. Thaw would doubtless hire a top criminal defense attorney and the trial would drag up all sorts of scandalous activities as the defense raised all manner of peripheral matters to justify, or, to obscure the plain act of cold-blooded murder. The press would have a field day.

He felt a momentary pang of sadness for the impending destruction of his friend's character. Oh well, thought Otto, Sandy is beyond reach of earthly retribution. Otto hoped that his circle would be spared besmirchment by the yellow press. The upper echelon of society always made fair game for the lurid press which loved to publish stories exposing the clay feet of the elite, regardless of the truth. The more lurid, the more papers sold. Simple economics.

But now, his thoughts turned to more pressing business. While at the opera the prior evening, he had overheard Lionel Stirnweiss raving about the new Waldstein collection of "intelligence" glasses at Tiffany's.

Otto knew that Jedrey, his favorite sales person, would have set aside the most striking monocles for his personal selection. Perhaps, Otto would buy them all to corner the market. After all, Otto had been nurturing his budding reputation as the arbiter of fashion and good taste for several years. He could not abide competition. Further, he did not want to miss his opportunity to make a fashion statement when he appeared at the opening of the upcoming season of the Metropolitan Opera.

Although he had been given a monocle by his mother when he graduated from military training school back in Germany, it only had sentimental value now. He had been known to impress nubile, young ladies with stories of military valor that left him with weakened vision in one eye, necessitating the use of a monocle. He traced many a feminine conquest to his tales of battlefield heroics and optic wounds suffered while he was with the Hussars. That was before he became a respectable banker.

Of course, his tales of military prowess ranged from exaggeration to fabrication depending on the perceived gullibility of the damsel he was trying to bed. Otto always had the ability to embellish a story. And, after the embarrassment with Countess Elisabeth Greffulhe when he emerged from an intermission at the opera wearing his monocle on a different eye than when the opera began, he took great care to keep his stories straight as to which eye had been injured.

So engrossed was he in the gorgeous array of new monocles that Otto almost forgot his lunch appointment. Fortunately, it was across the street at the Waldorf-Astoria Hotel. He dodged piles of horse manure left behind the hansom carriages. Muttering to himself about the need to eliminate horse-drawn conveyances from the better part of town, he hurried into the dining room just as his colleagues were being seated.

A crowd had gathered in the Waldorf's famed Peacock Alley due to the presence of a photography team taking pictures of the famous actress Sarah Bernhardt. She wore a red satin dress that was all tassels and sequins. The photographer was busy setting up his magnesium flash device while Bernhardt took a drag through her cigarette holder trying not to look too bored.

Otto nearly tripped over the legs of a tripod that had been set up near the mirrored entrance to the dining room. The camera was angled to avoid the reflection of the flash in the image. A muted "POOF" accompanied the flash. A blinding bolt of light bounced through a maze of chandeliers and crystal goblets, not to mention the multitude of diamonds gracing the ladies seated near the entrance. The acrid smell of magnesium and sulfur accompanied a white cloud of smoke which drifted upward in the lobby.

Otto scurried past the photographer and smiled at Bernhardt. She responded with a contemptuous scowl. Otto sighed, thinking that some day when he was in charge of the Met, the divas would be scrambling over each other vying for his attention. But for now, he approached the table where Jacob Schiff, the irascible chairman and patriarch of Kuhn Loeb, was seated next to J. Pierpont Morgan, the fabled head of J.P. Morgan & Company. Morgan rubbed his eyes, muttering, "Damn flash nearly blinded me. I've a mind to buy this wretched place just to have a peaceful lunch."

Across the table sat a gentleman Otto did not recognize.

"Allow me to introduce myself, Clarence Bennett Buckman, my friends call me C.B."

"A pleasure to meet you, sir," intoned Otto. With the exception of Pierpont, the others nodded. Buckman failed to observe the cue.

"As you all know, my friend Jacob here gave a speech at the New York Chamber of Commerce earlier this year," said Buckman, touching Jacob's sleeve. Looking down his bulbous nose, Pierpont raised an eyebrow.

"He warned that we were at risk of '*the most severe and far-reaching money panic in history*.[13]' He called for the establishment of a central bank with adequate control of credit resources."

"We know what I said in my speech. Why have you requested this meeting?" interjected Schiff.

Buckman gave him a wounded look of a star pupil who was not used to having his brilliance interrupted. He *fumfered*, "There are some who oppose a central bank and have tried to stoke up fear among the public against what they are calling the Money Trust. This type of talk will only breed resentment and hysteria. At the end of the day, it will not bode well for our plans. The most vocal of these critics is my primary opponent, Charles Lindbergh, Sr."

The Congressman had regained his stride and was warming to his task. He paused, looking for a sign of recognition. Pierpont rolled his eyes. He was no doubt calculating the money he could be making back at his office instead of sitting there. He had a well-earned reputation for being downright nasty to those whose egos surpassed Pierpont's plutomania. At a meeting of the Bankers Circle last year, Pierpont took a pitcher of ice water and poured it onto the speech of the Ambassador to Russia just when he was reaching a crescendo.

"Let me tell you about this fellow Lindbergh. He is a lawyer." Buckman spoke the last word as if it were a vile epithet.

"He is quite studious and thinks his role is to educate the bumpkins on monetary policy. He is actually telling farmers not to trust the banks. He wants them to set up farmers' cooperatives for the purpose of strengthening their independence from the banks. Can you imagine?"

When the expected reaction to this absurdity did not appear, Buckman plowed ahead.

"And, in Minnesota, he is in cahoots with lumber men who want to break the power of railroads to set shipping rates. Lindbergh is in favor of the Hepburn Act and the plan to have railroad transport rates set by the Interstate Commerce Commission. He has asked that 'trustbuster' Roosevelt to come speak for him. Lindbergh thinks that Roosevelt's support might elevate . . . ."

As the Congressman droned on, Schiff sensed an eruption of Vesuvian proportions building in Morgan. After many years of observation, Schiff could predict that the growing shade of reddish-purple on the knurly bumps of Pierpont's nose, meant trouble. Then it came.

"Enough with the palaver, Congressman, let me make one thing clear. We contribute handsomely to your campaign to insure your loyalty, but, we are not your friends. The solution here is obvious. Deluge this upstart with roorbacks, you know, rumors and slander to damage his standing in the community. Tell so many lies about him that his intimates, even his wife, will begin to doubt him. He will spend all his time defending himself and none attacking us. Do I make myself clear?"

Morgan's stentorian voice caused the conversational buzz in the room to stop. All eyes stared in their direction. Pierpont waited a second for effect. Then, with a gesture of pure command, he removed the napkin from his collar. "Now, if you gentlemen will excuse me, I have to go make some money."

When the 'Zeus of Wall Street' exited the room, it felt like he took the oxygen with him. Wide-eyed and slack jawed, Buckman quivered like a spotted fawn.

After a moment, Schiff said, "Don't just sit there, gentlemen. We have our orders. Otto, see that it is done."

$ $ $

A faint knock on his office door was followed by his secretary announcing, "Were you expecting anyone this morning, sir? You have a visitor."

C.A. continued to peruse his papers. "No. Who is here?"

"A Mrs. Fosseen. She claims that she met you at a campaign stop in Minneapolis."

"Fosseen . . . Fosseen? Oh, yes. Bring her in, but, after ten minutes interrupt us. I must finish this chapter."

Lindbergh crossed his office and put on his suit jacket just as Carrie Fosseen entered. Her step quickened and she bypassed the secretary. Extending her hand she said, "C.A. it is indeed a pleasure to see you again. Thank you for your time."

She was wearing a black dress tastefully trimmed with mauve ruffles. A stylish black hat highlighted with matching mauve roses completed her outfit. Her gray eyes darted around the room. As she advanced, she grasped and re-grasped her linen gloves.

"Welcome, Carrie. Please have a seat," C.A. said. "What brings you to our hamlet on this fine day?"

"Ordinarily, I am not this forward. However, after meeting you in Minneapolis, I felt an unusual bond with you. I wracked my brain to identify how I could help you. Then, it dawned on me. . ." She spoke so quickly that the words were a jumbled torrent. She took several shallow breaths and swallowed drily.

"Would you like some water?"

"Yes, please. Thank you . . . . I'm a bit nervous."

"Here," said C.A. as he handed her a tumbler of water. "There's no reason to be nervous."

Sipping slowly and peering over the rim of the glass, her breathing slowed. She fanned herself with a bird-like flutter.

"Whew," A deep breath. "Ok, here it is. I'm here to interview you for *The New York Times*. Well, actually for my cousin who writes for *The New York Times*. I've been sending my cousin copies of your speeches and my cousin wants to do a story on you. The editor does not think that you are important enough for national news. Oops, sorry. . . ."

"No need to apologize. The editor is right. I'm just a country lawyer."

"You see, that's the thing. I think that your ideas need to be broadcast across the nation. So, my cousin and I decided that I would draft an article about your quest against Mammon." Carrie said. "I am an English teacher after all," she said defensively. Lindbergh gave her the same nod he gave little Charley when the boy insisted that he could repair his tricycle.

"OK. I can give you the next half hour. Then, I must leave for a speaking engagement."

Carrie produced a pencil and stenographer's pad from her bag, smiled, and posed the first question on her list.

"I think this is going to be fun," said Lindbergh who was anything but rigid.

A week later, an article bearing the headline, "*Country Lawyer Tilts at Windmills*" appeared in *The New York Times* on page 17 just before the obituaries. The laudatory article submitted by Mrs. Fosseen's cousin had been transformed into a piece dripping with mockery and condescension. Carrie Fosseen phoned him, apologized profusely and promised to make it up to him. Lindbergh assured her that it was not necessary because no one in his district read *The New York Times*.

$ $ $

Wurthels and Lindbergh often breakfasted together in C.A.'s kitchen where they could get a head start on their day. In the comfort of the modern kitchen they were afforded privacy and the best flapjacks in Little Falls. You could say what you wanted about Evy Lindbergh, but her reputation for pecan cornmeal flapjacks was unsurpassed. The men would peruse the papers and linger over coffee discussing their plans for the day. This practice became more vital during the campaign.

"Listen to this," said Sam. "This from the *St. Peter Herald*: headline - 'Candidate Lindbergh Under Investigation'. 'The Herald has learned from anonymous sources inside the Attorney General's office that a grand jury is investigating C.A. Lindbergh's connection to the German-American Bank in Little Falls. The laws regarding grand jury secrecy have made it impossible to substantiate rumors of embezzlement at the bank. Mr. Davis Nessum of the State Banking Examiner's Office stated that bank embezzlement is a serious crime.' The article continues on an inner page."

"Ha! Can't you see that the article says absolutely nothing," laughed C.A.

"Dear, we may see that it is baseless, but many people think that where there is smoke there must be fire," said Evy.

"There have been several dozen articles like this in the last month. 'C.A. under investigation'; 'Lindbergh involved in questionable land deal'; 'Former client sues Lindbergh' and on and on. Can't you see that your reputation is being damaged? Even the town gossip Hattie Jorgenson remarked the other day at the market that 'Your poor husband is being abused in the papers.' Normally, she relishes this type of muck. She loves tearing people down. When she feels sorry for you, you know that the attacks have gone too far."

"Evy has a point C.A. Maybe we need a new approach. Standing silent regarding these slanders makes you look weak," said Sam.

"Stop, both of you. I am not going to dignify this trash by getting into an endless discussion trying to refute every lie against me. That's exactly what Buckman wants. He wants me to stop talking about the issues and waste my time with this drivel."

"It's not drivel, Ridge. You don't see the looks I get when I go to town. Disdain or pity. That's what I get . . . I can't take much more." She dropped her face into the handkerchief in her hands and sobbed, "I can't take it."

"Evy, don't cry. This is politics. It shows that we are getting to them, that they have to resort to muck slinging. When I speak on the stump, I can feel the enthusiasm for my ideas. No one has ever explained to them what is causing their problems. They are listening. They truly are."

Sensing another marital dust-up, Sam seized the chance to mediate.

"Let's focus on your book. I think that will help by keeping attention on the issues. Perhaps you can add a section on professional ethics and use it to defuse a lot of this nonsense."

Sam caught Evy's eye and had trouble fathoming her thoughts. He wondered whether he saw a glimmer of hopefulness or a look of resignation. It passed quickly. The conversation ended when Sam noticed that it was time for their meeting with major donors.

$ $ $

Lindbergh's brain trust sat on the porch arrayed around a small table. C.A. was on the front lawn rolling around with Charles Jr. and

Blake. The pup nipped at Junior's heels as he ran with a bright, red ball in his hands. His high-pitched giggle made the normally sour Drew grin. Just as the puppy was about to trip the boy, C.A. swooped in, grabbed him under the arms and twirled him skyward in a glorious circle. Junior's laugh was infectious.

"Daddy, make me fly again, please Daddy!"

Blake jumped and yelped as C.A. complied again and again until the three playmates collapsed in a writhing, giggling heap.

"Here's some lemonade and cookies for you gentlemen. The cookies are fresh out of the oven. This is my mother-in-law's secret recipe for Minnesota Munchers. Little Charley loves them. He calls them Minnesota Monsters."

"Drew, Big Charley, you are going to enjoy these. They are divine!" said Sam with a somewhat forced gaiety.

"Thanks, Evy. How are you getting on with this big, new house?" asked Weyerhaeuser.

"I like it just fine. We designed it for perfect family living. The main floor has the drawing and music rooms, the dining room and kitchen. You should see our larder. It's huge. The second floor has all the bedrooms and the third floor is C.A.'s favorite. It's got the billiard room and his office. He could stay up there forever and never come down. He's always up there writing and reading his books. Why a bomb could go off down here and he'd never know it."

"Drew here helped C.A. git them special cream-colored bricks. It looks grand from the mill."

"Well, once we finish all the decorating, we'll have you and the wives over for dinner. Might not be 'til Christmas, but, you'll be the first ones invited for sure."

"Why thank you, Evy. We'd be honored to dine with the next Congressman."

Evy nodded, lowered her eyes, and excused herself. Sam's gaze followed Evy as she disappeared into the house as if seeking sanctuary.

"That's the first time I've seen her smile in a month. This house is the only thing that brings her joy lately. You can see how she feels about C.A.'s campaign. I'll bet that in her heart she wishes he loses," said Sam. The men nodded.

"Damn, these cookies are good!" said Big Charley, breaking the silence.

"From what I hear, she may get her wish," commented Drew.

"Where are you getting that?"

"Now Sam, calm down. We want him to win as much as you do. We got him into this. But I've been to the last few rallies and I must say that the crowds have been disappointing. Maybe it's because the harvest is nearing, but...."

"I'm amazed at his stamina," remarked Sam. "He seems to thrive on the stump. He may be exhausted from the travel and his voice may be croaky, but he lights up when he gets in front of a crowd."

"That's good to hear," said Big Charley. "I've been hearing, shall we say, unkind things about C.A. Some of the men at the mill are questioning whether he has the character to win. You know that there line from Shakespeare,

Who steals my purse steals trash. 'Tis something, nothing:
'Twas mine, 'tis his, and has been slave to thousands.
But he that filches from me my good name
Robs me of that which not enriches him
And makes me poor indeed.[14]"

"I assure them that he is a man o' honor and they seem on board, but I'm not sure. There's a rumor that they started a pool, betting to see who wins. The odds against C.A. are rising, accordin' to my foreman."

Sam looked from one to the other. These were C.A.'s biggest supporters. If they were dejected, could defeat be far behind? He saw C.A. glance at them from beneath a tangle of little boy and puppy paws. A momentary frown appeared, then, disappeared when Blake and little Charley both licked his neck. He roared to life and hurled them both into the air.

"I hear that ole Buckman is fixin' to hold a big shindig on Labor Day. That's only three weeks before the primary. So I'm thinkin' that we gotta show that old German how to git votes," said Big Charley.

$ $ $

Labor Day, 1906, broke clear and sunny in Little Falls. Congressman Buckman wore a satisfied smirk on his leathery face as he watched the parade pass the reviewing stand. On the wall of the bank opposite the reviewing stand, in full view of everyone, was a banner proclaiming "Re-elect C.B. Buckman to Congress!"

Buckman forced a plaster smile when C.A. Lindbergh rode by the reviewing stand in an open-topped roadster. The incumbent's right hand twisted languorously as if it were a loose weathervane swiveling in the wind. He's such an amateur, thought Buckman. In three weeks when the primary results are in, Lindbergh will be a bad memory with a small-time law practice and I will be in my rightful place in the capital.

Later, when the parade ended, Clarence was looking forward to a frosted beer along with brats and potato salad. He licked his brushy, salt-and-pepper moustache in anticipation. He might even indulge in a piece of Bessie Johnson's apple crumb pie. His culinary thoughts were interrupted by the shout of "Heads up!"

A baseball whizzed past him followed by a zealous man in overalls chasing it for all he was worth. Ahead a large crowd was cheering, yelling and laughing as another man raced around the makeshift diamond on the edge of the business district. He tripped heading into third base and lay in a heap of dust gasping for air. A man with a megaphone announced, "Well, how about that. Dexter Tivoli just got hisself a triple. Next up for the Loggers is Nils Phillips. Give him a big hand, folks!"

Buckman paused. Although the speaker's face was obscured by the megaphone, something about the voice was familiar. Buckman continued walking past the "Free Beer" booth and the metal coal pit where the smell of roasting brats permeated the area. When he reached the "Fairy Floss" booth where spun sugar glass was being handed to the children, a feeling of dread came over him. Was that a calliope playing over by the gazebo?

"Jenkin Thompson, pitching for the Millers has his hands full."

Buckman slapped his forehead, admonishing himself for his own obtuseness. The megaphone voice belonged to none other than C.A. Lindbergh.

"Howdy, Clarence, can I git you a cold one? You look like you could use one." asked Big Charley.

Buckman mumbled assent, never taking his eyes off the festive crowd.

"Yeah, we figured that there should be a good old
fashioned rivalry ball game to liven things up around here."

"Yes, of course. Good idea. Who is playing?"

"The guys from the mill are playing the loggers now. Then, the farmers are gonna play the mechanics."

Buckman's nod had a stunned, wooden quality to it.

"And, then the winners play next week. The semi-finals are the following week and the finals on the Sunday right before primary day."

Buckman was silent.

"Oh, and did I mention that we are holding this tournament in every county in the district?"

Buckman eyed the sea of voters enjoying his rival's largesse. He was experienced enough to appreciate the enormity of the electoral implications. Clarence Buckman, self-anointed master politician, realized that he would rue the day that he underestimated Lindbergh. He, an incumbent Congressman, had been out-huckstered by a political novice.

More important, Clarence would have a lot of explaining to the New Yorkers who had invested so heavily, buying editors across the district, based on his assurances that the crusading Lindbergh would be stopped. A sharp headache formed over his left temple and he felt a queasiness in his stomach that he had not experienced since he stood over the ruins of his farm after the cyclone of 1886. The image of Pierpont Morgan's fiery black eyes made him shudder. Someone would have to pay; he just hoped it was not him.

As with most campaigns there was an ebb-and-flow that drove the participants from giddiness to despair. Although Buckman was only eight years older than his forty-seven year old challenger, years of too much whiskey in smoke-filled rooms on Capitol Hill had left him looking leathery and chafed, like an old, discarded baseball mitt. In contrast, Lindbergh appeared youthful and vibrant.

Sam seized on the contrast by sending out press releases along with photos of C.A. with his four year old son and puppy. The image of the young-looking father challenging the doughy grandfather was effective. For his part, Buckman used the power of incumbency and Money Trust lucre to thwart Lindbergh's gains.

As the hourglass to the primary dwindled, Sam wore the expression of perpetual worry that characterized all campaign managers. He had surveyed party leaders in all twelve counties and the results were not encouraging. The district-wide baseball tournament had been a stroke of genius; however, the effect had been blunted by a series of strategically placed editorials charging C.A. with rigging the outcomes. Of course, rather than admit to their own ineptitude, the teams that had been eliminated believed the charges.

Even more disturbing was that the railroads in the district had reduced their shipping rates so much that journalists in papers across the district started mocking C.A.'s insistence that there was a Money Trust out to destroy the common folk. The local farmers and merchants were experiencing an economic resurgence. Voters content with the status quo were not inclined to vote for a fire-breathing reformer like Lindbergh.

Moreover, the incessant torrent of scandalous articles against C.A. was like a river wearing down its limestone bed until a canyon forms. The relentless barrage eroded Lindbergh's reform platform and turned the contest into a war of attrition.

Perhaps the most damaging was a series of articles suggesting that C.A. had a wandering eye. Of course, these were flat out fabrications, but there were numerous pictures of C.A. in intense conversation with attractive female volunteers. Perhaps, these encounters were genuine, the result of Lindbergh's progressive views in favor of women's suffrage. Or, as Sam suspected, many of the young women campaign workers were opposition plants with instructions to maneuver C.A. into compromising positions.

Invariably, Lindbergh's passion for the issue was mischaracterized as another type of passion. Photographs of C.A. engaged in animated conversation with unaccompanied women, appeared in local reports of his appearances. Damaging innuendo and gossip attended these images of the handsome candidate and enamored young supporters. As C.A. became more astute at avoiding photos with unaccompanied women and there was a dearth of photos of C.A. with women supporters, the papers would invariably reprint the shot of Carrie Fosseen bear-hugging Lindbergh. The look of rapturous adulation on her face supported many an editorial accusation that Lindbergh was a rake and a cad.

To make matters worse, Evy rarely attended his campaign appearances, not only because of her responsibilities with little Charley, but due to her natural aversion to the erosion of her privacy that went along with public life. Where some political wives thrived in the spotlight, Evangeline Lindbergh cringed. As the campaign progressed and the attention grew, Evy withdrew further and her resentment festered. Rumors of marital discord between C.A. and Evy abounded.

Throughout it all, C.A. carried the battle to Buckman, revealing and challenging every vote the incumbent had ever cast. The record demonstrated that Buckman was a pawn of the entrenched power base. Despite these revelations, the Lindbergh campaign was having

difficulty gaining traction. Sam worried whether enough voters would see the truth. He worried that the attacks on Lindbergh were influencing the voters. The questions after C.A.'s speeches focused more on Lindbergh's character than his positions. They needed something to reverse the negative momentum. But what?

The campaign manager sipped his tepid coffee and choked back the acid taste in his throat. He secretly wished that the campaign would go away. Since the trip to Minneapolis, Sam had developed strong feelings toward Elisha Sharlette. He knew that he was acting like an infatuated schoolboy, but he could not get enough of her. On more than one occasion, he had driven to Minneapolis to be with her. Lately, she had taken up residence in a cabin he owned on Orono Lake. It was perfect – located between Little Falls and Minneapolis, it was secluded, yet accessible. Elisha, the beautiful Elisha, delicious Elisha, dominated his thoughts.

On some mornings when he left her asleep in the cabin after a night of amorous delight, he admonished himself for neglecting the campaign. By the time he reached Little Falls to resume scheduling campaign speeches, coordinating volunteers and charming newspaper editors, he vowed to abstain from Elisha. All it took was one late afternoon call promising intimacy and he was back on the road to Orono Lake and his goddess.

He looked around the Black and White Hamburger Shop hoping to see his friend. Sam pulled back his sleeve. His watch showed 4:45. If he could get rid of C.A. by five, he could be on the road and with Elisha before dark. Where was he?

Wearing his trademark fedora and three-piece suit, Lindbergh walked up the sidewalk. C.A. smiled and tipped his hat to the ladies who were on their way to market. Sam fumed. It was as if Lindbergh were deliberately dallying in order to torture him. C.A. was holding a manila envelope and his lips were pursed in a whistle.

"It took you long enough. The coffee is cold," said Sam in a voice dripping with resentment on account of his friend's jaunty attitude.

"Aye, Sam, it is truly a beautiful day."

"What makes you say that? Voting is in ten days and it is not looking good. The muck-slinging is taking its toll. We need a miracle to pull this one out of the fire." C.A. gave Sam an enigmatic grin.

"What has gotten into you, Ridge? You look like a bullsnake that just swallowed a gopher."

"Sam, our prayers have been answered," said C.A. placing the envelope on the tabletop after wiping it dry.

Lindbergh held the envelope with one hand and gently removed a photograph. It took Sam a second to orient the picture which was a reflected image. In the foreground he could make out that famous French actress, oh, what was her name? Sam looked at C.A. with a confused look. What is so exciting about a publicity shot of some French actress?

Lindbergh huffed, and then pointed to another section of the image with a gesture that said, back there, dummy. Sam focused on the people in the background reflected in the mirror behind the actress.

He recognized Buckman immediately. The bow tie and handlebar moustache were dead giveaways. Buckman was seated at a table with several other gentlemen. One was a dandy sporting a monocle, he was beside another man with a trim grey beard and appeared to be wearing a yarmulke. Sitting next to him was a scowling bull of a man. Sam shrugged. Then, it hit him like a camera flash. The other man was none other than J. Pierpont Morgan, his distinctive nose was obvious once you focused on the correct portion of the image.

"What *is* this? When was it taken? Where did you get it?" asked Sam, the words flowing out without breath.

"Slow down. This is a photograph that appeared in *The New York Times* last week in a story about Sarah Bernhardt appearing at Carnegie Hall. It was taken at the Waldorf Astoria Hotel in New York City. The shorter fellow with the white beard and yarmulke is Jacob Schiff, the head of Kuhn Loeb, investment bankers. And, of course, you recognize Zeus himself. They are having a cozy meal with our Congressman. Can you believe it?" said C.A., barely containing his glee.

"This is a picture from the national news?"

"Not exactly; only the portion with Bernhardt appeared in the paper. The rest of the image was cropped out."

"I see. But, how did you get this?"

"That's the strange part. It came in the mail in this envelope postmarked NYC," said C.A.

"Did it come with any note, or anything?"

Lindbergh handed Sam a piece of stationary. He read it audibly, "I thought you might be able to use this. Signed, a friend."

"The handwriting is definitely feminine. But I have no idea who might have sent it. I've never even been to New York City."

They lapsed into silence, each contemplating their good fortune and how to make the best advantage from this photo. Lindbergh retrieved the photo and note and returned them into the envelope. A slight aroma wafted from the envelope. What was it? Lavender, jasmine, maybe quince? C.A. shook his head quizzically.

$ $ $

Buckman was flustered when the photo appeared in every paper in the district. The *Little Falls Daily Transcript* bore the headline:

Buckman Meets With *Non-existent* Money Trust in NYC

The accompanying story told of Buckman's confused, deceitful, and contradictory attempts to explain the photo. Editors of five pro-Buckman papers withdrew their endorsements and shifted their support to C.A. Lindbergh. After publication of the shocking photo of Buckman dining with Mammon from Wall Street, the results of the primary were never in doubt.

With the Republican nomination secured at the end of September, Lindbergh rode a pulsing wave of momentum into the general election.

1906 New York City, NY

Why then tonight let us assay our plot.
~ William Shakespeare

"Patience is a virtue, patience is a virtue. If I hear that one more time I'm going to explode,"

"*Beruhige*, calm down, Otto," said Paul. They were seated in the Kuhn Loeb banquette at Marcel's, the fashionable restaurant around the corner from their offices in the financial district in Manhattan. Otto Kahn, a new partner at the venerable banking house, tugged open his napkin and the silverware wrapped within the careful folds jangled onto his cloisonné plate.

Otto Hermann Kahn was one of the youngest and most ambitious partners at Kuhn Loeb & Company. Born in Mannheim, Germany, he had come to New York more than twenty years earlier, married Addie Wolff, the daughter of one of the senior partners and had risen meteorically through the ranks of New York City bankers. He reminded his new bride that his mother had named him Otto which in German meant wealth, fortune.

In his time in New York, he had become something of a celebrity – an unusual trait in the normally staid and private world of investment banking where invisibility was considered a virtue. His gift for self-promotion bordered on genius. On one occasion, he held a closing of a multi-million dollar railroad merger in the lobby of the Metropolitan Opera House. The final signing of the papers was heralded by the famed tenor Enrico Caruso singing the "Hallelujah Chorus." Photos of Otto and the world famous tenor toasting with clients, E.H. Harriman and Leonor Fresnel Loree, were splashed on the front pages of the Wall Street Journal and all the NYC tabloids. The publicity garnered great attention for Otto's two passions, banking and the theater, specifically, The Met.

Of course, it simultaneously aroused the ire of Jacob Schiff, the chairman of Kuhn Loeb, who wanted to expel Otto from the firm. However, Otto's father-in-law, Abraham Wolff, a senior member of the firm, had persuaded Schiff that such drastic action against Otto was contrary to the firm's interest. Bram Wolff made his case to the pragmatic Schiff by reciting the roster of new clients garnered by what Schiff referred to as the "vulgar stunt." If anything would cause Schiff to abandon his dignity, it was an increase in the almighty dollars in his pocket. The motion for expulsion never saw the light of day and was replaced by a substantial bonus paid to Otto by a chagrined Schiff.

At the moment, Otto was preoccupied with another problem. In his right hand he twiddled his monocle. It shone bright gold as he handled it. The motto "Auri Sacra Fames" was emblazoned on the rim. Translated from Latin, it meant the "accursed hunger for gold" and Otto used it to remind himself of his life's ambition – to accumulate as much gold as possible. Otto Kahn was the perfect disciple of Mammon.

He and his partner Paul Warburg were in charge of the effort to gain enactment of a law to reform the banking and currency system of the United States, that is, capture the currency of the United States. During the Civil War, President Lincoln outsmarted Mammon and issued "greenbacks" on the credit of the federal government, effectively bypassing the private banks. Since the Civil War, the U.S. currency had fluctuated spasmodically, resulting in instability and periodic panics where customers demanded return of their deposits from banks that were incapable of returning their cash.

The New York banking interests, led by Kuhn Loeb and J.P. Morgan & Company, were determined to reduce volatility by "reforming" the currency. The most recent panic in 1893 had ended only when Morgan and the Rothschild banking interests in Europe loaned the U.S. Treasury 3.5 million ounces of gold.

The bankers were hailed as saviors of the Treasury, when in truth, they had profited obscenely from the crisis that they had created. The Holy Grail of the current generation of bankers, control of the dollar, was now within reach. Otto, for one, would not allow this opportunity to go to waste. He knew that the creation of controlled chaos was their most potent weapon. The last thing he wanted was for some rookie Congressman out of Minnesota exposing their game prematurely.

Otto straightened his French cuffs and tugged gently at his vest. He withdrew his monocle and perused the hand-calligraphied list of specials. A glimmer of refracted light danced on his cheek as he adjusted his gold monocle. Otto shook his head imperceptibly as he scanned his partner across the table. From Warburg's garish bowtie to the nubby woolen fabric of his formless suit, he was out of phase with fine *couture*; an inestimable failing in Otto's view.

"I have told him repeatedly that there were remnants of the Populists who were gaining strength in the Midwest. They could jeopardize our plans. Now that he has won the primary, he is more dangerous than ever."

Otto took a sip of water before continuing.

"Have you seen the latest speech of that lawyer in Minnesota who is running for Congress? Why it sounds like he was sitting in our boardroom, the way he described our plans," exclaimed Otto.

"Otto, you've got to be patient."

"There you go. Now you are starting to sound like Old Jake."

"You know that Jacob despises that nickname. If he hears that you've been calling him that, there will be hell to pay," said Paul rolling his eyes and tilting his head slightly toward Arnaud the waiter who was approaching, deftly balancing a tray with their aperitifs and salads.

"Yes, I understand. It's just that all my analysis on the likely members of the next Congress is being disregarded. This Lindbergh fellow could wreck our plans. You of all people should appreciate the importance of . . . ."

Paul was gobbling up his food as if he was breaking a fast. He realized that Otto had stopped talking only when he reached for one of Chef Jentoine's sunflower chive brioches.

"I'm sorry, please continue," said Paul gesturing with his fork, a piece of Romaine dangling precariously from the side of his moustache. Otto shook his head as if he were watching his dachshund puppy chew on a slipper, cute but incorrigible. Otto inhaled the shallow breath of a Talmudic tutor.

"Have you been out west, Paul? Have you seen the railroads being built? You should come with me on my next trip. They are blasting through the mountains. What they do with explosives these days is remarkable. Harriman employs the best. There is one fellow that you have to meet. His name is 'Nitro' Gleeson. He calls himself the maestro of dynamite. Such a colorful character; he's right out of a five cent cowboy novel. He's tall, wears a fortified black Stetson, you know, like the Plug Uglies wear as helmets. And, get this, he wears a leather string tie that has detonator caps on the tips of the rawhide. You would love him," said Otto, warming to his subject.

"I hope that is a nickname."

"It is. I gave it to him myself. His real name is Aloysius Gleeson the third. I told him that he needed something more catchy, more sinister," chuckled Otto.

"You succeeded. He does not sound like the kind of fellow that I would associate with," remarked Paul. A wry smile crossed Otto's face.

"Maybe so, Paul, but he is a good fellow to know."

"Whatever do you mean?" asked Paul.

"You'll see. You and Old Jake will see," replied Otto with a malevolent gleam in his eyes.

"Ah, look who just walked in," said Otto. "I'll be right back; I need to talk to her, excuse me."

Before Paul could open his mouth, Otto was across the room inviting himself to sit with a young woman and her companions. Anne smiled politely to Otto's incursion. She was a tall, slightly ungainly woman with dark, raccoon-like eyes and a sensitive mouth.

"Otto, you know Bessy and Elsie, of course."

Otto regarded Elisabeth "Bessy" Marbury with a critical eye. She was one of the most powerful literary and theatrical agents in the world, controlling many of the continental writers whose works had become the fashion in New York theater.

She was a large, buxom woman. With her fleshy face and porcine eyes, she reminded Otto of the neighborhood butcher from his boyhood days, whose ponderous countenance and thick features earned him the nickname of *saukerl*. Behind her back people called her Bossy, on account of her unladylike negotiating tactics. It was rumored that she nearly broke Flo Ziegfeld's wrist in an arm-wrestling match over royalties.

"Nice to see you ladies. Bessy, we need to talk about the rights to some avant-guard French plays that we are considering for a possible *Theatre Francais*."

"Sure, I'll let you know when I am free," she replied without lifting her eyes from the menu.

Otto turned to Elsie de Wolfe, a diminutive, former actress who had made her mark as a pioneer in interior design. She held her slender hand to Otto who gave it a slight buss, her ornate spider ring scratching his cheek barely.

"I hear that your designs for the Colony Club are a triumph of light, air and comfort. I would love to visit some day."

"Otto, sometimes you are guilty of extraordinary social obtuseness," she mocked. "You know that the Colony is for ladies only. You simply lack the requisite accoutrements."

A languorous sweep over her bosom with her alabaster hand produced a boisterous laugh.

"Surely, you ladies are not as obtuse as the male of the species. Would you be guilty of the same petty exclusions as men?" said Otto.

"Food for thought, Otto," said Anne.

"Yeah, that's it. The men can bring us the food on holidays," quipped Bessy.

"*Touchè*"

Tacking away from this volatile subject, Otto pulled an envelope from his jacket and handed it to Anne.

"Here are some tickets to our new production featuring Isadora Duncan. I thought you might enjoy her latest triumph."

"How thoughtful of you, Otto, I adore her. When does the performance begin?"

Otto withdrew a ticket and deftly removed his monocle from his breast pocket to read it. It was attached to his lapel by a chain made of turquoise and silver beads that was a gift from President Roosevelt on return from a campaign trip in the southwest. Otto had been "most helpful" in T.R.'s words in arranging the necessary railroad connections for the whistle-stop tour. Otto's partners had been most impressed with the stylish gift.

"What a distinctive chain you have there, Otto," remarked Elsie, her eyes widening.

"Oh, my," said Anne, clutching at her turquoise necklace. "It's the same chain that the Colonel gave to me and to Dad for his watch chain."

"I've got one from Roosevelt, too," said Bessy, raising her eyeglasses that were attached to her neck with a turquoise and silver chain.

Straining against the folds of her stout neck, the chain suddenly popped. Like the spray of champagne when opened, the beads scattered onto the marble flooring. As they bounced, accompanied by a staccato pinging, the bread boy stooped to gather them. An approaching waiter carrying a tray of champagne flutes failed to see the boy and tripped. The flutes flew with ominous accuracy toward Anne. Otto lurched toward her and caught two glasses, the others crashed to the floor and shattered. His monocle swung like a pendulum as Otto regained his balance.

"Well done, well done," commented a man at the next table.

Otto presented fizzing glasses to Anne and Elsie, while Bessy and the bread boy groped after the beads like children playing jacks.

$ $ $

The months of campaigning had finally reached an end. It was the night before Election Day, 1906. After his win in the Republican primary in late September, Lindbergh had gained momentum and the endorsements of most of the newspaper editorial boards in the District. C.A. and Sam shared a well-deserved evening of quiet together.

"You know, Ridgy, when I designed this billiard room, this is precisely what I envisioned. You, me and our buddy Hiram, enjoying a nice, sociable game of one pocket," said Sam, his index finger extending over his drink as it swept the room in a grand gesture. C.A. stood before the large fireplace filled with a crackling fire, the logs hissing steam. Blake lay on his side enjoying the warmth and proximity to his master.

Lindbergh's suit jacket was off, but he was still wearing his vest and the sleeves of his white shirt were rolled up to his elbows. Leaning on his pool cue, relaxed, one leg bent, he looked every bit the country squire, or, soon-to-be Congressman.

"This is one fine home Sam. You outdid yourself. Evy absolutely loves this place. I can't tell you how much we appreciate all of your efforts. You've been an amazing campaign manager. Regardless of the results, we are forever in your debt."

"Don't be so modest. You were the candidate; you made the campaign. You know that by this time tomorrow night, they will be calling you Congressman."

His wrist propelled the cue into the white ball which drove the green ball into the designated pocket. The sharp crack of the balls colliding synchronized with Sam's saying the word Congressman and provided emphasis.

"That's game, Sam. You win again. I think I'll call it a night," he said, stifling a yawn.

"Wait, C.A. There's something I must share with you. It's important."

"Can't it wait? I'm bone weary." Blake lifted his head and yawned. C.A. yawned, too. Then, he knelt to ruffle the fur behind the pup's ears.

"Actually, I wish it could wait," said Sam who poured himself another drink. "But, things are moving quickly and we have important matters to resolve . . . before I leave."

At the last phrase, C.A. swiveled from Blake to look at Sam. "What did you just say?"

"I said that I am going to be leaving."

"When? Where? What?"

"Wednesday. The day after tomorrow."

"I know when Wednesday is. Tell me, what the heck is going on?" C.A. was on his feet now, all vestiges of sleepiness gone.

"I've been meaning to tell you, but, what with the frenzy of the campaign there was never a right time. It's just that Elisha and I are in love. We are going to live in New York City."

"I hope this is a joke," said C.A., looking directly into Sam's eyes for sign that he was not serious. There was none.

"My goodness! You really are leaving. Hully gee."

"Now, Ridge, don't start with your lawyer's worst-case scenario analysis. Trust me, I have this under control. I have all the business files in order and scheduled a meeting with your brother Frank in the morning to pass the baton. We have to leave so soon because Elisha has been offered an opportunity to appear on Broadway."

Lindbergh collapsed onto an upholstered Morris chair and shook his head.

"Sam, I'm not concerned about the business. I know that between Frank and my expected new status, the business will be OK. No, I'm shaking my head because this is so unexpected. How long have you known E-lish-sha?" he said, exaggerating the pronunciation.

"I mean, what do you know about her? Have you met her family? Sam, do you know what you are getting into?"

"I appreciate your concern, Ridge. Listen, I'm a big boy. I can handle myself," said Sam. "I'm sure that you remember when you fell in love with Evy. Well, I'm experiencing the same feeling. I can't get her out of my mind. After what you've been through, you know that life is short and I'm going to take my chance at happiness with Elisha."

C.A. shook his head and gave Sam a patronizing look. Part of C.A.'s initial reaction was pure self-interest. He thought that the business would be in good hands while he tended to congressional assignments. Now, a degree of uncertainty had been injected into the equation. Who was he to tell a grown man how to live his life? He and Sam had been through tough times together. He loved him like a brother. Yet, Lindbergh struggled with the age old problem of watching a friend heading toward a train wreck relationship. Should he express his distrust for the potential mate and risk alienating his friend, or, remain silent and watch events unfold? Recognizing a Hobson's choice, C.A. opted to bite his tongue and be gracious. He cleared his throat.

"It seems that, with God's blessing, we will both be embarking on new paths. I'll be in Washington and you'll be in New York. Let's make sure that we wear out the road between the capital and New York City visiting each other."

For the first time, Sam realized the magnitude of his decision. He swallowed hard, blinked multiple times and reached to hug his friend. Lindbergh stiffened and extended his hand.

Sam shook C.A.'s hand and whispered, "Godspeed, Ridge."

"And, Godspeed to you – I fear that we will both need it," replied Lindbergh, with moist eyes.

1906 Little Falls, MN

It is the personality of the mistress that the home expresses. Men are forever guests in our homes, no matter how much happiness they may find there.
~ Elsie de Wolfe

The long campaign had taken its toll. C.A. was gaunt to the point where his suits hung on him like they were being supported by a wooden hanger. A full two inches separated his collar from his pencil neck. His right hand was swollen and mushy from all the handshaking. His voice had been reduced to a scratchy whisper.

The grind had been especially hard on his relationships. Sam was leaving for New York City. His brother Frank was so overwhelmed with the responsibility thrust on him that he barely had time to visit the bathroom, let alone confer with his brother like in the past. And worst of all, Evy was not there with him. She had begged off, saying little Charley had the croup and she had to stay with him at home. In their kitchen, C.A. had tried to convince her that little Charley would be fine at home with his grandmother. Evy pushed him toward the door.

"Just go to your precious victory party. Go!"

The last word was uttered with reproof, her eyes blazed with defiance. He shrugged his shoulders in a gesture of resignation. She glared at him as he let himself out.

Since they were political novices, they had not made plans for a victory party. Big Charley remedied that by clearing out the loading dock at the Westside Mill which was miraculously festooned with campaign banners and streamers purchased from the Engstrom's General Store. Nobody seemed to mind that the streamers were black and orange, left over from Halloween. Several kegs of beer were set up next to the outdoor grills that were soon sizzling with brats.

C.A. stood next to a beaming Big Charley, when they heard the sound of music approaching. Around the corner, the high school marching band strutted into the parking lot. Pandemonium erupted when a banner with the election results was strung across the front of the building.

"Hip, hip hooray," the growing crowd of supporters cheered.

"Congratulations C.A. you did it," shouted Sam over the din of the brass band and boisterous crowd.

"No, we did it, Sam. Thanks to you and Charles and Drew, we prevailed against the odds. I never realized how much effort it takes to get elected."

The crowd out front was restless. He could hear Caleb and some of the boys from Morrison County start chanting his name. The chanting effort faltered in the din. Then, it was picked up by a contingent from Brainerd. Soon the building reverberated with the chant, "C.A. Congress, C.A. Congress! We want C.A.!"

Lindbergh stood on the loading dock and addressed his friends. He recalled some of the highlights of his campaign. He pictured his family, friends and clients volunteering to work in his headquarters late in the evenings drawing signs, stuffing envelopes, and preparing lists. C.A. acknowledged the many people who contributed in so many ways to his victory. He concluded by vowing to represent them to the best of his ability and, God willing, accomplish real change to improve their lives.

Despite his exhaustion, his eyes shone luminous and fierce like a successful athlete at the end of a contest that forced him to expend all his resources. No longer the gentleman country lawyer, he was now a hardened advocate who knew how to deliver the decisive point. During the primary, he had stumbled in the early debates against an experienced incumbent. However, once he became familiar with the stump, C.A. simply worked harder, prepared better and out-thought his opponents. He won by a comfortable margin.

After the customary celebratory remarks, C.A. mingled with his joyous supporters. Sam watched his friend shaking hands and chatting amiably with friends and strangers alike. What was that old adage about victory having a thousand fathers, but defeat being an orphan? Looking out at this victory celebration, Sam had no doubt of its veracity.

C.A. was cornered by Hattie Jorgenson, the town gossip and phone operator. Taking pity on his friend, Sam hooked his elbow and, with perfunctory apologies to Hattie, whisked C.A. away into the Pine Tree Lumber Company executive offices. They reminisced about the campaign with C.A.'s inner circle. Sam insisted that C.A. recount the story of one of C.A.'s most memorable encounters.

After considerable prompting, Lindbergh relented. He recalled an appearance at Sand Dunes Forest, a state park of oak savanna and prairie. As the crowd at the rally dissipated and he was folding his notes into his breast pocket, he was approached by a dapper-looking gentleman. He had a friendly open face, sporting dark moustaches slightly upturned on the ends. The setting sun reflecting off his pincnez obscured his eyes.

"Hello, my name is Frank. I just wanted you to know that I, too, have researched the power-behind-the-throne and you are on to something. It is imperative that we try to expose such tomfoolery. We need people with vision to lead. *I believe that dreams – day dreams, you know, with your eyes wide open and your brain machinery whizzing – are likely to lead to the betterment of the world.*[15]"

Sensing a unique presence, C.A. stopped what he was doing and said, "Thank you. I have had difficulty in penetrating the depth of influence that is hidden from the public. I've heard some refer to the process as trying to peel back the layers of an onion, but I see it more like trying to fight an octopus. You have to wrestle with eight tentacles, while avoiding its venomous beak. Not an easy task."

"I see that I do not have to warn you about the perils of peering behind the curtain. Vigilance and care, my friend, vigilance and care," said Frank. With a wave of his hand, he departed.

C.A. recounted how he had shrugged at the cautionary statement and headed for the car. When they arrived back at Lindbergh's home, Sam could hardly contain himself. He sat next to C.A. without saying a word, waiting. C.A. looked up, squinting, "What?"

"I'll bet that you have no idea who you just spoke to," said Sam.

"So, should I?"

"Yes, of course."

"OK," said C.A., putting his papers into his briefcase with an abrupt toss. "Enlighten me." He said, exhaling loudly.

"Don't be so huffy," admonished Sam. C.A. tilted his head and stared.

"OK, I'm sorry. You're tired, I know," said Sam. "The mystery man was none other than L. Frank Baum, the famous author."

"The fellow who wrote *The Wonderful Wizard of Oz*?"

"The very same," answered Sam. The group grinned in appreciation, someone remarked that it was typical Lindbergh aplomb.

$ $ $

By the time he got home, the house was dark. C.A. was exhausted. His head drooped onto the pillow and gravity took control of his eyelids. He fell asleep thinking of the words of Frank Baum. The words swirled, gaining speed, "Vigilance and care, vigilance and care, vigilance and care . . . ." Like a vortex, vigilance and care, swept over C.A. who fell into a deep slumber.

C.A. dreamed that he was running through a field behind his house. A witch, flying on a rustic broom, was chasing him. She had a horrid, green nose that was covered with knurly bumps. Her features were masculine with dark piercing eyes and a white, brushy moustache. She wore a monocle. Could it be? His dream-self thought how strange it was that the witch was a combination of Morgan and Kahn. She was cackling and shouting threats and warnings at him. The witch swooped and swirled above him. The sky was black and foreboding, punctuated by brilliant flashes of lightning that were followed by fierce some thunders. C.A. shivered in the cold rain that drove down from above. The smell of ozone, like the odor given off by an electric engine, permeated the air. C.A. raced for the safety of a culvert that nestled near the driveway.

From a high altitude she dived downward, with the menace of a red-tailed hawk. The harpy reached inside her black cloak and retrieved a round object. With an ear-piercing shriek, she hurled it at him. It exploded. The concussion knocked him facedown to the ground. Spitting dirt, his ears ringing, he lifted his head off the pillow.

Where was he?

"Did you hear that?" said Evy.

He was home, in his bed. As the fog of deep sleep evaporated, he heard a sharp crackling and smelled burning timber. His first thought was the comfort of sitting before a blazing fire in the fireplace on a snowy night.

Lindbergh looked out the window and saw the carriage house lit with a bright, reddish-orange glow. The sun was reflecting off the white surface of the building. He thought, wait, it's too early for sunrise. Red in the morning, sailor's warning. The image flickered. It was not sunrise; it was a reflection - a bright echo of light coming from the house.

A thin haze of smoke infiltrated the room. A single word permeated his consciousness. He screamed as loud as he could,
"FIRE!"

"Evy, find Charley and get out of the house immediately. I'll call the fire company. Quick, go."

The fire company arrived in twelve minutes. In that time, C.A. and Bjorn, the Lindbergh foreman, made sure that everyone was safely evacuated. C.A. searched for his briefcase that contained his speech notes and the book manuscript he was drafting. He barely escaped from the burning house with it, when several joists near the kitchen collapsed sending a spray of embers fifty feet skyward.

"Stay back," commanded Lars Svenson, the chief of the Little Falls Fire Department and cleanup hitter of the Little Falls Pumpers champion baseball team. He had been in the stationhouse working the graveyard shift when he received the alarm. In an instant, his thoughts of baseball conquests and shiny trophies shifted to an adrenaline rush of action that all firefighters experience when the alarm sounds.

Now, he was standing on the running board of the bright, red pumper. The steam engine hissed and throbbed powerfully. Part of his crew skillfully directed water from the hoses onto the main house, while others watered down the carriage house and barn to keep the fire from spreading.

Bjorn came over to C.A. and reported that he had safely evacuated the horses and cows and the men were now removing the motorized automobile and tractors. C.A. nodded. He looked to where Evy was standing. She was clutching little Charley who was wrapped in his favorite blanket, the one decorated with fantastical flying machines. C.A. allowed himself a brief smile at the wondrous new century that his son would enjoy. There were so many frontiers to conquer.

Another crash brought him back to the unfolding tragedy. The house and all its contents had turned into an inferno. All their possessions were consumed by fire. His library, their furniture, family heirlooms were all gone. Although he was not a sentimental man, he mourned the destruction of the few mementoes of his parents, the daguerreotypes from his first marriage, the Bible containing the family lineage, some of it written in indecipherable Swedish. Except for some of the things that were in his law office, all of his material possessions were gone. He shivered in the early morning hours, thankful that Evy, the children and all the help had been safely evacuated.

Something nagged at him. He was missing something. What was he forgetting?

A trickle of cold sweat ran down the back of his neck. A panic gripped him.

Blakey, where was Blakey?

$ $ $

In the weeks after the fire, C.A. was consumed by unprecedented demands. What with the preparations for his term in Congress, the plans to transition his law practice and the hurried meetings with the architect who was redesigning their new home, C. A. never saw it coming.

"Sam, Sam have you prepared the Weyerhaueser/Drayton contract?" said C.A. as he dashed into the conference room.

"It's almost complete. Big Charley and Drew will be here tomorrow for the final OK," replied Sam. "They want to talk to you about arranging a meeting with Gifford Pinchot, the new head of the U.S. Forest Service. They are concerned about his efforts to manage national forest reserves. Whatever policy he adopts may significantly impact their business and they are anxious to present their side of the issues to him before the policy is solidified."

C.A. never looked at Sam who bore the harried look of an overworked beaver. His upper lip twitched over his protruding front teeth. His eyes rolled back in exasperation, "You have not heard a single word . . . ."

"Yes, – contract done, Charley and Drew here tomorrow, Pinchot meeting. See what I can do. I forgot to tell you. I will not be here tomorrow. I've been summoned to a meeting of the state Republican caucus in Minneapolis. Can you cover my meeting with the rep from the farmers' co-op? Thanks."

C.A. exchanged one stack of papers for another, stuffed it into his briefcase and was out the door before Sam could respond. Sam spun around in an effort to face the whirlwind. All he saw was the back of C.A.'s head and the flash of an over-the-shoulder wave. Sam sat down in a heap, shaking his head. Thinking that demands on his partner were enormous, Sam recalled the old adage about being careful what you wished for....

The pace only intensified in the months following the election. There were endless meetings in Minneapolis and Washington. There were receptions in Chicago hosted by the Speaker of the House and even one in Sagamore Hill to meet President Roosevelt.

💲 💲 💲

In the immediate aftermath of the fire, the Lindbergh family took refuge in a cabin by the river. When the house was under construction, the cabin had been their temporary home. Despite the cramped space, it was familiar and comfortable. C.A. decided that the cabin might just be a place of healing. He turned down other offers from family and friends to provide shelter. Unfortunately, his hope that a feeling of nostalgia might defuse the tension that had built up was wishful thinking. If anything, the loss of her precious home on the hill drove Evy into a dark place.

"I can't take anymore, Charles,"

"What do you mean Evy?"

"First, it was the disruption to our lives, your law practice, your business, our home life. I saw that you were committed. You needed something more in your life. My Dad told me that men feel the need for a quest in the middle of their lives. I understand. At least I thought I did."

She paused, looking directly into his eyes. With lowered eyes, he inhaled. He knew that she was just warming up.

"Then, it was those horrid stories. Day after day, insulting slander. So much vile filth spewed toward you, toward us. I'm glad that little Charley is too young for school. He would have been brutalized by the trash thrown at us."

Another pause, this time to gauge his contrition. C.A. obliged. His jaw tucked, he stood before her open-faced.

"But, when they try to kill us by burning down our home with us in it; that is beyond the pale. I have nightmares that the house is burning and I am running around the house looking for Charley. I can't find him. I just keep running through the smoke, calling his name. Never finding him; just searching, endlessly."

Tears flowed down her cheeks. C.A. handed her a handkerchief.

"And, I keep seeing the image of Sheriff Goff walking up the driveway from the culvert, carrying Blake. He was hanging limp, blood clotted on the side of his head. I thought he was dead. The sheriff said he found him collapsed in the culvert, whimpering. If the sheriff had not heard him down there he would have bled to death. And, for what?"

She knew that C.A. had been frantic while Blake was missing. She glared at him and pressed her point.

"You may think that this is worth it. You and your stupid male stubbornness may think that, as the farmers say, now is the time to tap the well deeper." Reaching a crescendo, Evy breathed deeply. Her normally gentle eyes flashed with emotion.

"I will not endanger little Charley or my own life, so that you can tilt at windmills like a crazy, old fool. We're done. Do you hear, we are done!"

Her stare was sharper than a Minnesota icicle on a wolf moon night. It had taken all of her strength to challenge her husband. But, she was desperate. She feared for her precious little son. She tried to catch her breath. Her heart raced. C.A. looked at her and sighed. He took both her hands in his.

"Don't you see that the worst is over? We have won. We are going to Washington, a new beginning. It is time to set things straight; our people deserve no less."

"Surely, you are not serious. You can't begin to comprehend the nature of the enemies you have stirred. Mammon will not rest until its minions destroy us."

"Aren't you being a bit melodramatic, Evy? Mammon stirring? This is not the apocalypse. We live in a nation of laws. I trust the law to protect and preserve our safety."

"You are such a fool, Ridge! You have challenged the money powers; do you expect them to stand idly by while you dismantle their means to fortune?"

"Let's say, for the sake of argument, that you are right," he said in his best lawyerly tone. "What would you have me do?"

"Quit. Announce that you have changed your mind and vacate the seat."

Her face shone with satisfaction that she had devised the perfect solution. She added a quick nod in affirmation; then waited. At the word quit, he flinched. It was like she had uttered an obscenity in some dark, visceral language. A look of sadness crossed his face. He dropped her hands. C.A. flexed and released his hands as if searching for something else to hold onto – something to bring the conversation back from the brink.

"You know, Evy, in the darkest days, my father would say, that to succumb is to die."

He faltered. His voice grew thick, almost a sob. The thought of all his father's suffering, and through it all, how his indomitable spirit shone. The vicious slanders that drove August from Sweden, and then, the excruciating pain of the mutilation of his left side at the mill that subjected him to a lifetime of debilitating handicap; he never succumbed.

With tears in his eyes, C.A. recalled his father wielding a scythe with one hand with a cyclone approaching. He refused the entreaties of his mother to get inside to safety. With C.A. at his side, his father shouted into the face of the storm, "I cannot stop. We do not eat if I stop!"

C.A. placed his hands over his eyes, then, wiped away the tears.

"Evy, I cannot and, will not, abandon what I . . . , what we . . . , have worked so hard to achieve. District 6 deserves us, it needs us and I would rather die trying to change things than stay back here in a flowery bed of ease. This is my destiny."

"You have made your choice. So be it. Mark my words, it is *you* who choose this path, not me and not little Charley."

November 1906 New York City, NY

In great houses dwell small people.
~ Maxim Gorky

Ever since he decided to run for Congress, his life had been an emotional rollercoaster. At first, the highs and lows of the campaign unnerved him. However, once he detected a rhythm, he learned to modulate the highs and lows. As he gained experience he used the vagaries of the campaign to his advantage and expended less useless energy chasing goals that were either ephemeral or worthless. His preparations and anxieties were controlled and efficient. He understood the importance of pace, momentum and of peaking at the right time. If only these principles could be applied to his personal life.

He feared that his relationship with Evy had been irreparably damaged. She had relocated to her family home with little Charley. For the first time in a long time, C.A. was faced with a problem that seemed insurmountable. His foray into public life had been rewarding on several levels so far. However, it had proven to be incompatible with his marriage. Perhaps, the campaign itself was the problem. He hoped that once he settled into the flow of his new position Evy would see that it was like any other job and relent. In his heart, he suspected that the public life of a congressman might never be normal enough for Evy. There were too many demands and pressures. All he could do was let it play out over time.

C.A. took comfort in the principle that God laughs at man's plans.

Look at Sam. Who could have predicted that his staid, dedicated business partner would fall head over heels for some showgirl and uproot his comfortable life in Minnesota for the theaters on Broadway in New York City. In the end, hadn't Sam done exactly what C.A. had done? A life truly lived required seizing opportunities which sometimes involved taking risks. He looked to the example of his father who left his position in the Swedish Parliament and traveled to America with his mistress and an infant. August Lindbergh's life certainly was an adventure filled with twists and turns. In varying degrees, all life is like that. With his election to Congress, C.A. Lindbergh embarked on a journey that would be full of unimaginable surprises and dangers.

As a newly-elected member of the Congress, C.A. was invited to a reception at the New York City mansion of J. Pierpont Morgan. C.A. arrived late, the result of an internal struggle over the wisdom of attending. The Congressman's initial reaction had been to decline, but he realized that knowing one's adversary was wise counsel.

He stood near the entrance, his eyes wide. Atop the impressive portico of the brownstone was a halyard bearing the flag of the United States, lit brightly, and below it a flag with a red field and indiscernible white symbols on the flag which hung limply in the still evening. In the waning winter light, the brownstone took on the color of dried blood.

As he entered the mansion, he was not prepared for the opulence inside. He had never been in such a magnificent structure. The marble columns and high-arching, domed ceiling covered with celestial angels of the reception area made him feel out of place. His right hand smoothed his hair, a response to a surge of nerves. An attractive server took his overcoat and handed him a flute of champagne.

As he watched the nation's financial and legislative leaders mingle, he thought that the scene rivaled the Christmas pageants taking place throughout the world. Pomp and the pompous paraded before him. There was Joseph Cannon, Republican, the fabled Speaker of the House. He was puffing on the longest cigar that Lindbergh had ever seen, all the while pontificating to a group of bankers in exquisitely-tailored pinstriped suits, remarkably, all of the same hue of charcoal.

Across the room he recognized Representative Carter Glass, Democrat, and member of the Banking and Currency committee. He, too, was holding court, widely gesticulating with a crystal tumbler that splashed expensive Scotch on the rapt listeners with each gesture. Attractive young ladies in evening gowns linked arms with men with distinguished gray at the temples. There was nothing paternal in the lustful looks exchanged.

On the other side of the room stood Senator Nelson W. Aldrich, Republican, a thick-waisted New Englander with thinning white hair and a bushy moustache. Corpulent, ruddy-nosed and lumbering, Aldrich was the epitome of a life of excess. Aldrich was from humble beginnings. The story was that he rose from cleaning fish in the local fishmongers as a boy in Rhode Island to one of the most powerful men in the country.

Recently, Aldrich had cemented his place in society on account of the marriage between his daughter and the only son of John D. Rockefeller, the billionaire who established the first great business trust with the Standard Oil Company. Aldrich was renowned for his prowess at buying votes and elections.

Lindbergh was repulsed by the man who would become one of his arch-enemies. Lindbergh recalled an exposè about the abuse of power by Aldrich in which Lincoln Steffens *wrote, "He is an inordinately selfish man, so selfish that in all the time I spent in his state I did not find, even among his associates, a single warm personal friend of the man.*[16]"

Fueled by the steady flow of alcohol, cigar smoke and power, the reception approached a level of gaiety that was at once intoxicating and predatory. From the fringe of the assemblage, Lindbergh felt the pervasive power of privilege and voracity that drove these men. Then, as if a switch had been flipped, the cacophony hushed and the host emerged from behind large gilded doors. A servant dutifully placed a stout wooden platform before J. Pierpont Morgan, helping him mount it. J.P. Morgan looked down on his guests the way a potentate would regard his subjects. Total silence prevailed.

"Ladies and gentlemen, welcome to my home. I see that many of you are making good use of the bourbon, scotch and rye whiskey being served on this festive occasion. There are some who say that a man is disguised by alcohol, but I think that is rubbish. Most men are disguised by sobriety. So my advice is to show your true selves, Drink up!"

There was an obligatory chuckle and a few 'here, heres.' Morgan smiled benevolently, his crystal rocks glass raised. Under bushy eyebrows, his steely dark eyes surveyed the crowd. Lindbergh had trouble reading the old man's expression. It was a combination of satisfaction, condescension, and rapacity. With his free hand, Morgan patted his belly.

"One of the privileges of wealth is the enjoyment of delicious food. As the French are wont to say, 'To eat is a necessity, but to eat intelligently is an art.' At the Chateau du Morgan, we excel in the art of food. We are pleased to present for your gustatory enjoyment a feast to rival the tables of Versailles. Sadly, we do not offer a vomitorium for those who overindulge. In other words, be judicious in your gluttony. All that said, Bon Appètit!" said Pierpont, waving theatrically toward drapes behind him.

On cue, the drapes parted to reveal a buffet of gargantuan proportion. The crowd gasped at the elaborate display of culinary delights, accented by ice sculptures for each food grouping – giant glistening lobsters for the seafood, a stunning chanticleer for the poultry, the head of a bull with a brass ring in the nose for the beef and a brilliant ice lily for the dessert. The momentary pause of appreciation was broken by the frenzied hobbling of Nelson Aldrich who surged forward, nearly upending the table holding the plates and silverware. By the time there was a semblance of order to the food line, Aldrich was ensconced on a sofa with several plates piled high with lobsters, filet mignon, and lollipop lamb chops dripping with mint jelly. Lindbergh's appetite evaporated.

C.A. spent the evening studying the affair with the imagined eye of an anthropologist exploring the Amazon. He did not formulate a favorable view of Morgan's guests. When Lindbergh tired of the spectacle, he retreated into the great man's study. With its high ceiling, Persian-carpeted floors and red-flocked wall covering, it presented a welcome respite from the chill hardness of the marble reception area. He looked at the massive, carved mahogany desk propped on lion's paws. Here is where the Zeus of banking moved economies.

Surveying the masterpieces that adorned the room with studied admiration, C.A.'s gaze fell on a putty gray object on a pedestal behind the desk. On close inspection, C.A. realized that he was looking directly into the face of an imposing personage.

"Stunning, isn't it?" said a feminine voice. C.A.'s shoulders twitched in surprise. He turned toward a young lady in a demure burgundy dress that blended perfectly with the décor.

"Yes, it certainly is. Do you know where it came from?"

"When George Washington was a gentleman farmer in 1785, he was visited by Jean-Antoine Houdon, a French sculptor who made a plaster cast of the General's face. This life mask is the truest, existing likeness of the Father of our country."

"Such a strong, honest face. He was the perfect man at the right time for our nation," said C.A. in a sober voice. His hand hovered over the cast. "Washington was an amazing individual. He accepted the challenges of an age with humility, relying on divine Providence to guide him. His life made a difference."

"Yes, and Washington's selflessness should be a beacon to us all. But, can any of us make a difference for good nowadays? The world is more complex; our society is so much more developed," she said.

"That is true; however, the basic values of freedom, individual responsibility and duty endure. . . Oh, dear, I sound like I am on the stump. It's become something of a habit," he sputtered.

"Excuse me, I have not introduced myself. C.A. Lindbergh, from the 6th District of Minnesota. It's a pleasure to meet you, Miss . . . "

She giggled at his sudden formality. With mock seriousness, she said, "Anne Tracy. . ."

Her lips pursed and she offered him her hand. He felt a shock through her silk evening glove as he shook her hand firmly. It must have been static electricity. Their eyes met and he saw something that caused him to pull his hand away.

"Is this your first time here? Let me give you a brief tour," she asked. Before he could answer, she crossed the room.

With a curator's expertise, she guided him through the priceless art that graced Morgan's study. C.A. found himself studying her as much as the masterpieces. She expressed a joy in her descriptions that enthralled him. Alone with her surrounded by so much beauty, he felt transported to an ethereal place.

"J. P. Morgan is an interesting man with many tastes. You should visit the library on the other side of the reception area. It is filled with innumerable treasures. He reportedly once said, *'No price is too high for an object of unquestioned beauty and known authenticity.*'[17'] Of course, with his money, that is easy to say," Anne said.

Looking at the clock above the mantelpiece, she said, "Oh, my, I am being terribly boring, like some obsolete docent at a museum."

"Quite the contrary, you are a breath of fresh air in a chamber filled with cigar smoke and politician's palaver," C.A. replied, gesturing with his head toward the noisiness outside the study. Anne regarded him with a coquettish glance.

"Yes, I see that you are very different from those men," she said.

She sat behind the desk and extended her hand in invitation for him to sit in the chair facing the desk. He hesitated briefly, fearing that they might be committing a breach of protocol.

Sensing his concern, she said, "Please do sit down. The entire first floor is open for guests to enjoy."

C.A. looked around and out the door to the noisy foyer. Deciding that the study was preferable to the smoke and clamor in other parts of the mansion, he eased himself into a padded chair. Nice, he thought indulgently.

"I've read your speeches about the Money Trust and sympathize with the dilemma facing the farmers and workers," said Anne.

Lindbergh raised his eyebrows in surprise that a woman of such obvious breeding would side with the working classes. His expression communicated his skepticism.

"Really, I do," she said, "I know it may come as a surprise to you that a woman sitting at the desk of the Zeus of Wall Street would dare to question the Money Trust."

C.A. nodded, showing a slight smile of incredulity.

"The truth of the matter is that the Trust is rapacious and its tentacles reach into every aspect of our economy. I do not think this is healthy for our way of life because it stifles initiative and robs the producers. We need brave men like you to champion the fight against this creature. If not, we are doomed to be just like the rest of the world – a nation dominated by a few monopolists, by Mammon."

He restrained his urge to applaud; but, smiled widely.

"I could not have said it better myself, Anne."

Now it was her turn to smile. "Those words are a paraphrase of your acceptance speech."

"Why thank you. I only wish that I could deliver those words with your grace and style."

Anne blushed and lowered her eyelids shyly. She reached into the wastebasket at her feet next to the spittoon. She retrieved a magazine and handed it to him. He raised his palms toward her with a look of disbelief. She pushed it forward.

"Come on, take it. No one will say anything; it's from the garbage for God's sake." He shook his head and let the magazine sit on the desktop between them as if it were toxic.

"It's an advance copy of Appleton's Magazine, the July – December issue. It contains a terrific article by Maxim Gorky, the Russian novelist, entitled '*The City of Mammon: My Impressions of America.*'"

"I recall something about this Gorky fellow having a difficult time in New York City...."

"Yes," said Anne. "Gorky wrote this article after he was run out of town. He called New York City, the City of Mammon because, in his view, it was populated by gold-obsessed thieves. He was so agitated by the treatment he received here that he wrote this diatribe."

"It's never good policy to agitate a writer with an audience. He can do much damage. The pen *is* mightier than the sword."

She folded back the magazine to read. "Here it is. Here's what this angry Russian wrote, *'This life of gold accumulation, this idolatry of money, this horrible worship of the Golden Devil already begins to stir up protest in the country. The odious life, entangled in a network of iron and oppressing the soul with its dismal emptiness, arouses the disgust of healthy people, and they are beginning to seek for a means of rescue from spiritual death.*[18]'"

C.A. leaned forward. The Russian certainly had a facility with words. C.A. tried to file away a few of the images. The one that resonated most was 'this horrible worship of the Golden Devil.' That certainly described the behavior of the Money Trust. It was Mammon at its worst.

Anne continued with the Gorky story, "He detested New York for the way he was treated. It was quite the scandal. Last April, Gorky arrived in the City to great fanfare. The novelist was here to raise money to promote revolution in Russia. The Czarist regime is repressive; it targets Jews in particular, with murderous pogroms that destroy Jewish businesses and homes. In advance of his trip, Gorky lined up dozens of fund-raisers. The Jewish community here is very influential and wealthy."

"Yes, I've heard that about New York," said Lindbergh.

"Gorky saw it as a great opportunity to raise money for the cause. Then came the scandal. It broke two days after he arrived and all the fundraisers were cancelled. Gorky left the country without raising a penny, and, worse, in disgrace. He never knew what hit him. You can understand why he was so bitter afterward."

"So what caused the uproar?" C.A. asked.

"Gorky arrived in New York, accompanied by a beautiful woman and they registered as Mr. and Mme. Gorky at the Hotel Belleclaire on the Upper West Side. The press learned that his companion was an actress and not his wife, who was back in Russia. The newspapers immediately reported the brazen, illicit relationship and claimed that it offended all notions of decency. Horrified by the bad publicity, the hotel manager was quite indignant and ordered them to vacate, *'My hotel is a family hotel, and in justice to my other guests I cannot possibly tolerate the presence of any persons whose characters are questioned in the slightest manner.'*[19] You can imagine the uproar."

"I recall that the story was carried in the national media."

"Well, Gorky of course, denied it; swearing up and down that the woman was his wife. He called it *'a slimy scandal'*[20] and declared that any insinuation to the contrary was a *'base calumny.'*[21]'"

Anne assumed the posture and voice of an indignant Gorky repeating the words "base calumny" with such solemnity that they both laughed hysterically. Anne effected a Russian pronunciation, extending the last syllable while thrusting out her chin in mock scorn. Lindbergh responded with a belly laugh that was so infectious that Anne was soon laughing so hard that she gasped for air between laughs. Her gasping contorted her face in the most comical way that he laughed even harder. Of course, his nasal, high-pitched guffaws caused Anne's head to rock back in hilarity. They laughed so hard that their sides ached.

In the midst of this laughing fit, a butler entered to announce that the conveyances had arrived to return the guests to their lodgings. Butler etiquette required him to wait until the laughter subsided before making his announcement. He stood quiet and motionless for seven minutes before they noticed him. By then, Anne and C.A. were teary-eyed and breathless.

All it took was for Anne to mouth "calumny" and the laughing spree erupted again. Like errant schoolmates, they peeked at each other and released laugh bubbles until they finally regained their composure. It took all of his British training to keep the butler from joining in. C.A. wondered whether 'a stiff upper lip' applied to this situation. He stifled a laugh.

C.A. stood, set his jaw and bowed slightly. "Thank you so much, Miss Tr . . ."

"It's Anne. Call me Anne."

"Annuschka, it is then," he said in a mock Russian accent. It provoked one last outburst. Their eyes locked and twinkled in mutual appreciation.

"Thanks for a most enjoyable evening, Anne."

Her gaze followed him, her eyes smiling.

Lindbergh funneled toward the exit with the last remaining guests, feeling exhilarated and confused. A trace of a scent lingered in the recesses of his mind. A surge of guests toward the taxis pushed him forward and shifted his attention to maintaining his balance as he went down the stairs. On the way back to the hotel, he wondered if, or, when, he would see her again.

With a wane moon illuminating the sidewalk, C.A. decided to walk back to his hotel. His mirth and well-being were short-lived. Where there had been moisture from the melting daylight, now a thin crust of ice had formed on the walk. A black limousine pulled adjacent to him and a short, energetic man popped out.

"Congressman Lindbergh. May I call you Charley?" he said.

C.A. thought, it's Congressman-elect; I have not been sworn in yet. He felt his arm entwined by the shorter man. Lindbergh felt like he was being suctioned toward the limo. Sliding on the ice, he braced.

"Allow me to introduce myself. I'm Otto Kahn of Kuhn Loeb and Company," he said, shaking hands and pulling Lindbergh to him with his right hand. C.A. recoiled slightly and Kahn released his grip sequentially, one clammy finger at a time.

"It's much too cold to walk. I'll give you a ride."

C.A. stared wide-eyed at the man. This type of familiarity was an affront. In Minnesota latching onto strangers without introduction was inappropriate. Dealing with these rude Easterners is going to take some getting used to, he thought.

"No thank you, kind sir. Since you obviously know who I am, you know that I am from Minnesota and this temperature is what we consider invigorating. So, I will bid you good evening, if it's all the same to you."

A dark look replaced Otto's smile as he watched Lindbergh trudge up Madison Avenue.

1906 New York City, NY

No grasp is like the sudden strain of the octopus....
The victim is oppressed by a vacuum drawing at numberless
points: it is not a clawing or a biting, but
an indescribable scarification.
~ Victor Hugo

C.A. woke up the following day troubled by his encounter with Kahn. The man was part of the Money Trust and he had the audacity to approach in the most awkward fashion. Well, thought Lindbergh, I'll be leaving this disturbing place tomorrow and will be home in time for Thanksgiving with my family. Today's agenda was topped by a reception/tour at the New York Aquarium hosted by Mayor George B. McCellan, Jr., the son of the Union general who so exasperated Lincoln for his reluctance to engage the enemy.

Lindbergh took a hansom cab down to Castle Garden at the Battery in lower Manhattan. The crisp briny air coming off the Atlantic Ocean was a tonic. The harbor bustled with activity. Sailing ships of every description crowded the broad expanse. It was a veritable Babel as stevedores and sailors roared polyglot shouts over the din while hoisting all manner of cargo to and from ships' holds. He admired the precision of the chaos. Crates and bales dangled from thick lines as stevedores manipulated booms and teamsters maneuvered wagons while superintendents orchestrated the activities with loud yells and whistles.

He stood to admire the large circular building that housed the aquarium. The building was surrounded by green lawns and intersecting promenades that provided access to the aquarium and the magnificent harbor behind it. The front of the ten-year-old facility was a tall crenulated structure that facilitated ingress and egress for the millions of tourists who visited each year. The building was capped by a multi-faceted cupola that gave it a regal bearing and served the more practical purpose of bringing natural light into the otherwise cavernous structure.

Entering through the nautically decorated entrance, Lindbergh approached a young lady with a clipboard who was standing next to a gentleman in a frock coat.

"Good morning, my name is..."

"Charles Lindbergh from the 6th District of Minnesota," said the young woman completing his sentence. She thrust several papers in his direction. C.A. leaned back slightly, in surprise. Gripping his elbow, she directed him to the gentleman in the frock coat.

"I'd like to introduce you to Mayor McClellan."

The mayor had a boyish face, clean-shaven and a thick head of dark brown hair. He made a military right-face and stood before Lindbergh with a broad smile shining across his face.

"Call me Max," said McClellan grasping C.A.'s hand and pumping it vigorously as if he was trying to wring out one more vote.

"Good morning, your honor," C.A. responded. Max adopted an expression of feigned injury.

"Now, now, Lindy, if you do not obey the mayor, I'll have no choice but to sentence you to spend an hour swimming with the cephalopods," he said, gesturing toward a large tank on the other side of the exhibition hall.

"You know that New York City is renowned for creatures with tentacles that entangle disobedient citizens and never release them," said the Mayor wriggling his fingers in mock terror.

"Yes, sir. I mean, yes, Max," replied C.A. winking.

"Duly noted," said the mayor who had already turned away to greet another visitor.

C.A. stood taking in the wondrous scene of tanks lining the walls of the exhibit hall. He looked at the papers in his hand and saw that one was a schematic map of the aquarium. Breathing deeply, he felt the humidity and salty scent in the air. Rays of sunlight from the cupola high above filled the hall. The tiled floor was covered with nautical motifs that matched the various exhibits.

A raucous barking drew his attention to the sea lion enclosure where a young attendant had just entered carrying the morning meal. The sea lions emerged from the pool and clambered onto the rocks where the man had placed a bucket. He reached in and withdrew a mass of bloody fish. The sea lions perched on their flippers motionless, except for their bobbing and shimmering heads. As the man fed each creature in turn, the baying subsided.

C.A. leaned against the wrought iron railing admiring the spectacle. The shiny fur of the sea lions was mottled gray, black and mauve. Their powerful muscles were evident beneath their coats. Flippers with claws that could slice the attendant; what magnificent creatures, he thought. And, yet, they had been trained to wait for their sustenance.

He felt a hand reach through the crook of his elbow.

"I've been assigned to be your docent and give you a custom tour of our wonderful aquarium," said a pleasant voice. C.A. leaned back and peered into the face of Anne Tracy.

"Oh, my, it's you," he said with a little more enthusiasm than he had intended. His stomach fluttered. "Anne, it's so good to see you. I wondered whether our paths would cross again."

She smiled with obvious joy. "You shan't be rid of me so easily. I consider it my civic duty to continue your cultural tour of our grand City. Last time, it was medieval art and sculptures; today, it is marine mammals and cephalopods. Her full lips widened on the last syllable in an endearing manner. He banished instantly the urge to discover how they would feel pressed to his. Her eyes lowered. She perused the schedule in her hand.

"Come, we must not dally, or we will miss the attendants feeding the octopuses. It's quite a spectacle."

Light from the cupola above streamed onto the marble floor reflecting beams into tanks filled with a dazzling array of sea life. Floating dust motes added to the ethereal atmosphere of the aquarium. He was wonder struck at the variety of shapes and colors of the creatures. His father would surely have appreciated the displays, abounding with God's infinite imagination, and, yes, humor – who else could conceive of a clown fish, or a blobfish?

Anne and C.A. scurried across the expansive hall to a large tank. Anne pointed.

"There's one. You see, under the rocky ledge."

C.A. squinted in vain. "Where?"

"The octopus can change the color and texture of its skin to match its surroundings and make itself nearly invisible. Marine scientists also believe that the skin of the octopus can mirror the colors of objects in its environment, allowing it to reflect back whatever it is attempting to mimic. Look to the left of the black rock. You can faintly see its outline."

"Yes, I see it. That is amazing."

"The octopus uses this to avoid detection by its predators, or to stalk its prey. It is a proficient hunter, using its tentacles to ensnare smaller creatures."

A crowd formed around them in anticipation of the feeding. Anne leaned imperceptibly into C.A. An attendant in crisp, navy blue overalls bearing the embroidered name "Bill," approached, carrying two containers stenciled in bright yellow with the words "N.Y. Aquarium." He stood before the tank facing the crowd and cleared his throat. After a suitable pause to garner their attention, he began.

"Welcome to our octopus exhibit. Octopuses are remarkable creatures. The octopus is an invertebrate, which means it has no skeleton. That makes it extremely flexible. The only hard part of its body is its beak that it uses to eat. An octopus can slide through any crevice that is only slightly larger than its beak. For that reason, we keep their tanks tightly sealed."

Then, mugging to the crowd, he whispered, "We've lost more than one night watchman to prowling octopuses. So, kids, better stay close to your parents."

He made a show of lifting the cover of the tank. With a long stick, he probed along the sandy bottom. An octopus emerged and jetted away leaving a black ink cloud.

"You have just witnessed a camouflaged octopus roused from hiding by this stick. The octopus moves by forcing water through its siphon. Of course, you also observed one of the creature's primary defense mechanisms. That's right, the ink cloud which the octopus squirts to confuse its enemies."

Bill bent down and removed the cover from a bucket and reached his glove hand into it. The crowd gasped as an octopus emerged, clinging to Bill's gloved with several tentacles swaying.

"This is Hector, one of our octopuses. Notice the suction cups on his tentacles."

"Yuck," shuddered a young girl near the front.

"The suction cups help the octopus move and to capture its prey. Oddly enough, the octopus also uses its suckers to taste what it grabs," said Bill, brandishing the animal toward the crowd. The crowd retreated, inhaling audibly. The girl hid behind her father's leg, only peeking out when he patted her head reassuringly.

"Hector weighs three pounds. The largest reported octopus was thirty feet long and weighed six hundred pounds. In mythology, the octopus is believed to have inspired the legend of the Kraken, a sea monster that attacks ships. The author of *20,000 Leagues under the Sea*, Jules Verne, has terrified generations of readers with tales of a giant octopus attacking the submarine *Nautilus*."

As Bill elevated Hector, the crowd shrank back.

"Should we return Hector to his home?" Bill asked. One child shouted, "Yes, hurry before he gets away."

Bill submerged his hand into the tank and Hector whisked away into a cave on the far side of the tank. The attendant bent to open the second bucket which contained an assortment of small sea animals.

"Does anyone know what octopuses eat?" asked Bill.

"Fish?" shouted a boy wearing a sailor cap.

"Yes. Anyone else?"

"Clams and mussels," answered the girl's father.

"Very good," said Bill. "The octopus wraps its tentacles around the shell and with its beak makes a hole and then injects toxic saliva into the shell. The poison is called Tetrodotoxin, or, TTX; it is toxic to humans. Once the clam or mussel is dead, the octopus eats the contents of the shell."

"That's disgusting," said the young girl. An uncomfortable chuckle rippled through the crowd.

"Lunchtime," said Bill laughing as he poured the contents of the bucket into the tank. Clams, minnows, shrimp and other sea critters drifted down in the octopus tank. Within minutes, Hector and his friends were feasting on the food. It was quite a display of nature and survival. As the prey dwindled, the crowd gradually dispersed, until only C.A. and Anne remained.

Anne's face showed signs of worry. She fidgeted with her papers.

"C.A. I want you to listen carefully to what I'm about to tell you."

His eyebrows raised in a question at the turn of the conversation.

"As Bill said, octopuses are extremely intelligent. They have the most complex brain of any invertebrate. Because their tentacles are capable of infinite degrees and directions of movement, each tentacle has its own brain-like organ that is independent of the primary brain's control. Some species of octopus have suckers that glow in the dark. The glowing suckers are used to signal other tentacles when defending itself or attracting victims."

"I gather that we are no longer talking about sea creatures," Lindbergh said.

"That's correct. The Money Trust is often depicted as an octopus precisely because it displays many of the same attributes. Be careful."

C.A. regarded Anne with solemn eyes. "Yes, I know," he murmured.

"One last similarity; the octopus has the ability to grow back its tentacles. Don't try to dismantle it piecemeal. Just when you think you've destroyed one tentacle, it will regenerate. You've got to destroy the entire body when you challenge Mammon."

Anne placed her fingers to her lips and then touched his cheek lightly.

"Success and good fortune," she whispered, then, she turned and faded into the crowd.

$ $ $

In life, there are random encounters with strangers that are destined to have great impact, but are not recognized as such at the time. Lindbergh was about to have such an encounter. As C.A. entered Grand Central Terminal, he sidestepped a construction worker carrying copper wire. The famous vaulted ceiling was obscured from view because work crews were installing electrical lines into the grand structure. C.A. pressed his overcoat to feel his tickets to Chicago for the first leg of his trip on the *20th Century Limited* and then home to Minnesota. The promoters of this express passenger line advertised it as the "Most Famous Train in the World."

Lindbergh mused that the luxury *Orient Express* between Paris and Istanbul might beg to differ, but he had to admire the brashness of turn-of-the-century America. Growing industrialization and over a decade of monetary stability had brought prosperity and ushered the United States into a position of world power. With optimism pulsing throughout the country, he hoped that the Money Trust would not derail a better life for the average American.

As Lindbergh scanned the archways for track 35, he was jostled by a man who glared at him and muttered, "Get out of the way, hayseed."

The blow knocked Lindbergh into a young woman carrying a basket of apples. Several rolled across the marble floor, being kicked and knocked this way and that. He put his valise down and chased after the fruit. He succeeded in corralling all of the apples but one that rolled down the stairs toward of all places, track 35. Well, I'll be, he said to himself.

Cradling the apples awkwardly, he searched for the girl. She was nowhere to be found. Then, it dawned on C.A. that he had left his suitcase behind. The realization that he might have fallen for one of the oldest tricks in the book made his heart sink. All of his belongings and his official papers, including the draft of his monograph on the Money Trust were in his suitcase. Could the girl have been a distraction to an unwary tourist as a ploy to steal his suitcase? It was close to his departure time. He doubted that he would even have time to find a police officer and make a report.

He wandered toward where he approximated the misadventure had occurred. The crowd surged this way and that toward various portals. He noticed an eddy in the stream of people. As he approached it, he heard sobbing. Like a cork popping to the surface of a fishing pond, he saw her sitting on the floor with the crowd flowing around her. Thankfully, she was propped on his suitcase.

He returned to the young woman who sat amid the bustle arranging her wares. Half-juggling the errant apples, C.A. deposited them gently in her basket. She raised her face. Her lips trembled and tears formed on her lower lids. She looked at him confused. There was something about that shape of her jade green eyes reminded him of his daughter Lillian. He knelt beside her. He noticed that she was wearing some sort of blue uniform with a red patch on which was embroidered a white crescent encircling a white five-pointed star. The symbol looked familiar, but he was unable to place it.

"What is your name?"

"Olivia," she replied.

"I'm so sorry, Olivia," he said. "I did not mean to knock into you. I feel like such an oaf."

She blinked the tears from her eyes and smiled at him.

"I'm so grateful that you retrieved the apples. They are for my mistress. She's having a soireè and the apples are for her famous apple *crème brulee*. She would have sacked me if I failed to bring the proper ingredients."

"Unfortunately, one of these rambunctious apples escaped down on to the tracks," said C.A., with a gesture of resignation.

"Oh, don't worry about him. We all are expendable in one way or another. He took his chance for freedom and escaped the Commodore's fiery ovens." She laughed softly.

"Listen, Olivia, I have a daughter your age and I would want someone to help her if she needed help. So, here's my card. If you need help explaining the Houdini apple to your mistress, just call and I'll see what I can do."

"Now boarding on Track 35, the *20th Century Limited*. All aboard!" bellowed a man dressed in a sharply pressed conductor's uniform. "Now boarding on Track 35, the *20th Century Limited*. All aboard!"

Olivia stuffed the card into her pocket. "Thank you, kind sir."

Lindbergh stood and entered the stream of passengers that thronged toward track 35. Before entering the stairway, he glanced back, but Olivia was gone. His heart ached.

Once on the platform he realized what the advertising meant when it proclaimed that the *20th Century Limited* provided "red carpet treatment." A wide crimson carpet had been rolled out to greet the passengers. When C.A. presented his ticket to the agent, a young black man in dark "Pullman green" livery stepped forward to greet him.

"Good day, sir. My name is James. Allow me to take your luggage and escort you to your Pullman." C.A. nodded and followed. James led him to a sleeper car where the porter stowed the luggage and tapped on a lower berth. "I see that you are travelling through our stop in Washington, heading on out west. This is your berth, sir. I will turn it down at 9:30 P.M. if that suits you. We are scheduled to arrive in Chicago's LaSalle Street Station in eighteen hours, at 9 A.M. sharp. From there you can connect to your train to Minneapolis.

"Each car has a name. This is the *President John Adams*. This car is the pride of the Pullman Palace Car Company. It has recently been renovated with electric lights and your own hot air furnace under the floor. Here is the regulator in case you would like to adjust the temperature. The wash room is at this end," said James pointing.

"You can relax in the drawing room over there. Or, if you prefer, you can relax in the Club Car. We have a secretary available in case you need that support. Would you like me to schedule an appointment with our barber, sir?"

"Yes, I'd like that, thanks."

"Actually, James, I could use a cup of coffee and would like to read today's papers. Where's the best place?"

"I have the perfect place for you, sir. Allow me to show you the Booklover's library which carries all the major newspapers and periodicals. It's located at the end of our Club Car. A coffee station is always stocked. Food service is available from 6 A.M. until midnight. Dinner is served between 5 and 8 P.M. Follow me, please."

They proceeded through several Pullmans until they reached the Club Car. When C.A. observed the decor of the Club Car, he said under his breath that George Pullman had truly transformed the ordinary railroad car into a rolling palace. Semi-empire ceilings painted in Nile green gave the car a spacious air. Black walnut woodwork with inlay graced the walls. Polished brass fixtures and framed mirrors between the high windows added to the palatial quality of the space. There was deep pile carpeting on the floor in a dark green and black tartan pattern. C. A. settled into one of the high-backed mahogany armchairs covered with plush, French upholstery in dark, green velvet. James brought him the Wall Street Journal and coffee.

"I'll be in the porters' room at the end of the car if you need anything, sir."

"Thank you, James. I'm fine."

With a slight lurch, the train moved forward. The car was remarkably silent. He could hardly feel the acceleration as the train headed out of Grand Central Station. C.A. went through the motions of reading the paper but soon, he was lost in thought, contemplating the long-awaited reunion with his family. He had been gone from Evy, Charley and the girls for too long. He could hardly wait to tell them of his experiences. Little Charley was going to love hearing about the octopuses at the aquarium.

"Damn that stenographer!" exclaimed a voice behind him. "I told E.H. that we could not trust her. Now, she is threatening to sell the letter to the rag sheet, the *New York World*," shouted a man who had just entered the Club car from the rear entrance. The back of C.A.'s chair was to the men, so he could not see them, and vice versa.

"Calm down, Maxwell. And, for God's sake, keep your voice down," said his companion. C.A. stopped reading. There was something about that voice.

"OK. It's just that there is going to be hell to pay if that letter gets out. You know how vindictive TR can be," said Maxwell, in an agitated voice. "Porter, you there, bring me another absinthe. Make that a double."

"Yes, sir, Mister Murly. Coming right up. Anything for you, sir?"

"Nothing, thanks." There it was again. He thought he recognized that voice – it was just beyond the edge of his consciousness. Darn, who was that?

"Maxwell, I think I can fix this. TR invited me to a little Christmas gathering at Sagamore Hill on the 12th. *Allow me to introduce...*"

With that phrase it clicked. C.A. realized that the voice belonged to Otto Kahn, the pretentious banker who tried to call him 'Charley' after the reception at the Morgan mansion. C.A. tried to shift in his chair so that he might see the reflection of the speakers in the windows. The speaker known as Maxwell was diagonally opposite him and could be seen clearly. He looked like the stereotypical lawyer-fixer – pinstriped suit, slicked back hair and corpulent face with pig-eyes. The reflection of the other character was obscured by the high-back chair. All he could discern was the man's hand which was gesticulating with a gold-trimmed monocle.

"*Allow me to introduce...* the entire problem in context. I'll explain everything to him. He'll understand that when Harriman made the contribution, he understood that Senator Depew would be appointed ambassador to France after the election."

"That's the problem. TR does not want to implement the *quid pro quo*. He knows that he received the Harriman money in exchange for the ambassadorship. But, now, he refuses to appoint Depew in return for the campaign money," said Maxwell in a harsh exaggerated whisper. "The President is undermining our entire system. Jeez, what a mess. I never thought I would see such a breach of faith."

Lindbergh almost flinched at the perfidy he was hearing. He looked out the train window focusing on the countryside speeding by and felt sadness at the institutional betrayal of the hardworking people who lived in those houses. How could these charlatans live with themselves?

"Don't worry, my friend. I'm sure that TR can be made to see the light. Trust me. Every bone in his body is political. He knows that commitments of this sort are the fuel that powers the system. He knows that if he wants to run in '08, he's got to play ball and honor his commitments."

"I hope you are right, Otto. I sure hope you are right," said Maxwell in a voice saturated with doubt. "I don't know about you, but I'm ready for dinner. Let's head to the dining car, we should eat before we arrive in D.C."

C.A. shook his head in disbelief. The depth of corruption seemed more pervasive that he had dreamt. By winning a seat in Congress was he entering a great, fetid cesspool? He stared blankly out the window.

The rhythmic rocking of the railcar was hypnotic. C.A.'s head leaned to the side flap of the armchair. An expanse of railroad tracks arose before him. Tracks split off into tributary tracks until the horizon was an endless array of tracks. The western sun lit the shiny steel rails, straight and strong. Or were they? The tips of the tracks began to writhe as if they were alive. The writhing tracks rose and twisted and C.A. saw suckers on their undersides. He watched as the writhing, suckered tracks engulfed passing towns. The track tentacles were everywhere, wrapping around buildings, warehouses and vehicles. He recoiled at the squishy, sucking sound made when the track tentacles engulfed its prey. One of the tentacles latched onto his window and forced it open. The humanlike eye of the octopus peered into the window ominously. The monster stared at him. Through the opening, a greedy tendril slithered toward him.

He felt a persistent tapping on his shoulder.

"Sorry to wake you, sir. This is last call for dinner. The dining car will be closing soon," said James, the porter.

"Thank you. You woke me not a moment too soon," C.A. said, shaking off the cobwebs and rubbing the dream from his eyes.

Thanksgiving 1906 Little Falls, MN

O how I laugh when I think of my vague indefinite riches. No run on my bank can drain it, for my wealth is not possession but enjoyment.
~ Henry David Thoreau

The long train ride home was complicated by the masses of people traveling for the Thanksgiving holiday. With the burgeoning growth of rail travel between major cities, he was able to schedule connections that took him from New York City to Chicago efficiently. With luck and no weather delays, Lindbergh was on schedule to arrive a day early.

He was bone-weary from his travels. It felt like he had been traveling for months. In point of fact, he had been traveling since the announcement of his candidacy in the spring. Nevertheless, he was buoyed by the prospect of seeing his family for Thanksgiving. He could almost smell the feast and feel the hugs of his family and, of course, the pleasure of nuzzling Blakey.

New York City had been everything he expected and then some. The encounters with Anne Tracy left him with mixed feelings. It had been a long time since he had been attracted to a woman who was not his wife. Perhaps, it was her intellect that intrigued him the most. Unlike Evy, Anne was knowledgeable about the Money Trust and, more important, interested in his views. Evy was always curt and dismissive whenever he tried to share some discovery or unique point about the Money Trust.

The other overriding impression he had from his trip was the revulsion he felt toward Otto Kahn. The man's arrogance was beyond description. His effrontery outside the Morgan Mansion was nothing compared to his corruption regarding the President. Henceforth, Lindbergh would identify Otto Kahn as the face of the Money Trust. As a lawyer, C.A. knew that it was terribly unfair to Kahn to personify him as Mammon; yet, it satisfied some visceral impulse to put the worst face on one's enemy.

His encounter with the vulnerable young woman, Olivia, in Grand Central Station fueled his homesickness. He pined to see his two daughters, Lillian and Eva. After the fire burned down the Pike Creek house, Lindbergh's family had moved into temporary quarters on the lower bank while a replacement house was built. It was a small but comfortable cabin down by the river.

As the hired carriage rounded the bend leading to the river, he strained for a glimpse of home. Had he been gone that long? He saw only darkness where the cabin should have been. He dropped the window and poked his head out for a better view. All he saw was pine trees swaying in the wind. At last, the carriage crunched to a stop.

"Don't look like no one's home," said the driver, as he spit a wad of tobacco juice.

"Somewhere else you'd want me to take you?"

"No, thanks," replied C.A. "I'm not supposed to be here yet. I thought I'd surprise them. I guess the surprise is on me."

C.A. paid the driver and bid him Happy Thanksgiving. On entering the cold, dark house, C.A. stifled a chill. Nothing a nice fire wouldn't cure. That's odd, he thought as he detected a musty smell. There are no ashes in the fire place. It's like it has not been used in quite a while. How could that be?

Once he had a fire crackling and candles lit, his mood improved. C.A. poured himself a drink and was just about to relax in front of the fire when he noticed an envelope tacked to the bedroom door. At least he would find out where everyone was. He recognized Evy's cursive and unfolded a note.

Dearest Charles,

I want you to know that regardless of what happens in the future, you are the love of my life. However, your election to Congress and the arson of our home has made our life together unsafe. As a mother of our darling boy, I must protect him with every fiber in my body. I wish that there was a better way to tell you that little Charley and I have gone to live in Detroit with my parents, but there is not. I see no other way out of this situation that you have created.

I understand your need to make a difference. I know that men of your moral fiber and temperament are compelled to joust at windmills. The people of Little Falls are fortunate to have you as their champion. Their nemesis, the Money Trust, is so formidable that I sincerely doubt it can be defeated. It pervades every aspect of the economy. Indeed, I fear that Mammon is too ingrained in human nature to be vulnerable. I also know that the more effective you are in damaging Mammon, the more violent it will be in defending itself and its prerogatives. I simply cannot stand by with little Charley and be a target for the backlash that will inevitably follow your efforts.

Remember always that little Charley and I love you dearly and you are always welcome to see us. Although my heart breaks to live apart from you, our safety depends on it. Hopefully, your quest against the tentacles of Mammon will bear swift success and we can reunite as a family. Until then, follow your heart and do not underestimate the power of your adversary. Stay strong morally and physically.

With all our love,

                    Evy & little Charley

P.S. The girls and mother are at your sister's house with Blakey. He is so totally devoted to you that I could not bear to deprive you of his loyalty. Take him wherever you go and he will be your best friend.

Lindbergh stared at the letter, rereading it over and over. In the flickering firelight he noticed several tear stains just below the signature.

Evy had correctly recognized his obsession with battling Mammon. Was she correct that he was an unrealistic idealist tilting at windmills? If he did not step forward to fight the monster, who would? Wasn't it Edmund Burke who said that all it is necessary for evil to prevail is for good men to do nothing? Should he retreat into comfort and security and allow the Money Trust to work its evil uncontested? Didn't the Founding Fathers risk everything to establish the great American Republic? Didn't the previous generation sacrifice much to eliminate the scourge of slavery? How could he fail to answer the call to his generation of enlightened citizens to suppress the control over hard-working people by the Money Trust? For God, family and country he had no choice. He resolved to sacrifice his personal comfort and family life in order to protect and defend the economic freedom of everyday Americans. C.A. had no idea just how much he would be called upon to sacrifice.

$ $ $

He had always been a hard worker. His father had instilled in him the necessity for hard work in order to survive. Despite his handicap, the old man had persevered and turned the family farm into a thriving economic unit. The livestock provided the muscle to conquer the farm acreage that in turn yielded cash crops that provided the money for better equipment and more land. The truck farm near the house supplied produce for the family. The dairy cows, chickens and pigs kept in the barn gave them products to sell. C.A. was no stranger to early morning chores. From milking the cows, to collecting the eggs, to slopping the pigs, he learned that self-sufficiency was the product of hard work. Indeed, their survival depended on hard work.

Minnesota was the frontier in the days of his childhood. He recalled warnings of Indian insurrections that required the entire family to relocate to the safety of Ft. Ripley. This was done on short notice and woe to the family that ignored the call to the fort. More than once he heard stories of families killed while trying to defend their homesteads against marauding Indians. During these times, he learned the importance of prayer. His parents stressed the need for devotion to God, especially in times of trouble.

These lessons served him well in law school. Although it was a different type of discipline, he applied himself to his studies. The distractions of college life at the University of Michigan never tempted him. He was often perplexed as one promising student after another fell by the wayside academically because they could not avoid the allure of the social life at Ann Arbor. He might have been considered boring by some of his classmates, but his professors regarded him as a first rate intellect and challenged him with extra-credit assignments. In his upper classman years, they sought him for research projects, some of which yielded a small stipend.

It was late and he felt extremely tired. Travel fatigue, the shock of Evy's letter and the gloom of an empty house, all contributed to his sense of lethargy. Within seconds after his head touched the pillow he was fast asleep.

It was so loud. The sound of the metallic blade whirring and biting through the bark and wood of the logs hurt his ears. Then, the blade would catch a knot or a stump and the screech would amplify until the knot was severed. He clamped his hands over his ears to drown out the sound. The smell of pine saturated the mill. Not even the pleasance of the fragrance could offset the shriek of the noise.

He was standing near a conveyor belt that was driven by gears propelled by the river. He could see under the building where the Upper Mississippi flowed through his home town of Little Falls. He was too young to understand the workings of the mill, but he was mesmerized by the cogs rotating into the interlocking gears. The foaming, splashing water reflected light onto the gears and the grease shone with tiny iridescent globs, forever rotating in place as the water surged downstream.

The Pine Tree Mill featured a round blade that was wider than he was tall. It was shiny, hard silver steel with pointy, sharp teeth that tore through logs faster than his father could drive a wedge through fire wood. When the blade was engaged with a log, wood turned into sawdust and boards. Behind him, men were driving wagons, lashing horses and shouting directions to the mill workers in an effort to load the planks that survived the encounter with the saw blade.

He was engrossed by the whiteness of the wood that came off the saw platform. Bright sunlight bouncing off the planks and the blade hurt his eyes. He could make out the curved ridges on the wood made by the blade. Suddenly, above the screech of the blade on wood, he heard an agonizing scream of pain more terrifying than anything he had ever heard. After a long moment, he saw red boards and there was silence as the blade slowed to a stop.

"Oh my lord, get Doc Willem up here quick. There's been an accident!"

Someone grabbed him by the shoulders and steered him toward the general store.

"Here, watch the boy. His father's hurt."

C.A. tried to run back to the mill, but strong hands held him. Edna Chester pulled him close, drawing him to her bosom and wrapping her pale hand around his head. Mats Henderson burst into the store exclaiming, "It's August Lindbergh. He fell into the blade. His left arm is gone. The saw cut into his side, you can see his heart beating through his ribs."

Edna tried to cover the boy's ears. C.A. pushed and wriggled to get free. She held him tight, so tight he could hardly breathe. When he finally cleared some space, sobs and tears wracked his body.

"Now, now, little boy, everything will be alright," she soothed. But it would not be alright. His father nearly died and would be an invalid in bed for the following year. Life for the Lindbergh family changed forever.

early 1907 Washington D.C.

It's a damned good thing to remember in politics to stick to your party and never attempt to buy the favor of your enemies at the expense of your friends.
~ Joseph "Uncle Joe" Cannon

Lindbergh embarked on his new career with conflicting emotions. On the one hand, he felt called to serve. He recognized that few comprehended the nature and scope of the danger to the Republic presented by the Money Trust. He truly felt that he was destined to confront the Money Trust. If not him, then whom? A myriad of images, ranging from Belinda, the malnourished daughter of his friend Jock, to the beleaguered faces of Minnesota's farmers, to the hopeful expressions of his supporters on Election night, fueled his resolve. As he prepared to enter the fray in Washington, Lindbergh was filled with a sense of obligation and mission.

On the other hand, Evy's words tore at his heart. Despite the cascading of events, C.A. accepted the fact that his choices led inexorably to the rupture of his family. In aggregate, the initial decision to run, the lonely separations on the campaign trail, the vile and baseless accusations, and the fiery arson of his home, comprised a terrible personal price. He knew in his heart that there could be no significant achievement without significant cost. Wherever the road ahead would take him, he was determined to do his father proud.

It was with this mindset that Lindbergh assumed the role as Congressman for the 6th District. His defeated opponent, Clarence Buckman had graciously agreed to provide him with an overview of how things worked in Washington. It was not the type of orientation he expected, but given his knowledge of Buckman as a man of low principle he was not surprised.

"The most important thing you can do is to cater to the whims and demands of Uncle Joe. Speaker Cannon insists that everyone call him Uncle Joe. Don't be fooled by this false informality. Uncle Joe is the most autocratic, status conscious Speaker that has ever held the office. If you don't bend over backwards to ingratiate yourself to him, you will find that all of your well-intentioned projects will be dead on arrival."

"What is your advice as to how I can get appointed to the Banking and Currency Committee?" asked Lindbergh.

Buckman withdrew a well-chewed cigar stub from his mouth and eyed it warily. He pondered how candid he could be with Lindbergh. The rising smoke from the cigar veiled his eyes. He decided, what the hell, this Crusader will find out soon enough.

"C. A., this is off-the-record. The best way to get appointed to the committee you want is to deliver a bag of cash to the Speaker along with an announcement of your desired appointment," said Buckman, exhaling a long puff of smoke in Lindbergh's direction.

Clarence relished the look of revulsion in CA's eyes and continued, "Of course, a middling size bag is no guarantee, if someone else brings a bigger bag to the Speaker." The old man relished bursting naïve bubbles. A jaded laugh and a look of amused pity ended CA's orientation.

$ $ $

C.A. fingered the invitation to the Republican caucus from Speaker Joseph G. Cannon while staring out the train window. His efforts over the past year in seeking election were over and he was about to commence the important work that he had talked about during the campaign. It was a few weeks before March 4, 1907 when he was scheduled to begin his term as a member of the 60th Congress.

The conductor shouted their arrival in Washington D.C. C.A. took the papers from his portable writing table and tapped them into neat order on both edges. He placed the papers and writing board into his briefcase. Then, lifting his suitcase from the overhead rack, he took a deep breath. He felt somewhat underwhelmed at the beginning of his Congressional career. After the excitement and anxiety of the campaign and the victory celebrations, actually reporting to work felt anticlimactic. With a wistful expression, C.A. searched his area for all of his belongings.

It was a clear winter day and he looked forward to an invigorating walk. The crisp February air reminded him of the delightful walks he had taken with Evy during their early days. CA thought of Evy and little Charley safely ensconced in Detroit and wondered whether he had made the right decision. Concluding that it was too late to second-guess his path, CA forged ahead.

Shouldering his baggage, he crossed the impressive hall of the New Jersey Avenue station of the B&O railroad. As he exited the Italianate-style depot, he checked the time on the clock tower and decided that he could walk to the capital in plenty of time for his meeting.

"I see that you are walking to the Capitol, do you mind if I join you?"

Mildly annoyed at the interruption, C.A. turned toward its source. Standing before him was a middle-aged gentleman in a cashmere overcoat that struggled to cover his ample girth. The slightly shorter man wore wire-rimmed spectacles that framed his magnet-gray eyes. His pudgy face displayed a wide smile, as he extended his bare right hand, "James Watson. It's a pleasure to meet you, Congressman Lindbergh."

When C.A.'s eyebrows adopted a how do you know who I am pose, Watson gestured with his eyes toward the gold-stamped engraving 'C.A. Lindbergh' on his briefcase.

"Of course. A present from my family. Gosh, I feel like a schoolboy attending his first day of class."

"Don't fret. You'll get the hang of it straight away. We lawyers have that knack of acclimating."

"Yes, thanks. It's a pleasure to meet you."

As they exited the terminal, C.A. pulled up his mental notes on James E. Watson. Lindbergh had received his invitation and orientation materials from Watson. According to Lindbergh's friend, Howard Bell, Watson played a critical role in the House. The affable Watson was a protégé of Speaker Cannon. Howard had encouraged C.A. to befriend Watson. He was a four-term representative from Indiana, but, more important, he was the Republican Whip.

The soon-to-be constituted 60th Congress was controlled by the Republican Party which held a fifty-seven member majority. The majority whip was the floor leader of the reigning party and he was responsible for corralling votes on important issues. If Watson was involved, he'd figure out a way to get a bill passed; if he was not involved, a bill stood no chance. Watson was said to be a master of utilizing inducements or threats, if necessary, to enforce party discipline. Members often parlayed their votes into appropriations for pet projects in their districts. Sadly, thought C.A., it was also true that they parlayed their votes into self-serving endeavors that lined their own pockets.

It was said that Watson did not have an ideological bone in his body, he was the ultimate pragmatist. Owing to his legendary poker games and his reputation as a garrulous, self-deprecating storyteller, Watson was well-regarded on both sides of the aisle. Watson was a horse-trader who used his relationships to get things done. In nautical terms, Cannon set the course, but, it was Watson who convinced, browbeat and cajoled the crew to complete the journey of any significant legislation.

By the time they arrived at the Capitol, Watson had his arm around Lindbergh's shoulder and they were conversing like lifelong conspirators. Jim Watson was a charmer, warm and genial by nature. C.A. expressed his concern about rumors that he had heard comparing legislating to sausage making; that you really did not want to know what went into producing either. C.A. considered this unpalatable. Watson assured C.A. that the process was not so distasteful.

"All legislation of consequence is a series of compromises, and there are many trades and deals among the senators in order to get important measures through. These trades are not of a sinister nature at all, but are entirely permissible by the highest standards of legislation and morals ... Every legislator understands that no measure of importance ever could be passed without this give-and-take policy being practiced to the limit[22]."

As Watson entered the building, the House Doorkeeper, Frank B. Lyon, hurried toward him to take his outer apparel.

"The Speaker is waiting for you, Congressman Watson." Shedding his coat, Watson said, "Mr. Lyon, this is my friend Congressman Lindbergh, please see to it that you take good care of him."

Turning to C.A., Watson smiled, "Truly a pleasure, sir. I look forward to working together. Make sure you introduce yourself to Jim Tawney. He is the senior member of the Minnesota delegation. He preceded me as whip. He knows everyone. Plus, he's chairman of Appropriations."

Watson let the last word linger on his lips as if it was the ultimate in seduction and winked slyly. "He'll show you the ropes. Gotta run. Let me know if you need anything."

And, with that he disappeared into a side doorway that Lyon held open for him.

Lyon then led C.A. into a large chamber that was filled with several hundred men. They stood in groups, mainly from their own state or committee. The noise level of the conversations was nearly deafening. C.A. walked along the fringes of the gathering, absorbing its pulse. A haze of cigar smoke gave the chamber a decrepit grayness. He passed shiny brass spittoons and was almost besmirched by an errant wad of chew being discarded by a feckless colleague.

Regional accents and nuances of dress in a field of almost universal black or dark blue business suits, helped C.A. differentiate the members. Lindbergh gradually identified the Minnesota contingent. He caught sight of James A. Tawney holding court in the center of Minnesotans. C.A. recognized Tawney's trademark black, handlebar mustache that was waxed to sharp points. Tawney's left hand clasped the lapel of his fashionable jacket while his right hand stabbed the air with the assurance of an emperor. Although Tawney was in his fifties, he retained the muscularity of the blacksmith that he was in his youth.

Before C.A. could introduce himself, a door in the rear of the chamber opened and a stentorian voice announced, "Attention, attention, the Speaker has entered the chamber."

After a suspenseful interval, 'Uncle Joe' Cannon emerged. With his thick, meaty hands Tawney led the applause; thunderous cracks erupted from the former blacksmith's hands. Tawney whistled as if he were back home at a county fair in Winona, Minnesota.

Thin and angular, Cannon approached the podium, smiling and waving to the adoring crowd with his ubiquitous cigar which sprayed embers like a new-fangled sparkler. Joseph G. Cannon started his political career by supporting Abe Lincoln's presidential candidacy and would go on to serve in the House of Representatives for almost five decades. He had been speaker during the last two Congresses and wielded power like a broad axe. For Uncle Joe, there was no room for subtlety or nuance. Either you were with him or *agin'* him. He demanded absolute allegiance and enforced his will by controlling the agenda, restricting floor debate, directing the flow of patronage and funding. Under Cannon's orchestration, Watson and Tawney played good cop, bad cop like virtuosi.

C.A. watched the seventy-year-old navigate the stairs to the podium. Lindbergh nearly rushed forward to assist the rickety Speaker who teetered, but Watson's extended hand caught and guided the Speaker into position. Uncle Joe's craggy features were partially obscured by a wispy white beard. Cannon appeared taller than he actually was – he extended his five-foot-eight inch frame by always wearing a stovepipe hat and by standing ramrod straight. When he was in the throes of an excited speech, which was frequent, he rose on his tiptoes. He wore a stiff, starched collar with a bow tie and an unstructured, three-piece black suit. He looked like a benign grandfather as he surveyed the assemblage with his sharp blue eyes. Despite his insistence on being called Uncle Joe, when he was out of earshot, the Speaker was known by the colorful moniker of "Foul Mouth Joe."

Cannon raised his hands palms down seeking silence. The volume of conversation melted away to nothing as the Speaker cleared his throat. He welcomed the new Congress with flowery words that predicted unprecedented success. Warming to his subject, he championed legislative prerogatives over executive adventurism. It seemed as if every other word from Cannon was profane. Ridge Lindbergh felt like wincing with each profanity. His mind wandered to the time in his teenage years when he got kicked by a cow at the Morrison County Fair and he let loose a string of blue language that would have embarrassed a pimp. He thought about how his father had admonished him by simply saying, "Son, a gentleman does not cuss in public. Cussin' ain't Minnesota nice."

Cannon droned on. His well-known antagonism toward President Theodore Roosevelt came through when he vowed to thwart the President's vision of conservationism. He thundered that no Congress under his leadership would enact legislation to preserve open spaces. He promised that on his watch there would be "*Not one cent for scenery*[23]" A forced, nervous laugh rippled through the crowd at that line.

Next, he turned to Roosevelt's platform to reign in corporate power under the guise of reform. Cannon's eyes blazed as he warned, *"I* am goddamned tired of listening to all this babble for reform. America is a hell of a success.²⁴ "

C.A. felt that Uncle Joe's ire was aimed directly at him. This was so contrary to the conciliatory tone expressed by Watson on their walk from the train station that C.A. felt confused. It was about to get worse. The foundation of his public service was about to be blown to smithereens.

"OK, gentlemen, it's time to get down to practical business. We are going to line up according to our interests and we will then see about committee assignments. Alright, listen up. All those who represent the banks head on over to Bob Bonynge. Raise your hand higher, you lazy bastard," shouted Uncle Joe.

"Now, all those who represent the railroads go stand by Clay Van Voorhis, the bald asshole with his hands up over there."

"All those who represent the lumber interests git your butts over to my friend, Jim Tawney."

"Good, good. Next, all those who represent manufacturers, go over to John Dalzell, the asshole with the handlebar mustache."

"OK, all those who represent other corporations get your asses over to my good friend, Sereno Payne."

"That does it. Wait a goddamn minute. What are you guys in the middle doing? Are you deef? I rattled off all the interests, how come you're still standing there with your thumbs up your asses?" That provoked raucus laughter. A dozen or so stood in the center of the chamber wearing sheepish, bewildered looks.

"Calm down, men. Let me git to the bottom of this." Cannon gestured genially, if condescendingly, "You there. Yes, you," he indicated C.A.

"Now, you are from Minnesota, right, son?"

"Yes, your honor," replied Lindbergh who answered in his best lawyer demeanor.

"I see we have a new lawyer with us," said Uncle Joe, to a gaggle of chuckles.

"Well, Mr. Lawyer from Minnesota, we've gone through the banks, railroads, manufacturers and corporations and you ain't chosen one. So, pray tell, who do you represent?"

C.A. reddened as a chorus of catcalls fell on his ears. He steeled himself for what was about to happen. When the catcalls died down,

C.A. said in an unwavering voice, "Mr. Speaker, I am proud to report that on November 6th, I was duly elected to represent the people of the 6th District of Minnesota. So my answer to your question is that I do not represent any special interests. I represent the people, all the people and only the people."

C.A. thought he heard a pin drop. After an uncomfortable pause, Uncle Joe scoffed, "Suit yourself."

PART TWO
Crisis

early 1907 New York City, NY

In our studies this will become as plain as the noon day sun on a clear day.
~ C.A. Lindbergh, Sr.

His indoctrination in the ways of Washington was rapid. Speaker Cannon ran Congress like his own utility. Individual Congressmen were summoned to meetings or votes on Cannon's erratic schedule. The pace in Washington was frantic. He ran from caucus to committee meeting to ceremonial duties. His life was a blur of activity. C.A. soon came to the realization that deliberate chaos was the Speaker's way of asserting control. Lindbergh's innate resisitance to bullying resulted in his gravitating to a group of like-minded rebels who came to be known as the Insurgents.

At the same time he was adapting to his new career, C.A.'s estrangement from Evy continued. It appeared on its way to becoming permanent. He was so distracted by the crush of important issues that the nightly telephone calls he pledged to make to Evy and little Charley soon became weekly and then monthly. His conversations with Evy were awkward and one-sided. Over time as his calls became sporadic, their relationship evaporated. Evy seethed and found it difficult to be civil with her husband. The frequency of Lindbergh's calls lessened. At some point she was so angry and resentful, that whenever she heard her husband's voice on the telephone, she simply handed the receiver to little Charley without uttering a word. Despite the pain he felt when Evy refused to speak to him, C.A. was unfailingly cheerful and upbeat with his son.

The one area which did not suffer from his workload was his letter writing. He wrote frequently to his daughters, Lillian and Eva, and sent cards and doodles to little Charley. While other Congressmen coveted social standing and reveled in the high life of Washington, Lindbergh derived his greatest pleasure from reading notes from his children. He adored accounts of their juvenile struggles growing up in the Midwest and reports of their progress.

Due to their intertwined business interests and longtime special relationship, Lindbergh stayed in communication with Sam Wurthels. C.A. instructed his partner to divest Lindbergh's real estate holdings, lest he be accused of interests that might conflict with his legislative responsibilities. Sam obeyed C.A.'s directive even though they both lost money on the sale of certain properties. When the accounting came, he found it disconcerting and worrisome. It was almost as if Sam had given the properties away, rather than negotiate the best deal. Prior to this divestiture, Lindbergh had believed that his investments would be sufficient to educate his daughters and support Evy and little Charley. Now his finances groaned under the weight of meeting his obligations on his meager Congressional salary. Lindbergh vowed to get answers from Sam who was in New York

It was snowing when Lindbergh arrived in New York City to meet with his friend and reconcile their accounts. He met Sam at the White Horse Tavern on Hudson and 11th Street. The pub had been built some thirty years earlier as a watering hole for longshoremen who labored at the west side docks. Since the turn of the century there had been an influx of writers, actors, and bohemians that changed the character of the establishment. Now, instead of fisticuffs and late night brawls, the most lethal object thrown was a sarcastic barb from a drunken would-be writer.

C.A. settled into a worn wooden booth and waited. The wood in the venerable tavern was darkened by age, smoke, and wasted ambitions. Sam entered from a back staircase. C.A. could not believe his friend's appearance. Expecting to see his neatly attired, clean-shaven partner, Lindbergh suppressed his shock at Sam's unkempt appearance. He wore a grimy, patched work shirt that reeked of smoke and some unidentifiable sour smell. It was evident that Sam had not been to a barber since he had left Minnesota. C.A. wondered whether his friend had even bathed since he last saw him. His hair extended in a disheveled mass spilling over his collar. A stubby beard crept up his face toward bloodshot eyes.

"I see you found the place," Sam bellowed. He twisted a chair around so that his elbows rested on the back of the wooden chair. Over his shoulder, Sam ordered the barkeep, "Hey, Sedgwick, my friend here needs another round of suds and a plate of sandwiches and pickles."

"Right, Cap," said Sedgwick.

"They serve the best pickles in town here. Crunchier than a virgin on a winter's day."

C.A. winced at Sam's crudity. He watched as Sam chugged down a beer, wiped his mouth on his sleeve and belched loudly.

"Ah, that's sweet. Bring another, Lassie," he said to a passing waitress. "So, tell me how you like Washington."

"The transition has been challenging. The leadership is intellectually and morally corrupt. But there is still the opportunity to serve honorably. I'm doing important work, trying to protect the farmers and regular folks from the parasites. I'm writing a book about how the banks and the railroads conspire to suppress commodity prices while raising shipping costs. The Money Trust's manipulation of interest rates is destroying the farmers and other working men. Our constituents are falling into greater debt each year. I fear that the family farm may soon become extinct. I add to my manuscript every evening in my warren of an office."

"Good for you," said Sam, raising a new tankard of beer. "Down the hatch!"

"How's Elisha? Where is she?" asked C.A., trying to steer to a topic that might interest Sam.

"Oh, she's upstairs sleeping. She had a late night with her producer. You know these artsy types. That Kahn really works them hard."

"Is that so?" said C.A., his interest piqued.

"Yeah, that banker guy - I'm sure you've heard of him – he's financing Elisha's new show. Otto Kahn is rumored to be the most influential person in show biz. You would not like him. He's not direct like Minnesota folk. Otto has affectations."

"What do you mean 'affectations'?"

"He has this monocle that is his trademark. It's gold and has a saying on it that he calls Otto's motto. Something about the hunger for gold. When you are with him, it's like he uses the monocle to hypnotize you. He's always twirling it, or pointing it . . . . It can be unsettling; but that's not the main thing. Otto is a real judge of talent and he thinks Elisha is the most talented showgirl he's ever met. He thinks that she's gonna be a real star. He's a real taskmaster. He's got her comin' and goin' – all hours. But, she's happy...."

"And how about you?"

"You want the truth? I'm not sure. This world is far different from Minnesota. There are so many delights, so many distractions so many new and wild experiences. Elisha has expanded my senses in so many ways. I never thought that I could be so deeply in love with anyone."

"Well, then, my friend, I am happy for you. Although I'm not sure that I understand your comment about expanding your senses."

"C. A., she has introduced me to some writers who are experimenting with the boundaries of human emotions. Nothing too strong, you know, just enough to alter the consciousness. Some are rather the aphrodisiac." Sam lowered his eyes.

"Another beer here. How about you Ridge, another beer?"

"No thank you," muttered C.A. He had a strange feeling behind him that he was being watched. He turned quickly only to see the swinging door to the kitchen moving back and forth. This place and his friend's ramblings were giving him an uneasy feeling.

"Listen Sam, I'm planning to return to Minnesota in a few weeks. Why don't we plan to go back together and tie up any loose ends?"

Sam eyed his friend over the rim of his newly-arrived beer and said, "Sure, sure, that's a good idea."

Lindbergh knew from the decided lack of enthusiasm in Sam's voice that he would never return to Minnesota. He realized that Elisha's hold over Sam was much too strong. C.A. also knew that he could expect very little, if anything, from their joint holdings. Hopefully, his brother Frank could salvage what was left of the joint property.

"So, what's up with Evy?" asked Sam.

"It's the same as it was. She wants no part of me as long as I am involved in public life. She just doesn't understand that I *need* to do this."

Again, Lindbergh felt eyes on his back.

Sam saw something in his friend's eyes. Was it sadness, or something else? Wariness, perhaps? Sam wrestled with whether he should tell C.A. about the satchel from Commander Hyatt. He knew that it was a lie by omission, but he could not bring himself to reveal what Hyatt told him. It wasn't the right time. Anyway, Elisha had made him promise to keep the secret until after she had sorted out her career.

"Well, Sam, I must be going. You take good care." Lindbergh stood then extended his hand. Sam staggered to his feet and grabbed CA's hand and pulled him toward him into a beery, bear hug.

"You, too, Ridgy. See you soon."

C.A. hailed a hansom cab to take him back to his hotel. As he reached for the door of the carriage, he saw reflected in the window, the image of a young woman looking at him from the tavern. When he turned his head she was gone.

The meeting with his partner had not gone as he had expected. He could not believe how Sam had become so slovenly in such a short period of time. He was worried about the effect that Elisha was having on Sam. It was obvious that Elisha was leading Sam on a path of dissolution. Moreover, he worried about Elisha's relationship with that banker Kahn. Maybe she really was working to perfect her performance, but it sounded more suspicious than that. Yet, Sam seemed oblivious to the likely infidelity. The circumstances saddened C.A., but he felt at a loss over how to change things. He made a note to himself to contact Sam's mother when he returned to Minnesota next month. He wondered whether she might be able to get through to him.

The cab traveled north on 12th Street and turned right on 44th Street. As they proceeded across town, C.A. noticed a building flying several distinctive flags. One caught his attention. It was a red pennant bearing a white crescent encircling a white 5-pointed star. Where had he seen that symbol before? Yes, it was on the blouse of that young girl that he had bumped into at Grand Central Station the last time he was in New York. He had helped her pick up the apples. What was her name? Olida? Ophelia? No . . . Olivia, that's it, Olivia. What had she said as she walked away? It had something to do with ovens. He couldn't recall whose ovens, some officer's . . . . It's funny how the mind works, he mused.

"Excuse me sir, what is that building?" asked Lindbergh pointing toward a distinctive building on the north side of the street.

"That grand structure, Sir, is the home of the New York Yacht

Club. It was built about 5 or 6 years ago as a clubhouse for the rich, yachting gentlemen of the city. It's got a nautical theme. You see those 3 windows there? Thems supposed to be the ass-ends of 17th-century Dutch yachts. You see the seashells, angry dolphins and draped sea weed under the sterns, that's ocean stuff. And, there, above the entrance to the building that's old Neptune," he said, gesturing toward a menacing, concrete visage which hovered in the facade above the front entrance.

"Some say that the builder modeled Neptune after the Commodore, but I don't see it. The Commodore is much uglier," said the cabbie quite content with his own irreverence.

"Who is the Commodore?" asked Lindbergh.

"Why that would be J.P. Morgan hisself," said the driver.

"Can you tell me about that red pennant hanging next to the door?"

"No, Guv'nor, I haven't the foggiest. Maybe it means there is a storm a brewin'."

$ $ $

Her feet ached. The blister on her heel had broken halfway through the rehearsal. By the last dance number, her stocking was soaked with blood from the raw wound. She had not realized how much hard work went into a Broadway production. The director was a perfectionist. If one girl mis-stepped and disrupted the symmetry of the number, they heard the director shout from the balcony, "No, no, number six. Take it from the top and let's get it right this time!"

Miss Angela, the choreographer, rushed out from the wings and whispered encouragement as they reformed the dance line.

"Come now, girls, practice makes perfect. No crying Mary Ann. Hilda, chin up. Elisha, smile," she cooed, *sotto voce*.

After dancing for three hours, they were finally dismissed. Miss Angela applied a salve to Elisha's tortured heel. She placed cotton wadding over it and taped it loosely before swaddling her foot in a clean, cotton sock.

"Leave this on until tomorrow's rehearsal. See me before and I'll bind the wound with some moleskin, before you go on."

"Thanks, you're such an angel," said Elisha.

"That's how I got my name," replied Miss Angela, with a laugh. Elisha reddened and laughed as well. It would be her last light-hearted moment of the afternoon. She packed her bag and ate a banana as she hurried to a drama lesson with her acting teacher. Otto had insisted that she take drama lessons if she was going to become a star.

However, her acting coach was a dreadful human being. She had never encountered such a perpetually negative person. Boris Belinkovich Vulpinyena, a disciple of the famous Russian physiologist, Ivan Petrovich Pavlov, a Nobel laureate for his work in Physiology. Pavlov's study of how dogs could be conditioned to salivate by exposure to a stimulus that accompanied their feeding-time, resulted in his theory of conditioned reflex. His revolutionary work proved that canines could be conditioned to respond to a stimulus even after the reward, the food, had been eliminated.

Boris applied this theory to acting, but instead of providing a reward, he used negative punishment. He reminded Elisha that she would perform to unprecedented emotional heights if she would focus on the disdain and humiliation that would follow if she failed. As a consequence, a typical acting lesson would have Elisha reading a dramatic part only to have Boris submit her to sustained verbal abuse.

She arrived at his studio on Fourteenth Street to find Boris in a pensive mood.

"Miss Elisha, I have been thinking that my methods are not working. You have not improved as much as hoped." Elisha breathed a sigh of relief. Maybe her prayers that he abandon his negative approach had been answered and he would adopt the opposite method and shower her with praise. She thought that a positive reward would certainly motivate her to do her best. Alas, it was wishful thinking.

"I have talked to Mr. Otto and he suggested that in Shakespeare's time, audiences spurred the actors to great dramatic heights by means of the threat of tossing overripe fruit at them. Therefore, I have decided to take a more physical approach to your training."

She could not believe her ears.

"So, starting today, every time you fail to evoke the desired emotion, I will pelt you with a rotten tomato."

Looking at the basket of tomatoes partially obscured by a cloud of flies, Elisha recoiled. My God, he's serious, she thought. She dropped to her knees, with her hands clasped in exhortation. "Please, Mr. Vulpinyena, no, don't throw those foul tomatoes at me. I can't bear it," she cried. Tears streamed down her face.

"Brava, brava!" clapped Boris. "I think it is working. OK, let's go to Act one, scene three where Rosalina learns that her father has been murdered."

Elisha stood, shocked. It was the first positive reaction Boris had ever directed toward her. And, the old fool thought that her plea was an act and that she had been motivated by his threat. When, in actuality, her plea was not acting, but genuine fear. Boris proceeded with *elán*, much to Elisha's dismay.

Two hours later a stinking, tomato-splattered Elisha left the studio and headed to meet Otto at what he called the Fire Rescue Station. She would barely have time to clean herself and change into something provocative before he arrived. The aspiring actress was on the verge of despair. The humiliation she had experienced with Boris was unbearable. Her mood was so dark that she contemplated abandoning her dream and returning to Minneapolis. Only the riches that Otto promised kept her from running away. By the time Otto entered the retreat, she had recovered her equanimity. It was amazing how a couple of Brandy Manhattan cocktails and one of Otto's magic, white pills made her feel euphoric.

A typical day for Otto was spent at his office at 52 William Street conducting his investment banking business. When the working day was over, he shifted to his true passion, the theater. The firm's chairman, Jacob Schiff, expressed great disdain for Otto's theatrical pursuits and forbade him from using Kuhn Loeb facilities for "those goniffs." Rather than press the issue and endure an atmosphere that was decidedly prudish, Otto preferred to conduct theatrical business away from the office. He devised the Fire Rescue Station as the perfect alternative.

In 1906, when the City built the new Fire Patrol Station No. 2, on West 3rd Street, Otto purchased the decommissioned firehouse that it replaced. He renovated it to accommodate his needs. The façade of the exterior was brick with a large limestone central archway with ornamental doors that previously opened for passage of the fire wagons. Otto painted these ebony black and trimmed them with shiny brass hinges and the numerals 19 for the house number on St. Luke's Place. Balancing the main central archway were two smaller entrances. One was for Otto's office and was appropriately marked with a brass sign. The other door was for guests. It was an elaborate, carved wooden door with stained glass panels depicting scenes of New Amsterdam.

The second story featured ornamental, arched windows and a frieze decorated in an early Dutch motif.

The street level floor was what Otto referred to as the public area; upstairs was the private area. The office was unconventional, featuring couches and Queen Anne style armchairs along the perimeter. The only concession to business was a large credenza that had been modified to hold files relating to Kahn's theatrical endeavors. A small marble bar and walnut icebox rested unobtrusively in the corner. Gaslight sconces, walnut paneling and oil paintings of the Mariinsky Theater in St. Petersburg and the *Wiener Staatsoper*, the Vienna State Opera House, adorned the walls. In addition to the front entrance, there were two additional doors in the office. One led to the adjacent public space on the first floor. The other, seamlessly concealed in the paneling, opened to a secret stairway leading to a bedroom suite upstairs. This stairway led to Otto's lair in case a business meeting with a female turned amorous. The door to that suite was locked from the inside. Only Otto had the key.

The remainder of the first floor was a large open area with high ceilings and wood floors. Plush upholstered couches, armchairs and chaises graced the floor which was covered with Persian rugs of varying sizes. The walls were wainscoted to the chair rail and painted above that with a pastel shade of rose that was at once sultry, yet classical. The room could have easily passed for a salon at one the finest hotels on the Continent save for one unique feature. Otto had retained the brass fireman's pole connecting the two floors and the basement. During the renovation, Otto directed that flooring be built around the pole on the first floor. Thus configured, the pole provided a creative prop for Otto's erotic fantasies.

There was one other feature that differentiated this pole from the standard firemen's pole. He delighted in having his paramours exhibit their dancing skills, using it for balance. Before his untimely demise, Stanford White had suggested that Otto install a perch midway up the high-ceilinged wall so that several girls could 'dance the pole' simultaneously. It was a stroke of genius.

Otto missed his friend, the prominent architect who used his considerable design talents to create opulent lairs where moneyed men could indulge in carnal pleasure in style. They had shared many a bacchanalia at White's love nest. It was hard to believe that White had been murdered by the husband of one of the women that White had ruined. Otto took pride in the statement by that old degenerate White, who begrudgingly admitted, "Otto, I must say that your pole is more conducive to debauchery than my red velvet swing." Otto tipped his glass in silent tribute to the master.

The remainder of the Fire Rescue Station consisted of the second floor which Otto gutted and made it into a luxury apartment with two suites, including twin bathrooms, each outfitted with a steam room and a shower with a rain showerhead and multiple body massage jets. The two bedrooms were sumptuously appointed, as might be expected as a place designed for sexual dalliances.

When Otto's extramarital activities kept him from his mansion on 91st Street, he opted to stay at the Fire Rescue Station. Otto told his wife, Addie, that he was a sponsor and honorary member of the West Village Fire Brigade. She understood that his devotion to duty required him to spend nights at the Fire Rescue Station. After all, many socially prominent people generously gave their time and money to worthy causes. What could be more altruistic than helping keep the City safe from the ravages of fire. One need only look across the continent to see how fire had destroyed much of San Francisco just one year earlier.

For many years Addie Kahn was unaware of Otto's deceptive use of the Fire Rescue Station. She only discovered it by accident when she was seated next to Fire Chief Dixon at a charity fundraiser and she asked proudly about Otto's achievements with the West Village Fire Brigade. When the Fire Chief professed ignorance of such an outfit, her expression of disbelief and anger was epic. The Fire Chief nearly choked on his filet mignon as he surmised the nature of her dismay. He shook his head ruefully at another alibi busted. In the end, it did not matter because by the time she discovered Otto's years of perfidy, their marriage had become one of convenience only.

"Otto, I'm so glad that you are home. Have I got a surprise for you. But first you relax and have this Bronx cocktail I've made for you. Just stirred, to keep it from clouding," cooed Elisha.

She greeted him with a buss on the cheek. He removed his suit jacket and settled onto a chaise. She limped slightly over to the polished mahogany bar and returned carrying two drinks. Hers was a Brandy Manhattan that she had acquired a taste for in Minnesota. His was a bright orange mixture of gin, sweet and dry vermouth and orange juice, with an orange slice perched like some exotic bird on the rim of the glass. If he noticed her injury, he paid it no mind.

"So tell me how, was your lesson with my friend Boris?"

"He may be your friend, but he's not mine. The man is an absolute beast!" said Elisha, adjusting herself on the edge of Otto's chaise.

"I'm told by veteran theatrical folks that he is an absolute genius."

Elisha scoffed, "If throwing rotten tomatoes at someone is genius, then Boris is a reincarnated Leonardo da Vinci. Seriously, Otto, the man is an absolute beast. He delights in making others suffer."

"My little Elisha, don't you know that all true artists suffer for their art." When she started to reply, he shushed her and pulled her head to him for a kiss. The kiss turned passionate. Soon they were lying parallel, Elisha's leg draped over Otto's hip.

"Well then, I need something to relieve my day of suffering," she whispered hoarsely. They made love so violently that they landed on the Garrus Bijar, a rug so dense and cushioned that they barely noticed the drop.

Later, they rested, each lost in thought. The door knocker rapped three times.

"Perfect timing," exclaimed Otto, pulling on his robe. "I ordered dinner from Cobble Court's. They make the best *coq au vin* in the City. I'm famished."

They dined without utensils, tearing at the chicken with their fingers, and mining cremini mushrooms from the tasty mélange. Fingers, chins and necks were alternately licked. Otto and Elisha tippled chilled Italian prosecco with their repast. The culmination of the meal was a tartine with tawny, caramelized sugar gracing the apple slices. After another bout of lovemaking, they lay sated.

Otto asked, "What's the news with our friend Sam? Did he meet with that clown from Minnesota, yet?"

"Yes, be nice Otto. Lindbergh is not a clown; he may be a little misguided, but he is a fine gentleman. They met yesterday."

"OK." Otto took a cigar from a wood and mother-of-pearl clad humidor proffered by Elisha. Deftly clipping the tip, Otto lit his stoogie.

"I need to know more about Lindbergh," said Otto tilting back and expelling a cloud of smoke.

"There is news. Sam told me that C.A. is working on a manuscript.

He has done extensive research on the impact of monetary practices on the farming community in the Midwest."

"Is that so?" said Otto, raising an eyebrow.

"Yes, according to C.A., the Money Trust, as he calls the banking establishment, is conspiring with the railroad interests to raise shipping costs and interest rates. The result will be the destruction of independent farmers."

"Tell me more about his manuscript."

"It's called *'Banking and Currency and the Money Trust.'* He is obsessed with it. He spends all his free time in his office working on it. He literally sleeps in the office, so that he can spend all his waking hours writing this book." Otto gave her a bored look. Except for the title, this was stale information that his operatives had already told him.

"Tell me something I don't already know," snapped Otto who flashed his nasty side. Elisha bit her lower lip. She was torn between her loyalty to Sam and her desire to satisfy Otto's insatiable need for intelligence about Lindbergh. Maybe she could divert his attention by dancing with the pole. Otto always enjoyed her twists, spins and gyrations. Not tonight.

He read her mind. When she attempted to rise, Kahn seized her wrist tightly.

"Later for that. You are holding something back from me. Tell me now!"

After a long pause, she said "OK," in a small voice.

1907 Washington D.C.

The real menace of our Republic is the invisible government, which like a giant octopus sprawls its slimy legs over our cities, states and nation....
~ John F. Hylan

Lindbergh's trip to New York had been unnerving. His dear friend Sam was in trouble and he did not even realize it. C.A. was a man who avoided temptation. He had learned from his father that a man had to control his appetites otherwise they would control him. Under the guise of discovering himself, Sam was recklessly heading toward a dark place with Elisha leading the way.

What was so frustrating to C.A. was that although he could see the impending personal fall of his friend, C.A. had neither the temperament nor training to halt the progression of Sam's descent. Normally, the lessons of self-reliance, stoicism in the face of adversity and moral uprightness that C.A.'s father had pressed into his personality were virtues. However, when it came to helping his friend avoid the downward spiral of his new life style, these attributes were useless.

Moreover, Lindbergh had no way of knowing the true malevolent force behind Sam's predicament. Perhaps, if he had known the invisible hand directing Sam's dissolution, C.A. might have been able to avert the impending disaster. But, he had no idea of the depths of depravity of the Money Trust and could only react to events as they unfolded.

Back in D.C., the pace accelerated. He threw himself into the mountains of material that piled onto his desk at an astonishing rate.

There were committee reports, transcripts of public testimony and marked drafts of legislation. It wasn't long before he realized that the only time he could work in peace was after the building emptied and his colleagues left to fill the salons and restaurants of the Capital. The social circuit of wining and dining with industry representatives and all sorts, reputable and otherwise, did not appeal to him. He politely declined most invitations, until they trickled down to only the most perfunctory. He developed a reputation as a loner. And although he was considered brilliant and always prepared, traits not in great supply on Capitol Hill, C.A. had another trait that was in short supply in D.C., he burned with the desire to make a positive difference for his constituents.

With increased access to information that came with being a Congressman, he threw himself into researching and analyzing data, especially economic information that impacted his constituents in ways that few understood. His most productive hours were after the building had emptied and he could delve into problems in great depth. There were many occasions when he worked so long into the night that he ended up sleeping on the couch opposite his desk.

Blakey was with him constantly, his sole source of companionship. The dog had matured into a powerful Labrador retriever. He was pitch-black from tip to tail, with a sleek coat that made him appear like a shadow in the night. Blake's demeanor was calm and gentle, except when he sensed trouble. On those occasions, his ears perked up, his nose rose to capture the slightest scent and his keen eyes scanned the scene with an eagle's acuity. Blake was so well-behaved that most staffers in the building did not know he was present. The only exception occurred when an inebriated representative from Texas tried to show C.A. how to 'rassle a steer to the ground. Before he could say Sam Houston, the representative was on the floor with Blake standing over him, his back bristling and his teeth bared. There was a decided wet spot near the Texan's crotch when C.A. helped him to his feet and dusted him off.

C.A. took to using the black, leather couch in his office for, in his parlance, naps. On occasion when his staff arrived and found him asleep on the couch, they tiptoed through the office so as not to awaken him. On most mornings, however, he was wide awake and had already put in several hours' work before the staff arrived. In a strange way, this new life style suited him. He lived like an aesthetic, eating and drinking sparingly. On some days he consumed only a bowl of oatmeal for breakfast, an apple for lunch and a bowl of soup from the House kitchen for dinner at his desk.

C.A. absorbed the research material like a meadow absorbs the spring rain. He correlated and connected disparate pieces of information until he discerned a pattern of interrelationships. C.A. became obsessed with the role of the Money Trust; its tentacles were everywhere. He began drafting an analysis of the Money Trust that would explain the dangers to freedom posed by this creature. He realized that it had all the attributes of a living organism. It grew, it replicated itself and consumed what it could – farms, shops, factories – to feed its growth. Anne Tracy's analogy to the octopus was certainly apt. In his manuscript, he referred to the Money Trust as an octopus to be slayed. He fixated on a sketch drawn by another critic, of an octopus winding its tentacles through the government and economy.

Often when he fell asleep on the office couch, he was haunted by a recurring dream. C.A. dreamed that he was at the Pine Tree saw mill and he was being pulled into the saw. From his vantage point above the scene, he witnessed himself as a young man held down on a conveyor belt by tentacles. He was being drawn towards disaster. His father stood by passively. Standing next to him was a short, mustachioed man using his cane to whip an octopus while he exhorted it to squeeze its prey more tightly. The loud, whirring blade ripped through his arm, grinding through the bone. No matter how hard he tried to scream, he could not make a sound. C.A. would invariably awake as the blade tore at his ribs, exposing his beating heart through his chest. The dream would leave him shaking, with his shirt drenched in sweat.

$ $ $

From the way it began, C. A. could not have predicted the way it would end.

As usual, he was asleep in his office. A half-typed sheet of his manuscript was in the roller of his typewriter. The manuscript was on the desk, cinched with a rubber binder. Blakey lifted his ears and turned his head toward the outer door that was C.A.'s private entrance. It was around the corner from the public entrance to his congressional suite. It was unmarked and directly abutted the exterior hallway.

A low rumble, not quite a growl built in the dog's chest. C.A. awoke. As his eyes focused, he saw two shadows beneath the door. He stroked Blakey to be quiet. A slim envelope appeared under the door sill and Lindbergh heard footsteps retreat down the hall.

Blakey bolted from his grasp and sniffed the intruding missive.

"It's OK, boy," said Lindbergh, rising from his torpor to retrieve the envelope. It was addressed to him in an assertive, but definitely feminine hand. As he brought it up to open it, he detected a faint perfume. He could not place the aroma except to recognize that he had smelled it before. Lavender? Jasmine? Or quince? The musty smell of his lived-in office interfered with his olfactory powers. He chuckled and vowed to air out the place.

At his desk he withdrew the replica Civil War sabre letter opener that he had received as an election victory gift from Crow Wing County Veterans of the Civil War. It bore the inscription "The Pen Is Mightier Than the Sword." This motto reinforced his belief in the power of words to effectuate change. That was why he was writing his book. Of course, history has demonstrated that the targets of the pen often respond with the sword.

The blade sliced the flap open, emitting the scent. Now it came to him. The last time he smelled it, he received the photo of Clarence Buckman meeting with the Money Trust in New York City. He wondered if this missive would be as momentous. Like a baby in a cradle, a single sheet of paper rested in the envelope. With a flourish of mental fanfare, he opened it.

"Take the electric car to the Riggs House, opposite the Treasury, Thursday, 2 P.M. Follow the lavender rose. Come alone."

C.A. turned the note over looking for a signature or some other identifying mark. There was none. It was the same handwriting and scent from the missive that he had received along with the photo of Buckman and Morgan during the campaign. The next day was filled with anxious speculation.

Later in the day, C.A. went to research in the Library of Congress Building. This majestic edifice was his favorite place in Washington. Directly across from the Capitol building, it was built between 1890 and 1897. It was rightfully dubbed "America's Palace." Its soaring interior, capped by a series of six stained glass skylights and adorned with murals, statues, and mosaics, is as magnificent as any palace ever conceived. In C.A.'s estimation, the grandest aspect of it was that it belonged to the people, not some potentate.

He approached the research librarian at the information desk with his request. She was a tall, lithe woman with long, straight blonde hair which she swiped away from her face several times a minute. This nervous habit was more endearing than distracting. C.A. thought of the many Scandinavian women in his district. A pang of homesickness struck him. He wondered what his daughters, Lillian, Eva and his wife Evy were doing today. An image of little Charley, his hands covered with red finger paint, chasing the girls through the house flashed into his mind.

He smiled at the boisterous commotion that he imagined. The persistent doubt that plagued him resurfaced. Had he chosen wisely?

"May I help you, Congressman?" she said, recognizing him from his frequent visits. He noticed the catch light reflected in her blue eyes as she smiled at him. She admired his research tenacity; most of the other elected officials left the work of data analysis to staff members. Congressman Lindbergh was a welcome contrast to the rest of his colleagues.

"Yes, Emma. I'm looking for materials relating to the history of mortgage foreclosures of family farms since the Civil War. Can you help me find them? I'll be at my usual desk."

"Yes, I'll tell Mary the reference librarian assigned to Congress. She'll bring you everything you need."

C.A. knew that it would take a while for the requested materials to be assembled and brought to him in the reading room. He used these intervals to explore the amazing building. C.A. climbed the stairs, the sound of his leather footfalls echoing slightly against the marble. At the top of the stairs, he turned and stopped in astonishment. There, on the west wall, he beheld the motto, "The Pen Is Mightier Than the Sword."

The prior evening he had focused on the motto on his letter opener. Now, he just saw it on the wall in the Library of Congress. This could not be happenstance. The message twice delivered helped dissipate his doubt and reinforced his resolve. Invigorated, he made his way back to the reading room.

Thursday morning's committee hearing ran long and finally adjourned for lunch.

"C.A., you have a minute?" asked Jim Watson, buttonholing him in the rotunda.

"Sure, what can I do for you?"

"I'm drafting legislation that will enable farmers to form locally owned cooperatives without fear of prosecution under the Sherman Antitrust Act. I know that you have established a cooperative in

Minnesota and I wanted to hear about your experience, so that I can understand some of the nuances."

"When would you like to meet?"

"How about over lunch? I'll buy," said Watson, steering Lindbergh by the elbow toward the cafeteria. C.A. knew that his new friend liked to imbibe a few during lunch and he would miss his rendezvous if he set foot in the cafeteria. At the risk of alienating the Whip, C.A. decided to rebuff his invitation.

"I'm so sorry, but I've got an appointment across town. I'll take a rain check."

Watson feigned a hurt expression. "I get it, you're heading for a tryst and don't have time for ole Jimmy." C.A. tried to wriggle his arm free, but Watson had other ideas. He decided to have some fun at C.A.'s expense.

"Hey, James Albertus," Watson called in a commanding voice to Minnesota Congressman James A. Tawney.

"This here rookie just told me that he's too busy to discuss legislation with me. I think he's got a date. What should we do with him?"

A glint lit Tawney's eyes, signifying that the hazing had begun.

"I think that our freshman should sing his state song during our lunch break."

A chorus of "Make him sing!" rang through the dining room. A table and chair for C.A. to stand on was carried over. By now, all eyes were on Lindbergh, except for those of a few other freshmen who were endeavoring to become invisible. As uncomfortable as he was, C.A. knew that his rendition of "Hail, Minnesota" would lead his tormentors to flee the room.

With mock seriousness, he mounted the impromptu stage and mimicked tuning his vocal chords. Then, throwing his arms wide he screeched:

Minnesota, hail to thee!
Hail to thee our state so dear!
Thy light shall ever be
A beacon bright and clear.

His voice resembled a caterwauling tabby with its tail caught in a washer wringer. It lingered in the air at the end of each line. As Lindbergh took a breath in preparation for the second stanza, a barrage of boos, hisses and pleas to stop filled the room. Sensing that his goal had been achieved, Lindbergh bowed deeply and stepped down, hands raised triumphantly. Watson and Tawney held their hands over their ears. His eyes watery from laughter, Watson gestured for C.A. to leave quickly. Watson mouthed to C.A. that he would see him the next day.

Lindbergh nodded his thanks and exited the Capitol without glancing back. Who knew that his un-angelic singing voice would become an asset? He broke into a jog and was barely able to board the electric trolley heading toward the Treasury Building. Much like the country itself, the nation's capital was transforming into a bustling, modern center. To be sure, it retained elements of its genteel southern roots, but steel and urgency were replacing magnolias and parasol-carrying strollers along the Potomac. The Treasury Building was a case in point.

Over the last half-century, there had been numerous expansions to accommodate the ever-expanding power of the Treasury Department. He stood beneath the shadow of the latest iteration of the Treasury Building. With its colonnades of fluted Ionic columns, it was a pretentious manifestation of the Money Trust and its never-sated influence at the center of the Republic. C.A. thought back to one of his orientation sessions about the evolution of the nation's capital. The original plan was for there to be an unobstructed view between the White House and the Capitol Building. He considered the faux grandiose intrusion of the Treasury Building between the President's home and the People's house, the Capitol, to be a gross effrontery. He gritted his teeth at the thought of the challenges that lay before him.

It was with a determined frame of mind that C.A. entered the Riggs House, an elegant hotel located across the street from the Treasury Building. The Riggs House touted itself as the "home of statesmen and rendezvous of *bons vivants*." He was struck by the opulence that assaulted his senses. The lobby was a study in marquetry tastefully combining cherry, mahogany, and rosewood in intricate patterns punctuated by sparkling beveled glass panels. He followed the main corridor past two of the largest mirrors he had ever seen. A magnificent velvet carpet cushioned his every step.

Definitely feeling like he was out of his element, an awkwardness enveloped him. What had he gotten into? Maybe Watson was right. The mysterious note might have been sent by a misguided admirer, or worse, a scandal monger looking to catch him in a compromising position. Better to leave now before he became entangled in something he could not control.

As he retreated toward the lobby, a waiter in a short-waist white jacket and black trousers approached him. The waiter was carrying a tray with a crystal bud vase containing a single lavender rose.

"Follow me, sir," he said. Intrigued, a wary Lindbergh complied. They made several turns along a private hallway decorated with murals of biblical scenes. At the end of the hall C.A. eyed a mural depicting the Last Supper. The leather bag of silver coins clutched by Judas appeared magnified.

Without knocking, the waiter opened the door while balancing the bud vase. He gestured for C.A. to enter the darkened room. Supple, leather lounges lined the perimeter of the room. The waiter set the tray down on a circular serving table and proceeded to uncork a bottle of champagne. A lone figure with her back to him waited until the waiter completed pouring and left the room. She was wearing a floor length dress that gave him no clue as to her identity.

C.A. folded his arms across him chest. It was so quiet that he thought he could hear the champagne bubbles bursting to the surface. He sniffed a faint touch of lavender, just like the fragrance on the envelopes. Patience, he told himself as he tried to restrain his curiosity. Let it happen.

"I hope that you do not mind my precautions. When you know the entire story, you will understand."

She still had not turned toward him. That voice, her stance, could it be her?

With a grace borne of the finest ladies academy, she pivoted and walked to him. She offered a flute and took one herself. He found himself bowing slightly as if they were engaged in some ritual. They sat facing each other and clinked glasses.

"It's nice to see you again, Anne."

"Yes, C.A. I've been looking for an opportunity to see you again. For the record, in case you have not connected all the dots, I was the one who sent you the photo of that buffoon Buckman with the Money Trust."

"Of course," he stammered, "I should have figured it out sooner. I was thrown off the scent because I thought it might have been from Carrie Fosseen's cousin as a gesture to make-up for the disastrous article in the New York Times comparing me to Don Quixote tilting at windmills."

They both chuckled at the imagery of Lindbergh in knight's armor astride an emaciated charger.

C.A. raised an eyebrow and regarded her with an expectant look that said, OK, then, the ball is in your court. She blinked her eyelids rapidly as she gathered her thoughts.

"Oh, dear, I did not expect to behave like a tongue-tied school girl."

"Take your time. My calendar is clear for the rest of the afternoon; although I do have much work to do this evening."

"Oh, yes, your book . . . ," she stopped with a sheepish look. He leaned back and shook his head.

"I guess there are no secrets in this town," he said, chagrined. She let loose a quiet laugh.

"No, there are not," Anne whispered. "Actually, the reason I wanted to see you has precisely to do with your book, at least, the subject of your book."

C.A. hunched forward with his elbows on his knees.

"I'm all ears."

"Mammon is on the move. There has not been a panic since '93. That's fourteen years. There is a storm of events forming that will dwarf the last monetary panic." A frightened look came across her eyes.

"What do you mean? Are you suggesting that there are people who are manipulating events to cause a panic? That's impossible. How can they know that they will not be consumed by it? The very definition of panic is an irrational, out of control event."

His voice trailed off as the realization hit him. His enemy, whatever you called it, Mammon, the Money Trust, must be far stronger and more evil than he had previously imagined. She saw the realization in his face and nodded affirmatively that his epiphany was true.

"Don't ask me how I know this, but events are being manipulated to create an extremely dangerous situation. You are well aware of the annual agricultural money cycle. Each fall during the harvest season, there is a significant outflow of money from the New York banks to purchase farm products. In normal times, this outflow of cash leads to a shortage of money in New York and other financial centers. To counteract this shortage, the banks typically raise interest rates. It's basic supply and demand – fewer available dollars results in the banks charging more for the dollars they have. Higher interest rates depress borrowing and hence business expansion suffers. In the coming fall, the usual cycle will be artificially manipulated by attempts to corner the markets of various commodities. The end result will be an overextended money supply, higher interest costs and massive dislocation of resources and a resultant panic."

"When is this going to happen?"

"When the harvest comes."

"We've got to stop it. We've got to warn the farmers."

"There's nothing you can do at this time. The enemy is too big and too strong. Your time will come, but, not now. It's too dangerous. We must work together to expose the evil monster, then with public opinion on your side you will prevail. Remember what I told you, you can't wound it, you have to kill it."

March 1907 Little Falls, MN

The senseless craving for money and the shameless craving for power that money gives is a disease from which people suffer everywhere.
~Maxim Gorky

Sitting at the desk in his office, C.A. unbuttoned his collar. He had heard about the enervating heat of Washington, but it was only March and he was beginning to experience it firsthand. He longed for the crisp, clear air of his native state. Instead, the humidity of D.C. sapped his energy. A smile came to his lips as he contemplated the recent course of events that had provided the answer to the mystery of the origins of the Buckman photograph, the release of which helped reveal the hypocrisy of his opponent in his first election.

He had to admit that the involvement of Anne Tracy had come as a complete surprise. She certainly intrigued him. The prospect of Anne collaborating with him on the book was welcome. It did not occur to him to question the source of her insight into the Money Trust; all that mattered was that she would be a valuable sounding board to help provide the proper perspective for his research conclusions.

A trip back home soon would be the tonic. He planned a trip at the end of March to celebrate Easter. The visit started well, then turned drastically bad. He would later reflect that it marked the unofficial death of his marriage.

He had returned to Little Falls in the last week of March. When he arrived back home, the first call he made after checking in with family was to Jock Pierz and the second was to Big Charley Weyerhaeuser.

C.A. entered the office of the Pine Tree Lumber Company and heard the booming voice of Big Charley.

". . . So I says, 'Well, don-chya-no, she's pregnant?' Get it?" thundered Weyerhaeuser, simultaneously slapping his knee.

Raucus laughter emanated from the office.

Lindbergh smiled at the warm camaraderie. He missed the gruff naturalness of his native Minnesota. Hearing Big Charley again after so many months produced a swell of affection for his friend and primary donor to his successful congressional campaign. He thought about all the good times they had together.

"I best be headin' out, Big Charley, the missus needs help for the big Easter celebration. Got the famly comin' to town."

C.A. heard a slap on the back. The door to the inner office swung open.

"Well, I'll be. If it ain't our 'steemed Congressman. You gonna come in? Or, just stand there grinnin'?" shouted Big Charley.

"Big Charley! How are you, my friend? I didn't want to interrupt. I was waiting for you to finish up."

"You would have been standing there 'til Ole stopped gropin' Lena down behind da barn," joked Big Charley. "Come on in, come in. Have a bit a medicine?" beckoned Charley with a bottle of sloshing, tawny liquor.

"I guess you could twist my arm a bit," said Lindbergh. "Whoa, whoa, not so much," he protested when Big Charley filled his glass to the rim.

"What? (pause) I heard that you congressmen are big drinkers (wink)," said Weyerhaeuser passing the glass.

"To your health, welcome back, Ridgy!" said Big Charley. They both raised their glasses and clinked. Amber liquor sloshed over the rims onto the wooden floor.

"Don't pay that there no mind. Tell me, how the hell are you?"

"I'm good, thanks. I think the pace and life as a legislator agrees with me. I've met a great number of influential people."

They settled into well-worn armchairs.

"You remember when we were seniors in high school and while everyone was in the gym for the pep rally for the big game, we snuck three goats into the gym?" asked Ridge.

"You're dern-tootin'! We painted numbers on 'em – 1, 2 an' 4," exclaimed Big Charley.

"Ha! Principal Spencer spent the whole day lookin' for number 3."

"That was quite the prank," said C.A. grinning at the thought of ol' Darren Spencer, a Boston transplant, scurrying around the school with a bunch of carrots, crying, "Here, goaty, goaty. Come out, come out wherever you are."

They laughed at the memory so hard that tears streamed down their faces. It was good to be home. Big Charley refilled their glasses and the conversation turned serious.

"Big Charley, I want you to know that I've had several sessions with Director Pinchot of the Forest Service. He is not quite the conservation zealot that the President is. Pinchot recognizes the importance of lumber to the development of the west. I brought you a copy of the new book, *The Use Of The National Forest Reserves*. In here, he states right up front that, *'We know that the welfare of every community is dependent upon a cheap and plentiful supply of timber.*[25]*'*" C.A. handed the book to his friend. Weyerhaeuser smiled.

"Here's the bottom line. There has never been a Forest Service before; so, he's kind of making it up as he goes along. The major focus for the next generation is acquisition of forest lands in the far west. He has ambitious plans to more than triple the number and acreage of forest reserves. He always emphasizes that forest management involves long term decisions. You will be happy to know that Pinchot believes, *'The prime object of the forest reserves is use.* [26]*'* He is all in favor of cutting timber from forest reserves just like any other timber."

"That sounds good, C.A., real good," said Big Charley, easing back in his chair, his shoulders relaxing.

"I think that you two would get along. Would you like me to arrange a meeting with him next time he's out this way?"

"Yeah, sure, you betcha. You ready for another drink, then?"

C.A. nodded and mimicked, "Yeah, sure, you betcha." Big Charley gave C.A. a playful push on the shoulder.

"Charley, there is another thing you should know. It looks like the Money Trust is going to engineer another bank panic this fall. Be careful. Make sure that you are not over-exposed and have plenty of operating cash available."

"Is that so?"

"Yessir. All research and my sources point in that direction."

Weyerhaeuser gazed out the window. He sipped on his 'medicine.'

"You know, in all these years, I used to think I had the advantage. I worked hard like me Pappy. Business comin' from the woods is good, honest work. Then the railroads joined the banks in workin agin' us. Now, I don't know," he said, in a somber voice, his head nodding from side to side.

"Charley, don't be glum. There's lots of good happening. There are members in Congress who care deeply about this country and we are doing our best to make things right. There's a group that meets every Monday morning to pray. We are called the Insurgents and already have made the Speaker back off on some of the proposals from the banks and railroads. We are making progress and I see good things in the future."

"I trust you, Ridge, I do. You let me know if I can do anything for you. I mean it."

A long silence ensued. The sun was low in the sky. Charley got up and tilted the blinds in order to block the sun from their eyes. C.A. sat there, half-lit in bright sunshine. For a moment Charley saw the Lindbergh of his high school days, young, with the world before him. Then, in the shadowed room, the older, mature Lindbergh returned. Charley paused, thought better not to get maudlin, and spoke.

"It's sure been a long, cold spring, eh? Why don't we go fishin' an stuff out west of the lake? Jock told me he found a new fishin' hole there. I'spoze black fly season is still weeks away, so we'll be safe from those ishka pests," Big Charley said, swatting at imaginary winged tormentors.

"I won't take no for an answer. I'll have Jock make all the arrangements. We can go after them there walleyes tomorrow at dusk. You be ready at the cabin at noon. I'll pick you up."

Although the day was unseasonably brisk and the night promised to be colder still, the three men enjoyed an evening of old friends and simple pleasures. Big Charley and C.A. met Jock at Pine Tree where they loaded the gear into Weyerhaeuser's truck. Jock directed Big Charley to a secluded spot on the Little Elk River, west of Fort Ripley. Jock brought all the equipment for shore casting at night. As they put on their waders and set up their rods, Jock advised them.

"Them there walleyes like to feed along the weed edges especially when the water is cool, like now in early spring. Look for two things. They like to swim upstream to feed while they are looking for good spots to spawn. The trick is to swim the bait in the mid-water column.

That's where they'll be lookin' for food."

"Are you gonna start a campfire to cook the first big-ass walleye I nab?" said Big Charley who was sloshing through the weeds.

He turned and smiled at Lindbergh, "Hey, C.A., how do you like my new hat electric lamp?"

"I like it. Maybe your men can wear them when they go night logging, eh." He saw Big Charley pause to process the possibility, then, he let out a loud laugh.

"That's a good one. Night logging, ha. I'll have to tell Drew to recruit a night logging crew." He laughed again at his own joke.

As C. A. waded out into the stream, he said, "Hey, Jock. You said there were two things we needed to know. What is the second?"

Jock cupped his hands around his mouth so that both me could hear him.

"Look for the eyeshine. Them fishes got eyes that face out and their eyes gives off a shine at night, especially when there's some light like from your hat lamps. So you got to look for the eyeshine to see where the fish is hiding."

Lindbergh and Weyerhaeuser fished well past sundown without much luck. Cast and retrieve, cast and retrieve, cast and retrieve. They waded along the shoreline, exchanging stories and reminisces. Occasionally, they would break from the routine to re-bait or refresh themselves.

C.A. had forgotten how squishy and slimy bait minnows were. More than a few times, he pricked his hand while baiting the hook. His damning expletives hurled toward the innocent creatures in a fit of pain brought raucous guffaws from Big Charley. Even Jock hid smirks at C.A.'s misfortune.

"I guess your days in the Capitol softened your hands. Here, a snort of beer from that there growler will make the pain disappear," said Big Charley. He bent over and lifted a blue mottled can from the creek. Steadying himself on the rocks, he poured three cups of foamy beer from the growler. The men toasted to the noble walleye they hoped to catch for dinner.

Several hours later, just about the time they were about to resign themselves to a meal of baked beans and potatoes, Big Charley made the catch of the day, a three foot long walleye that must have weighed over twenty pounds. Charley admired the fish and the light from his hat lamp swept down the olive dorsal back, sparkled off the golden hue on the flank which blended to white on the belly. C.A. wished that they had a camera to capture the magnificent image of a grinning Big Charley holding up the beautiful specimen. C.A. thought that it was as grand a sight as he had seen since little Charley was born.

"Hully gee, will you cast your eyes on that there fella. He's gonna make a grand dinner, eh."

"Whoa, Big Charley, you got to watch out for the sharp teeth, so he don't eat you first, eh?" said Jock.

Jock prepared a delicious dinner over the open fire. He melted fresh butter in his cast iron skillet, seasoned the walleye fillets with salt and pepper and then, sauteed the fish in a mixture of caramelized onions and bacon from his own smokehouse. Jock pulled some steaming baked potatoes from out of the coals underneath the fire. Some fresh-baked skillet cornbread rounded out a meal that rivaled any table in Washington D.C. They washed it all down with another growler of beer. Big Charley and C.A. leaned, sated, against a tree trunk in front of the campfire.

"Now, that was a fantastic meal, Jock. You would make a fortune cooking like that in Washington," said C.A. Big Charley bit the ends off three cigars and handed them to his buddies. He withdrew a burning branch from the campfire and the men leaned forward to light their cigars.

"Didn't you grow up near here, Jock?"

"Yessir."

"What was it like when this was Dakota country and the Civil War was being fought? I remember hearing stories when I was a kid about a Confederate invasion from Canada. Was there anything to that?"

"My grandfather told me about a battle that took place pretnear here. I used to come here to look for artyfacts from the war. You know, Miniè balls, belt buckles and the like. Once I found a tommyhawk. It was all rotten, but I think there was blood on the stone blade."

The sounds of owls and insects echoed through the woods. Ridge could see Big Charley through the haze. His eyes had a faraway look of remembrances past. He spoke,

"I used to have nightmares about Chief Hole-in-the-Day riding around my house with his band of warriors screaming war cries. They carried bows with lit arrows ready to set our house on fire. I have never been so afraid in my life. Good thing it was only a dream."

Jock shifted uncomfortably.

"About them stories of rebs coming here from the north country, there is some truth to that there. Towards the end of the war, there was some folks in Canada who wanted to help the rebs. So they made a plan to attack a wagon train out of Fort Ripley that was carryin' payments for the timber companies that supplied lumber to the Union. The wagons were heading ta San Francisco with some valuable cargo. They was ambushed pretnear here. Captain Rumblelow was in command. When the attack began, he ordered Lieutenant Hyatt to go for reinforcements. When he arrived at the fort, the only force available to go on a rescue mission was Chief Hole-in-the-Day and his warriors. By the time they got back here, the wagon train was all blowed up."

"I thought Chief Hole-in-the-Day was a bad Indian who fought against the settlers. What was he doing at Fort Ripley?" asked Ridge.

"In the beginning, Chief Hole-in-the-Day liked the settlers, but then he got tricked into joining the renegades. Then, after the Dakota Wars was finished, he joined up with the Union soldiers. Guess he figured he had better side with the winners," said Jock with a chuckle.

"What happened to the cargo headed for San Francisco?"

"Ain't no tellin'. Nobody knows. It could have been taken, it could have been blowed up. All they saw when they got back was a big, smolderin' hole."

Lindbergh looked toward Big Charley and watched his head bob as he tried to stay awake.

"Charley, you've had a long day. What say we put you into the tent to sleep?" said Ridge, carefully guiding Weyerhaeuser to his feet and toward the tent flap. Without too much trouble, C.A. got his friend onto his cot. Before C.A. returned to the campfire, he heard the rumble of Big Charley sawing wood.

"Jock, did they ever find out who the attackers were?" asked Ridge, his forehead twisted in a knot of confusion.

"It makes no sense. The war was lost for the Confederates, right? It was after General Lee had already surrendered. Who were they? And what were they looking for?"

"Like I said. According to me Pa, there was some folks in Canada who wanted to help the rebs. They was priests, I think I heard it said. They took up with John Surratt. They hid him. Maybe they wanted what was with the wagon train to help Surratt. I don' know."

"Wait a minute. Do you mean John Surratt, the one whose mother was hanged for conspiring to assassinate President Lincoln?" asked Ridge, incredulously.

"Yessir, the very same," said Jock.

$ $ $

After much cajoling, Evy had agreed to come to Little Falls by midday on Good Friday. His time with Evy was strained and awkward. She had encased herself with an invisible barrier. Every attempt at conversation was met with silence or sarcasm. Evy was deft at deflating any effort by C.A. to explain the satisfying nature of his work. She had no use for his tales of minor Parliamentary victories or his enthusiasm for his manuscript. Her emotional detachment was so complete that they might as well have existed in different dimensions.

She saw to it that they had separate bedrooms. Hers was always locked. They shared no meals or activities. On Easter Sunday she took little Charley to an early mass at the Holy Family Catholic Church in Belle Prairie, just north of Little Falls. C.A. knew that she did this out of spite because he had expressed his desire to attend services at the Dutch Reformed Church with his brother and sisters and their families.

Evy showed up late for family dinner at his brother Frank's house. She professed to have lost track of time while Charley participated in the Easter egg hunt. At the urging of his older daughter Eva, C. A. put aside his hurt and offered Evy an olive branch in the form of a visit to Washington, D.C. "You and little Charley will love Washington in the spring, the flowers will be in full bloom. I'm told that the city is magical in April. Charley will love the museums and he will benefit from seeing the buildings in our capital."

Her reply was so abrupt and rude, that even the children's table which moments before had been a scene of sugar-fueled hilarity, fell into awkward silence. She rejected his olive branch and any hope of reconciliation by rebuffing his invitation with a defiant shout, "Why would you think that I had any interest in your life in Washington? I'm perfectly happy in Detroit. Everything I need is there."

A stunned silence at the vehemence of this proclamation enveloped the dinner table and cast a pall over the rest of the day. She left with little Charley for Detroit the following morning without saying goodbye.

midyear 1907 Washington, D.C.

Nothing in life is so exhilarating as to be shot at without result.
~ Winston Churchill

The Little Falls Depot was one of many small depots along the Northern Pacific Railroad. To promote local pride, the railroad allowed each hamlet to construct its depot to be consistent with the town's own unique ambiance. For some reason, the town fathers of Little Falls chose to model their depot after an Old English style station clad with black half-timbering, red soffits and window sashes, and cream-colored stucco. With a two-story center section which served as the waiting room, the depot offered oak bench seating arranged perpendicular to a large black, cast iron stove. There was an open porch at the end of the building featuring stone columns supporting a Tudor gable beam.

Although the morning was cold, C.A. waited outside under the covered porch. If he had any doubts about the state of his marriage, the Easter Sunday outburst as the family called it, had shattered any hope of reconciliation. Evy's blatant hostility in front of the entire family was inexcusable. He struggled with how to handle the situation.

On the one hand, Evy appeared to be a loving, conscientious mother, little Charley seemed happy. C.A. knew now that he could thrive without her. On the other hand, she was utterly disrespectful, and, well, hostile. Now that he was in public life, he had to consider what impact, if any, she and the situation would have on his career.

C.A. concluded, with mild surprise, that her abandonment of him to Detroit actually ameliorated the negatives.

Out of sight, out of mind. Her absence from any campaign activities could be explained away easily. She hated campaign events and she was in Detroit caring for family. All of which was true.

The big locomotive hissed to a stop. C.A. felt a sense of relief as he and Blakey boarded. They headed directly to the dining car for breakfast and the morning papers.

"And, how are you today, Mr. Congressman. I hope your Easter was all that you expected. I'm sure that your family appreciated having you back," said James, the porter.

"Just fine, James. We got to feast on some walleye in the great outdoors. What could be better?" he smiled.

$ $ $

Lindbergh proceeded directly to his office and worked himself to exhaustion until he fell asleep on the couch. There was a barely audible metallic noise from the front door of Lindbergh's congressional suite. The sound of metal probing, followed by tumblers clicking, signaled the unlocking of the lock. The door knob twisted. Blakey lifted his ears and turned his head toward the anteroom. Blakey tensed, gathering his legs under him. He was ready to defend his master. A rising hint of a growl awoke C.A.

As his eyes focused, he saw a shadow slip into the suite. The anteroom was lit faintly by moonlight streaming in from the large window adjacent to the secretary's desk. The door clicked shut with a faint reverberation. Lindbergh was on the couch, still wearing his suit. He folded the book that rested on his chest, a victim of his over-tiredness.

With a stranger in his office, all of C.A.'s senses were on full alert. He saw a burglar wearing a Stetson, dressed totally in black. The figure was orienting to the layout of the suite. He held a hand-held electric light using it to scan the outer office slowly. Satisfied that the room did not contain what he was after, he moved toward C.A.'s inner office.

C.A. circled his hand around Blakey's snout, signaling him to be quiet. Then, Lindbergh slipped off the couch and crawled behind the desk. C.A. remained out of sight behind the desk as the intruder entered Lindbergh's private office. At his side, Blakey was coiled, but quiet, with C.A. holding his collar.

The burglar shined the flashlight across the bookcase along the back wall, searching row by row for something. From his kneeling position, Lindbergh eased the pull on one of the drawers. A tiny squeak caused the intruder to halt. He listened, holding his breath. His hand slipped into his jacket. A bead of sweat rolled into C.A.'s eye; he blinked it away.

C.A. lifted the pull slightly to relieve the pressure and resumed pulling the drawer open. With his right hand he reached in and grasped a metallic handle. Wriggling his index finger past the trigger guard, he tightened his grip. A beam of light passed over his head to the wall behind him. It swept slowly across and then down. The light stopped at the manuscript on the desktop.

The floor creaked as the burglar advanced toward the desk. The steps halted. C.A. turned to see the light stop at Blakey's tail extending beyond the edge of the desk. C.A. grabbed the pistol and sprang up.

"Who are you? What are you doing here?"

The light flashed toward C.A.'s eyes. He heard the rustle of cloth and the scrape of leather as the intruder withdrew something from beneath his jacket. C.A. dived to his left just before the crack of a revolver sent a bullet toward him.

The burglar snatched up the manuscript and ran toward the outer office. Some pages slipped from the center of the thick pile. They fluttered behind the burglar as C.A. rose and took chase.

Unfettered, Blakey made maximum use of his voice box, releasing a deep, full-throated bark. The dog sprang into action, his paws skittering on the wood floor. Foamy spittle flew from his mouth. Blakey reached the intruder at the front door. He leaped and knocked the man off balance, sending him crashing into the door. C.A. heard distant shouts; no doubt security men aroused by the sound of gunfire.

Blakey clamped onto the arm of the intruder's coat. In a panic, the man swung his arm violently and smashed Blakey into the door frame. The blow knocked him senseless.

Free of the dog, the man turned and ran toward the window. C.A. raised the pistol and fired. A flash of flame erupted from the Colt. In the confines of the office, the report of the .45 was deafening. The burglar jumped and barreled through the window. C.A. ran to the window only to see a dark figure scrambling through the shrubbery and out of sight.

C.A. raced over to Blakey and cradled his head. His breath was raspy and irregular. C.A. stroked his head and sobbed a prayer. After a long moment, Blakey's eyes fluttered open. Gaining his senses, he wriggled free and bolted toward the window, sniffing and howling.

"Put the weapon on the floor, sir," said an armed officer in a firm but quiet voice.

C.A. bent at the waist and placed the gun on the floor. Now that the drama was over, he started shaking. The acrid smell of cordite dominated the room. The officer looked at the outer door.

"Are you Congressman Lindbergh, sir?" C.A. nodded, dully.

"Have a seat on this bench, sir, and I'll get you some water."

Lindbergh sat and collected his thoughts. Blakey followed him with his eyes. Then, in that strange way that dogs have, Blakey waddled over, with his tail wagging faster than a windmill in a tornado. C.A. grabbed Blakey around both ears and pressed faces while whispering words of endearment and gratitude.

By the time congressional employees arrived to begin their workday, the United States Capitol Police had interviewed C.A. four different times. They cordoned his office off and labeled it a crime scene. Since the crime involved gunfire, an officer from the U.S. Marshall's office visited Lindbergh. Sergeant Sylvester Dawson questioned C.A. about his weapon and would have confiscated it as evidence if Lindbergh had not clamped onto it with his hand and asserted Congressional privilege. The officer, a former Marine gunnery sergeant, had enough sense not to wrestle over a loaded revolver with a superior officer.

"Well, Sir, we have removed the slug from the paneling in your office. We will examine it to see if it provides any information about who the burglar might be; but, between you and me, it's just a formality. Don't get your hopes up."

C.A. nodded in assent.

"I'll bet you don't get many shootings in the Capitol, then?"

"No, Sir, at least not since before the Civil War. I've heard stories that things were wild back when tensions were high before secession and everyone came armed. Congressmen were made of different stock back then. You would have fit right in," he chuckled. "I'm afraid that not many of your colleagues would have handled themselves as well as you did. We found blood on the window frame, so there's a chance that you got a piece of him."

"The light was poor, but I thought I saw him grab for his right ear before he leapt out the window. The blood might be from that, or, from a bite on the arm from good old Blakey, here."

The dog at his side lifted his head upon hearing his name. He twisted his head to lick Lindbergh's hand, which patted his head in obvious affection. Blakey thumped his long, black tail in contentment.

Throughout the day, C.A. was consoled and pressed for details by his colleagues. C.A. tired of the endless repetitions and seriously contemplated preparing a written account to be shown to the curious. By lunchtime, the story as retold in the halls had grown to mammoth proportions. Members were referring to it as "Lindbergh's last stand" or the "Shootout at C.A.'s corral."

Majority Whip Jim Watson stopped by to ask him how in God's name, had he had enough ammunition to fight off five armed men. When C.A. tried to convince him that nothing of the sort happened, Watson brushed his protestations aside and accused him of false modesty.

Unlike other Congressmen who would have embellished the story in heroic terms of self-aggrandizement, Lindbergh's version became terser and terser with each retelling. By the end of the day, all C.A. would say was, "Blakey and my Colt took care of a burglar."

C.A. was about to leave for his boarding house when a liveried messenger delivered an envelope to his secretary.

It read, "The usual, 5 P.M. Blakey welcome."

Lindbergh read the missive with mixed feelings. On one hand, he was exhausted physically and mentally. The day had been a grueling ordeal of interrogation, viewing mugs shots and fending off inquiries from colleagues and the press. The prospect of sleep alone with Blakey in his own room offered great appeal. On the other hand, a part of him wanted to discuss the burglary with someone who was familiar with his current projects. He suspected that the burglary had something to do with his research on the Money Trust, but his intuition told him that there was something more. Perhaps, Anne could provide insight that eluded him so far. He concluded that his weariness could wait. It was more important to explore the possibilities before his memory of the event faded.

With Blakey by his side, he walked to the Riggs House. He turned over the events of the previous night in his mind. There was something about the burglar's actions that made no sense. If his objective was to steal the manuscript, why did he search the bookcases? What was he looking for? He gave in to mental fatigue and walked the remainder of the way in a trance-like state.

When she opened the door to the room, Anne rushed into his arms.

"Oh, Ridgy, I was so frightened when I heard that you had been shot at. How terrible!"

Lindbergh sagged into her embrace. The pent up emotions of the day flowed out.

"Anne, Anne, I'm so glad you sent that note. I - I - I . . . ."

The relief that he felt rendered him speechless. Her hug tightening, she drew him into the room. Blakey barely made it into the room, as they collapsed onto the door closing behind them. As if sensing the couple needed privacy, Blakey took refuge across the room, beside the room service table.

Anne shushed Ridgy when he tried to speak. Her lips covered his with such force and passion that Lindbergh surrendered to the comfort of her kiss. They stood pressed together; both lost in gratitude for a disaster averted. This first kiss also symbolized the feelings for each other that had developed over the months of collaboration. Both realized that they had crossed the point of no return. When their lips parted, they stared into each other's eyes, both acknowledging the new bond between them.

"Oh, Ridgy, when I heard about the attack, I was distraught. I don't know what I would do if anything happened to you," said Anne, the words flooding out in a torrent of emotion.

"Don't you worry, Anne, Blakey and I know how to handle bad guys," he replied in a jocular tone.

"I *do* worry about you. We are challenging forces beyond your imagination. You need to exercise vigilance and care."

Those were the same words used by the author of the *Wizard of Oz*. Perhaps, they were right. He should take more precautions. He vowed to lock up his manuscript in the office safe whenever he was out of the office.

Blakey pawed the tablecloth which drew the plates precariously toward the edge. His whining for the food on the table broke C.A. from his reverie. And so, their relationship blossomed.

"Look, the poor little fellow is calling us to dinner," laughed Anne. "Come, you both must be famished. I've ordered special meals for all three of us."

C.A. thought how wonderful it was that Anne had considered Blakey's needs. For the first time since he had come to Washington, the shroud of loneliness that had engulfed Lindbergh vanished. The three ate with a zeal and gusto fueled by release from tension. When he finished his meal, Blakey shuffled to a spot under a table in the corner. Ridge and Anne pondered the meaning of the attack and concluded that the burglar was searching for a particular book. They wondered whether any book could hold such treasure to justify attempted murder of a Congressman. Eventually, drowsiness prevailed and they both moved to the bedroom.

It was dark outside when Lindbergh awakened with Anne entwined with him on the bed. He felt an urge that he had not experienced in many months. He kissed her face gently and pulled the covers over them. She responded with a sleepy hug. Clothes were loosened and soon they were wide awake, tentatively exploring each other's bodies.

"Actually, Ridgy, I am a little uncomfortable. You see, I do not have much experience with men. I have been quite cloistered."

Ridge found her lack of experience all the more captivating. He replied, "Don't be afraid we can go slow."

She gave him a wary look, but presented no obstacles. What started out slow and gentle gradually, after much coaxing, had turned passionate. Ridge found the pace excruciating. She was so timid. Nevertheless, he refused to rush; after all, he thought, he had more or less despaired of ever being intimate with a woman again. Anne had awakened feelings that he had pushed into dormancy, and for that, he was grateful.

After they had been intimate for the first time, he wondered whether their working relationship would change. His trepidation faded when Annie quipped, "Ridgy, are you sure that you told me the truth about how you got your nickname? After tonight's marathon, I can think of a more accurate reason for that name."

1907 Washington D.C.-New York City, NY

> I am thankful -- thankful beyond words -- that I had only $51,000 on deposit in the Knickerbocker Trust, instead of a million; for if I had had a million in that bucket shop, I should be nineteen times as sorry as I am now.
> ~ Mark Twain

In the immediate aftermath of the burglary, Lindbergh found it impossible to accomplish any work in his office. There was a constant stream of investigators tramping through the office. Some were dusting the doorknobs and others were examining all manner of debris with magnifying glasses. At first, C.A.'s interest was piqued and he questioned Sergeant Dawson about the investigative methodologies.

"Here, look, here, Congressman," said Sgt. Dawson, holding a magnifying glass up to the outer door knob. Lindbergh leaned over the officer's shoulder and discerned a swirl of lines highlighted by a contrasting powder on the brass knob.

"What am I looking at?"

"Most likely it's a palm print from our burglar."

"I remember reading Mark Twain's novel – the name escapes me now – where the main character solved a crime by using fingerprints. I thought that only fingerprints were used for identifying criminals," said the legislator.

"Generally speaking, Sir, that is true. However, there are reports that the Chinese used hand prints as evidence in criminal investigations several centuries before Christ," replied the Sergeant. The hefty policeman got on his back on the floor and looked up to the doorknob.

"I think that we have a clean thumb print on the underside of the knob here," said Dawson, pointing.

C.A. crouched down, craning his neck toward the bottom of the knob. Blakey joined in, licking his master's face while he was bent down.

Lindbergh stood, straightening his vest. "So, what's the next step?"

"Recently, the police chief's association established a national repository for fingerprints. It's called the National Bureau of Criminal Identification. A few years ago, the Army started collecting fingerprints as well; so now there's a larger pool of prints. We send the National Bureau a copy of the prints and they search their archives for a match. They wire us the results. Like I said, it's a new system that is far from perfect; it's worth a shot.

"Also, I'll send an all-points-bulletin to DC area hospitals and local police for any information about persons seeking treatment for a gunshot wound and/or dog bite. Sometimes we get lucky. Our communications are getting better all the time and we might just find our man."

"Sounds like you are targeting with a shotgun in the hopes of striking a flea at one hundred yards," said the Congressman in a dubious voice.

"That might be so, Sir. However, I have not mentioned our secret weapon."

"And what might that be?" asked Lindbergh.

"Why, it's our SB."

"Excuse me?"

"Our snitch brigade. We roust out informants and put the word out about our search. They are mostly skels, you know, unsavory types," said Dawson.

"You would not invite them to court your daughter, but they know how to find out information, especially when they are properly motivated, if you know what I mean," said Dawson, tapping his nightstick.

"Well," said Lindbergh, stifling a yawn, "Keep me posted on the progress of your investigation. I am most concerned."

Sitting at his desk in his D.C. office, Lindbergh barely raised his eyes when the congressional page slipped a large envelop into his inbox. The pages had been instructed not to interrupt the congressman from

Minnesota.

"Don't you dare interrupt Congressman Lindbergh. He is immersed in important work and he don't need you to break his thoughts," admonished Elias Stephens, the chief of pages.

It was Friday afternoon and he was working in shirtsleeves and vest at his desk. C.A. was puzzled over the absence of any communication fron Anne. Had they crossed some forbidden line? Was she frightened or embarrassed at the prospect of intimacy with a man who was still married? He did not even know if she was still in Washington. The memory of that night lingered. Admonishing himself that he could not moon like a love sick cow, he decided to continue drafting the chapter on speculation by eastern bankers. He would reward himself with a walk before dinner along the National Mall down to the Potomac.

This was his second autumn in the nation's capital and he had come to appreciate the botanical delights of Washington. He loved the fragrance of the fall-blooming chrysanthemums and the variegated foliage of Japanese maples. For the moment, he concentrated his attention on his manuscript. Based on his research and work with Anne, he sensed a coming economic storm. The manuscript was his only weapon; without it he would lapse into helplessness. With it, he was empowered.

C.A. completed a section of his manuscript, placed his pen back into the inkwell, and rubbed his eyes. Unlike most of his colleagues, he had chosen to remain in the capital for the weekend in order to refine his manuscript on currency and banking. He walked around his desk, stretching toward the ceiling and wind-milling his arms to restore circulation.

He had been so busy writing that he forgot to open his mail. Hoping to find a lavender-scented missive, he searched the pile of papers strewn on his desk. A hefty envelope poked out from under some papers. There was a scent, but it was not the one he wanted; it was more like pine. He recognized the handwriting of Big Charley Weyerhaeuser. Wielding a letter opener with a little more force than necessary, he withdrew a document on stationery of the German American Bank of Little Falls, Minnesota. Both he and Big Charley were on the bank's board of directors.

According to the handwritten note on the cover, it was a draft status report on the bank's reserves. The bank served the local farmers and lumbermen in Minnesota. Lindbergh cringed as he read that the preponderance of the bank's reserves were deposited in eastern banks. If his analysis was correct and eastern banks began to fail, the bank would be dangerously exposed to catastrophic loss that would hurt his constituents.

Lindbergh often railed against the speculative practices of banks that gambled with the reserve funds deposited by small rural banks in large eastern (mostly New York) banks. Realistically, there were no limitations on how reserve funds could be "invested." The New York banks ignored their fiduciary duty to handle reserve accounts conservatively and had adopted a culture of speculation that disregarded risk in an irrational quest for quick profits. Lindbergh struggled with the dual problem of publicizing the danger and crafting legislation to outlaw the pernicious practices that threatened to destroy the nation's financial system. The absence of institutional safeguards would devastate the U.S. economy numerous times in the ensuing decades.

$ $ $

The Knickerbocker Trust building on 34th Street and Fifth Avenue in New York City was a true temple to Mammon. Designed by Stanford White and opened in 1904, the headquarters of the Knick, as it was commonly known, was modeled after a Roman temple. The grand structure was built with white Vermont marble formed into Corinthian columns. Bronze grillwork and massive double doors adorned the exterior. The building radiated stability and reverence for the Almighty dollar. The common belief was that 'If Ol' Knick was behind you, it was as good as gold.' As with most slogans, it would prove to be more hype than reality.

The interior reflected the values of the modern banker. It was attractively clad in Italian marble and Italian walnut interspersed with bronze tellers' cages. The coffered ceiling of the public banking room rose thirty feet high supported by twin, glistening columns.

Otto Kahn walked into this marble palace as if he owned it. He had traveled too much to be awed by the Knick; nevertheless, he silently thanked his deceased friend Stanford White for this impressive ode to banking.

"Otto, my good friend, you are early," said Charles T. Barney when his secretary guided Otto into the President's office. It was tastefully appointed, paneled with Brazilian mahogany and lit by a circular chandelier of Savorski crystal.

"A sherry, perhaps?" asked Barney, brandishing an ornate crystal decanter. Sitting erect with his gloves held in his hands which rested on his cane, Otto nodded. Barney walked over and closed the door. Then he sat across from Otto and raised his glass in silent toast.

Charles T. Barney was in his mid-fifties, stout and balding with a full salt-and-pepper beard. In his youth, his appearance imparted the impression of solidity and dependability. Now, he imparted a stony impression. From his phlegmatic movements like the shifting of tectonic plates, to his dull charcoal eyes peering out from rings of lunar-like dust, Barney came across as some primordial rock person, devoid of color or energy.

Over the preceding decade, Barney and his wife Laurinda "Lily" nee' Whitney, had risen to the pinnacle of New York society. Barney owed his meteoric rise in New York banking circles to the support and guidance of his brother-in-law, William Collins Whitney, patriarch of the prominent Whitneys whose ancestors had come over on the Mayflower. Unfortunately, when William Whitney died in 1904, his business acuity and sound advice died with him.

Left to his own devices, Barney began to consort with unsavory types. When the stock market experienced a steady downturn in 1906, Barney sought to bolster returns by entering into a scheme to corner the market on the shares of the United Copper Company. His co-conspirators were Charles W. Morse, who had spent time behind bars with Charles Ponzi, and F. Augustus Heinze, a principal of the United Copper Company.

His thick hands engulfed the sherry *copita* which he brought to his lips and drained. Fortified, Barney dispensed with pleasantries and dove right into the reason he had asked to see Kahn.

"Otto, I know how astute you are at investing. I have a proposition for you," said Charles Tracy Barney, the president of the Knickerbocker Trust, one of the largest and most respected banks in the country. It served as trustee for many of the country's wealthiest individual and corporate clients.

"We have an opportunity to make a killing. I've been working with Augustus Heinze, who along with his brother, owns a majority of stock in the United Copper Company. He believes that many of the outstanding shares have been sold short by shareholders who are betting that the price will decline. We intend to aggressively purchase

United Copper stock in order to drive up the share price. Once that happens, we will squeeze the shorts and they will have no alternative than to buy our shares at the inflated price. We reasonably expect to double our money in a matter of weeks. I am authorized to admit you into our plan as a participating purchaser."

As Barney explained the nature of the scheme, Otto Kahn regarded him with a jaundiced eye and wondered whether he would be involved with these nefarious types if his brother-in-law William Collins Whitney had still been alive. Since the death of the conservative Whitney three years earlier, Barney had engaged in increasingly risky endeavors. If anything, Otto had his finger on the pulse of Wall Street.

"My good fellow, we have known each other for years and I appreciate your trust. However, I have reason to believe a war is coming and I want to keep my powder dry if you know what I mean."

Barney sat and stared blankly as Otto collected his bowler and put on his gloves.

"Otto, don't leave. We were counting on you to contribute a million. Would you consider a half million? . . . *please*," pleaded Charles Barney in a trembling voice. Otto departed without glancing back. It was the last time he would see Barney.

$ $ $

Lindbergh wished that Anne would contact him. They had so much to discuss. Tracking the events of that October was surreal to Lindbergh. Each day brought news of bank runs by everyday people trying to withdraw their life savings. The all-too-common narrative was that the banks lacked the liquid funds to satisfy the withdrawal demands of their depositors and had no alternative but to close. The succession of bank closings accelerated and an imminent financial collapse loomed.

The panic reached a fever pitch when the venerable Knickerbocker Trust got rid of its president, Charles T. Barney for his role in the effort to corner the market on United Copper stock. When the bank was unable to satisfy withdrawal demands, confidence in the Knickerbocker Trust evaporated and correspondent banks refused to honor its checks. The Knick descended into a death spiral.

As events careened toward financial chaos, C.A. wished he could discuss them with Anne. Her insight was so profound that he felt adrift without her. He berated himself for not having a way to contact her. He wondered what she was doing that prevented her from sending him a message. He thought about going to New York to look for her, but he had no address, no relative to call, and nothing but her name to locate her.

He thought briefly of making inquiry at the Riggs House, but, then, rejected the idea when he realized how ridiculous he would sound to the desk clerk. "I've been having an affair with one of your guests and I'd like you to help me locate her." It was not a comfortable predicament for someone who was trained to be Minnesota nice. Since he concluded that he would have to wait for Anne to contact him, Lindbergh immersed himself in his manuscript.

The volume of frantic calls from constituents had overwhelmed and shut down the House switchboard. The Congress descended into eerie doldrums. Outside, the Panic of 1907 raged like the howling blaze that devastated San Francisco a year earlier.

November 14, 1907 New York City, NY

Crash Crash Crash
~ Boston Post, October 18, 1907

"Otto, that's balderdash and you know it!" exclaimed Charles whose voice rose as he lurched to his feet. Spittle from the mouth of Charles T. Barney sprayed onto the handset of his candlestick phone. He had recently resigned under duress from his position of president of the Knickerbocker Trust.

"Charles, there is no need to shout. What you are asking is, well, .. it's just not possible," Otto replied in a low tone. He was seated in his Wall Street office surveying the bustling New York harbor.

"You keep saying that; but we both know that it's not true," said Charles. This obviously is not working he thought. His tone changed. His voice was now almost sweet, cloying.

"Otto, remember last month when I nominated you for the board of the Met? Remember how you told me how much being on the board meant to you. That being on the board was the gateway to your dream to transform the Met, to transform the City into a cultural mecca?"

"Yes, that's true, Charles. I have great plans." conceded Otto.

"Remember how you promised that if I ever needed anything, all I had to do was ask you. Remember saying that Otto?" said Charles, his voice cracking.

"Yes, but, you are asking for a loan of millions of dollars. You know that in these times, that's just not possible."

"Otto, you know I'm good for it. I'll put up my house. You've been here. You know how wonderful it is. This neighborhood, Murray Hill, is prime. You met my family here. You know, you know," his voice trailed off.

"I'm sorry, Charles, it's just not possible," Otto heard a sound like an ear phone hitting the desk.

"Charles, Charles, are you there?" Otto raised his voice, then, lowered it to quell the anxious gazes from the office staff.

"Charles, Charles, don't do anything rash . . ."

In the drawing room downstairs, Mrs. Lily Whitney Barney was entertaining her friend, Susan Abbott Mead.

"Lily, I'm worried about the declining value of our portfolio," said her closest friend whose eyebrows were knotted together. "Our holdings are down thirty percent in the last year."

"Not to worry, Suzy. My Charles says that every dip is an opportunity to fleece the timid who are so afraid of their shadows that they sell whenever it gets cloudy," she chuckled.

"I heard that Morgan rushed back from his retreat in Richmond? And, is holding court in his library. . . . My husband says that bankers are being hauled in before that man with the hideous nose. Have you seen his nose lately? It's like a huge red door knob covered with pustules. It's disgusting. And his breath! Between the cigars, whiskey and gum disease, the man nearly asphyxiated me when I sat next to him at the Governor's Ball.

"And, to think that he is calling bankers into his library, as if he is some Persian potentate. Peggy Alderson's husband calls him Pierpont the Powerful. Good grief! And I hear that he spews such dreadful language. Why the man cannot put together a sentence without blaspheming. Has Charles been called before his majesty?" asked Suzy.

Lily Whitney Barney picked up her rose-tinted teacup, took a sip, sighed, and said in hushed tones, "He met with the Old Man the other day and came back from the meeting a little . . . unsettled. To be honest, since his meeting with Pierpont, Charles has been moping around, not eating or sleeping much."

She paused at the sound of shouting coming from upstairs. It was Charles. Susan gave her a look of concern. In their long friendship, Susan had never heard Charles use such a loud, shrill voice. Lily was uncomfortable with her friend's look of pity and decided to act as if nothing were amiss.

"Charles is going to meet Pierpont again and I'm sure everything will be resolved. Charles is upstairs getting ready. He usually handles his telephone calls first thing, then, leaves for his meetings."

Upstairs, Charles pulled his vest down and straightened his regimental tie in the mirror. His eyes were puffy and ringed with dark circles evidencing his lack of sleep since his meeting with Morgan. A wave of melancholy swept over him as he considered how he would tell Lily that he had resigned the presidency of the Knickerbocker Trust. Shame and darkness engulfed him. If only he had not been beguiled by that rascal Fritz Heinze. He should have known better than to trust that huckster. Charles' vanity trumped his judgment when he accepted a position on the board of Heinze's company and threw the financial resources of his venerable company behind the scheme to corner the copper market.

And it worked at first, when the stock of United Copper soared to an all-time high of $62 per share. That was one month ago. Three days later the stock price crashed to $15 per share. What possessed him to think that they could corner the market on copper? Charles' throat constricted when he thought of his last meeting with Heinze.

CRRAACCKK!!

"Ohh, no! Oh, God, Noooo!" Lily burst to her feet tipping over the table holding the tea set. The bone china shattered like the veneer of calm that had encased Lily a second earlier. Now, all she could feel was an animal urgency to race toward the report that rebounded through the house. The horrible, deafening sound of a single gunshot reverberated with each step as if mocking her effort to get upstairs.

Otto spat into the receiver, "Charles? Charles? Where are you Charles?"

"No, no no...," her voice trailed off.

"Mother?" She heard someone say.

She could not identify the voice. Her only desire was to get to the upstairs office. When she bounded into the room, Charles was standing, his back to her, unmoving. A flicker of hope surged, then, she saw his image in the mirror. A stain was spreading across his belly turning grey pinstripe vest a ghastly color.

For an instant she wondered why Charles would spill burgundy wine so early in the day. Their eyes locked in the mirror for a frozen second. Charles shrugged almost apologetically as his eyes shuttered. He slowly sank to his knees and collapsed backward into her arms. His weight forced her down with him and she cradled his head.

"Help, Help, oh my God, Help!"

"Mother? Oh, no, Mother!" Her son, Ashbel was next to her now. His face was half-covered with shaving soap and his undershirt struck her as oddly clean and white. The stain on Charles' chest was turning purplish.

"Is he . . .?" Ash shouted.

Racing toward the desk, his foot kicked the gun. It spun and clanked noisily into the metal bedpost.

"Where is it, dammit!" he exclaimed fumbling through the directory on the desk. After what seemed like an eternity he found what he was looking for and rotated the dial. His father coughed a ragged cough. His mother was on her knees cradling his father's head as she murmured "Why? Why?"

The phone was ringing now.

"Dr. Dixon, Dr. Dixon, this is Ash Barney. There's been a terrible accident. My father's been shot. Get over here as quickly as possible!"

The domestic staff at the Barney residence stood immobile along the stairs, their hands to their mouths and eyes wide with shock at the scene before them.

"Mrs. Timmons, please help me bring him to the bed." Ash pleaded. Another cough racked his father. It seemed to awaken the onlookers. Suddenly, a stout woman wearing an apron and folded sleeves plowed through and was at his father's side.

"Lift," Ida Timmons yelled, "for God's sake, Mr. Charles, don't die!"

Together they lifted and tugged until his father's body lay on the bed. He breathed hoarsely. Lily stared vacantly at Ash, noticing the blood stain that marred his shirt.

"It's Dr. Dixon," someone murmured.

"Where is he?" shouted a large man with a florid face. His eyes locked on Charles.

"Get me some boiling water. Quickly!"

The morning turned to afternoon, as they watched the doctor work frantically to stop the bleeding and remove the bullet. After several slippages, the surgeon used his forceps to grip the deformed

November 14, 1907: New York City, NY

metal slug and yank it out. A tinny clang on the bone china dish that had been commandeered for use by the doctor reverberated through the room.

Later, outside the now-darkened room, Dr. Dixon described the internal damage.

"The bullet entered the abdomen on an upward trajectory. It pierced the intestines and lung before lodging in the left shoulder. It missed his heart by a quarter of an inch. He has lost a lot of blood. I just don't know...." his voice trailed off.

A former military surgeon, he knew that the wound was fatal. But, he had learned practicing medicine for the wealthy was best tempered with plastic optimism.

"We've done all we can do now. Let him rest (in peace, he thought). He's in God's hands now."

November 1907 New York City, NY

I owe the public nothing,
~ J. Pierpont Morgan

"It was inevitable," remarked J. Pierpont Morgan. He folded the New York Times that he was reading. Otto wondered whether he was referring to the collapse of the Knickerbocker Trust or the suicide of Charles T. Barney. Or, maybe the Old Man thought that both events were inevitable. Whichever it was, the financial system was approaching total collapse.

Otto had been summoned from the opera to Morgan's library in his mansion. Morgan returned his attention to playing cards on his desk.

"Nothing like a game of solitaire to enliven the old noggin," he said absently to no one in particular. A rasping cough emerged from deep within his chest.

"The damn doctors are useless. They can't cure a stupid cold," he groused, while taking a swig of *Dr. Winston's Elixir*, a vile-looking green concoction in a pint bottle manufactured by C.F. Boehringer & Soehne (Mannheim, Germany), "largest makers in the world of quinine and cocaine." The main ingredients listed on the labels were sugar, caffeine and cocaine. There were four empty bottles strewn on a serving table next to the desk.

In the massive three-story library filled with leather-bound first editions, Otto bit his lip trying to fight back his annoyance. There was a sweet young soprano whom Otto had planned to bring to his Fire Rescue Station after the opera. The call to duty, especially from Pierpont Morgan, came first. The delicious soprano would have to wait.

The selection of books revealed Morgan's deep interests in theories of finance and fine art collecting. The latter interest was on prominent display throughout the mansion. The former would be displayed by Zeus himself. Resigning himself to a long night trapped in Morgan's museum of a mansion, Otto removed his monocle. He thought that this just might be the night Morgan salvaged the nation's financial system, or the night everything collapsed. Either way, thought Otto, positioning is the key and he was in position to benefit regardless of which way events turned.

Throughout the night, Morgan summoned his staff into his office to discuss their detailed analysis of the liquidity and solvency of a particular banking institution. Otto's job was to occupy the bank officers in the library while Pierpont decided their fate in the office.

The cigar cutter was shaped like a hand-held guillotine. Pierpont wielded the shiny gold mechanism deftly as he clipped the end of his *Monte Cristo*. He ran the cigar under his nose. Disgusted at his inability to smell the aroma of the expensive cigar due to his cold, he bellowed like a wounded water buffalo for his attendant. Jasper Braithwrite, Pierpont's personal valet, appeared beside his master instantaneously, wielding a gilded lighter that was shaped like an octopus.

"May I, sir?" he said, holding the octopus head back as a sliver of yellow flame rose toward the tuck end of the hand-rolled cigar. Morgan drew furiously and puffs of smoke rose toward the ceiling. The effort was followed by a bout of bone-wracking coughs. When Morgan settled back into his tufted chair, the valet ticked a checkmark in his notebook. Dr. Schilling, Morgan's internist, had insisted that Morgan stop smoking during his illness. The old bull refused to obey doctor's orders. Finally, Morgan relented and compromised. Until he was rid of 'this damn annoying cold,' Pierpont promised to smoke no more than twenty cigars per day.

"So you see, my friend, we must excise your company like the tip of this cigar," proclaimed the rather corpulent man whose red, scabrous nose was crisscrossed with purplish capillaries.

"You must be joking . . . we have serviced our clients since the time we helped finance Jefferson's Louisiana Purchase over a hundred years ago," snorted Edgar Pentleton who wore his elitism on his countenance as naturally as the way most men wore a Windsor knot. He was as close to royalty as possible in the United States. His great grandfather had signed the Mayflower Compact and his family of bankers had financed the presidential campaigns of at least one dozen presidents.

Morgan replied with the stare of an eagle that was locked in on its prey. Morgan's leonine head tilted and his eyebrows rose. Now in his seventies, Pierpont, as intimates addressed him, was able to turn men to his will by sheer force of personality. As more than one such intimate recounted, a test of wills with Morgan invariably led to a surreal capitulation. "It's as if he took control of my mind and compelled me to sign the agreement despite my serious reservations."

Pentleton straightened his carriage as if he had been ordered to attention. He complied as Pierpont ordered and as simple as that the bank that his family had controlled for over a century ceased to exist. Pentleton Bank was one of many that fell victim to the Panic of 1907.

$ $ $

While the financial world tottered toward chaos, President Roosevelt was in the Louisiana canebrakes hunting black bear. TR relished the opportunity to hunt in one of the most striking and interesting landscapes in the country. The canebrakes were vast stands of canes, a native form of bamboo that stretched for miles in the moist rich bottomlands of the river floodplains. Except for vines and occasional trees, the canes choked off other vegetation. Feathery and graceful, the canes frequently grew fifteen to twenty feet high. Often intermixed with vines and scrub trees, the canebrakes were nearly impenetrable. Scouts and guides used heavy bush-knives to hack through the vegetation. Canebrakes provided the perfect environment for black bears and other desirable game.

Theodore Roosevelt took meticulous notes of his exploits. "*I was especially anxious to kill a bear in these canebrakes after the fashion of the old Southern planters, who for a century past have followed the bear with horse and hound and horn in Louisiana, Mississippi, and Arkansas.*[27]"

He deflected questions from reporters about the growing financial crisis. Instead, he regaled them with reports of the party's catch of *"three bears, six deer, one wild turkey, 12 squirrels, one duck, one opossum, and one wildcat.*[28] *"* To allay concerns, Roosevelt dispatched his treasury secretary, George Cortelyou, to work with Morgan in New York.

As the crisis worsened, pressure grew for Roosevelt to return to Washington. Ever the hunter, TR refused to leave until he had bagged a black bear. Later he would write a magazine article recounting how he shot a black bear in the canebrakes:

"Peering through the thick-growing stalks I suddenly made out the dim outline of the bear coming straight toward us; and noiselessly I cocked and half-raised my rifle, waiting for a clearer chance. In a few seconds it came; the bear turned almost broadside to me, and walked forward very stiff-legged, almost as if on tiptoe, now and then looking back at the nearest dogs. These were two in number--Rowdy, a very deep-voiced hound, in the lead, and Queen, a shrill-tongued brindled bitch, a little behind. Once or twice the bear paused as she looked back at them, evidently hoping that they would come so near that by a sudden race she could catch one of them. But they were too wary.

All of this took but a few moments, and as I saw the bear quite distinctly some twenty yards off, I fired for behind the shoulder. Although I could see her outline, yet the cane was so thick that my sight was on it and not on the bear itself. But I knew my bullet would go true; and, sure enough, at the crack of the rifle the bear stumbled and fell forward, the bullet having passed through both lungs and out at the opposite side. Immediately the dogs came running forward at full speed, and we raced forward likewise lest the pack should receive damage. The bear had but a minute or two to live, yet even in that time more than one valuable hound might lose its life; so when within half a dozen steps of the black, angered beast, I fired again, breaking the spine at the root of the neck; and down went the bear stark dead, slain in the canebrake in true hunter fashion. One by one the hounds struggled up and fell on their dead quarry, the noise of the worry filling the air. Then we dragged the bear out to the edge of the cane, and my companion wound his horn to summon the other hunters.

This was a big she-bear, very lean, and weighing two hundred and two pounds.[29] *"*

Once his trophy had been dispatched to the taxidermist, the President returned to Washington in no apparent rush. On his arrival, he explained that he returned to Washington with due deliberate speed in order to avoid exacerbating the situation. The reality was that he did not want his hunting vacation to end – or miss killing a bear.

$ $ $

During the President's adventure, Treasury Secretary Cortelyou traveled to New York City and reported for duty to J.P. Morgan. George Cortelyou was a native New Yorker who traced his lineage to Dutch immigrants from 1652. To say he was austere was an understatement. From his black suit, wire rimmed spectacles, black-brush mustache and dark hair brushed straight back, George Cortelyou exuded seriousness. No one could recall ever seeing him smile. In his mid-fifties, he had served in the Roosevelt administration in various cabinet posts and was as establishment as he could be. Although Cortelyou had been Treasury Secretary for only six months, he had read accounts of how Morgan single-handedly saved the U.S. Treasury during the Panic of 1893 by personally supplying millions of dollars of gold bullion to back government obligations. Anecdotes of Morgan's domineering personality swirled through his head. An involuntary tremble ran through his hands as he stood in the foyer of the Morgan Mansion waiting to be announced.

The septuagenarian Morgan was sitting behind his desk as he had been for most of the last week. His eyes were glassy and runny. He held a discolored handkerchief under his bulbous nose that wheezed a liquid gurgle with each breath.

"Sit down for God's sake," Morgan rasped almost inaudibly.

"Yessir, of course," said Secretary Cortelyou, scurrying to a chair in front of Morgan's massive desk that was cluttered with thick reports bearing the names of various financial institutions.

"Jasper, bring the secretary some coffee. He's going to need it," croaked Morgan to his attendant.

"You, Cortelyou, what is your salary? For that matter, what does the President earn?" muttered Morgan.

"I'm sorry, sir, I'm afraid that I did not hear you correctly," stammered Cortelyou.

Morgan straightened in his chair and blustered.

"You damn well heard what I said! I want to know what you and the President earn. You want to know why? I'll tell you why . . . because when this mess is over, I'm going to submit a bill in the amount of both your salaries. Since I've been doing both your jobs, I'm entitled to both your salaries!"

Cortelyou averted his eyes and blushed in embarrassment.

"The G-ddamn country is collapsing. Banks are failing and people are jumping out of buildings. What kind of damn fool goes riding around Louseyanna on his horse lookin' to shoot a bear that ain't ever done nothin' to him? When I see the President again, if I last that long," he said, smothering a cough in his handkerchief. "I'm going to rip him a new one."

Cortelyou was silent. Only his eyes moved. He realized that if he fixated on Morgan's nose which had turned bright red, he could distract himself enough to maintain his composure. The infamous Morgan nose was pitted with what seemed like pomegranate seeds, bone-colored stones oozing a deep red sludge. Cortelyou's relief was short-lived.

"What the hell are you staring at, you damn fool," thundered Morgan.

"Well, sir . . . I'm sorry, sir," said the Secretary, dithering his hands. Then, recovering his equilibrium somewhat, Cortelyou said, "I'm here to help, sir. The President instructed me to provide any assistance necessary."

"Good. You will deposit twenty-five million dollars in these institutions by close of business tomorrow," Morgan ordered, sliding Cortelyou a scribbled list across the desk.

Cortelyou saw his chance to escape. He stood and put the note in his portfolio without looking at it. Edging toward the door, he said, "I'll take my leave then."

A sly smile creased Morgan's face.

"The twenty-five million is just the beginning, George. Check in with me here again tomorrow afternoon . . . Oh, by the way, tell TR I send my regards."

$ $ $

Most of the country followed the crisis in the daily newspapers. Lindbergh anxiously awaited the morning edition of the Washington Times as though the reportage of the Panic of 1907 were 'part issues' of a Charles Dickens novel. A new drama unfolded each day. One day there were reports of J.P. Morgan locking bankers in his library until they agreed to loan much-needed cash to ailing banks. The next day's edition chronicled how J.P. Morgan wagged his index finger under the nose of Ransom H. Thomas, the president of the New York Stock Exchange, while ordering him not to close the Exchange one minute before the clock struck 3 P.M.

Lindbergh read with fascination the innovative, if unlawful, efforts of the banking community to create the liquidity necessary to infuse the system with cash and cash equivalents. The New York Clearinghouse Association, a trade group privately owned by member banks, stepped into the fray by issuing clearinghouse loan certificates that artificially increased the supply of currency available for member banks to dispense to customers seeking to withdraw money from their accounts. The only problem was that there was no such legal instrument as a clearinghouse loan certificate. Nevertheless, the country's financial system remained intact.

After several months, the banking system stabilized, so that by the following January a shaken system resumed relative normalcy. Lindbergh burned to see Anne so that he could craft a replacement for this obsolete, volatile banking system. He also craved her physical comforts.

Spring 1908 Washington D.C.

> Paper is poverty ... it is the ghost of money,
> and not money itself.
> ~ Thomas Jefferson

He stood at the railing where the accommodation ladder joined the Presidential yacht, the *U.S.S. Mayflower*. The sleek, white vessel had twin masts for sails and a large black smokestack to exhaust the steam-driven diesel engines. President Theodore Roosevelt gazed down the deck of the 275 foot yacht that had recently been commissioned for his use. He had admired the *Mayflower* since the first time he laid eyes on her during the Spanish American War. So much had happened to him since 1898, that he sometimes wondered whether it was all a dream. TR knocked the highly varnished wooden railing with his knuckles. This was definitely real. He was definitely the President of the United States; and the country was definitely facing an existential crisis.

Only months before, the country's financial system had almost collapsed. Disaster had been averted only because he had capitulated to that scoundrel Morgan and prevented the collapse by using dollars from the people's treasury to prop up some damn fool bank speculators. The President regarded the financial system the same way that Captain Nemo regarded the giant octopus. It was inexorable, insatiable and only through the grace of God could it be tamed to any degree. He hoped that tonight's meeting would lead to a solution. TR had found that there was something about the tranquility of a dinner cruise down the Potomac River that helped the cognitive processes, as he liked to say. Time would tell.

Roosevelt regretted that he had *"never studied elocution or practised debating[30]"* as a preparation for public life. So when it came to policy decisions, he liked to hear debate on issues by people with ardent convictions. To foster a full discussion during that evening's cruise, TR invited Congressman C.A. Lindbergh to round out the guest list. In a white linen suit, sporting a straw fedora, Lindbergh strode up the accommodation ladder. When he reached the deck, he smiled and grasped the President's hand enthusiastically.

"It's a pleasure to see you, again, Mr. President. Thank you for having me."

"Welcome. May I call you Lindy?"

"Yes, of course, Mr. President," said C.A.

"Let's repair to the fantail while we wait for our other guests. They are late, but you and I can have a cold beverage," said TR. Lindbergh's eyebrows raised, wondering who the other guests might be. The President signaled to the steward with two fingers.

Sipping on mint juleps, they stood at the stern enjoying the picturesque vista. The Presidential flag beneath the Stars and Stripes, barely stirred in a light breeze. The *Mayflower* gleamed white in the late afternoon sun as the light bounced off the tranquil Potomac, reflecting the bright, spring flowers and green foliage. It reminded C.A. of the waterways back home. He had spent many joyful afternoons as a youth walking through the springtime wonderland of the Minnesota lake country. The riot of colors after the dreary grayness of winter was pressed indelibly in his memory. He was entranced by an image of Silver Lake, appearing through the dappling leaves, covered with flashing prisms of pink, yellow and purple wildflowers. Lindbergh was jarred back to the present by the President's use of his name.

"So you see, Lindy, the fantail is the largest open area on the *Mayflower*. All my guests agree that it is a divine spot to observe the hurly-burly activity of the estuary. Ah, my glass is empty," said TR, signaling to the steward. Almost immediately, the steward was standing before them offering the President and Lindbergh mint juleps, along with a bowl of cashews.

TR raised his glass, "Cheers!"

The President moved energetically around the deck. He could not sit down; he was like a restless schoolboy. No wonder, thought Lindbergh, the president had been described as a "steam engine in trousers."

"You know, the first time I sat on the fantail of the *Mayflower*, I was a young colonel in the 1st Cavalry Volunteers, the fabled Rough Riders. She was a warship then, painted battleship grey and outfitted with plenty of firepower. She took part in the blockade of the port of Havana and later was dispatched to Santiago de Cuba. That was on the eastern end of Cuba where my unit was positioned. We had just conquered San Juan Hill and many of the officers who had participated in the battle were invited on board for a celebratory dinner.

"There were some wonderful soldiers at that dinner: Brigadier General Leonard Wood, Major General Joseph Wheeler, Brigadier General Hamilton S. Hawkins, Major General William Rufus Shafter, to name a few. There were two others of note. Lt. John J. "Black Jack"Pershing, and Lt. John Henry "Blackie" Parker who used three, rapid-fire Gatlings to provide covering fire for the assault. We'd never have been able to take the hill if it hadn't been for Parker's Gatling guns.[31]"

The President removed his *pince-nez* and wiped a speck from his eye. "And, to think, Lindy, now, I am their commander-in-chief."

From the bridge Commander Cameron Winslow signaled welcome to an incoming launch. The President and C.A. watched from their vantage point on the fantail, as two passengers boarded the *Mayflower*. The first guest was a large man dressed in a striped seersucker suit. His face was obscured from view by a wide-brimmed Panama hat. He appeared to be in his late sixties and he waddled up the accommodation ladder with the assistance of a white-uniformed sailor.

From the first person's bulk, Lindbergh could barely discern another person behind him. In his haste to board the Presidential yacht, the second man tried to wedge past the first. Chief Petty Officer Galloway stopped him short with a strident, "Stand down, sir. You are making the ladder unstable."

With C.A. a few steps behind, TR bounded back across the deck to welcome the other guests. C.A. recognized Senator Nelson Aldrich, but still could not see the person standing behind him.

"C.A., I'm sure you know Senator Aldrich," said the President, gesturing toward the portly legislator who suffered from gout and other maladies attributable to his gluttonous spirit.

"Howya doing, Nelly?" said TR, flashing his famous buck-toothed grin and patting the old man solidly on the back. C.A. saw a flash of pain in Aldrich's eyes before he responded with a feeble punch to the President's shoulder, accompanied by "I'm just bully. Now, I've been on this vessel for three whole minutes and still do not have a drink in my hand. You are slipping, Mr. President," Aldrich huffed.

Roosevelt waved to the steward for more drinks. Lindbergh stood expectantly, his hands clasped at the small of his back. After a long moment the other guest emerged from the shadow of Aldrich. It was none other than Otto Kahn, the New York banker who embodied the Money Trust. He wore a double-breasted navy blue sport jacket, white duck trousers and a white forage cap with gold oak leaf embellishments on the visor. C.A. saw himself reflected in the monocle in Kahn's right eye.

"Good to see you again, Congressman," said the banker, extending his hand. C.A. recalled the slimy sensation when he shook hands with Kahn the first time they met. He wished he had brought gloves. He grinned and shook hands with his adversary.

"Likewise, I'm sure," he heard himself saying.

The chief steward announced dinner and the President led them into the dining room where they settled down for a delicious dinner of TR's favorite – fried chicken smothered in white gravy.

During dinner the conversation was devoted to the latest Washington gossip. Feeling like the new preacher's wife dropped into a ladies quilting circle, C.A. mainly observed the interplay among his fellow guests. He nodded occasionally and chuckled when appropriate, but he had nothing to contribute. C.A. found the Washington social scene alien.

"Let's retire to the lounge and enjoy cigars and brandy," said their host. They followed the President to a stateroom and sat in armchairs arrayed so that each had a spectacular view of the sunset.

"Gentlemen, we have survived a financial panic and banking crisis for the last time. I aim to fix the problem and reform the banking system so that nothing like this recent panic happens again. I've called you together for a discussion that will lead to a solution. Everything said in this room tonight stays here. Think of this as our own little bunker," said the President.

"Before we get to your suggested fixes, I want to understand a few basic aspects of our monetary system. Nelly, would you provide some historical background on the nature of money?"

The Senator stuffed the remains of an éclair into his mouth and licked each finger clean.

"Mmmm, my compliments to the pastry chef, TR. He has outdone himself. Let's see . . . where to start? Well, money is a medium of exchange. Any agreed-on item can be used to procure goods or services. For example, the American Indians used wampum – sea shells of a certain grade or uniformity as currency. The ancient Egyptians utilized a system of value that fluctuated according to the weight of certain metals like silver and copper which were readily available. While this had the advantage of uniformity, as you might imagine, it became unduly cumbersome as commerce developed throughout the ancient world. Around 1500 BC, the Phoenicians invented metal money and actually minted coins that were accepted as currency in commerce."

He paused to gulp a delicate glass of port that had been placed on a serving table next to him. A comforting thrum of the *Mayflower's* machinery enveloped them as the yacht glided along heading back in the darkness.

C.A. could see the lights of farmhouses twinkling and thought of the people at the end of their day preparing to rest for the next day's arduous labor. The image of his father, drenched in sweat and dirt entering their cabin at dusk inspired him. Providence had presented the chance this night to improve their lot. He prayed that he was up to the task. Meanwhile, Aldrich droned on.

"Coins were a significant advancement, but they still suffered from the disadvantage of transporting large amounts. Coins were so cumbersome that merchants sought a better way to transfer wealth between trading partners. It was the Chinese who invented paper money in the seventh century A.D. They developed a system that used privately issued bills of credit or exchange notes which evolved into an acceptable, recognized form of payment. In today's parlance we would call these instruments issued by merchants the first banknotes."

"Thank you, Nelly. That was clear and concise," said the President. "Which brings me to my next question: Can one of you explain the types of money that exist in America?"

Not wanting to appear too anxious, C.A. let Kahn answer.

"When we talk about money, especially paper money, we are talking about negotiable instruments. In this country several different types have developed. I will give a brief overview, avoiding annoying and mundane details. I must note that this development has been strongly influenced by the exigency of war."

"War is the horrible plague of humanity," muttered the President. Otto continued.

"First, there was the 'Continental.' This was a bill of credit issued by the Continental Congress that in essence promised to pay to the holder on demand, the face value of the bill in silver. Since the Congress lacked sufficient silver to pay the outstanding amount of bills, the market lacked confidence in the 'Continental' and its value as a medium of exchange diminished. Ultimately, it spawned the phrase 'Not worth a Continental,' in other words, worthless. This demonstrated the folly of printing money that has nothing of value to support it.

"Next came the banknote. There was a well-established network of banks within each of the states. These banks issued paper money that were promissory notes by the bank promising to the bearer to redeem or pay the face value in specie, usually, gold or silver. These banks issued paper money with a printed legend that, for example, the Farmers Exchange Bank of Gloucester, Rhode Island will pay the bearer on demand a specified sum of dollars in specie. The bank was required to have sufficient specie to redeem its banknotes.

"During the Civil War, the Union was broke, yet needed money to prosecute the war. So, in 1862, Congress authorized the Treasury to issue 'United States notes,' so-called greenbacks because of the color of the ink used. These greenbacks had two unique features, one, they were not redeemable for specie, and, two, they were declared to be legal tender, meaning that the government mandated that they be accepted in satisfaction for debts public and private.

"In 1864, Congress engineered the demise of state chartered banks by imposing a prohibitive tax that soon made state banknotes extinct. Simultaneously, Congress established the Comptroller of the Currency and authorized national banks. These banks would issue currency that provided for redemption in specie by the issuing bank. The seal of the Treasury was added to national bank notes."

When Otto paused to sip his port, the President seized the opportunity to interrupt.

"Thank you, Otto. Very informative," he said.

Turning toward Lindbergh, the President asked, "Lindy, I want to hear your view on the recent Panic and how we can prevent future panics."

"Thank you, Mr. President. I am writing a book about our monetary system, so I relish this opportunity," said C.A. glancing at Aldrich and Kahn as if to say, now for the truth.

"As you know, I come from an agrarian district that depends on credit from banks to plant crops, finance equipment purchases and get their products to market. The Money Trust has perpetrated a triple whammy on my constituents. They purchased new machines to increase yields, but they found out that the prices on machinery and equipment were exorbitant because Congress imposed protective tariffs at the behest of the Money Trust. Then, the banks raised interest rates so high that no one could afford them. Yet, they still had hope because the harvests looked good. When my constituents produced bumper crops, the prices fell through the floor. The result is more unmanageable debt and greater control by the few people running the Money Trust."

"In my research, I have seen that the banking system is unfairly rigged. The people deposit their money in banks for safekeeping and to support investment in their communities. However, the banks, in conjunction with the speculators, appropriate and manipulate the credit based on those deposits. The depositors receive a nominal amount of interest on their money, while the banks take that money and lend it out multiple times, in effect, to the people making the deposits. The end result is exorbitant profit for the banks and ruinous payments imposed on the people.

"All too often in an effort to woo Mammon, the banks engage in ever-more speculative investments. *The speculation and gambling that is incidental to our banking and currency system is simply appalling, and it is absolutely ridiculous that we should tolerate it, and pay the cost of its continuance.* [32]

"When the bank speculators overreach as they did last fall with the attempt to corner the copper market, the average person gets spooked and tries to withdraw his life savings. But the banks did not have sufficient money on hand; the people's money had been invested and was unavailable when the depositors sought its return. That led to bank runs, bank failures and heart-rending loses for average people.

"The most insidious feature of our monetary system is that it is controlled by a small group of men. *There is a man-made god that controls the social and industrial system that governs us. We know him as the Money Trust.*[33] By means of positions on the governing boards of banks, key industries and investment companies, these men dictate the fate of our economy. The Money Trust operates like a giant, malevolent octopus, with its tentacles slithering through banks, manufacturers, transporters and government with the sole goal of enriching itself."

Like the experienced lawyer he was, C.A. focused his persuasive powers on the judge, in this forum, the President. He held eye contact with TR while vaguely registering the uncomfortable shifting of Aldrich, disparaging mutterings and Kahn's angry, demonic stare. C.A. felt a dark force seeking to distract and intimidate. In his peripheral vision, he sensed Otto's monocle catching the light as it swung hypnotically from his index finger.

"Of course, every effort is made to disguise and deny the existence of the Money Trust. *Thousands of newspapers are supported by the [Money Trust] for the very purpose of beguiling us into believing things that these interests want us to believe. This question of who owns and who uses the money is the one on which they expend the greatest efforts in order to deceive.* [34] But the Money Trust does exist. I have seen traces of its manipulation, stifling competition, and restraining trade.

"I know that you, Mr. President, abhor trusts. Your efforts against the beef, sugar, and railroad trusts are the stuff of legend. What we need is a congressional investigation of the governing boards of the banks and key industries to prove that the Money Trust exists and is strangling progress. The Money Trust *is offended if given or called by his true name, and being jealous of his power, he oppose[s] an investigation of its sources.* [35] We need to put to rest the narrative that the Money Trust is a myth. It is real and extremely dangerous to our country."

Senator Aldrich harrumphed as he leaned forward with some difficulty due to his girth.

"Mr. President, I feel like King Saul listening to the witch of Endor conjuring the spirit of the prophet Samuel. That's what my esteemed colleague is doing by conjuring up the so-called Money Trust. You and I know that it is a figment of an overactive imagination.

"The problem we have is an obsolete currency system. My recommendation is that we form a study group to evaluate the monetary systems of modern economies in order to reform our system with the best aspects of the world's systems. At least, when the study group is finished with its analysis we would have a new monetary model suitable to our economy."

The President scratched his temple and squinted at Aldrich. C.A. had appeared before many inscrutable jurists in his career, but TR topped them all. Kahn cleared his throat.

"Mr. President, if I may . . . ?" Otto hesitated. With the aplomb of a great horned owl, TR turned toward Kahn.

"Since the Civil War the United States has been hampered by its monetary system. We should look to Europe for ideas to modernize."

The silence that followed was finally broken by the sounds of the crew bringing the *Mayflower* into her berth.

"Gentlemen, this evening has been quite stimulating. I appreciate your candor and insight. I plan further discussions in an effort to resolve this dilemma. Good evening."

After dinner on the yacht, Otto and Aldrich huddled together in the rear seat of a cab.

"Nelly, did you see how TR reacted to Lindbergh? I think he was persuaded. That damn Congressman is likely to upset everything. I wish that I could make him disappear."

"Otto, why don't we deal with him the way we deal with all the other irritants? We just spend enough money to overwhelm them," said Aldrich.

"We've tried. That won't work in this case. We've spent so much money in his district trying to lick Lindbergh that the district has become too prosperous to care about a change. We've even tried . . . how shall I phrase this . . . more aggressive attempts to take him out of the equation. None have worked . . . yet," said Otto, his voice decreasing to an ominous whisper.

When Lindbergh debarked, the President clasped his hand and said, "Well done, my friend. You acquitted yourself well. I will certainly take your comments to heart."

C.A. left re-energized. A few days later, his elation disappeared when he received a copy of a draft bill to establish a National Monetary Commission. The bill was sponsored by Senator Aldrich. Lindbergh forced himself to swallow his disillusionment over the *kabuki* theater played on the *Mayflower*. He vowed to use the new bill to promote his monetary ideas.

On the eve of Decoration Day, 1908, President Roosevelt signed the Aldrich-Vreeland Act establishing the National Monetary Commission. In a Republican dominated Congress, the legislation passed through Congress mostly along party lines.

With renewed determination, Lindbergh redoubled his efforts to complete his manuscript. At the same time, Aldrich contemplated his wardrobe for an extended junket to research European banking systems.

1908 Little Falls, MN

> I know of no safe depository of the ultimate powers of society, but the people themselves, and if we think them not enlightened enough to exercise their control with a wholesome discretion, the remedy is not to take it from them, but to inform their discretion by education.
> ~ Thomas Jefferson

If anything, the American public is resilient. The Panic of 1907 passed into history and was followed by an uneasy serenity. Unfortunately, the Panic left a trail of devastated lives in its wake. Thousands of people lost their life savings and some lost their lives. The fragility of the financial system was obvious to thinking people. The problem was that there were not enough thinking people wrestling with solutions.

Lindbergh realized that his years of work would be ignored, or fall on deaf ears unless he got re-elected to Congress. So, he rolled up his sleeves and set about his re-election campaign.

Congress was winding down as members prepared to return to their districts to mount their respective campaigns for re-election. The system of two-year terms, kept Congressmen in perpetual campaign mode, which was an exhausting and expensive endeavor. When his colleagues complained about this, C.A. reminded them of the wonderful opportunity it presented to mingle with their constituents and listen to their concerns. The typical reaction from an incumbent congressman was a prolonged groan.

C.A. Lindbergh was a man of principle who soon learned the cost of adhering to principle in the rough-and-tumble of national politics. Shortly after he entered Congress, he aligned himself with a group of

Republican Congressmen who were known as the Insurgents. These brave, or the foolhardy, depending on your point of view, legislators challenged the autocratic rule of Speaker Cannon. They objected to the rules giving the Speaker final say on which legislation would go to the floor for a vote and the nature and extent of debate on pending matters.

The Speaker was merciless in punishing those who resisted his priorities. The Speaker and his leadership cadre were vindictive in enforcing party discipline. Committee chairmanships and the accompanying budgets and staff were denied to those who failed to tow the party line. The plums of patronage that traditionally went to the victors were dangled parsimoniously to recalcitrant Congressmen. The Insurgents chaffed at Cannon's dictatorial approach.

Lindbergh took his oath of office seriously and he considered the Speaker's autocratic approach to be a grave infringement on his sovereignty as an elected official. When the Speaker or Watson denied a reasonable request, Lindbergh took it as a personal affront. During his campaign for re-election to Congress, Lindbergh issued a pamphlet which set forth his guiding principles. The brochure opened with the unequivocal declaration that, *"I am opposed to bosses and professional politicians administering the government.*[36]*"* There was no doubt that C.A. was not afraid to cross swords with the Speaker.

C.A. recalled a meeting with the Speaker early on in his career shortly after the Speaker had ridiculed him in public for not aligning with the special interest of his choice. Early one Monday morning, C.A. and all the new Congressmen were summoned to the Speaker's office. While all the freshman congressmen waited in Cannon's anteroom, a side door opened and a gnarly finger beckoned C.A. to enter. He walked into Cannon's expansive office. The shades were drawn and in the darkness, it was difficult for C.A. to see the Speaker. He was hunched down in a tufted, leather desk chair. Lindbergh was surprised at how diminutive the Speaker looked, leaning back in the chair so far that Lindbergh thought he might fall backwards.

For a long moment, C.A. stood before the Speaker who puffed his trademark cigar. Judging from the length of the cigar, C.A. calculated that it was Uncle Joe's first of the dozen he would smoke that day. The gray pallor of the Speaker's face glowed intermittently when he dragged on his cigar and the tuck end flared. With a nicotine-stained hand, Uncle Joe invited Lindbergh to sit in one of the armchairs across the desk from the Speaker. The desktop was cluttered with piles of documents and rolled scrolls, yellowed on the ends from the incessant smoke. From his seated position, C.A. shimmied the chair to the right to get a better angle in order to see the Speaker.

"Ah, my friend from Minnesota, how are you this fine morning?" said Uncle Joe in a raspy voice.

"I'm fine, Sir."

Cannon's flinty blue eyes regarded C.A. who could feel the old man calculating the best approach to take with him. The crow's feet around the Speaker's eyes deepened. A swirl of smoke rose from his nostrils and drifted across his craggy features filtering white and gray. Lindbergh presented a tough puzzle for Cannon. The freshman Congressman lacked the usual pressure and stroking points. Unlike most of his colleagues, Lindbergh was neither avaricious, nor vainglorious. Cannon assessed him as the mature, accomplished, successful attorney that he was. Lindbergh was not insecure and thus could not be wooed by titles and adulation. The speaker had to admit that Lindbergh was the most dangerous type; he was a man of conviction who sincerely wanted to serve his constituents. As such, he was immune from the lure of money, fame, or power.

"I'll be honest with you, Lindbergh. I do not know you from a hill of beans. Nor, do I have the time or any great desire to know you," said Uncle Joe in a bored tone.

C.A. leaned forward slightly, trying to anticipate where the conversation was headed.

"You defeated Buckman, right?" asked the Speaker. C.A. nodded.

"Now, I *knew* that there Buckman. I knew that he was a greedy, sonofabitch. Once I figgered his price, I knew I could work with him. That bastard never disappointed me. Never once screwed me." Uncle Joe paused, drawing on his cigar. C.A. wore a noncommittal mask.

"But, you? I don't know you. I don't know if I can work with you."

At this part of the Speaker's indoctrination, as he called it, the typical Congressman professed great ability to work together with the team assuring the Speaker of their dependability. The cherry on the tuck end of Cannon's cigar glowed brighter with each draw. In a gesture that Cannon considered insolent, Lindbergh half-nodded suggesting that he was still listening. The cherry flamed redder.

"I understand that you have been meeting with our *friends* on the other side of the aisle to garner support for your legislation regarding timbering rights. Is that true?" said Cannon, sarcasm dripping from his pronunciation of the word friends.

"Yessir, I have. There is a group of representatives from the agricultural areas that believe we can advance the interests of our constituents by . . . ."

"*It's a damned good thing to remember in politics to stick to your party and never attempt to buy the favor of your enemies at the expense of your friend,*[37] " admonished the Speaker in a thunderous voice.

"The only friends you have are Republicans. I'm sure that my friend Jim Watson has explained to you the way it works. Democrats are like herds of bastard cats that flit around helter-skelter, chasing butterflies while the goddamn business of the country goes to hell. On the other hand, we are disciplined. We Republicans caucus on issues and stick to the plan developed by the caucus. We can't have damn fools doing things on their own!"

Cannon winced slightly when his hand pounded the desk. "Do I make myself clear, Lindbergh?"

"I'm afraid you do, Sir," replied C.A., pausing before continuing.

"Now, I will make myself clear. *Any Member who surrenders his action to the control of a caucus, whether it be one party or of the other, violates his oath, is a traitor to his constituency, and commits treason against his country.*[38] "

Drawing furiously on his cigar, Uncle Joe glared at Lindbergh. With practiced calm, C.A. watched the cherry glow screaming red. He rose to leave. The Speaker was used to getting his way and did not take kindly to being challenged by men like Lindbergh. The old man gave C.A. the smile of a fox who watched the chicken-hawk fly to safety, knowing that he would catch him the next time, or the time after that. Eventually, the fox prevailed, always.

"You know, Lindbergh, I will tell you what I told those asshole reporters at the effin' Waldorf Astoria banquet in New York City when I was asked if we should shoot you insurgent bastards. I said then and I'll say it to your face: '*Shoot them? That would be too honorable. Hang them.* [39] '"

He took a length of rope from his desk and, in deliberate fashion, formed a noose. With his flinty blue eyes blazing, Cannon thundered, "Now, if you are not out of my effin' office before I can say Rumpleeffin'-stilskin, I *will* summon the hangman."

$ $ $

Lindbergh knew that he and Cannon would never see eye-to-eye. However, C.A.'s star was ascending and Cannon's was waning. Electoral victories in next several cycles would solidify Lindbergh's role as the leading spokesman against the Money Trust.

"All aboard!" shouted the conductor who signaled the all-clear to the engineer with a green-lensed lantern.

With a chuff-chuff-chuff of steam driving the wheel pistons, the passenger train accelerated out of Washington's New Jersey Avenue Station. He felt the thump-bang as the locomotive yanked the cars forward. Lindbergh gazed out the window at the disappearing platform. Clouds of smoke from the engine's funnel obscured the bustling scene. He could see a few isolated faces, oddly disconnected from hands waving goodbye. Some of the faces he thought, or, perhaps, wished that he recognized. For the most part, he saw the backs of passengers following porters to the terminal and the street beyond.

Despite his public life as a Congressman, he felt isolated. Confrontations like the ones he had had with Uncle Joe sapped his energy. While in session, he barely slept and certainly lacked the time to meditate deeply on the import of these changes. Except for the late night research sessions, his time was consumed by a never-ending barrage of demands and obligations. He knew that he must sacrifice in order to achieve his goal. With a feeling of melancholy, he thought of how each passenger had a distinct destination and destiny.

During the train ride back to Minnesota, Ridge was lost in thought. Everything about his life had changed since the last election and now he was returning home to conduct another campaign. It seemed like yesterday that he was in his billiards room with Sam, Drew and Big Charley considering the prospect of him running for Congress. Were they so persuasive, or, was it his own sense of emptiness that fueled his decision to challenge that old windbag Buckman? His wife could not understand his longing for meaning. She was content with their life in the Pine Creek house and, therefore, he should also be content.

That house, their home was the first victim. Burned to the ground. At the time, he thought it was caused by a careless accident; a misplaced candle, an errant ember escaping from a poorly tended fireplace, a faulty gas valve. In retrospect, it might well have been arson. If only

Blakey could speak.

C.A. never did understand how his brave, canine companion had ended up in a drainage culvert with a gash on his head. The report of the fire marshal was inconclusive. It read: "Although the presence of several areas of extreme high-temperature burning is unusual and possibly indicative of some sort of accelerant, there is insufficient evidence to support a conclusion other than accidental combustion due to unknown failure."

His marriage was the second victim.

The insurance company was satisfied and paid the claim. Of course, there was no recompense for the sentimental value of so many things – family photographs, the family Bible, his childhood doodlings. The loss of their home devastated his wife Evy. She was convinced that the fire was related to his election and his persistent attacks on the Money Trust. Her sense of personal and emotional security was irreparably damaged. She would never say it, but she blamed C.A. for the disaster and resented his refusal to abandon his seat. The Congressional seat he had worked so hard to attain became to her the symbol of all that was wrong with their marriage. His heart ached when he recalled the letter she had left him on that first Thanksgiving after the election when he had returned from a freshmen congressmen orientation in Washington, D.C.

The estrangement from Evy during his first term was torture. He missed little Charley and his family. His work researching the manuscript of his major exposè of the Money Trust made him even more reclusive. At least, there was solace in the potential for reconciliation and a return to familial normalcy.

Those hopes were obliterated when he traveled home for Easter recess. C.A. still felt the pain of Evy's nearly violent rejection of him the following Easter. The angry, twisted rage on her face that afternoon was indelibly etched in his memory. He closed his eyes and rubbed as if he could erase the scene, the pain, the loss.

At the end of the day, his attacks on the Money Trust were the cause of his estrangement from Evy, the cause of their marriage in name only. It was a steep price indeed. Was the battle with Mammon worth the price? He could not say; the battle was still raging.

"Good morning, Congressman," said James, the porter. The young man knew the importance of recognizing distinguished passengers. The railroad hierarchy constantly drummed the necessity of customer satisfaction into the staff. Being a bright fellow who never wanted to return to the cotton fields of his home in Alabama, James took the railroad's exhortations about satisfied customers to another level. Not only did he pride himself on his dedication to service, he recognized the direct impact on his wallet by virtue of handsome tips.

"Would you like some willow bark tea, Sir? It is a right proper tonic for vexations."

Lindbergh smiled at James and nodded his assent. Maybe the porter had made the right career choice. All he had to do was to anticipate needs of travelers and satisfy them. In contrast, a Congressman like Lindbergh was charged with saving his constituents from the evil tentacles of a rapacious Mammon. C.A. chuckled; he doubted that he would make a very good porter. He was too clumsy.

"Here you are, Sir," interrupted James, presenting a tray with a teapot and cup and saucer. "Would you like some honey? There are some that believe this tea provides too much bitterness."

C.A. waved away the honey; he would sip the beverage in its natural form. A cup of bitterness seemed appropriate to his mood.

"Yes, Sir. Will there be anything else?"

"Thank you, James, nothing for me; but I think Blakey here would appreciate some water," he said, barely audible over the screech of the wheels negotiating a sweeping curve. The high-pitched sound unsettled the dog who repositioned himself on the seat next to his master. Lindbergh patted Blakey and thanked the Lord for him. Blakey wriggled onto his back, fairly begging for a belly scratch. C.A. obliged, grinning at Blakey's contentment.

C.A. opened his briefcase and withdrew his manuscript. It had taken him weeks to reconstruct the manuscript after the burglary. He recalled a conversation with his father about his troubles while he was a legislator in Sweden.

Although his father was generally reticent about this period of his life, he told C.A. that, "You can tell what your enemies fear by what they attack. In my case, they feared my rectitude and my disdain of their attempts to buy my allegiance. So, they attacked my financial integrity; they framed me and accused me of embezzlement. We fled to America to escape the dishonor – a decision I regret. I should have stayed and fought for my reputation. I did not; I was driven to protect you and your mother."

C.A. was too young to understand the words his father used. He wished that he could continue that discussion with his father now.

There were so many unanswered questions about the circumstances of his father's emigration from Sweden. He probably would never know the truth.

At least now, all these years later, a mature C.A. understood the point that his father had made with a hard edge in his voice. Lindbergh knew that the Money Trust feared the findings and warnings contained in his manuscript. Yet, there was something else that he could not explain.

The arson, the burglary . . . something did not make sense. Just behind the range of light, something lingered and nagged. Whoever was behind these crimes had an ulterior motive beyond just the manuscript. The burglar was looking for something else; he grabbed the manuscript during his escape, almost as an afterthought. C.A. felt as if he were enveloped in an inky cloud. If only he could see what was eluding him. He prayed that the answer became apparent before someone got mortally injured.

He hefted the manuscript in his hands. It was bulky. In the short time that Anne had assisted him, they had made substantial progress. Her grasp of the issues, her insight into patterns and her knowledge of structure were uncanny. Whenever he was stumped, she was there to solve the riddle. Her explanations were lucid and cogent. She was fearless with a red pencil; forcing him to write precisely and persuasively. The manuscript was going to expose the grip of Mammon's tentacles on every aspect of the economy. Too often, he paused while they worked to marvel at her intellectual keenness. He doubted that he would have made substantial progress without her.

Riffling through the pages, a sense of pride of accomplishment and excited anticipation filled him. His book would expose what Mammon wanted hidden. Mammon would succeed when it controlled all aspects of the currency. When published, this book would provide a roadmap for reform that would revolutionize the monetary system and liberate it from the clutches of Mammon.

Then, his thoughts turned to turn his personal life. He considered his relationship with Anne. The rhythmic clickity-clack of the rails comforted him, much like Anne's presence in his life had. Before his collaboration with her, he had been adrift. He missed his first wife, May. Her untimely death left a perpetual hole in his heart.

He recognized now that his second marriage to Evy was an ill-conceived attempt to replace his beloved May. His loneliness after May's death led him to an infatuation with Evy. She was young, pretty and intellectually attractive. Unfortunately, over time, he realized that she was also petulant, spiteful and that she did not share his goals.

Lindbergh was a private person by nature. He was analytical and cerebral which helped explain why the reclusive life of a conscientious legislator suited him. When Anne came into his new life to collaborate on his passionate battle against the Money Trust, he was quite unprepared for the flood of emotion that ensued. Their relationship had evolved from collaborators to colleagues to intimates. Even though she was shrouded in mystery and disappeared *incommunicado* at times, he relied on her. When she explained that her absences were due to trips abroad, C.A. recognized disconsolately that he had no hold over her. He had to accept whatever she was able, or, willing to give him.

$ $ $

The remnants of flyers and posters from the 1908 campaign swirled through the air like so many bits of torn hopes and tattered dreams. C.A. won election to his second term handily. Without a primary to contend with he campaigned strongly throughout the district. His Democrat opponent, Dr. Andrew Gilkinson, was weak and ineffectual. During their one debate, Dr. Gilkinson candidly admitted that C.A. Lindbergh was an outstanding public servant. If the campaign had been a heavyweight boxing match, it would have been stopped in the first round.

While in Minnesota, C.A. sought the company of his good friends. None had stronger ties than the owner of the Pine Tree Lumber Company, Charley Weyerhaeuser.

"How's business, Big Charley?" asked C.A. on a brisk October morning while sharing a cup of coffee near the potbelly stove in the big man's office. Big Charley was leaning back on a wooden chair with the heels of his work boots resting on the stove. Steam from the melting snow rose from his boots and rivulets of water sizzled as they hit the cast iron. He savored a long swallow of coffee.

"I can't complain too much, Ridge. We're knockin' down timber faster than ever. We just ain't makin' any more money. We work harder, produce more and make the same. It's like we are runnin' in place."

"You know, Big Charley, it's not right. Everywhere I travel around the District people are suffering. In town squares, grange halls and churches, I speak to people who have lost their life savings. Agrarian debt has skyrocketed and the future looks dismal; they are losing hope," said a somber Lindbergh. He sipped his drink, his expression taut.

"Well, Ridge, the last few years ain't been easy. Folks have struggled with a triple whammy. They was all excited about the new machines to increase yields, but they found out that the prices on machinery and equipment were exorbitant because of the protective tariffs. Then, interest rates got so high no one could afford 'em. They still had hope because the crops looked good. Then, kaboom! When they produced bumper harvests, the prices fell through the floor," said Big Charley shaking his head.

"I know. The final nail in the coffin was when they went to the banks to withdraw their savings, and the banks failed. Their money was gone. It's a disgrace!" C.A. lamented.

"You can say that agin. The cops got called out to stop a riot at the Little Falls S & L. Marjorie Engstrom and her kid was almost trampled. I never thought I'd see such violence in Little Falls."

"How's Jock? I have not seen him since I've been back."

"He's gone. He packed up, took his kids and headed west. That's right, and he ain't the only one. Lots of families are leaving. They think that there's more opportunity out west. They want to get as far away from the eastern parasites as they can. And I don't blame 'em," said Big Charley, chuckling at his line about the parasites.

"It's got to change. There is a growing faction in Congress called the Insurgents who are agitating for reform, but the Speaker, Uncle Joe, squelches every attempt we make. This next session is going to be a war."

Lindbergh stiffened visibly at the thought of the impending battles with Cannon. The polar opposite of C.A., the Speaker was a crude bully, autocratic and devious. Worse, Uncle Joe controlled every cog and pulley of the machinery of the House. C.A. knew that his second term in Congress would be challenging, especially with the clarion calls for reform of the banking system. It would take every ounce of his strength to combat the Money Trust's corrupting influence.

His second term rushed by so fast that before he could turn around he was running for re-election. Many years later he would reminisce about how the years flew by, blurring into an accelerated farrago of experiences. The one constant was his battle with the Money Trust.

1910 New York City, NY

I took my power in my hand
And went against the world;
'Twas not so much as David had,
But I was twice as bold.
I aimed my pebble,
But myself was all the one that fell.
  ~ Emily Dickinson

During the autumn of 1910, monetary reform was the issue of the day. As the public discourse increased, Lindbergh felt pressure to complete his manuscript. Although he had made great progress with Anne's help, he needed to resolve in his mind the proper role of the government. Too much government control would stifle the free market; too little government control would lead to predations that victimized the average citizen. He struggled to identify the proper balance.

One private institution that seemed to work efficiently without government control was the system for clearing checks and private notes. C.A. arranged to do analytical research at the New York Clearinghouse in New York City to gather comparative statistics to test his hypothesis that the private sector was performing the check clearing function admirably.

An essential part of Lindbergh's discipline was his devotion to routine. In law school he had learned to balance his obligation to study hard, with the necessity to earn his tuition by selling the hides of animals he had trapped. He established a routine of studying from dusk until midnight and trapping from dawn until it was time to attend classes. He would often remark in later years that the discipline of routine was essential to success.

While Lindbergh lived a monastic existence, his adversaries indulged in a quite different approach.

$ $ $

Paul Warburg stood on the bridge of the *RMS Mauretania* straining to see their destination, but New York City was invisible, shrouded in thick clouds. The *Mauretania's* voyage to New York City from Fishguard, England was the culmination of several excursions to the continent on fact-finding missions into the intricacies of the various monetary systems in place in European nations. The project, called the National Monetary Commission, was President Roosevelt's response to the Panic of 1907. He urged Congress to send him a bill that would authorize the expenditure of public money to explore firsthand the banking practices of successful economies. Roosevelt signed the Aldrich-Vreeland Act. Nelson Aldrich was appointed chairman and Representative Edward B. Vreeland was appointed vice chairman.

On the continent, the outdated autocracies were oblivious to the approaching Armageddon. In Germany, the Kaiser fostered a rising militarism that threatened to embroil the decrepit Dual Monarchy of Austria-Hungary in battles for which it was unprepared and which would fatally splinter the old dynasty. There was grave unrest in Russia after its humiliating defeat to Japan in the Russo-Japanese War which ended in 1906. Revolutionaries threatened the government of Tzar Nicholas II. The seven-century old Ottoman Empire was heading toward its fatal decline.

Despite all the political turmoil, several European countries had recently overhauled their banking systems. Britain, Germany, Switzerland, and France had modernized their banking laws in efforts to accommodate financial and economic changes wrought by the Industrial Revolution and the rise of the nation state. Congress saw the European banking changes as an opportunity to learn and sent the National Monetary Commission to glean best practices that could be adapted to the banking system in the United States.

For their part, Kahn and Warburg had the forethought to see that Europe was a bomb waiting to explode and they wanted to position

American banking interests to take advantage of the coming conflagration. The work of the National Monetary Commission and their scheme to establish a central bank for the United States was proceeding according to plan. They just had to make sure that their nemesis from Minnesota did not upset their carefully-honed conspiracy.

After the Commission's first junket, it became apparent that the members of the Commission were incapable of framing cogent questions to the banking authorities whom they interviewed. Worse, yet, they were unable to comprehend the answers they received. The Americans' ineptitude with foreign languages made matters worse.

One evening over dinner at Delmonico's, Senator Nelson Aldrich, the chairman of the Commission confided in his friend Otto Kahn that the National Monetary Commission was doomed to abject failure because the members lacked the technical expertise to unravel the intricacies and nuances of the banking systems that they were studying. Otto seized on the opportunity to influence the work of the Commission. He suggested that the Commission retain the services of his brilliant partner Paul Warburg. With Warburg's background in German and English banking, he was the perfect expert to guide the work of the Commission.

"Of course," said Otto, winking slyly over his brandy snifter at the corpulent Senator, "He will not come cheap."

"Not to worry, Otto, my friends in Congress have given our Commission a blank check."

"What do you mean?" asked Otto.

"I *mean*, exactly what it sounds like. My old buddy Jim Tawney's Appropriations Committee has given us continuing, unlimited funding to complete our mission to study various banking systems."

"Unlimited *and* continuing . . . how delightful," purred Otto, savoring the thought. Puffing on his fat Cohiba, Aldrich added, "And, there is no obligation to report details of our expenditures." The cigar smoke formed perfect circles as Aldrich exhaled. To Otto, the smoke rings seemed to form perfectly shaped dollar signs.

"Well, then, Senator, Paul Warburg is the right man for your Commission. I guarantee it; you won't be sorry."

Born Paul Moritz Warburg in Hamburg, Germany in 1868, the young banker immigrated to New York in the early twentieth century. He was raised by the Warburg family that controlled M.M. Warburg &

Company, a Jewish banking dynasty with roots reaching back to the great mercantile interests of Venice in the eighteenth century. Paul was destined to be a banker and soon became a partner at M.M. Warburg. Then, he made a fateful trip to New York where he was the best man at a wedding. The maid of honor was Nina Loeb, the nubile daughter of Solomon Loeb one of the founding partners of Kuhn Loeb and Company, a prominent New York bank. Like his good friend and partner Otto Kahn, Warburg married the daughter of one of the senior governing partners of the New York investment firm of Kuhn Loeb and Company.

Unlike Kahn, Paul Warburg lacked the same flair, *savoire fair* and dynamic personality of Kahn. With a bald pate, bushy moustache and introverted demeanor, Paul Warburg blended into the background as if he were a human chameleon. Warburg was a short man who was undistinguished in every aspect of his persona save one, his prodigious intellect. The force of his ideas on central banking were about to change the course of history.

Standing on the bridge of the *Mauretania* puffing his pipe, Warburg reflected that it felt good to be returning to his adopted home. As a consulting expert for the National Monetary Commission, the three month sojourn through the capitals of Europe had been exhausting. It was an endless profusion of interviews, meetings and studying dry, academic papers. In every country, their study of the banking system was complicated by the diversity of business conditions which were peculiar to that locale. Yet, the one constant throughout the process was his driving ambition to install a central bank based on government credit in the United States.

Warburg was relieved that the so-called fact-finding phase of the National Monetary Commission had concluded. Actually, relieved was a gross understatement. The basis for his relief was not as might be expected – a conclusion of the tedious, never-ending study. Rather, he was relieved that he no longer had to witness the gluttonous depravity of the members of the Commission. A naturally conservative and scholarly man, he abhorred the prevailing attitude of the elected officials on the Commission who viewed their time in Europe as a license to overindulge at taxpayers' expense.

His Orthodox upbringing resulted in his constant embarrassment, even shame, due to the antics of the Commissioners, which ranged from juvenile to downright criminal. In Berlin, several of the members got so drunk playing beer drinking games that they had to be hospitalized. The charges for that evening of 'innocent revelry' as Senator Aldrich called it approached five figures.

The Parisian affair, as it became known within the group, was even more deplorable. Several members were captured on film in a brothel. They were dressed, or, more accurately, half-dressed, in *Follies Bergere* costumes and photographed *in flagrante delicto* with a bevy of fifteen year-old prostitutes. The cost in legal fees, bribes, and hush money was appalling.

Senator Aldrich had the audacity to secure a picture of himself dressed as a can-can girl with legs flailing, drinking from a champagne bottle while dancing with a topless girl who could have been his granddaughter.

To add to Warburg's discomfort, Aldrich relished mortifying the diminutive banker by displaying the photograph whenever the two happened to be in the same room. The degenerate Senator's hairy chest and spindly legs made him a perverted caricature of a French dancer. In his thick New England accent, Aldrich would chide Warburg, "Come on, Paulie, show some vigor. The party last night was wicked fun! Life's too short to be such a prig." When Paul invariably grimaced, Aldrich would give him a teeth-rattling slap on the back, accompanied by, "I love, this lil' Kraut."

The *Mauretania* was one of two superliners built by the Cunard Line in conjunction with the British government as part of a not-so-subtle competition with Germany to see who could build the largest and fastest ships. Britain had long prided itself as master of the seas, but Germany had usurped that title in 1897 when it launched the *SS Kaiser Wilhelm* which was capable of cruising at 22 knots. In less than a decade, Germany had built five "Kaiser class" superliners. To Britain's chagrin, the *Kaiser Wilhelm* held the Blue Riband, an unofficial accolade given to the world's fastest passenger ship. In an effort to regain the Blue Riband and supremacy of the Atlantic, the British government lent the Cunard Line several million pounds to build the superliners, with the proviso that the ships be capable of being refitted for war and that they be turned over to His Majesty's Navy in a national emergency.

Along with her sister ship, the *RMS Lusitania*, the *Mauretania* sported revolutionary twin turbine power plants that drove four screws capable of propelling the vessels to unprecedented speeds. Spewing dense, black, coal-smoke from four black funnels rising above the bridge, the *Mauretania* presented a formidable profile. The powerful engines created a faint vibration throughout the vessel. Passengers reported that, after a period of acclimation, the thrum of the engines combined with the nautical motion of the vessel produced a comforting, womblike sensation.

Shortly after its christening, the *Mauretania* snatched the Blue Riband for Britain by crossing the Atlantic at a speed in excess of 26 knots per hour. It would hold the coveted title for the next twenty years. The builders of the *Mauretania* were not just obsessed with speed. The vessel was a state-of-the-art luxury liner. It was equipped with electric illumination throughout and modern elevators between decks. The first class decks were sumptuously furnished and provided more expansive passenger space than any of its competitors. By far the innovation most appreciated by Warburg and the members of the National Monetary Commission was the ship's wireless telegraph.

A sheet of yellow paper in his hand flapped in the stiff breeze that buffeted the upper deck. With both hands he stretched the page and read. It was from his partner at Kuhn Loeb, Otto Kahn, who advised that he would be boarding the *Mauretania* when the tugboats reached her to guide her through Ambrose Channel into New York harbor. The contents brought a smile to his face. Otto would be hosting a *ben tornati* party to welcome their group back to the United States.

Their initial *bon voyage* party seemed like yesterday. Then, Otto had orchestrated a grand bacchanalia, rich in caviar, champagne, and courtesans. The Congressmen and their consultants were in high spirits when their steam-liner headed for Europe for their first fact-finding tour. Except for the hired experts, none of the Congressmen had expertise in finance, banking, or currency matters. Now, after several years of fact-finding, they could point to over 9,000 pages of translations, monographs, and transcripts of interviews devoted to the intricacies of European banking systems that were soon to be published. It could be said without dispute that after years of study and hundreds of thousands of taxpayer dollars spent junketing in the capitols of Europe, the members of the Commission had developed zero banking expertise. The same could not be said about their expertise in the wines, luxury hotels, and spas of the capitols of Europe – the expertise that the Congressmen gained in that regard at taxpayer expense was indeed impressive, and extensive.

Aldrich's chief aide was a chubby young man also named Nelson who was the Senator's nephew. He burst into the salon where a shapely young female attendant was administering a pedicure to Uncle Nelson. The Senator flashed a baleful look at the aide for interrupting his contemplation of the girl's ample cleavage.

"Senator, he's here."

"Who is here?"

"Sir, you must come topside. Otto Kahn has arrived on one of the tugs..."

"So what?" bellowed Aldrich. "Can't you see that I'm busy?"

"But, sir, Kahn's entrance is, well, majestic. You've got to see it to believe it."

"Nelson, calm down. Just tell me what is going on."

"The seas are choppy and the fog is dense. But, the cargo crane has been activated. Kahn is on the deck of a tug astride a huge wooden container..."

"What is that damn fool up to?"

"He's wearing an opera cape. It's flapping in the wind. He's waving his top hat to everyone on deck. There's quite a crowd. You will want to see this spectacle."

"Oh, alright," said Aldrich. He lurched to his feet and grunted in pain. The aide was about to remind his boss that there were balls of cotton between his toes when Aldrich disappeared from the salon onto the upper rear deck. With impeccable timing, like an apparition, Kahn appeared out of the grayness, balanced on a huge crate. A startled Aldrich stepped back as Otto passed him at eye-level.

"Hallo, Senator, hallo," bellowed Otto, waving from the crate swaying in the wind. Aldrich waved wanly, suddenly realizing how ridiculous he must have appeared. He was barefoot with cotton-stuffed toes and wearing a pastel-colored smock. Much to his chagrin, the image of the debonair Otto waving to the absurd-looking Senator splashed across the New York daily newspapers the next morning.

Later, after Aldrich had recovered his dignity, he sat with Otto in what had come to be known as the Congressional Lounge. It was a beautifully appointed luxury ballroom for first class passengers that the Captain had designated for the exclusive use of Commission members at the outset of the voyage. Aldrich had used the necessity for confidentiality to convince the Captain, who soon realized that the need for confidentiality stemmed more from the members' sexual indiscretions than to Commission deliberations. Despite persistent complaints from the entertainment and housekeeping staffs, the Captain continued to cater to the salacious demands of the Commission.

"Otto, the tour was a trifle long. Yet, who can complain about two years of taxpayer funded junkets in Europe?" preened Senator Nelson Aldrich. He wobbled as he approached a divan in the opulent private ballroom on the first-class deck of the *Mauretania*. It was hard to tell whether Aldrich's unsteadiness was due to the sway of the ship or an over-indulgence of the bubbly that flowed so freely.

"Do be careful, my dear fellow. It seems that your legs are betraying you," said Otto Kahn, who braced himself to catch the unsteady Senator in the event of a fall. To have both hands free to catch the corpulent fellow, Otto released his monocle and it swung on its chain like a pendulum.

"It's the damn gout," grumbled Aldrich. "The ship's Doc tells me that I've got to stop eating all the rich French food they serve on this floating palace. But, the sauces, *Hollandaise, Bèarnaise* and *Crème Anglaise,* are all so irresistible!"

"It is a pity how you suffer for your service. It's a shame that your constituents are unaware of your sacrifice," said Otto whose irony was lost on the Senator.

"Yes, we must chalk it up as an occupational hazard," sighed Aldrich, coming to rest on the plush, velvet divan which creaked ominously under the load. The Senator had always battled a weight problem; however, with all his over-indulgences while boondoggling in Europe, it was safe to say that Aldrich had lost the battle once and for all.

The bottom three buttons on his vest refused to close and his blubbery chin so resisted the edges of his collar that he had abandoned all hope that they would ever connect again.

"Oh, Otto, I'm afraid that I've added a few pounds to my fat stomach, or, *grosse brioche*, as the French call it," said Aldrich, patting his ample girth. He summoned a waiter passing with a tray of canapés and grabbed several with his fat fingers. With crumbs falling from his lips, Aldrich gestured for Otto to partake in the feast. Otto winced imperceptibly at the gluttonous exhibition and patted his own stomach indicating that he had not yet acclimated to the rocking of the ship.

"So, tell me, Nelson, how is the work of your Commission progressing?"

"Quite well; your man Warburg is a gem. We are formulating a plan for a Reserve Association comprised of member banks with some government representation. In reality, it will function as a central bank, without calling it that. Warburg understands the aversion throughout the public to a central bank. All the bad blood from the Second National Bank of the United States that resulted in the battles with President Andrew Jackson and the abolishment of a national central bank. Times have changed. We think that if we can install a central bank disguised as a Reserve Association, then no one will be the wiser until it's too late," said the portly Senator.

The banker turned toward the Senator and said, "The trick will be to accomplish this by stealth. Our biggest concern is that annoying Congressman from Minnesota. He seems to be one step ahead of us. However, plans are in motion to neutralize him . . . permanently."

$ $ $

Back in New York City, the Congressman was a creature of routine. Each morning he enjoyed a breakfast of a bagel slathered with cream cheese, piled high with lox and and a cup of hot coffee at a kiosk in Grand Central Station before heading to his research target of the day. He owed his appreciation to this New York classic to Rosie, the woman who ran the bagel kiosk. When he first came to the City, he restricted his breakfast to plain bagels, toasted, with butter. Then a revelatory moment occurred.

"Good morning, guv'ner," said Rosie. "How's about trying something different on your bagel today?"

"What are you suggesting, Rosie?" said a cautious Lindbergh.

"Here, try this, it's our most popular bagel," said Rosie, who rapidly dispensed bagels to customers rushing by like snowflakes in a blizzard.

"What's that on the bagel?" he asked.

"Cream cheese and lox, a New York classic, guv'ner," said Rosie, handing him one shrouded in a paper wrapper.

Lindbergh sipped his coffee as he contemplated the ring-shaped roll, filled with fluffy, white spread covered with beautiful, translucent pink flesh. When he bit into the bagel, the taste was wonderful. The chewy texture of the bagel was the perfect vehicle to carry the blending of a creaminess with the slightly smoky, salty flesh. Eyes closed, C.A. chewed slowly, savoring the flavors.

"So, what d'ya think? I was right, huh?" said Rosie. Lindbergh continued chewing; then washed it down with his coffee.

"This lox, as you call it, is quite delicious. To me, it tastes quite a lot like salmon," said C.A.

"Ah, that's a funny one, right there, guv'ner."

He planned to spend the day at the New York Clearing House on Cedar Street and then meet Anne for dinner at Fraunces Tavern before catching a train back to Minnesota for his re-election campaign. C.A. asked the desk clerk at the Waldorf to arrange for transportation that evening. He did not want to be stranded in lower Manhattan on what was expected to be a bitter cold night.

After his breakfast, Lindbergh boarded the IRT line heading downtown. C.A. enjoyed watching the passengers entering and exiting the train, as the subway rattled and clanked. There was no distinction among the riders; mechanics in worn overalls carrying toolboxes, literally rubbed shoulders with dapper businessmen carrying leather briefcases. He found the democracy of the subway inspiring. Engrossed in people-watching, Lindbergh failed to notice the drama developing behind him.

A malevolent force in a black Stetson had boarded Lindbergh's car as the doors closed at the 42nd Street station. As the man surreptitiously glanced at Lindbergh, a frown crossed the face of a young woman in a blue uniform coat holding a leather strap near the rear door. Having followed the Congressman for quite a while, Olivia had developed a proprietary interest in him. She resented the stranger's intrusion into her domain. There was a tug on her sleeve.

"Would you like a seat, young lady?" asked a gentleman wearing a bowler hat as he rose from his seat. She gave a furtive glance toward Lindbergh, then, nodded her thanks as she sat. Since she knew his destination, there would be no harm in sitting. At every stop, she craned her neck to glimpse the black Stetson. He was stationary, blending in as an ordinary straphanger. Her instincts, aided by her observation that he never turned a page of the newspaper he held, told her different. She had to admit that her years on the streets as an orphan had honed her awareness of danger to a sharp edge. She sized up the black Stetson. He wore a loose black coat that was longer than the eastern fashion and black pointed boots. He was above average height, muscular in a rangy way with large, gnarly hands. She figured that he was a westerner, and, judging from his erect posture, probably ex-military. A lot of veterans from the Spanish-American war had gravitated to New York in recent years. She had seen first-hand that they could handle a weapon in a scrape.

Exiting the subway, C.A. consulted a handwritten map that the desk clerk had drawn and walked downtown. He walked in his brisk fashion, his leather briefcase swinging in cadence with his gait. The black Stetson ambled behind, occasionally stopping to window shop, but, never for too long. Lindbergh was always in his sight. Olivia dawdled and even considered going ahead to C.A.'s destination. She decided against going directly to the clearinghouse; it would be better to keep an eye on the black Stetson.

The New York Clearinghouse was the oldest and largest bank clearing house in the nation. This temple of commerce had been completed a decade earlier. When the cornerstone was laid in 1894, the *New York Times* reported, *"The new building will be four stories high, 96 feet long and of substantial and attractive architecture. It will have a marble front and a sweeping dome. Strongly built vaults will occupy the basement.*[40]*"* Lindbergh thought to himself that the elaborate Renaissance Revival building was truly a temple to Mammon.

Scaffolding encased the entrance and C.A. nodded to the workmen who scurried across the façade repairing windows and repointing mortar joints. The Congressman entered, showed his credentials to the receptionist and was directed to a small room containing a desk piled high with ledgers. C.A. settled in for a tedious research session. Within minutes, he was lost in thought, analyzing and comparing the volume of clearinghouse transactions since the turn of the century. He was unaware of the drama developing outside.

Olivia slowed and blended into a vestibule of the building opposite the Clearing House. She figured that her mark would be inside for several hours if his past behavior was predictive. As an un-credentialed woman, Olivia was unable to follow the Congressman into the building. She stationed herself in a coffee shop across the street where she viewed the entrance. From a table by the window Olivia sipped her coffee and watched with interest as the man in the black Stetson spoke with some workmen who were working on the building. They were working on scaffolding in the front of the building, adjacent to the entranceway. The man in the black Stetson gestured toward the coffee shop and walked to it. Olivia averted her gaze, pretending to fuss with the contents of her purse. He sat at the counter and ordered breakfast.

Olivia loosened her coat and settled in for what might be a long wait. She pretended to read a newspaper while she puzzled over the black Stetson and what he might mean to her assignment. After an hour or so, the cups of coffee she had consumed had their natural effect. When she returned from the ladies room, the black Stetson was gone. Panicked, her eyes swept across the coffee shop. Nothing.

She stared through the front glass. Through the condensation on the window she discerned the figures of the workmen on the scaffolding. One scraped around the edges of the window frames on the second floor adjacent to the entrance. The other was on the ground securing a large, thin flat object that was wrapped in some kind of burlap. He loaded the object onto a sling and hoisted it up the scaffold where he unwrapped it. The large pane of glass caught the sun, sending a ray of light that nearly blinded her. Her hand reflexively shielded her eyes.

She started at the noise of a door closing behind her. She was so engrossed in watching the workmen that she had forgotten the black Stetson who emerged from the men's lavatory adjusting his trousers. Straining to see him from the corner of her eye, Olivia saw him pay his bill and gather his belongings. A small notebook fell from his coat pocket. Olivia turned to see him bend to pick it up. Something dark and black swung from under his armpit. She brought the tips of her fingers to her lips to stifle a gasp. He was armed.

When her gaze lifted, she saw him looking at her. With her loveliest ingénue smile, Olivia returned his look. A look of wariness flickered behind his eyes, he shook his head and his clean shaven face turned into a placid mask. He nodded to her and touched the brim of the black Stetson. She would report to Lady Anne later that his eyes were cold and deadly like predators she had seen at the aquarium. Olivia watched him check his watch and talk to the workmen again.

Inside the building, C.A. stretched and rubbed his eyes. He checked his pad which had a list of numbers corresponding to years going back to the turn of the century. Satisfied that the data supported his hypothesis that the volume of transactions handled by the clearinghouse was increasing dramatically, he made a note to cross-check the geographic distribution of transactions over the years. His stomach told him it was time for lunch. He packed his materials into his briefcase.

"I'll return after lunch," he said to the receptionist. "I have a few more hours of research this afternoon."

She smiled and said, "The materials will be here when you get back, Congressman. Once you've eaten lunch, everything will be alright."

There was something about her demeanor and phraseology that reminded him of a face from a long time ago. Of course, he chided himself, the receptionist resembled Mrs. Chester, the matron from Little Falls who grabbed him so tightly when his father had been critically injured in the saw mill accident over forty years ago. The anguish of that memory swept over him, bringing with it a dark premonition of impending danger. He stood motionless, staring into the bright sunlight streaming through the glass entrance. How fragile it all is; in the blink of an eye life can be radically changed. C.A.'s shoulders slumped. Suddenly, he was unable to face whatever was on the other side of the door. Engulfed by an irrational fear, he froze. Then, he could hear his father saying, "To succumb is to die."

"Is everything alright?"

"Yes . . . of course, the sunlight blinded me for a second," said Lindbergh. "I must go on."

It was nearly noon. If Olivia knew anything about the Congressman, she knew that he was punctual and would be emerging from the building shortly. A moment of panic gripped her as she searched to re-sight the black Stetson. Then, she saw him stationed within eyesight of the workmen and the entranceway. A realization invaded her brain. A flash of steel told her that one of the workmen wielded a knife. The Congressman would soon be walking directly under the heavy glass poised over the entrance. If it struck him, it would cleave him from head to toe.

Olivia told herself to be calm. She knew what she had to do. She raced out of the coffee shop, reaching into her blue winter coat. Behind her she heard the shopkeeper shouting, "Miss, Miss, your bill!"

The black Stetson looked at her with a perplexed expression, then, at the man with the knife. He was reaching toward the rope above the glass. Olivia fingered a smooth round marble and loaded her weapon. She watched as the Congressman emerged and the black Stetson signaled to the man on the scaffold. Fighting the urge to scream a warning, Olivia set her feet and aimed. A slight gust of wind twisted the glass flush toward her. Olivia pulled her slingshot back as far as she could and unleashed the marble.

A sharp reflection of light glinted off the catseye as it raced across the street at the exact instant the workman cut the rope that released the glass. The heavy pane fell toward the Congressman.

The sound of glass hitting glass was followed by a shattering sound. The pane exploded into a thousand pieces. At the sound, the Congressman covered his head with his briefcase. The shattered glass fell harmlessly to the sidewalk.

The black Stetson glared at her with a look that could best be described as astonished hatred.

With an unfocussed gaze, the Congressman looked toward Olivia, then up toward the workman, then to his feet. The workman, a sheepish look on his face, held his hands out palms up in a gesture of guilty apology. Lindbergh was surrounded by broken glass. His eyes fixed on something. He bent and picked up a catseye marble and put it into his pocket. When he straightened and looked across the street, the girl in the blue coat was gone. He was not quite sure what had just happened, but he knew that his young son would love the marble.

1910 New York City, NY

*If perchance a friend should betray you;
if he forms a subtle plot to get hold of what is yours;
if people should try to spread evil reports about you,
would you tamely submit to all this without
flying into a rage?*
~ Moliere, *The Misanthrope*

When C.A. reflected on the events at the Clearing House, he was beset by raw emotions. Although dreams of his father's tragic accident had recurred throughout his life, he had never experienced the terror of that event while awake in broad daylight. The resemblance of the receptionist at the clearinghouse to some long-forgotten person who had comforted him when his father was mangled at the saw mill was odd and probably triggered the flashback. He attributed it to fatigue.

Nevertheless, C.A. could not ignore the premonition of something evil coming toward him. Was Evy correct that his efforts were awakening some monstrous presence that was intent on destroying him? No, he would not, could not, accept the possibility that she was right.

Later that evening, he met Anne at Fraunces Tavern. The sun had deserted the city and the wind had burrowed through his overcoat leaving him chilled. Anne was already there when he had arrived. She was drinking a hot toddy.

"How was your day, dear?" she asked.

When he had told of the flashback, the premonition and the near disaster with the glass pane that could have sliced him in two, she had given him a strange look, as if she already knew about it. She dismissed his concerns by conjuring up an imaginary headline:

Death by Glass, Minnesota Congressman Sliced in Half
– City Orders Transparent Investigation.

C.A. failed to see any humor in her jocularity and resented her immediate retreat to the ladies room. He could not understand her insensitivity, especially in light of her prior warnings about the Money Trust. When she had returned her eyes were red and she steered the conversation toward the results of his research. After dinner, C.A. bade her an awkward goodbye at Grand Central Station and boarded a train heading for Minnesota.

$ $ $

Back in Little Falls, the press of his re-election campaign drove the events in New York City from his mind. On the positive side, he was so popular with his constituents that everyone wanted to hear about the progress of his work on monetary reform and his role with the Insurgents as they challenged the Washington establishment. The negative side was that his popularity engendered an endless procession of appearances and speaking engagement that occupied his every waking hour. The result was another landslide victory.

Now, with the election successfully behind him, his thoughts turned to his former partner. He had not seen, or, heard from Sam in months. The last time he had seen Sam, C.A. was shocked at his deterioration. Sam's clothes were grimy and tattered. He was unkempt, malodorous, and undernourished. There were dark circles under his bloodshot eyes and his beard resembled a bird's nest. C.A. worried about his friend's obsession with Elisha and their dalliance with experimental drugs.

Most worrisome to C.A. was Sam's last communication. Lindbergh's eyebrows knotted when he unfolded a note handwritten on coarse, fibrous paper. He read the stained and smudged note repeatedly trying to discern its meaning.

Ridge, I am following Elisha to Baden Baden for treatment. Don't worry, (smudge) safe. Always, Sam

C.A. whistled silently under his breath. The note was barely legible and the smudges made it impossible to comprehend. Neither Sam, nor

Elisha had responded to C.A.'s attempts to reach them. He dismissed as unfathomable an impulse to contact Elisha's employer, Otto Kahn, for information about his friend. The man repulsed C.A., who refused to humble himself to a charter member of the Money Trust.

The smudge on the note was irritating. He could see that it consisted of five letters. He interpreted it to say 'we are.' However, the first letter seemed more like a 'b' than a 'w.' But, C.A. could not fit any word into the space that made more sense than 'we are safe.' In any event, Lindbergh would have to trust his friend's statements not to worry and his inclusion of the word *safe* in the letter. If Sam told him not to worry that he was safe, C.A. had no choice but to trust his friend. Sam was resourceful and C.A. believed that he would return soon enough. At least he hoped so.

$ $ $

When the lavender-scented invitation had been delivered to his Washington office, his mood elevated immediately. Gently opening the envelope, he smiled at her neat, compact handwriting. He had not seen her for quite a while. The demands of his re-election campaign required him to travel throughout his district in Minnesota giving one speech after another. Anne missed him and now that Election Day had passed, she wanted to meet him in New York. Anne hinted that she had dramatic news for him that she could only tell him in person. His curiosity piqued, Lindbergh decided to reward himself on his third election victory by traveling to New York City for a rendezvous with Anne.

Their relationship had developed nicely. Anne filled a void in his heart that Evy's small-mindedness had created. With his continued estrangement from Evy, he had grown to appreciate his new life. The manuscript exposing the Money Trust was developing nicely thanks to the collaboration with Anne. He believed that he could rely on Anne no matter what.

Yet, there was a nagging doubt in his mind based on Anne's strange reaction that needed to be addressed. C.A. vowed to move past whatever troubled Anne during their previous meeting at Fraunces Tavern right after the attempt on his life.

During his walk from Grand Central Station to their rendezvous point, he inhaled the unseasonably mild air. There was a crisp autumnal quality to it that invigorated him. In the initial stages of their relationship, they had kept in the shadows, avoiding crowded places.

Although he still preferred privacy, he realized that New York City was so vibrant and bustling, that no one noticed them. Anne had explained to him that being in New York City was much like being in a large school of anchovies; there were so many silvery, mirrored individuals that he was indistinguishable from the mass and functionally invisible.

Over time, he realized it was true and he was able to relax with her in New York. This confidence would prove misguided. His world was about to be shattered by an earthquake followed by a tsunami.

His re-election to his third term was so satisfying that he could not wait to celebrate it with her. Anne was equally joyous and had arranged for a sumptuous luncheon at the Plaza Hotel. The prestigious hotel had been totally rebuilt a few years earlier and now displayed all the pomp, and gilded opulence of a grand French chateau. Although it violated his conservative financial habits, C.A. had become accustomed to Anne's expensive taste. They had a unique arrangement; when they were in New York, she picked up the tab and when they were in D.C. he did likewise.

Since she had set the ground rules, it never occurred to him to question the arrangement. In any event, most of their time together was spent in D.C. working on the book. Anne acquiesced in his aesthetic existence in Washington. She rather enjoyed the austerity of the scholar; it was a welcome change to the pace from her hectic life as a socialite in New York.

The only time C.A. doubted the sanity of their arrangement was during the Panic of 1907 when he could not reach her and had no idea where she was. However, when Anne arrived in Washington that December with souvenirs and the explanation that she had been traveling in France, his doubts evaporated. After all, he had no claim on Anne, especially since he was still legally married to Evy.

When Lindbergh spotted Anne sitting in the Palm Court under the towering, stained glass dome, his heart leapt. She was wearing a blue dress that was so dark it appeared black. A matching hat with a stylish brim arched over her forehead. A mink coat in a similar shade draped the back of her chair. His step quickened and when she half-rose to greet him he took her hands. He was about to kiss her when the hat interfered. For an awkward moment, he hesitated, then, he bowed rigidly, muttering, "I'm sorry I'm late. The train was delayed on the New Jersey side of the Hudson."

"Not to worry. I've started without you," she said, raising her glass. "What are you having?"

"A Manhattan, darling," replied Anne. She signaled the waiter to bring two Manhattans.

"Tell me about the campaign. I'm sure that you had fun. You must tell me all about it."

"For the most part, the campaign was uneventful," he remarked with an expression that betrayed no emotion. When she gave him a skeptical look almost imploring him to share his experiences with her, he relented.

"The campaign was a farce. Speaker Cannon and Senator Aldrich convinced some local legislator to challenge me in a primary. His name was Pat McGarry. He's a real standpatter; he wants nothing to change. How can you go before the people without any ideas to make their situation better?"

"What is a standpatter?" asked Anne.

"It is a person who is perfectly content to have things continue as they are. He kowtows to the bosses and steadfastly opposes fresh, new ideas that will promote progress. He is the opposite of an Insurgent," gushed C.A., warming to the task.

"In contrast, I am considered an Insurgent. That is, a representative who is for progress and against the balky defenders of the status quo. The Insurgents are threatening the establishment and their stranglehold on the machinery of government. With my resounding victory over Cannon's puppet, the electorate has proclaimed that our Insurgent movement against the establishment is for real. In the primary, I defeated McGarry in a landslide, winning seventy five percent of the vote. The donkey Democrats are afraid of me and so I was unopposed in the general election and won every vote cast. How's that for victory?

"It gets sweeter. Remember Congressman "Big Jim" Tawney, the former Speaker who hazed me mercilessly when I first arrived in Washington? He is one of Cannon's staunchest allies. Well, guess what? Finally, after eighteen years in Congress, he got his comeuppance. Tawney lost in the primary. Imagine that! All because the Insurgents fought Cannon and the bosses. We definitely are making strides to return this country to the people."

"That's such exciting news!" she declared.

"Wait, it gets better. The old guard has been ousted. In the last session, the Insurgents led by my good friend, Nebraskan George Norris, broke Uncle Joe's stranglehold on the legislative process. We voted to change the rules by stripping Uncle Joe of his power to assign committees and by removing him from the powerful Rules Committee. But Uncle Joe was still the Speaker and not to be trifled with; ain't nothing more dangerous than a tomcat that's been cornered. Well, thanks to the good people of Danville, Illinois, Uncle Joe is no longer their representative. He lost his bid for re-election. Ain't that something? Even more amazing, the Democrats gained control over the House, so Uncle Joe's henchmen are out of power also."

"With Uncle Joe Cannon no longer in control, who will be the next Speaker?" asked Anne.

"We won't know for sure until the new Congress convenes and votes. The early scuttlebutt favors Champ Clark from Missouri as the next Speaker. He's got some strange ideas. For example, he wants the United States to annex Canada. The Chicago Tribune accused him of letting his *imagination run wild like a Missouri mule on a rampage*.[41] I love that description."

"Where does he stand on monetary reform?"

"On more than one occasion, he told me that he opposed a central bank. He believes that the Aldrich faction is the Money Trust, trying to cement control over the banks and currency by the Wall Street interests," said Lindbergh.

"What is the status of the Aldrich Commission?" asked Anne.

"They are still compiling information for their report. It's an endless boondoggle on the taxpayers' nickel. Half of the members of the National Monetary Commission are no longer elected officials, yet, they continue to receive salaries from the Commission for traveling in luxury throughout Europe. The word is that the new leadership in Congress is going to order them to conclude their work and issue their report by early next year," said C.A.

Leaning forward, Anne whispered in his ear, "Congratulations, Ridgy, I see great things ahead for you." Her tone of voice was filled with the promise of delights to come. Momentarily distracted, C.A. sipped his drink and he cleared his throat.

"Thanks, Anne. It *is* bully, isn't it?"

He peered at her across the table. She was such a mystery. He barely knew anything about her. It was as if she were an apparition sent to help him with his most important work at his lowest moments. She had become indispensable to him, his work. His thoughts reverted to his obsession - the manuscript that would expose the corrupt tentacles of the Money Trust.

"The stage is set for us to publish this book at long last." He raised his briefcase proudly, a wide grin splayed across his face.

Smiling knowingly, Anne said, "Wait until you hear what I have to tell you. I'm sure that you will want to write another chapter."

His curiosity aroused, Lindbergh straightened to get a good look at her face. She returned his gaze intently, there was no guile. He leaned forward as if to say, out with it. Anne toyed with him, shaking her head from side to side slowly. She caught the waiter's eye and he approached their table from behind C.A.

"My goodness, woman, don't keep me dangling like an opossum in a tree." She smiled at his quaint expression. Her eyes shifted to the waiter who placed two Manhattans, glistening with condensation, on their table.

"Marco, do you have that striped bass dish I had last week? It was exquisite."

"Yes, madam, shall I bring two orders?" Anne looked to C.A. for confirmation, her hand resting on his arm. His eyes assented. He knew that she liked to tantalize him and would not reveal the surprise until she was ready. C.A. sipped his drink and engaged the casual sport of people-watching. Anne had schooled him in this pastime. He had to admit that her running commentary on the characters passing through the Palm Court was entertaining; but, only in small doses. She was careful not to overdo it and offend his mid-western sense of propriety.

After a tasty repast of baked striped bass with fennel and chanterelles served with flaming Pernod, they sat sipping cappuccinos.

"That was sinfully delicious," said C.A. patting his stomach. "I may have to loosen my vest."

"I know that when you are alone in Washington, you are too distracted to eat properly. I have to fatten you up while I can." They both laughed; their eyes engaging. The toe of her stockinged foot caressed his calf. He blushed.

"For dessert, here is news that will curl you hair."

Lindbergh reflexively brushed his straight hair back from his forehead. Anne gave him a look of appreciation.

"Well?"

"The Money Trust was shaken by the last election. They believe that their plans for a central bank and control of the currency are in jeopardy. You have really scared them," Anne said, smiling with an earnest look. Her smile reminded him of the smile his mother gave him when he retrieved his father's axe from some thieving Indians. That was a harrowing experience for a ten year-old; but, he was fearless in protecting the axe that his family needed to survive. His upbringing with a pioneer family on the frontier gave C.A. a fearless confidence that would serve him well in his fight with Mammon. In light of what Anne was about to tell him, he certainly would need every ounce of courage he could muster.

Anne reached for his hand and squeezed it with a sense of reassurance. She took a sip of her Manhattan as if to steady herself for the news she was about to deliver.

"I think that the Money Trust is about to resort to desperate measures. They plan to continue to support the Aldrich Plan; but, they are realistic enough to question whether the new Congress will ever pass it. They expect the Democrats to force Aldrich to produce a written plan. Mammon is preparing to write the Aldrich Plan for him. The financial titans are determined to have the central bank in place before war comes to Europe. They consider the current time a unique, once-in-a-lifetime opportunity to seize control of the economy of the United States and the world."

Lindbergh had never seen Anne so intense. Her demeanor was defiant and fierce as if to say, "Not on my watch!" C.A. admired her resolve. She took a deep breath and looked directly into his eyes.

"The Money Trust has scheduled a secret meeting in Georgia at the Jekyll Island Club. Are you familiar with the Jekyll Island Club?" C.A. gave her a bewildered look.

"The Jekyll Island Club is '*the richest, the most exclusive, the most inaccessible club in the world.* [42]' It was established toward the end of the 19th century as a winter retreat for some of the weathiest people in the world. One-sixth of the total wealth of the world is represented by the members of the Jekyll Island Club.[43]"

"You are telling me that the Money Trust is going to this Jerkyll Island club. Who exactly is going there?" There was a measure of disbelief in his voice.

Anne giggled, "Not Jerkyll Island; it's Jekyll Island."

"Alright, alright, stick to the point. Who is going to be there?" snapped Lindbergh.

"It's all very secretive, hush, hush. But, so far, I can tell you that Nelson Aldrich and Paul Warburg will definitely be there. Probably Otto Kahn and Frank Vanderlip, the government bond expert and, oh yes, Abram Piatt Andrew, Assistant Treasury Secretary, will be there. A couple of other bankers have also been invited. I'm not sure who exactly..."

"Tell me, what do they plan to do at this luxury hotel?" said Lindbergh. She could feel the mental wheels of the trained lawyer assessing each piece of information, trying to judge whether it was credible.

"Their goal is to write currency reform legislation that will establish a central bank... under their control, of course. The plan is to lock themselves on the Island for two weeks, if necessary, to draft legislation establishing a central bank with the power to issue currency that will be legal tender of the United States."

Anne paused to let what she had just said register. "Once Mammon gets the ability to print currency that obligates the government to honor, the United States as we know it is finished. Control over the currency is the Holy Grail to the Money Trust. They believe that they are close to seizing it. Lord help us!"

"Wait, what about the National Monetary Commission?" asked C.A.

"I think that Mammon is tired of waiting for Aldrich. He's too busy junketing around Europe and Mammon sees a window of opportunity before war engulfs Europe. Mammon's goal is to be in charge before the first shot is fired in Europe. Once the proper system is in place all the gold will flow to Mammon. Europe will be bled dry."

Lindbergh slumped back in his chair as if he had been struck. A quizzical look crossed his face. He thought, how could this be? The shock of her revelation was nothing compared to what was about to happen.

"Surely, you are not serious? he said.

"I am dead serious. I am absolutely certain that a cabal of bankers and the two public officials I mentioned will be embarking from a train yard in Hoboken, New Jersey next week – destination Jekyll Island, Georgia. They will be there over the Thanksgiving holiday to write the legislation."

"A meeting like that would constitute a criminal conspiracy of the gravest order. Why, it's downright treasonous. It is a virtual coup," said

C.A.

His arms limp at his side, C.A. sat staring vacantly at the floor. She could see his mind racing through the implications and possibilities. He shook his head.

"Wait, how do you know this? How can you be so sure? It's so . . . mind-boggling, that . . . they would be this audacious," he said, his voice trailing off. Again, his thoughts crowded out his speech.

"Trust me, Ridge, I know," Anne said in a firm tone.

Lindbergh was speechless, his lawyer's mind racing. Who could he tell? Who would have the authority to stop this traitorous conspiracy? Who could he trust? He had to muster all his resources to defeat the Aldrich Plan. C.A. was exultant; he finally had the upper hand. With this inside information he could defeat the Money Trust and he owed it all to Anne, his dear Anne.

The two were so engrossed in conversation that they did not notice a diminutive redhead walk by their table. It was Elsie de Wolfe, a prominent doyenne in New York, Paris, and London society. She was dressed to the nines, dripping diamonds and pearls. Her silk, emerald green dress was partially covered by a luxurious red fox coat that matched her hair perfectly. She stopped and, with a look of recognition, broke into a huge smile.

"Anne? Annie? Anne Tracy Morgan? Is that you? My goodness gracious, where have you been hiding? How long has it been?" said Elsie. Exuding elegance, she glided over to Anne and smooched loudly as she air-kissed Anne on both cheeks.

Elsie grasped Anne's hands and raised her, giving her an approving once-over.

"You look radiant, my dear. I have missed you so much," she said.

"Aren't you going to introduce me to your friend?" Elsie crooned, winking salaciously at C.A.

A scowl creased his forehead and he felt a heat rising to his ears. With a tight jaw, he rose stiffly.

"Charles A. Lindbergh, ma'am," he said in a wind-chill tone.

"Hi, there," replied Elsie. "Do you mind if I join you and Annie Morgan here?" she said, sitting down next to Anne before either could reply. Anne's eyes pleaded to him. He stared, stonily, as if he had just seen Medusa.

"So, how's Pierpont?" asked Elsie.

"Has he taken his yacht south for the winter yet? I'll bet that his crescent and star flag is waving in the breeze heading toward Bermuda, or maybe Rio de Janeiro. Yeah, I can see ole Pierpont with a red rose in his mouth doing the samba with some sensual *lindeza*. Your old man certainly knows how to live in style, Annie. Jeez, I wish I had his 'book and swag.'"

Anne blanched, wide-eyed. C.A. wanted to scream, 'Shut Up,' but he couldn't; it wasn't in his nature. He gritted his teeth and Elsie prattled on, her words were like unknowing arrows piercing Anne and C.A.

Elsie beckoned the waiter. "I'll have a champagne cocktail. And, bring Miss Morgan another Manhattan. What would you like Charley?" said Elsie.

C. A. tried to mask the betrayal he felt as he bent to retrieve his briefcase.

"I must be going. I have much work. Good afternoon, ma'am, . . . Miss Morgan," said C.A. His voice was clipped and hard. After flashing a stern look of disbelief toward Anne, he headed out the exit without glancing back.

"What just happened?" asked Elsie, feigning concern. "I hope it wasn't something I said."

"You could not possibly know how you munged things up, how much damage you've caused," said Anne into her monogrammed handkerchief which she used to dab her eyes.

He took refuge in a study warren in the rare book room at the New York Library, fraught with the aching realization of betrayal and his own self-loathing at his reckless stupidity. Emptiness overwhelmed him. How could he have been so blind? From the moment he first met Anne, he should have realized that she was the daughter of J. Pierpont Morgan, the epitome of the monster he sought to slay.

C.A. recalled their first encounter in the study of J.P. Morgan. She was so comfortable in the study that she gave him a detailed tour of the artwork. Her knowledge of the provenance of the priceless artifacts and the history of the paintings was indeed superb. In hindsight, how he failed to connect her to the Morgan family was incredibly dense on his part. Even her ease in the study, sitting in the great man's chair was a dead giveaway. The deference of the servant was another sign that she was a family member. He berated himself for being a foolish rube.

Maybe he was being too harsh. Maybe it started out as an innocent mistake and the longer it lasted the harder it was to rectify. He had to remember who she was. No, he thought, she was J.P. Morgan's daughter, lying, cheating, and stealing were inherited traits. This devilish charade was deliberate. It was a cunning plot to infuse his work with misinformation. His manuscript would be easily discredited.

Lindbergh withdrew the manuscript. All of this work, years of research and analysis, was it all a lie? He thought of the countless hours spent with Anne debating, weighing, and synthesizing his positions on the Money Trust. Ah, there's that word again . . . trust. After this afternoon's revelation, what could he trust? C.A. lurched toward a waste basket and vomited, purging himself of the expensive Plaza meal. He gazed blindly into the receptacle and thought that it would make the ideal container for a fire to consume the manuscript.

Not far away, Anne Tracy Morgan sat in her suite at the Plaza, crying uncontrollably. She had wanted to tell him her true identity on more than one occasion, but she couldn't. The deceit, and she had to admit that deceit it was, started as an innocent mistake on his part that she conveniently condoned and even nurtured. After all, what harm could come from letting this hayseed Congressman believe that she was Anne Tracy? It was kind of liberating to be Anne Tracy and not bear the burdens of being the great J.P. Morgan's youngest daughter.

As time passed, she realized that her relationship with him would never have blossomed if he had known the truth. He would not have accepted her or desired her to assist him in exposing the Money Trust. How could he? He simply would have been repulsed by her blood ties to the enemy he so fervently despised. He would not have let her into his confidence and certainly would not have allowed the relationship to become what it had become. And, now, she had nothing.

PART THREE
Dread

November 22, 1910 Jekyll Island, GA

In all conspiracies there must be great secrecy.
~ Edward Hyde, Earl of Clarendon

They met the chief guide in the lobby of the resort at four in the morning so that they could be at the duck blind before sunrise. A tall, slope-shouldered young man dressed in brown, mottled fatigues stood in the center of the lobby. His complexion was ruddy and weathered. A noticeable lump in his right cheek evidenced a healthy-sized chaw of tobacco. As he looked around for a spittoon, the head butler handed him a new-fangled Dixie cup. Earl looked quizzically at the paper cup.

"It's for expectoration," said Clinton the butler.

"Say what?" drawled Earl.

"It's for spitting, my good man," stated Otto Kahn.

"Oh, thanks y'all," muttered Earl, as he spit a gob of viscous, brown saliva onto the ground where it splashed onto his scuffed boots.

With a supercilious air, Clinton checked off the names of their party (first names only) on his clipboard and announced that everyone was present and provisions had been loaded in the backpacks of the guides. Waiting for the adventure to begin were seven men dressed inexpensive new hunting outfits. They followed Earl outside and stood on the frosted grass that was illuminated only by the beams of light streaming from the first floor of the large 'hunting lodge,' otherwise known as the Jekyll Island Club.

The resort was built in the late 1880s on a barrier island off the coast of Georgia and was owned by the Jekyll Island Club, a consortium of America's wealthiest families. It had been conceived as an exclusive hunting club for the wealthy to escape the harsh winters of the North. Within a few years after it was completed, it had developed into the most exclusive social club in the United States.

The main building on Jekyll Island was called the 'Clubhouse.' It stood on a rise, overlooking salt marshes known as the Marshes of Glynn and a beautiful stretch of Atlantic Ocean beach. The island was originally called the *Isla de Ballenas*, Island of the Whales, by the Spanish due to the whale breeding grounds in nearby St. Andrew's Sound. In 1733, James Oglethorpe, a member of the British Parliament, received a charter from King George II to settle the eponymous colony of Georgia. Funding for the colony came in part from Sir Joseph Jekyll, Oglethorpe's fellow Member of Parliament. The *Isla de Ballenas* was renamed Jekyll Island by Governor Oglethorpe.

The 'Clubhouse' was set among live oaks draped with Spanish moss and magnolia trees. Built with deep red brick in the Queen Anne style, the window trim was painted the color of dried blood, giving the building a distinctive masculine aura. The Clubhouse featured a turret that was over eighty feet tall and had two cantilevered balconies, one on the conference room level and another at the highest level with stunning vistas in every direction. The architect, Charles Alexander of Chicago, incorporated multiple verandas and balconies into the structure to take advantage of the spectacular natural setting and the salubrious ocean breezes.

The interior of the Clubhouse was the opposite of rustic with its decorative Ionic columns, handcrafted cherry wood millwork, and wainscoting. There were over ninety marble fireplaces and antique, hand woven rugs abounded. The architects designed the building to bring the natural setting inside via countless bay windows and clerestory panels of stained glass depicting colorful local flora. The Clubhouse had every spa amenity imaginable, from saunas and steam rooms to heated sea water swimming pools and Roman baths. It was strictly for men and soon became a destination for all sorts of private events like stag parties and other bacchanalia. In November 1910, it was the site of one of the most momentous events in American history. The participants took every measure possible to insure that there would be no plaque celebrating this event to future generations. Like the thieves that they were, they worked in secret.

Outside near the path to the marshes, the pack of Labrador Retrievers waited in the dark, panting steamy puffs and straining restlessly in anticipation. Earl patiently reviewed the safety rules and their plan for the hunt. He told them that they would wear chest-high waders when they got to the marsh, so that their butts would stay 'as dry as dust in a smokehouse.' He explained that they would be given facemasks once they were situated in order to keep them hidden from their flying prey.

"A hunter's mug facin' them ducks flying by is like a mirror reflecting the sun, screamin' 'Skedaddle.'"

He revealed the tips for success. Foremost among these was the admonition to avoid sky busting, the mistake of firing at ducks that were too far away. He explained that the ideal distance is twenty to thirty yards.

"Any thang farther than that, and you're just wastin' powder. Unnerstood?"

Satisfied that his party was ready, Earl led them into the marsh. Muck clung to Otto's waders as he followed the guide. Despite wearing two pairs of heavy woolen socks, he was beginning to lose feeling in his toes. Fortunately, he did not have to carry his shotguns and ammunition. The assistant guides carried all the equipment. A faint pinkish glow was growing in the sky before them.

Cresting a rise, he saw the ocean in the distance and a beautiful, secluded pond surrounded by the low brush of the coastal plain in the foreground. They arrived at a dry spot and squatted in the dim light drinking hot coffee and eating fresh-baked cinnamon rolls, while the guides set up the decoys and distributed the weapons and ammo. A large black Lab brushed against his leg leaving a wet swatch across his brown waders. Otto inhaled deeply, absorbing the aroma of coffee mingled with the pungent smell of wet dog.

Before him in the dawn light was a group of seven men sitting in a circle. As far as Earl their guide and any other outside observer was concerned, they were a group of businessmen on a hunting excursion. However, looks were deceiving. This was no ordinary group. Two were highly-placed government officials. The remaining were men who controlled banking and the economy by means of an intricate web of directorships, trusts, and stock ownership. Lindbergh would have identified them as the Money Trust. They represented one quarter of the world's wealth.

They had set aside two weeks from their busy schedules to perform the arduous task of writing the legislation that would secure their dominance over the American banking system. These men considered power and influence to be their ordained right exclusively and intended to seize this opportunity to codify their objective. They had spent the last several days setting goals and organizing into subgroups based on expertise. Since their venture had gotten off to an excellent start, they had decided to reward themselves by going duck hunting.

At dinner the previous evening they had christened themselves as the Mammon Mob. The meeting of the Mammon Mob had been organized in utmost secrecy by Senator Nelson Wilmarth Aldrich, a portly New Englander. Among Aldrich's more notable achievements was the fact that his daughter had married the only son of John D. Rockefeller, Sr.

Nelson Aldrich considered himself a gifted leader and during his twenty-nine year career in the Senate he had pulled, prodded, cajoled and bullied many fellow Senators and Presidents. His self-proclaimed forte was monetary policy and, as he approached his seventieth birthday, he desperately yearned to cap his career with the Holy Grail of bankers. It had been three quarters of a century since they had controlled the dollar and he believed that it was high time that they were restored to their rightful place. After all, the issuance of currency was too important to be left to the amateurs in Congress; only the professional banking class knew what was best.

Next to Aldrich was a brilliant, young economist with sterling credentials whom Aldrich had recruited to work on the National Monetary Commission. He was currently serving as Assistant Secretary of the Treasury after a stint as Director of the U.S. Mint. His name was Abram Piatt Andrew and he was the youngest of the group. Clean-shaven, with deep set eyes and a penetrating stare, Abe was miserable. His thin lips were purplish blue against his pasty white skin.

"I hope those damn ducks are as cold as we are," said Abe through chattering teeth.

"Quit your bellyaching, Abe. Just focus on how delicious they will be when roasted by our world-renown chef," said Ben, a.k.a. Benjamin Strong, Jr., who at thirty-seven was the second youngest in the Mob. His great grandfather had served with Alexander Hamilton when the first U.S. National Bank was established. He was a vice president at the Bankers Trust Company, and, a protégé of Henry Pomeroy Davison.

Known to intimates as Harry, Davison was the founder of the Bankers Trust Company and, was now a senior partner of J.P. Morgan

& Company. Davison had saved the group's anonymity when he charmed a group of reporters into silence when the group had arrived at the Brunswick Station. Davison convinced the newsmen that 'there was nothing to see here' by promising them a free vacation at the Jekyll Island Club before Christmas. Normally shunned by the elites, the reporters happily tore up their notes and packed their cameras.

"Hey, Orville, look at Paul. He's holding his shotgun by the barrel. I'm going to make damn sure that he is in front of me at all times," said Harry, elbowing the man next to him. Davison was sitting beside Frank Vanderlip, president of the National City Bank of New York who represented the interests of the Rockefeller family and Kuhn, Loeb & Company.

With an elongated face, wire rimmed glasses and a thick mustache, Vanderlip presented an austere mien. However, his personality was quite the opposite. The former news reporter possessed a wry sense of humor. When Aldrich dictated that the group would use only first names to insure anonymity, Vanderlip leaned over to Davison and said, "Since you and I are always right, we will be the Wright brothers. You can be Wilbur. Call me Orville." They both giggled like school chums and maintained the charade for the entire Jekyll Island mission. They even developed secret hand signals so that they could communicate surreptitiously during discussions.

"You may want to rethink that, Wilbur," quipped Orville. "That's the direction the barrel is facing."

A nervous laugh spread through the group. Although each of the men knew others in the group, they were by no means a cohesive team. They were embarking on a momentous task under significant constraints and pressure to achieve something unique. Tension was inevitable.

To avoid scrutiny from the press or the public, the party had rendezvoused at an infrequently-used railroad siding in Hoboken, New Jersey. They had surreptitiously boarded private, unmarked cars with windows shuttered from prying eyes. The train had traveled through Raleigh, North Carolina to Brunswick Georgia, where the passengers disembarked and took motor launches to the Jekyll Island Club.

As the eldest and titular sponsor of the endeavor, Aldrich insisted that the highest level of security prevail, lest the outside world get wind of the nefarious plan that was being concocted. So intense was their fear of discovery that the regular staff at the Jekyll Island resort had been given a two week furlough. A new complement of temporary staff had been brought in to run the facility. To ensure that they remained ignorant of the identities of the guests, there was a strict protocol against uttering last names. For the entire stay, the secretive group used only first names in conversation. No record of the attendees was kept and at the end of each day, all notes were collected and burned in the big fireplace in the lodge's conference room.

The reason for the secrecy stemmed from their mission. The ostensible purpose of the meeting at Jekyll Island of the Mammon Mob was to complete the directive to the National Monetary Commission to report on banking and currency systems throughout the world. In reality, they were there to draft legislation that would provide the small cabal of bankers with nothing less than complete control over the currency and credit of the United States. The plan was to create a central bank comprised of private banks, known as the Federal Reserve Bank, and endow it with the power to print money backed by the U.S. Treasury.

The Mammon Mob formed at Jekyll Island consisted mainly of New York financiers who had three different, but very real concerns. First, the Panic of 1893 had shaken them to their cores. The United States government would have gone broke had not certain members of the Mammon Mob stepped forward with their resources to bail out the government. The prospect of the government failing was so potentially calamitous to their considerable fortunes, that they vowed to prevent it from happening again. That debacle had been followed by the Panic of 1907 when ruinous bank runs threatened the stability of the financial system. They recognized that the current banking system was antiquated and unable to respond to the demands of the economy.

Second, they were gravely concerned about the growing influence of the banks of the western states whose coffers were swelling with Klondike gold. Unless something drastic was done, the dominance of the New York banks was destined to fade as the deposits and reserves of the western banks outpaced their eastern competitors. Third, they anticipated as inevitable a European war and wanted to be in the best position to maximize their profits from financing the major belligerents.

The serious brain power behind the efforts of the Mammon Mob was provided by Paul Warburg, the diminutive German immigrant. He was barely five feet tall and was completely bald. With a thick, black mustache and piercing brownish-green eyes that turned dark and foreboding in artificial light, Paul looked every bit the martinet who intended to drive this group to complete the task before them.

Whenever he sensed that the group's attention was flagging, he berated them in ever-rising stridency that this was a once-in-a-century opportunity and failure was not an option. His manner was condescending and pedantic. After only two days on the Island, his clipped, heavily accented voice was grating on a number of the 'guests' like a fingernail on a blackboard. Otto and 'Orville' served as moderating influences when tempers threatened to flare.

The issue of whether the United States should have a national bank had plagued American political leaders since the inception of the country. The first Secretary of the Treasury, Alexander Hamilton, was the prime proponent of a national bank for the fledgling country. Hamilton modeled his national bank proposal after the Bank of England. He reasoned that all major countries had their own national bank as a natural outgrowth of their sovereignty. Among the principle benefits of a national bank were a ready source to finance government operations, a repository for government revenues and a clearing house for repayment of government debt. He believed "... *that banks are an usual engine in the administration of national finances, and an ordinary and the most effectual instrument of loan, and one which, in this country, has been found essential, pleads strongly against the supposition that a government, clothed with most of the most important prerogatives of sovereignty in relation to its revenues, its debts, its credits, its defense, its trade, its intercourse with foreign nations, is forbidden to make use of that instrument as an appendage to its own authority.*[44]"

Hamilton's plan was opposed by James Madison, Secretary of State Thomas Jefferson, and Attorney General Edmund Randolph. The Southern leaders argued that the establishment of a national bank not having been specifically enumerated as a power of the national government was an unconstitutional usurpation of power that rested in the various States. Further, they believed that a national bank would encroach on the prerogatives of the local banks. Since the nation was in its infancy the argument centered on the Constitutional issue of whether Congress had the power to create a national bank.

Nevertheless, Jefferson issued a dire warning about the evils of a central bank, *"If the American people ever allow private banks to control the issuance of their currency, first by inflation and then by deflation, the banks and corporations that will grow up around them will deprive the people of all their property until their children will wake up homeless on the continent their fathers conquered."*

The First National Bank of the United States was established in the Bank Bill of 1791. It consisted of charter banks that were owned jointly by private interests and the Federal government. The bill was sent to George Washington for signature. Both sides zealously pressed their arguments on him. After considering all the ramifications and his determination to pay every cent owed to the young nation's creditors, President Washington signed the bill into law. The Bank had a twenty year charter that expired in 1811.

After the charter of the First Bank expired, the United States experienced dramatic fluctuations in the value of its currency. In 1816, the Second Bank of the United States was chartered by Congress for twenty years. Andrew Jackson was President when the charter of the Second Bank of the United States was waning. In 1832, the money interests attempted early renewal of the charter of the Second Bank of the United States. The pro-bank legislators reasoned that Andrew Jackson would not challenge the early re-charter bill because he was up for re-election. They miscalculated.

President Jackson vetoed the bill. A death struggle, known as the Bank War (1832-1836) between Nicholas Biddle, President of the Bank and Ole' Hickory ensued. After a particularly virulent economic panic, monetary chaos, the first-ever censure of a sitting President by the U.S. Senate and a recession, Jackson prevailed. The Second Bank of the United States died a natural death by expiration of its charter. For the remainder of the nineteenth century there was no national bank. Memories fade and now in the beginning of the twentieth century, the circumstances were more propitious than ever for a national bank to rise like a Phoenix from the rubble of the Bank War.

This history was known by all the men present and they were determined to avoid the mistakes of the past. Their creature would be immortal, not subject to a charter that would expire after a period of time. They knew that their creature would be adverse to sunlight and honest debate. No, their creature would slither below the surface, operating in the murky shadows. They schemed to use misdirection, misinformation, and marginalization to achieve their goals. They vowed to attack opponents personally in order to discredit them, polarize them and ultimately eliminate them, if necessary. As an action item, Otto prepared an enemies list. Prominent at the top of the list was Congressman Lindbergh. Had C.A. known about the consternation that he was causing the Mammon Mob, he would have taken a perverse delight in knowing that he had them so worried.

This conspiracy was devised in the sumptuous environs of the Jekyll Island Club where no luxury was denied. Thanksgiving dinner was nontraditional. Chef Sebastian had been brought in from New Orleans to create culinary delights for the first-name crew, as he called them. They began with an appetizer of Cajun crawfish soufflé that was airy and briny. A tureen of Jekyll Island terrapin bisque with champignons was well-received. The *piece d' resistance* was the *entrè*. It was a Southern-inspired creation: barbequed duck with Georgia peaches and basil, served with wild rice pilaf and creamed okra.

With their appetites sharpened by the exertion of the hunt, the members of the Mammon Mob wolfed down dinner and asked for seconds. The sommelier paired the *entrè* with hearty *Chianti* that held up to the fatty richness of the duck. Dessert was a pumpkin pie infused with Frangelico and topped with crème Chantilly in the shape of a rose and dusted with chocolate espresso powder. It was served with a fine German Riesling.

After this exquisite meal, they retired to the veranda that had been winterized for their use with glass panels and a fire pit. Cigars and port were passed through the group. Senator Aldrich commended them on their sacrifices for their country by leaving their families behind on this important holiday. Over the next week they would write the Federal Reserve Act in excruciating detail. But on that evening they were content to discuss how they would sell their creation to the public.

In the mellow atmosphere punctuated by cigar tucks glowing red, they discussed practical political considerations. A concern was expressed about how to limit expected opposition to the legislation. Nelson suggested that the best way was for the friendly banks to flex their muscles. He explained that credit could be denied to those who were vocal in their opposition to establishing a central bank. He volunteered to visit various banking industry leaders and persuade them to flex their credit muscles, or more properly, their credit-denying muscles.

Otto opined that the Mammon Mob could supercharge their efforts by establishing a Fund. He explained, "Once we establish a Fund for banks to contribute to, there will be significant pressure to get on board rather than risk being ostracized. The unstated implication would be that contributors to the Fund would be treated favorably and non-contributors would be …. You get the picture. People suffer from a herd mentality. The tendency to follow the herd increases with the complexity of an issue. Nobody wants to be an outlier, or worse, deemed too dense to comprehend the nuances and benefits. Our job is to exploit the herd of bankers toward our goals."

"We could call it the Exploitation Fund," said Nelson warming to the idea. "We can visit bankers personally and solicit funds for our war chest. We could also use it with politicians. Those who do not 'see it our way' will find large campaign contributions made to their opponents in the next elections."

"That's right. In addition, when the time comes to push the legislation over the top, we will have money to spread around to influence those on the fence," offered Wilbur.

"The next thing we have to do is control the terms of the discussion. *The name of Central Bank is to be carefully avoided, but the 'Federal Reserve Association', the name given to the proposed central organization, will be endowed with the usual powers and responsibilities of a European Central Bank.*[45]" Nelson admonished them.

"I propose that we establish a Business Men's Monetary Reform League with the object of "carry[ing] on an active campaign of education and propaganda for monetary reform. [46] To avoid the taint of any banking reform associated with New York, we should establish the headquarters in the Midwest. I suggest Chicago. The League will orchestrate a massive education program with a blitz of addresses and pamphlets written in non-technical jargon," said Paul.

"Do you mean to say that we can influence public opinion by misdirection and misinformation?" asked Orville.

"That's right. We can use the newspapers, the wireless radio, and pliable members in public office and academia to condition the public to view the Reserve bank system favorably. We call this process propaganda, you know, like the way the churches propagate their religious faiths. We can massage the facts, provide misdirection and misinformation to bolster our message," said Paul.

"I would not call that propaganda, I would call that crapaganda," commented Orville, to the boisterous laughter of the Mammon Mob.

January, 1911 Warwick, RI-Little Falls, MN-New York City, NY

*The harder the conflict,
the more glorious the triumph.*
~ Thomas Paine

Newly returned from Jekyll Island, Nelson Aldrich spent Christmas at his Warwick, Rhode Island mansion. He contemplated the events of the last few weeks as he climbed the private staircase from his suite to the Great Terrace. From his impoverished beginnings, Aldrich had made good on his vow to his fiancé lo so many years ago. He told his future wife, Abigail Chapman that he would succeed in amassing money "... [w]illingly or forcibly from a selfish world."

By most measures he had succeeded. His mansion, built on seventy five acres overlooking Narragansett Bay, was tangible proof of that success. It took several hundred craftsmen sixteen years to build the seventy-room mansion that had once been known as Indian Oaks. Finally completed, the Aldrich Mansion was so adorned with Italian marble of such diversity and color that one architectural critic reported that the Senator's mansion was reminiscent of the Golden Palace of Nero, the depraved Roman emperor, except that it lacked the legendary rotating dining room where Nero held his orgies.

On reading the review, Aldrich told his architect to draw up plans for a rotating dining room. The harried architect concluded that a replica of Nero's dining room would be cost-prohibitive and impossible technologically.

The construction of the mansion became an obsession to Aldrich. When he was not on some taxpayer junket, he spent most of his considerable spare time supervising all aspects of the design, and insisted that the lobby, banquet hall and music conservatory be constructed with vaulted ceilings to accentuate the spacious layout of the main floor. The Senator engaged the services of the country's most renowned interior designer, Elsie de Wolfe. At his urging, she selected ornate paintings of Renaissance masters and intricate woodcarvings to complete the public areas.

A magnificent marble staircase ushered guests to the luxurious living suites. The master suite contained a private staircase to the Great Terrace, a cantilevered affair with panoramic views of Narragansett Bay. The sharp, burning pain of his gout seared through every joint in his legs as he struggled to climb the stairs. The private staircase had seemed like a grand idea when the architect proposed it; however, neither had anticipated the debilitating effects that gout would inflict when he grew older. Now, he convinced himself that the pain was a small price to pay for the transcendent experience of brandy and a cigar while enjoying the most spectacular view from the Great Terrace. He wished that someone would invent a modern stair-lift, like the one used to carry King Henry VIII up the stairs at Whitehall Palace.

Catching his breath, Nelson surveyed the horizon and concluded that the ordeal was worth the effort. He leaned on one of two marble sphinxes that flanked the terrace. The crisp winter air, bearing a familiar touch of salt, ruffled his wispy white hair. Aldrich decided to fortify himself with one of his favorite spirits. His view from the pinnacle of his career was intoxicating. Inhaling from a crystal snifter filled with Vieux Cognac Clos de Griffier 1788, the Senator gazed out from his Great Terrace. In the distance, he could barely see the fishmonger's shop where he had worked as a teenager. He had come a long way from that stinking dock.

The true measure of his success, however, was intangible. It was captured in the various titles he had acquired during his rule in the Senate. In Washington circles he was known, variously, as "the boss of the United States," "the power behind the power behind the throne," "the general manager of the United States." While he knew that these appellations were often uttered with a measure of sarcasm, he also knew that they were used with a large dose of fear and respect, two qualities that he admired and strove to engender.

At Jekyll Island, the Money Trust had finalized plans to commandeer the treasury of the strongest, most promising economy in the world. Most incredibly, the grand theft Mammon, as Aldrich referred to it, would be accomplished without a shot being fired and without the populace realizing that the result would be perpetual servitude to the Money Trust. He grinned.

One of the dilemmas they tackled on Jekyll Island was how to handle the report of the National Monetary Commission. For the last two years, Aldrich and his cronies had engaged in a fact-finding mission ostensibly to study other banking systems. They had traveled through the grand capitals of Europe experiencing every extravagance at taxpayers' expense without doing much analysis. To cover their sloth, the Commission reproduced thousands of pages of translations of academic articles about different European banking practices.

The new Democrat-controlled Congress was demanding that they conclude their work, issue a report and introduce legislation based on their extensive studies. Aldrich knew that this was a fool's errand because the Democrats would never allow any plan attributable to him to be enacted. On Jekyll Island, Otto Kahn had devised a strategy to address this problem.

In the meantime, the Money Trust would incorporate a National Citizens' League for monetary and currency reform. The organization would be headquartered in Chicago, rather than New York City. The propaganda effort would continue until they could elect a new president in 1912. By then, support within from the banking community and the public would be solidly behind their stealth legislation. Otto was the mastermind of this strategy and Paul Warburg was his chief tactician in charge of implementation.

Aldrich had to give Otto Kahn credit. The plan was ingenious and it could only be accomplished by intense secrecy and sworn oaths of silence. Their plan could be derailed if someone saw through the ruse. However, there were precious few people in the country who really would understand the true purpose of the Jekyll Island legislation and blow the clarion call alerting the public to the danger. Before the conspirators left Jekyll Island, Otto guaranteed them that he would eliminate the threats.

$ $ $

Meanwhile, halfway across the country, Lindbergh sat in his modest home in Little Falls, Minnesota. Although he welcomed the time with his family celebrating Christmas, he was emotionally exhausted. The tragic end of his relationship with Anne had made him moody and listless. Only after she was gone did he realize the depth of the bonds they shared. He lost his appetite. Not even a batch of Minnesota Monster cookies baked by his daughter Lillian could rouse him out of the doldrums.

Lindbergh tried to go ice-fishing with little Charley and was so distracted that the boy almost fell through the hole in the ice. Bored by the slow pace of ice-fishing, the boy was chasing the shadow of Blakey who was romping outside the canvas shelter. Little Charley tripped and went head long toward the hole in the ice. C.A. was fortunate that Big Charley was watching little Charley. He was inches away from falling in when Big Charley saved the boy from danger by grabbing him by the scruff of the neck at the last second.

"Dang it, Ridge, you need to stop wallowing in self-pity," shouted Big Charley, as Charley dangled over the ice hole. He put the boy down and told him to go outside the shanty and play with Blakey. Fearing a tongue-lashing, the youngster high-tailed it out of the shelter.

"I know, Big Charley. I just can't shake this feeling. It's not only the betrayal by Anne that has got me flummoxed. I feel helpless. I dread what this new system will do to our country. These evil men are at some resort in Georgia plotting to steal the U.S. Treasury and I haven't the slightest idea as to how to stop them. It's like fighting a giant octopus. There are too many tentacles, spreading everywhere, latching onto one industry after another. It's too much without Anne. Maybe Evy is right. I should quit Congress and practice law in Little Falls and live happily ever after," said C.A.

He was slumped over and there were deep shadows under his eyes. Big Charley was saddened by the loss of vitality in his friend's eyes.

"Listen to yourself, Ridge. I can't believe I'm settin' in this here shanty with the C.A. Lindbergh, I growed up with. That fella did not know the meaning of the word quit. He came from better stock than that there. Just think about how your pappy persevered. What did he always say?" Lindbergh gave his friend a blank stare.

"Oh, yeah, his famous saying was, '*no degree of adversity can conquer the unconquerable*[47]'. I can hear him loud and clear. 'Now Charles August, quit your sniffling. Always remember, *no degree of adversity can conquer the unconquerable.*' There you have it Mr. Congressman. *No degree of adversity can conquer the unconquerable.*

You, sir, are unconquerable as far as I can tell," said Big Charley, who clasped C.A. on both shoulders with his massive hands.

Lindbergh smiled at his friend's imitation of his father's voice. He knew that Big Charley was right, but it would take more than a pep talk to defeat the Money Trust. He needed a spark to rekindle his passion. Ezra, the letter carrier, delivered the spark the next day.

$ $ $

Senator Aldrich left his snowy palace on the Bay with a pronounced spring in his step. His gout had subsided. His spirits were soaring as he walked into his senatorial office after the Christmas recess. He was early for the meeting that would begin the next phase of the plan. Seeing that the Senator had removed a cigar from the humidor on his desk, his aide, Arthur Shelton, said, "Let me get that for you, Sir."

Aldrich bit off the end of the cigar and held it up to the flame Shelton held. Nelson knew that Pierpont would be appalled at the procedure; but, what the heck. True, the cigars were a gift from the Zeus of Wall Street and if Pierpont wanted to guillotine the ends of his cigars, then that was his prerogative. Aldrich had not grown up in hoity-toity Connecticut like Pierpont. Aldrich had grown up on the docks of Warwick, Rhode Island and, goddammit, if he wanted to bite off the end of a one hundred dollar cigar the way he learned growing up, then, he would do it.

It was time for the meeting of the *de facto* steering committee of the National Monetary Commission. There were three members - Nelson Aldrich, Ed Vreeland and Paul Warburg. They intended to formulate a plan of banking and currency reforms that would be proposed to Congress. The plan would be called the Aldrich Plan, and would be disseminated under the auspices of the National Monetary Commission.

When several of the Commission members learned of the *de facto* steering committee, they raised objections. The principle complaint was that there had been no deliberations by the Commission as an entire body. Ever the savvy conciliator, Aldrich gave the objectors an option. They could either join the steering committee and spend the winter months in New York City, pouring through the minutia of the comparative banking systems, or, travel to Geneva and Zurich for supplemental research during the winter festival season. Aldrich sweetened the choice by adding tickets to the Grindelwald Snow Festival, an ancient celebration of winter featuring fantastical ice sculptures and snow sports. Needless to say, the composition of the steering committee was unchanged.

$ $ $

C.A. sat in an armchair in his living room in Little Falls watching his son play with his favorite Christmas present, a wooden aero plane. Purchased in a general store in Washington, the plane was an exact replica of the Wright Brothers' first flying machine. The *Flyer* was a wooden biplane that had twin propellers behind the wings and a working rudder. Little Charley spent every waking hour since Christmas Day navigating the white and red model throughout the house. He would spin the propellers and take-off, then, cruise with the plane held with an outstretched arm over imaginary hills, mountains and oceans. The boy's enthusiasm was a balm to the wounded father.

As little Charley was performing maintenance on his treasure there was a knock at the door. C.A. pushed aside the curtains and saw the mailman holding a bulky envelope.

"Sorry to bother you, C.A. but I have a package that needs your signature," said Ezra the letter carrier. Lindbergh had known the man for as long as he had lived in Little Falls and did not know his full name. Everybody just called him Ezra the letter carrier.

"Why thank you, Ezra. I wasn't expecting anything."

Handing the package across the transom, Ezra said, "It's not from anyone I know. The return address is in New York City. It's from a D.G. Phillips, there then."

"Don't think I know anyone by that name. Thanks, Ezra. You have a good day there."

Lindbergh stood for a few seconds watching Ezra pad down the street to his next appointed round. C.A. was trying to decide whether to interrupt watching his son play with the toy plane or open the package which would undoubtedly entail some level of work. The decision was made for him when Mother Lindbergh called from the kitchen asking Little Charley if he wanted some Minnesota Monsters. The prospect of fresh-baked cookies drew the boy to the kitchen like Icarus to the sun.

Curious about the package, C.A. slit the top with his pocket knife and withdrew a stack of papers. He read the cover letter on top with increasing interest. The writer explained that he was an investigative journalist and novelist. A few years earlier he had written an exposè series entitled "*Treason of the Senate*" that chronicled corruption in the Senate. He had read Lindbergh's speeches on the Money Trust with interest. He suggested that they might have a mutual interest in exposing and defeating the Money Trust. He proposed meeting the next time Lindbergh was in New York City to discuss possible collaboration. It was signed, David Graham Phillips.

The next hour raced by as Lindbergh was engrossed in the contents of the package which consisted of articles written by Phillips and Lincoln Steffens for *Cosmopolitan* magazine, plus copies of correspondence among various banking and governmental officials. This was a treasure trove of material that would supplement his manuscript. Excited, Lindbergh put on his overcoat and went to the telegraph office to confirm a meeting in New York City the following week.

The unsolicited package accomplished what none of his family or friends could; it rekindled his creative and competitive juices. He could hardly wait for the train to take him to New York City. Watching little Charley mimic flight with his model plane made Lindbergh think about how his grandchildren would probably be able to fly from Little Falls to New York City in a matter of hours.

$ $ $

New York City was unseasonably mild in January 1911. C.A. Lindbergh had not felt this energized since the end of his relationship with Anne Tracy Morgan several months earlier. The material sent by D.G. Phillips was exactly the sort of evidence that Lindbergh needed to support his case against the Money Trust. His collaboration with Anne had been theoretical and conceptual. He was at the point in drafting his manuscript where he needed to bolster his conceptual model with hard facts. Given Phillips' track record as an investigator, C.A. tingled with anticipation at the prospect of working with the talented journalist. C.A. could not help but think that Phillips' approach to him was providential.

He was scheduled to meet Phillips at Healy's Tavern near Gramercy Park at 1 P.M. Since it was a Sunday afternoon, they agreed to an informal ice-breaker at the well-known pub. Lindbergh arrived early so that he could explore the fashionable residential neighborhood. Blakey strode at his side, strong and inquisitive. His canine companion loved walking in the City. Between the multitude of hydrants and the ethnic food shops, he was entertained by the endless array of intriguing scents.

Built around a unique park, the area lived up to its reputation as a tranquil jewel set in the midst of the hurly-burly of the nation's largest city and financial capital. Several blocks of brick and brownstone houses with small, well-tended gardens and shade trees provide a graceful and quiet atmosphere. His attention was drawn to Gramercy Park, a unique property in the center of the neighborhood. He estimated that the park covered about two acres. When he tried to enter the park, the wrought iron fence was locked. There were people inside the park, but they ignored him. He wondered how New Yorkers could be so discourteous; Minnesotans would have tripped over themselves to open a gate for a stranger. He was somewhat befuddled by this behavior. Then, he heard his name being called and walked over to greet his appointment.

David Graham Phillips was a tall, earnest-looking man in his mid-forties. With dark close-cropped hair, a strong, clean shaven chin and sincere blue eyes, Phillips exuded openness. Despite it being January, he wore a cream-colored suit with a red chrysanthemum in his lapel. From the man's demeanor, Lindbergh sensed that Phillips' strongest attribute was determination. Not a determination defined by doggedness, but rather, a determination to right injustice regardless of the personal cost.

Phillips crossed the street, greeted C.A. with a perfunctory introduction and showered attention on Blakey who showed his delight by almost wagging his tail off. C.A. found himself drawn instantly to the intense man.

"You are a lucky man to have such a beautiful companion. What's his name?" said Phillips.

"His name is Blakey. He's named after the English poet, William Blake," replied C.A.

"He is grand, a beautiful specimen, he is," said the journalist, thumping Blakey on his side.

"I hope you don't mind my asking, but Blakey would love a romp in the park. Unfortunately, the gate is locked and the people inside are most rude. They won't let us in."

Phillips laughed, his blue eyes twinkling.

"Welcome to Gramercy Park, the only private park in New York City. Some eighty years ago, an urban visionary named Samuel Ruggles donated this land as a perpetual park. It is owned by a corporation that maintains it for the exclusive use of the surrounding property owners. They pay an annual assessment and receive a key to the gate, entitling them to use the park. The park has been locked since 1844. Sadly, even if you were one of the fortunate few with a key, Blakey would not be permitted inside. No dogs allowed."

"This City is certainly an endless source of innovation and wonder," said Lindbergh.

"It surely is. Let's go to Healy's and drain a few," said Phillips, with a sweeping gesture in the direction of Healy's Tavern. They entered the venerable tavern and were escorted to the second booth from the front. The irony at the transition from bright sunlight to the murky, darkness of the pub was not lost on either man.

"Congressman, it is indeed a pleasure to make your acquaintance. I have been following your travails in exposing the Money Trust and commend you for your valor," said Phillips who raised two fingers to the bartender, signaling for two beers.

"Please call me C.A. I must say, that the pleasure is all mine. You have greatly distinguished yourself with your exposés and dramatic novels. You do your country a great service."

"Unfortunately, our President does not agree with you," said Phillips. C.A. raised a questioning eyebrow. Phillips took a mug from the waiter and gulped a healthy swig.

"Ah, that first one always tastes grand," he said licking the foam from his upper lip. "Anyway, when I wrote my series on *Treason of the Senate*, our beloved Teddy called me a 'foul-mouthed, coarse blackguard.' And that's not all. Do you know that I inspired the President to invent a new word to describe my style of journalism? You have the honor of sitting across from a genuine muckraker."

"That deserves a toast," said C.A., raising his mug. "To muckrakers everywhere, may their muck besmirch the corrupt and expose them to shame!" Phillips clinked glasses a bit too loudly and both men took healthy swigs.

"Let me tell you something else that you probably do not know. You are sitting in the exact seat where my friend Will wrote the famous short story, *The Gift of the Magi*."

"David, that cannot be. That story was written by O. Henry. I know because I gave it to my sister for Christmas."

"You are correct, my friend, except that O. Henry is his *nom de plume*. His real life name is William Sydney Porter. Will, to his friends."

C.A. smiled. He was enjoying the writer's company. When David signaled for another round, C.A. noticed a young man with unkempt hair glowering at them. C.A. nodded to David toward the man and whispered, "Do you know him?" With discretion born, no doubt, of numerous clandestine meetings, David glanced at the mirror behind the bar to view the man.

"No, never saw him before in my life. Why?" asked David.

"I don't know. I got a strange feeling in my gut from the way he looked at you," said C.A.

"Welcome to New York, Congressman. We have all types here. He's probably harmless. This City has more than its share of lost souls. Oddly enough, Gramercy has plenty; I live in the National Arts Club down the block and plenty of failed, tortured artists come there to stay. See, he's already leaving," said David. They watched the man in the dark coat put on a grey fedora and pick up his violin case. He left the pub without glancing back.

Lindbergh was silent. He was thinking about certain episodes in his life since he had embarked on a political career. The fire that burned down his home in Little Falls, the burglary at his congressional office, the bizarre shattering of the plate glass in lower Manhattan were all suspicious events. Were they part of some pattern? Or, were they just bad luck?

"A penny for your thoughts?" said David.

"Oh, I'm reflecting on certain suspicious events in my life since I've entered this battle. Have you had the same type of suspicious experiences?"

"Sure, I get occasional threats from kooks. If they are ominous enough, I take them to the police who without fail, tell me not to worry. They say that the crazy letters actually defuse the emotions of the writer. I used to walk around looking over my shoulder until I decided that I did not want to live that way. Now, I use it as motivation to write as much as I can with the time given to me. I grind out 6,000 words a day. If I were to die tomorrow, I would be six years ahead of the game."

Neither man appreciated how prophetic that statement would be.

Phillips and Lindbergh were cut from the same cloth – extremely bright, dedicated, and prodigious workers. They spent the rest of the day squirreled away in booth two sharing documents and insights. Although there were occasional meal and bathroom breaks, the pair worked until Tom Healy interrupted them to inform them that it was closing time.

"This has been most productive," said Phillips. "There is so much more to cover. When can we resume?"

"I must return to Washington tomorrow, David, for committee work. But, I am available the week after next. Are you free?" Phillips consulted his appointment book.

"I could meet you again on Monday, January 23rd? OK?"

"Consider it a date. Here, at 1 P.M., Monday after next."

WINTER 1911 Baden Baden, Germany

> No, it was not the money that I valued—what I wanted was to make all this mob of ... hotel proprietors, and fine ladies of Baden talk about me, recount my story, wonder at me, extol my doings, and worship my winnings.
> ~Fyodor Dostoyevsky

While Lindbergh was experiencing rejuvenation by virtue of his collaboration with David Graham Phillips, Otto decided to take a victory lap to celebrate the success at Jekyll Island. He travelled to Baden Baden to spend time with his newest protégée, Elisha Sharlette. He had not seen her since the previous fall when he paid for her and her worthless consort, Sam Wurthels, to go to the spa to overcome their unsavory dependence on alcohol and drugs.

Otto had an ulterior motive. Although he was repulsed by Sam's pliable character and soppy devotion to Elisha, Sam was Lindbergh's closest friend and longtime business associate. The devious banker considered Sam a potentially valuable source of intelligence about Lindbergh, especially details of the secret that Elisha had revealed to him. If anyone could reveal the Congressman's clay feet, it was Sam Wurthels.

None of Kahn's usual methods employed to discredit, control or corrupt a politician worked with Lindbergh. He was immune to the usual monetary incentives bestowed on compliant legislators. Attempts at bribery, blackmail, and extortion had failed to produce a scintilla of proof connecting Lindbergh to anything scandalous. Indeed, in his cynical, mocking way, Kahn had begun to refer to the Congressman as St. Charles.

A frustrated Otto thought that Lindbergh might be vulnerable to electoral defeat if his best friend and confidante were removed from his inner circle. In the grand scheme of things, Kahn considered it a relatively small expense to send Sam and Elisha to Germany for a few months. Practicing the fine art of discerning a character flaw or stubborn strain in an adversary that could undermine him in the future, Otto reasoned that, given Lindbergh's loyalty to his friend, Sam might yet prove to be a useful pressure point to be applied to the Congressman at a critical legislative juncture.

In the meantime, Otto intended to enjoy the pleasures of the famous spa with one of his favorite hedonists, Prince Felix Yusopov. Heir to the largest fortune in Russia, Prince Felix was handsome in a delicate way. Small-boned with alabaster skin, he could display a coquettish charm that was quite captivating to either gender. There were some in the aristocratic set that frequented the playgrounds of Europe who whispered, in the parlance of the day, that Felix was prone to "errors in grammar," that is, he preferred male liaisons to female. Otto knew from direct experience that Felix was equally adept with the anatomy of either persuasion.

Otto was dressed in his usual evening attire, a tuxedo, monocle, top hat and opera cape with red satin lining. Felix was more flamboyant, wearing a black velvet tux accented by French lace cuffs and collar, accessorized with a flaming red and neon blue cravat topped by a diamond stickpin the size of a robin's egg. As they headed toward the main building to indulge in *bread and circuses*, as Felix called the ritual pre-dinner imbibing, Otto plotted.

He had just learned that one of his former lovers, Countess Elisabeth Greffulhe, was staying at the resort and he needed to find a way to divest himself of Elisha for the duration of his stay so that he could rekindle his affair with the countess. He needed a plan. While he was sorting through his machinations, Felix interrupted his train of thought.

"Otto, I can see why the Romans built a *thermae* at Baden Baden. The attendant gave me a tour of the ancient Roman vapour baths, or *thermae*, before my session. It was quite interesting. I feel invigorated after my soak in the hot springs."

"The Roman baths were communal in every sense of the word. These baths were a central part of a complex that included libraries, lecture halls, gymnasiums, and formal gardens. In short, they housed every form of social and recreational activity," said Otto.

"Tell me, are your plans for the bank progressing?"

"As long as I can keep a certain Minnesota Congressman from interrupting our plans, I am confident that the United States will have a central bank by the time you silly Europeans have your next war," said Otto.

"Otto, you make war sound like a bad thing. You know that war is when the wealthy exploit the poor to build our fortunes," chuckled Felix.

"That may be true, but, it's a lot easier to steal with a pen than with a gun. It's also not as messy."

"Otto, you disrespect centuries of bloody plundering with your comments. What good are the poor, anyway? War helps keep the vermin from multiplying and prevents starvation by eliminating all those hungry mouths to feed." Felix paused, affecting a dejected look.

"Who is this fellow who threatens you so much?" asked Felix.

"Charles A. Lindbergh. He is a lawyer-legislator who is one of the very few people in America who truly understands the magnitude and audacity of our plan. He is dangerous because he is smart and fearless. We have various schemes to eliminate this threat."

"In my country, he would just disappear. Poof! Problem gone."

"America does not have your secret police, your Okhrana. We have to be more imaginative. Tonight, you will meet one of our assets to help neutralize Congressman Lindbergh," said Otto. This remark prompted a raised eyebrow from the Prince.

"Let's talk of something more uplifting. For example, I am anxious to join the *Rennen von Blut,* the 'Race of Blood', tonight, are you?"

"Most definitely," said Otto. "Gaming at the Kurhaus Casino is one of the highlights of the season."

Glancing at his pocket watch, Otto said, "I do believe that it is time for our pre-game sustenance."

They ambled, arm-in-arm through the famed Kurgarten, spa garden, on their way to the dining hall in the main building. A marvel of Roman engineering, the colonnaded path was covered with a cobalt blue silk awning that shimmered from a current of warm air piped through the columns from the *thermae*. To counterbalance the slight mineralness of the air, pots of Tonquin musk adorned the tops of the columns. The barely detectable aroma was rich and subtle, the essence of a sybaritic meadow. Some Baden regulars swore that it was an aphrodisiac that stimulated a variety of appetites.

A majestic row of Corinthian columns graced the front of the main structure. At the grand entrance a frieze of double griffins greeted guests. The liveried doorman welcomed Otto and Felix with obsequious respect. A spacious lobby reception area was awash in crystal and rich damask. The room was filled with the sound of lively conversation, of friends beckoning to dine at their table and the toasting and clinking of flutes and tumblers. Attractive servers, wearing black tuxedo trousers and open-necked blouses tailored to emphasize their physical endowments, carried trays of champagne and sumptuous gourmet morsels for the hungry guests.

Otto and Felix sidled across the room to Elisha who was charming a group of French businessman with tales of theatrical triumphs in New York City. Her gown in caramel and green silk was clingy enough to showcase her assets nicely without crossing the line into *déclassé*. The palette accentuated her sultry eyes. Her honey-blonde hair was pinned in a *chignon* at the nape of her neck and she wore a choker of four strands of pearls.

Elisha attracted the attention of every man in the room as she sauntered toward Otto and Felix. She walked with a dancer's litheness and vitality. When Elisha held out both her hands to Otto and kissed him on both cheeks, a subdued quiet of envy passed through the room.

"Elisha, allow me to introduce my good friend, Prince Felix Yusopov."

Bowing smartly from the waist, Felix lifted Elisha's hand and brushed it sensually with his lips. "*Enchantè, mademoiselle*," he whispered, holding her eyes with a ravenous gaze. For a long moment, Elisha felt as if the world had stopped. His glacier blue eyes possessed a primal charm unlike anything she had ever experienced. Her hand tingled and her arm fell limply to her side when he released it.

The instant synergy between Elisha and Felix did not escape Kahn's attention. He sensed an animal attraction that he just might parlay into a plan that would free him to bed the wanton Countess Greffulhe.

"Shall we?" asked Otto, gesturing toward the banquet hall.

The guests dined like nobility, which, after all, most of them were. A terrine of *foie gras*, followed by a specialty Casino salad containing marinated Alpine elderberries, dried currants, walnuts, and a velvety, crumbled *chèvre*, were merely prelude to an entrée of either lobster thermidor or succulent prime ribs. Elisha drank a perfectly matched Chardonnay with her lobster, while Felix and Otto enjoyed a 1904

Bordeaux with their beef. A *limon sorbetto* cleansed the palate before a bowl of pears and apples was served along with a creamy, walnut gourmandize.

"Elisha," said Otto, "tell me how your friend Sam is faring."

"He's faring quite well. The ascetic program that you recommended is working wonders. Yes, at first he resisted – the abrupt detoxification – where the client lives on bread and mineral water for fourteen days, is extreme, I'll admit. But, he needed it; he was so addicted to alcohol and drugs that an extreme remedy was warranted. He hallucinated for five days – screaming about snakes and scorpions crawling under his skin. They had to sedate him."

"What a tragedy," said Otto. "And, now?"

"For the next week he will be in the Ward of *Wasser und Abführmittel* (Water and Laxative)."

Felix whispered to Otto in Russian, "Does that mean what I think it does?" And he made a flatulence sound with his tongue. Otto nodded solemnly and mouthed the words water and laxatives to the Prince. Elisha wanted to ignore the coarse sound, but the tension and too much wine caused her to burst into laughter. Felix and Otto joined her and the trio enjoyed a bit of frivolity at Sam's expense.

When they regained their composure, Otto said, "After that, I will need a double espresso."

"*Da*, I may need a double wodka," laughed Felix, who eyed Elisha as if she were the next course.

Otto feared that unless he deflected the sexual energy, Felix might ravish Elisha right there in the banquet hall. He had to temper Felix's ardor until the right moment. Otto launched into a boring dissertation on the history of the spa. It was originally developed by the Romans who believed that the thermal springs promoted physical and spiritual healing. He told them that the Kurhaus Casino was built in 1824, as a veritable temple dedicated to Mammon.

Its games of chance were designed to lure aristocrats and *noveau riche* to gamble for the highest stakes. Fyodor Dostoyevsky no stranger to the addictive nature of gambling was inspired by the Kurhaus Casino to write *The Gambler,* his novel about the downward spiral caused by compulsive gambling.

"Elisha, you are fortunate to be here tonight for the legendary *Rennen von Blut,* the 'Race of Blood,' a game of chance that is not for the faint-of-heart," said Otto.

WINTER 1911: Baden Baden, Germany

Before Elisha could ask what it was, Otto explained, "This game is unique to Kurhaus. It is by invitation only. The game, it's really two games in one, involves simulated horse racing and a game called *Trente et Quarante*, Thirty and Forty. Basically, if you think of Thirty and Forty as a combination of Black Jack and roulette, you will be OK."

"What are the stakes?"

"Each player must bring at least $250,000 to each round."

"Whew," whistled Elisha. Felix smiled as if to say, it's *only* $250,000.

"We start with sixty-four players and there are four rounds. After four rounds have been completed, there will be four players remaining. The final four, if you will. That's when it gets interesting."

"All these fours are making me dizzy," quipped Elisha. The heads of several guests turned and looked reprovingly at her. She shrugged with her palms facing toward the ceiling.

"Are you with me?" asked Otto. Elisha nodded.

"There are two croupiers at each table, one to handle the cards, the other to handle the tiles. The game is played with a stack of six decks of cards to limit card-counting. A round is over when the stack has been depleted. The player with the most money in tiles at the end of the round is declared the winner and moves on."

"I still don't understand. How is *Trente et Quarante* played?" asked Elisha. At the adjoining table, there was an attractive brunette in a fashionable black gown studded with smokey-ink pearls. She was wearing a tiara with more diamonds on it than Elisha had ever seen on one person. Elisha made eye contact with her and they smiled politely to each other.

Looking down through his monocle, Otto regarded Elisha with a condescending look, and proceeded slowly as if speaking to a toddler.

"It's simple. These are standard playing cards which are counted at their face value – including the ace, which counts as 1 -, and picture cards which count as 10. The croupier deals out two rows with as many cards as necessary for each row to total over 30 points. The winning row is the one with the point total closest to 30. You with me so far? Now for the betting."

Otto continued, "There are four possible bets: Red and Inverse OR Black and Inverse OR Red and Color OR Black and Color. In each hand, a player can make no more than two bets. The first row dealt out is the black row; the second row is the red row. The row that totals closest to thirty is the winner. So, if the cards in the black row total 34 points and the cards in the red row total 37, the black row is the winner. Next, color and inverse are determined by the first card in the first row. If it is the same color as that of the winning row, color wins and inverse loses. If the first card is a different color than that of the winning row, inverse wins and color loses."

"I think I get it," said Elisha. "Once I see it played, I think I will follow it."

"When we get to the final four players, the rules change somewhat. I will explain how when we get there," said Otto.

"How long will this take?" asked Elisha.

"Typically, between three and four hours," said Otto.

"Don't worry, my precious one, there is a separate gallery for the spectators and the casino provides an open bar and there is even a *stehimbiss*, snack bar, in case you develop a hunger," purred the Prince.

As the players entered a large room lit by extravagant crystal chandeliers, they displayed their invitations to the "*chef de partie*" or, game supervisor. He consulted a list of invitees who had deposited at least $250,000 with the cashier, the *casino kasse*. Once he approved a player, the *chef de partie* handed him a stack of tiles of different colors that were debossed with a dollar denomination: gold tiles = $10,000; black tiles = $5,000 and red tiles = $1,000.

One unfortunate invitee was denied entry because his cheque had been declined for insufficient funds. Before he could protest too loudly, he was ushered out the door by two large Alpine types who grabbed him under the arms and guided him away. The players went to their pre-assigned seats at the special tables. Otto and Felix were at opposite sides of the room. The players faced the front of the room where the *chef de partie* stood with such martial stillness that he could have easily been mistaken for a mannequin. An expectant quiet settled over the ballroom. The spectators settled into a gallery that encircled the room.

"Mademoiselles and monsieurs, welcome to the eighty-seventh campaign known as the *Rennen von Blut*, or, the 'Race of Blood,' for our English-speaking guests. This is a modern version of the ancient Egyptian game called Senet. In essence, it is a racing game with the players passing through stations on the way to the empire of the dead. The original contest involved an arduous journey that was a struggle to the death. At the Kurhaus, of course, the "Race" is symbolic. That is not to say that the stakes are insignificant. Tonight, the entrance stake is

$250,000; the amount of tiles represented on the tables is $18 million."

The crowd gasped. The *chef de partie* withdrew a sistrum, an Egyptian rattle, that he shook with increasing intensity, building tension.

"Without further *adieu*, '*Que les jeux commencent*' 'Let the games begin!'" At the last syllable, he crashed the sistrum on a kettle drum with bone-shaking force.

At the resulting boom, the players took their places and the croupiers yelled, "*Faites vos jeux*," "Place your bets." The players slide their tiles quickly onto one or two of the betting layout. As the game progressed, slow or indecisive bettors drew the ire of the other players and croupiers alike. It was not uncommon for croupiers to push late bets off the layout, thereby disadvantaging the bettor. Experienced players increased their bets later in the round in an effort to amass a winning pile before the stack emptied.

"*Rien ne va plus*," "No more bets," entoned the croupier.

Not wanting to appear overly interested in Felix, Elisha took a seat behind Otto's table. To her surprise, the pace of betting and card flipping was frenetic. Groans of loss and squeals of delight punctuated the room. As the games progressed, she noticed that the more successful players were stoic. Otto was calculating and decisive. So intense was his concentration that he never lifted his eyes from the table. Soon, his methodical betting and unflappable demeanor produced a pile of tiles that rivaled the leaning tower of Pisa.

"Your friend is quite the strategist," said the diamond tiara brunette who sat slightly off her left shoulder. Elisha was so engrossed in the action that at first she did not realize that the comment had been directed to her. She flushed.

"Oh, I'm sorry. I was mesmerized . . . yes, he is," she replied. "Er, nice to meet you. My name is Elisha."

"It is a pleasure to meet you. I am Contessa Raffaella Elizabetta di Mattanza. My friends call me Lizzy. I lived in New York for seven years of schooling; so, that's where my mastery of English comes from . . . oh, a dreadful dangling participle," she said with a spirit of self-mockery. Elisha felt at ease with the garrulous young countess.

Lizzy waved at a passing waiter, and said, "*Due Campari e soda, per piaciere. Grazie.*"

"Is this your first Race of Blood?" Lizzy asked, in a voice dripping with mock drama.

"Well . . . yes, I must say that it is quite fascinating." Just then there was a loud thud. Elisha turned to watch a tall man in a military uniform storm out of the room, leaving his upturned chair where it had fallen. An adjacent player lifted the chair and waved to her. It was Felix, smiling a triumphant smile. He pursed his lips and blew a kiss in her direction. Embarrassed, she averted her gaze; then, snuck a peek at the debonair Russian. Felix pretended not to see.

"Watch out for that one. He's got quite a reputation," observed Lizzy, pantomiming an 'ooo-la-la.' The waiter arrived with their drinks just in time to deflect the conversation.

Sensing Elisha's conflicted feelings, Lizzy asked, "Did Otto tell you about the final round?" In response to the unasked question, Lizzy added, "Everyone knows Otto the Magnificent. He is quite the celebrity . . . on both sides of the big pond, as they say."

"Back to the final round; that's when it really gets tense. You see that oval table over there. That is where the final round is played. If you go over there you can see that the oval represents a race track, including quarter posts. The head croupier gives each of the four finalists a crystal knight that looks like a chess piece. These are fine Bohemian crystal; one is black, one white, and one red. These are the colors of the flag of the German Reich, in order from top to bottom. The fourth one is green, the color of the land. They are probably worth a couple of grand each. The crystal horses mark the player's progress around the track. At each quarter-post, one player is eliminated. When that happens, the leader with the most value in tiles has the option of taking that ceremonial hammer over there and smashing the loser's horse. It's quite humiliating."

Before she could stop herself, Elisha said, "That seems like kind of an extravagant waste."

Knotting her eyebrows and looking down her nose, Lizzy said, "In case you have not noticed, honey, this whole place is over-the-top extravagant. I mean, they are playing (finger quotes) for 18 million dollars here." She exhaled a puff of air that ruffled her lips, emitting a low, equine-like snort.

During the awkward silence that ensued, Elisha wracked her brain for a way to restart the conversation without appearing foolish. A low rumble of conversation in the casino prompted her to ask, "Why do the *chef de partie* and croupiers use French when giving directions while the casino staff uses German?"

"Good question. The French claim to have originated the game in the 17th century. Thus, in most European casinos, *Trente et Quarente* is officiated in French. But, I will let you in on a little secret," said Lizzy in a low whisper, gesturing for Elisha to move closer.

"It was invented by the Italians at least two hundred years before the French. The first written reference to the game is in an anti-gambling sermon by St. Bernardine of Siena. We Italians humor the French in this and so many other things," said Lizzy with a loud guffaw. Elisha giggled at the silly national jealousies. Lizzy peered past Elisha and then arose, announcing that she was going to powder her nose. Elisha hesitated, then, motioned for her new found friend to go on without her.

In reality, Elisha was transfixed by the spectacle of rich and powerful men waging monetary combat. The atmosphere in the casino crackled as fortunes were gained and lost. Her eyes darted from Otto to Felix as she rooted for them. Elisha released a sigh of relief each time they survived another round and advanced. There was no clock in the room, but she spied the time from a wristwatch on one of the players. It was after midnight; three hours had whizzed by so quickly. Half the field had been eliminated. Only the most skilled players remained.

Carrying a French horn, a young man, wearing an ornamental, purple beret, marched up to the *chef de partie*. He saluted and stood at attention. On cue, the young man played a hunting tune, signaling the conclusion of the next round. As if a spell had been broken, a clatter of chairs and rising buzz of excited chatter filled the room. Friends and well-wishers surrounded the remaining sixteen players. To Elisha, who in her younger days was no stranger to boxing arenas, the scene was reminiscent. The same exhortations, admonitions and attaboys were showered on the combatants. The only difference was that in this arena the blood and cuts were not visible; they were in the wallet and the psyche.

Otto and Felix approached Elisha from their tables on opposite ends of the room.

"My dear Otto, you look so drained. Here have an espresso. I ordered it just the way you like it."

"Thanks, Elisha. A pick-me-up is most welcome. The Race of Blood surely tests one's endurance, eh, Felix?"

"The night is young, Otto. Perhaps, we will test each other in the final battle?"

"Yes, Felix. It would be an honor to pit the sage Odin against august Adonis," said Kahn, with a maleficent wink. A blast of the horn summoned the players back for the finale. Felix bowed to Elisha and whispered, "Wish me luck, my precious one." Something about his manner gave Elisha a dark, uneasy feeling. It was a fleeting premonition that evaporated as quickly as it had come. She turned and like an apparition Lizzy re-appeared at her side.

"Now, let me tell you what makes the final round so special. When there are just two players remaining, the *chef de partie* convenes the *blottir,* in English, the huddle. During the huddle, the players get to challenge each other to side-wager something especially valuable or dear to them. If the challenge is accepted, the *chef* holds the collateral and the game is played. As you can see, a sort of blood fever possesses the players. Over the years the stakes have ranged from ancestral homes to a sheik's harem. The stakes are not revealed until the game is over."

With just a few highly skilled players, the action accelerated in the round of four. Soon, Otto's brilliant red crystal knight stood alone facing Felix's inscrutable black crystal knight. White and green crystal shards were all that remained of the markers of the other players. Otto and Felix braced to face-off in the final round; but first, the *blottir.*

January 1911 Chicago, IL-Washington D.C.

No League, no bill!
~ Congressman Carter Glass

Aldrich winced as his feet touched the floor. His gout had flared again and bolts of debilitating pain shot through his legs with each step. He was already in a foul mood on account of being in Chicago in the winter. When the Money Trust met at the Jekyll Island Club in balmy Georgia, they agreed to establish a nationwide propaganda organization headquartered in Chicago. Here he was in the Windy City in February, the coldest month on record.

When he had arrived yesterday, the temperature was minus ten degrees. The damn fools lacked Yankee common sense. The formational meetings for the National Citizens' League for the Promotion of a Sound Banking System should have been held in Florida. Just because the League was headquartered in Chicago did not mean that the meetings had to be in this frigid outpost. Damn fools.

At least, the accommodations were first rate. The Nickerson Mansion on Erie Street was the most expensive and, elaborate residence in the city. It was built in 1883 by Samuel Mayo Nickerson, the president of the First National Bank of Chicago. The current owner had enough sense to winter in warmer climes. He graciously made his house available to the members of the steering committee to hold the meetings. Aldrich was grateful for the accommodations. He appreciated the varieties of marble, onyx, carved exotic and domestic woods, glazed tiles, and stained glass that rivaled his own mansion.

The room that Aldrich considered the most striking was the drawing room. The entire ceiling was covered with a stained glass dome depicting the tree of life. The dome was backlit so that the cathedral and opalescent glass shone jewel-like above them. The Senator, Otto Kahn, and Paul Warburg had spent the last two evenings planning the event calendar in this splendid room.

Today was the first actual meeting of the National Citizens' League for the Promotion of a Sound Banking System. The secret Jekyll Island conspirators conceived the plan to advance a program of education as a means of building public support for banking and currency reform.

They enlisted the aid of the National Board of Trade and the Chicago Association of Commerce as pawns to develop the structure for the new organization. In an example of linguistic duplicity that would be hard to match, the foundational documents described the object of the organization as: *to give organized expression to the growing public sentiment in favor of, and to carry on a campaign of education for an improved banking system for the United States of America.*[48]

The altruistic language was deliberately crafted to conceal the true purpose of the propaganda campaign – the establishment of a central bank owned and controlled by private banks with power to issue currency backed by the government.

Otto Kahn addressed the assemblage of bankers and businessmen.

"We recognize the clamor of opposition to a central bank. It is the political bugaboo of our time. The Democrat Party has a long tradition of opposition to a national central bank. With all due respect to our banking brethren, many bankers appreciate the art of banking, but are deficient in their understanding of the science of banking. So a campaign of education is imperative."

"Here, here," commented someone in the crowd.

"I would be remiss if I did not single out our esteemed Senator from Rhode Island. Nelson Aldrich has devoted years of his life promoting a sound banking system for this great country. What has his reward been? He has been subjected to a steady stream of approbation and editorial anathema. The press calls him an old warhorse; he considers it a term of endearment.

"We all know that he has served this country with distinction. History will show that he was a stalwart leader who helped us navigate some of the worst economic conditions of our generation. For that we owe him our sincere gratitude. Please join me in giving Senator Nelson W. Aldrich a well-deserved round of applause."

The room erupted into boisterous cheering. Aldrich sat milking the moment. Removing his spectacles, he dabbed his eyes. When the applause waned, Aldrich stood and waved his arms in appreciation. A second pulse of clapping exceeding the initial wave, followed. The Senator pantomimed a hug to his heart.

With a smiling nod toward Aldrich, Kahn took a sip of water, cleared his throat and continued.

"My friends the task before us is crucial. We all have heard the drums of war in Europe. No one knows where or when it will begin. As bankers and business leaders it is our patriotic duty to make sure this great country is ready to serve the financial needs of the combatants."

Not wanting to overplay this angle Otto changed gears.

"We need to rally the people to the cause. Although there has been much public discussion about the deficiencies of our banking system since the recent Panic, the topic is considered an impenetrable mystery. Our task is to educate the populace by simplifying the issues and moving banking and currency reform to the top of the public agenda. This effort is unprecedented, but necessary in this era of participatory democracy.

"Leading this effort will require mastery of banking science and understanding of the mentality of the people. We are fortunate to have someone who possesses both. Allow me to introduce my partner, Paul Warburg, one of the great bankers of our time" said Otto with a vocal flourish that turned Warburg an embarrassed shade of red.

Approaching the podium, Warburg unfolded a sheaf of papers.

"Thank you Otto. Gentlemen, we are at a crossroads. At one end is prosperity and success; at the other is panic and poverty. I have here," he said, holding the papers above his head, "the map to prosperity and success. Our plan is simple – that does not mean it will be easy.

"The first component will be to establish state organizations for the education program. Our plan is aggressive, as it must be. We will have distinct offices in forty-four of the forty-six states by the summer. Each state office will tailor the program to the particular situation of that state, whether agricultural, mining, or manufacturing, etcetera.

"We will implement the program on two levels: publicity and political.

"First, publicity; the backbone of our campaign will be a monthly magazine called *Banking Reform*. To supplement the impact of the magazine, we will prepare educational pamphlets and distribute millions of copies via mailing lists that are being specifically prepared for our League. We will supply material for millions of newspaper columns. We will supply thousands of speakers to civic groups, schools, and fraternal organizations. This effort will create a groundswell of support for an improved banking system.

"Second, political; we will publish a book with the same title as the magazine. Our text book, *Banking Reform*, will be distributed to members of all political parties. We will engage in a concerted effort to influence party platforms at state conventions. Our goal will be the inclusion of terms like 'revision of our antiquated banking system' and demand for 'creation of a system of elastic note and credit system.' This will foster an atmosphere of openness to reform.

"I must emphasize that this effort will be strictly bi-partisan. It is critical that the League appear neither Republican nor Democrat. It is imperative that banking reform be a neutral issue, an issue of national interest.

"In a moment, we will now separate into subgroups. Please consult the lists that are on tables around the room. In conclusion, we are embarking on a mission of critical importance to this Republic. The future depends on each and every one of you. Now, let's get to work."

Enthusiastic applause followed Warburg's exhortation. The usually staid bankers and businessmen surged toward the committee sign-up tables. The remainder of the day was a frenetic blur of activity. With inflated chests and greedy smiles, Otto and Aldrich surveyed the scene.

The day concluded with an eloquent benediction from the esteemed Senator from Rhode Island.

"As we all know, gentlemen, we are on the path of truth and righteousness. It is therefore fitting that I draw from the Holy Bible as we embark on this campaign. In the Book of Deuteronomy, we learn *'But the LORD your God will deliver them over to you, throwing them into great confusion until they are destroyed.*[49]*'* In the spirit of Deuteronomy, I offer a solemn toast," he said.

Raising his goblet, he admired the brilliant rainbows flashing off the Baccarat stemware. After a dramatic pause, Nelson Aldrich bellowed, "Confusion to our enemies!"

$ $ $

While Kahn and Warburg tackled the thorny issue of garnering popular support from a public that was extremely suspicious of the Money Trust, C.A. Lindbergh walked down Pennsylvania Avenue in Washington D.C. The Congressman had just left his office in the

Capitol. He had spent most of the day editing the manuscript that he was convinced would educate the public and thereby rebuff efforts by the Money Trust to gain power over the U.S. currency. C.A. was filled with a burgeoning confidence that the Aldrich Plan would be stillborn in Congress. Victory was in sight.

Just as he was about to slay one monster, another reared its ugly head. He was headed for a meeting at the Riggs House with one of his staunchest supporters. Lindbergh had no idea of the barbarity of this new monster; nor that both monsters answered to the same master.

The sight of the Riggs House brought memories of his liaisons with Anne Tracy. Those were good times he thought. They had worked well together and shared a sense of commitment to expose the Money Trust and its efforts to take over the nation's currency. Due to an unfortunate turn of events she was out of his life. It was painful to think about it.

When Lindbergh entered the hotel and proceeded to the private conference room, he received an exuberant welcome from Big Charley Weyerhaeuser. He wore a buckskin jacket over a plaid shirt. Big Charley's hair and winter beard were characteristically unkempt. His only concession to civilization was a string tie that was drawn loosely around his blocky neck.

"There he is! There's my favorite Congressman," said Big Charley with genuine affection. He crossed the room and enveloped C.A. in a bear hug that expelled the air from C.A.'s chest.

"Hully gee, Ridge, don't they feed ya in this town? Ya's skinny as a rail. Not to worry, I made sure that we had a big spread for our meetin' tonight," said Big Charley, motioning toward a mountain of food in platters on the conference table.

Swigging on a drink, the lumberman passed a generously-filled tumbler to C.A. They clinked glasses and simultaneously said, "*Shål!*" Big Charley smacked his lips loudly and sat down near a bowl of cashews. He grabbed a handful and plopped a few into his mouth.

"Big Charley, I thought your message said that there would be you, me and one other. There's enough food on that table to feed the entire Congress."

"Them pigs would devour this spread as quick as a Minnesota lightning strike," Charley howled, slapping C.A. on the back.

"So tell me, why all the secrecy? I've been wracking my brain trying to figure out what you got to tell me in a place where there won't be any nosey-bodies."

"I'll let the General tell you. That should be him there then," said Charley, turning toward a firm knock at the door.

A tall, dignified man in full military regalia entered the room. His dark, double-breasted jacket with colored piping bore a cluster of gold oak leaves, indicative of the rank of General in the Imperial Russian Army.

"Ridge, this here's General Tikhon Kracilnikov. He is an intimate friend of the Tsar and serves as liaison with foreigners for natural resources. We've been working together on monetizing Russia's vast timber reserves."

"It is a pleasure to meet you, Sir. I am C.A. Lindbergh, representative of the 6th District of the great state of Minnesota. Please have a seat."

The General unbuckled his ceremonial sword and the men settled into upholstered armchairs. They exchanged pleasantries and ate some of the food. Although C.A. found the General interesting, he failed to see why Charley had arranged this unusual meeting.

"Can I get you a drink, General?" asked Big Charley.

"Wodka, neat, if you please," he said in impeccable English that betrayed a slight Slavic lilt.

"Ridge, let me set the stage here. I met the General in St. Petersburg while on a trade mission last month. He had just returned from a short holiday in Baden Baden where he encountered Sam Wurthels and his girlfriend, that Elisha dame. When he learned that I was from Minnesota, he shared the most amazing story with me."

The General finished a serving of *brie en croute* and wiped his lips with a dainty movement that belied his military bearing. After a sip of vodka, the General spoke,

"I was in Baden Baden for the Race of Blood. I met your friend Sam in the spa. He told me that he was there to cleanse his body and spirit. He said that he was staying there with a woman named Elisha Starlette, also from Minnesota. I was to meet her later during my stay."

"She's quite a hotsy-totsy, that there," said Charley, earning a look of reprove from C.A. Big Charley smiled sheepishly, then, poured himself another drink.

"On the evening in question, I sat at dinner with Otto Kahn, whom I believe you know." Lindbergh nodded.

"Prince Felix Yusopov was at our table as well. As you will see, he is a despicable little degenerate. He is a disgrace to Mother Russia."

The General's eyes blazed with indignation.

"Yusopov's behavior toward Mme. Starlette at dinner was abominable. He undressed her with his eyes and addressed her with such salacious comments that I was tempted to thrash the pervert right then and there. Perhaps, I should have. Now, I regret adhering to my sense of decorum," he said, his voice choking with emotion.

After a short respite, the General continued.

"Permit me to provide background before I describe the tragic ending of that evening," said the General, awaiting C.A.'s approval to proceed.

"Congressman, are you familiar with the *Rennen von Blut*, the 'Race of Blood,' that is held once a year at the Kurhaus Casino?"

Resisting the urge to say *nyet*, C.A. shook his head from side to side.

"The Race of Blood is a high-stakes gambling match, based on the French card game called *Trente et Quarante*, Thirty and Forty. Basically, Thirty and Forty is a combination of Black Jack and roulette. The Race of Blood is an invitation-only tournament with a field of sixty-four, that is divided into sixteen groups of four players. The entry fee is $250,000 each, for a total of $18 million at stake this year."

"Whew-ee, that is one humongous card game" exclaimed Big Charley. The General exchanged an amused glance with Lindbergh.

"The game is deceptively simple. The croupier deals out two rows with as many face-up cards as necessary for each row to total over 30 points. The row that totals closest to 31 points is the winner. There are many nuances in betting. Suffice it to say, players win if they bet on the correct color of the lead card in the winning row. The round ends when the stack of cards is depleted. The player with the most money at that point is declared the winner and moves to the next round. The others at the table are eliminated."

Kracilnikov raised his empty glass to Charley. The big man complied by refilling the tumbler to the brim.

"I apologize for being so long-winded. The Race of Blood progresses with players being eliminated until only two remain. I was eliminated in the penultimate round when that little weasel Felix cheated by moving my bet. The croupier did not penalize him and I lost," he paused, emitting a frustrated growl.

"One of the unique aspects of the Race of Blood is that the last two players engage in a challenge bet, where the players identify something of extreme value belonging to the other and challenges him to add it to the stakes. Over the years, the challenge items have ranged from vineyards in France, to an island in the Aegean Sea. But, never before has it sunk to the level of depravity that we saw this year," said the General his voice nearly cracking.

Big Charley and Ridge leaned forward in their seats.

"Of course, the gallery does not know the subject of the side bet until the game is over. That adds to the suspense and excitement. The sense of anticipation is heightened in this way. The crowd stays to the end just to find out.

"I sat in the gallery across from the Prince. I watched as Otto Kahn slipped a vial to Felix who then passed it to an accomplice. This strange behavior was done so swiftly and with such dexterity that I noticed it only because I was focused on Felix. Most of the spectators were getting their last drinks at the bar before settling in for the final play. Needless to say, I was most curious.

"My eyes were glued to the young countess with the vial. Just before the players returned to the table, Otto approached Mme. Starette and embraced her. During this hug, the countess poured some clear liquid into the other woman's glass. As the round progressed and the excitement built, Mme. Starette drank the tainted liquid freely," he paused to let the facts sink in, watching the faces of his audience.

"As the Race to Blood reached its conclusion, Mme. Starette's eyes became glassy and her movements seemed sluggish. When Felix won the last round, he jumped in celebration. I watched in disgust. Then, something perverse happened. Felix hugged Mme. Starette and pulled her toward the exit. She wobbled and leaned heavily on him as he half-dragged her from the room. It appeared to me that she was not in control of her faculties. She walked stiffly, as if she were under the influence of some substance.

"In the excitement of the final victory, this behavior went unnoticed. I moved toward her, but was blocked by a flood of spectators. While trying to pass, I heard the *chef de partie*, the game supervisor, remark that he had never seen a player challenge another player to wager a woman as the challenge bet. When his companion expressed incredulity, the *chef* repeated that Kahn put up the American woman (Mme. Starette) as his collateral and that Prince Felix had already collected his prize."

There was another pause and another raised glass. A sense of shock and concern filled the room.

"General, how can this happen in this day and age?" asked

Lindbergh who was visibly shaken.

"That night and later that morning, I inquired about the whereabouts of Mme. Starette and Prince Felix. After considerable prodding, the concierge told me in confidence that the Prince had departed and was accompanied by the American woman who was barely conscious. My subsequent inquiries have been fruitless. Due to the many palaces the Prince owns, no one knows where he and the lady could be. Such a dastardly crime; and there seems to be no recourse. God help her immortal soul," he said crossing himself.

"That is outrageous. Can't the American ambassador help us?" an animated Lindbergh said.

A forlorn look from the General was his answer.

$ $ $

C.A. was glad to leave Washington behind. The incredible news about Elisha and Sam was difficult to digest. He wondered whether he had time-lapsed into some prior century. How could an American woman be a prize in a card game in a casino in Germany and just disappear?

There was no trace of Elisha Starette. She could be in Russia or any one of a dozen other countries where Prince Felix Yusopov maintained palaces. No one knew whether she was even alive. According to the U.S. embassy in Berlin, until a family member registered a formal missing persons report, their hands were tied. Informal backchannel communications had proved unproductive.

To add injury to outrage, his friend, Sam Wurthels, was also missing. According to the desk clerk at Kurhaus of Baden-Baden, Mr. Wurthels had checked out after inquiring about rail transportation to Odessa on the Crimean Peninsula. The clerk recalled that Wurthels was agitated and frantic when he left.

All of Lindbergh's subsequent inquiries had been futile. There was no further evidence of the fate of Elisha and Sam. C.A. despaired of ever seeing them again. Reports on the Russian Prince were that he was cruel and capable of unspeakable depravity.

January 23, 1911 New York City, NY

*Actions are sometimes performed in a masterly
and most cunning way, while the direction of the actions is
deranged and dependent on various morbid impressions - it's like
a dream.*
~ Fyodor Dostevsky

With Blakey at his side, C.A. tried to keep a brisk pace down Lexington Avenue. Unfortunately, Blakey loved New York City almost as much as his master, but for a different reason. There were fire hydrants on every corner and Blakey stopped to sniff each one. The intermittent pace gave C.A. a chance to think. He realized why he liked New York City so much more than Washington D.C. New York City was vibrant, pulsing with activity. In the City, people made things, built things and added to the economic health of the country. In contrast, Washington D.C. was essentially the seat of government that specialized in pushing paper. If he had to choose between host and parasite, he would choose the host every time.

For the first time in months, he felt back on track. His meeting with David Phillips at Healy's Tavern had inspired him to re-examine his manuscript. The dread he felt toward the Fed was dissipating. The insights provided by Phillips cast certain matters in a new light. Since their last meeting, C.A. had devoted much time to restructuring his argument. He could not wait to share his latest draft with his new collaborator. He hoped that Phillips would have the time to give him solid editorial input.

Time was of the essence. The elections of the past fall had resulted in the complete replacement of the leadership in both chambers of Congress. That fact alone might provide the opportunity to derail the plans of the Money Trust. He doubted that the Democrats could be in the pocket of the Money Trust as much as his Republicans. Time would demonstrate that Mammon was bipartisan.

As Blakey tugged him toward his meeting, Lindbergh reflected on the fragility of the personal relationships in his life. The disturbing news about Sam's disappearance into the wilds of Russia was disconcerting. He worried about the fate of his longtime partner. Sam Wurthels had been missing for weeks. C.A. feared the worst. With limpid enthusiasm, he convinced himself that he should remain optimistic that Sam would somehow prevail and return.

His estrangement from his second wife Evy was as close to permanent as possible. Oddly, he did not miss her and rarely thought of her. He wished he could say the same about Anne Tracy Morgan. A day did not pass where he did not miss her company, wit, and intellect. His conflicting emotions about Anne were difficult to reconcile. C.A. could not have imagined twists and turns his life would take over the next year.

At least in David Phillips, he seemed to have found an intellect powerful and dedicated enough to assist him in completing his *magnum opus* – his great work on *Banking and Currency and the Money Trust*. His pace quickened; he did not want to be late for his 1 P.M. meeting with the brilliant author.

When he arrived at the corner of Lexington Avenue and 21st Street, he saw David walking in his direction toward a building with a large black and orange Princeton University flag. C.A. remembered David mentioning that he would be picking up his mail at the Princeton Club before their meeting.

Suddenly, a man accosted David. It looked like the disheveled young man from Healy's Tavern. He was yelling and gesticulating wildly. Barking his most menacing growl, Blakey pulled free and ran toward the young man. He was too late.

David stared at the lunatic with an uncomprehending look, as if to say, 'listen, buddy, you've got it wrong. I have no idea who you are.' A look of horror crossed David's face. C.A. saw the gun. The madman screamed, *"Here you go!"*

The gun flashed four, five, six times. David jerked backward with each blast of the pistol. Red splotches seeped through David's cream-colored suit. He crumpled to the ground.

The gunman watched Blakey running toward him with teeth bared. The man lifted the weapon, shouted, *"Here I go!"* There was a blast of gunfire. The gunman fell back with Blakey on him, gripping the man's arm. It was no use.

Lindbergh raced to help Blakey subdue the assassin. When he pulled the dog off the man, he saw that the lunatic was dead from a gunshot to his brain. C.A. rushed to David.

"Hold on, David, an ambulance is coming," C.A. pleaded. He could tell by the waning glimmer of David's blue eyes that he knew that he was dying.

As he was hoisted into the ambulance, he said, *"I could've won against two bullets,"* he said. *"But not against six.* [50]*"*

$ $ $

"If you wasn't a Congressman, I'd have to send your mutt to the pound as a material witness," said the detective from the 13th Precinct.

C.A. did not know if the man was serious and did not much care. As a lawyer, Lindbergh knew that he was obligated to cooperate. However, after three hours of redundant questioning, his patience was stretched to the breaking point. He wanted to be with his friend at the hospital. This detective was the third person to ask him for his recollection of the attack. C.A. rubbed Blakey behind the ear and wondered how much longer he would be there.

Eventually, policemen realized that they should not trifle with a Congressman. They brought him into the lieutenant's office to wait. This was better than the windowless witness room. There was coffee for him and water for Blakey, but the growing darkness outside increased his anxiety.

Blakey's ears perked up before approaching shadows against the frosted glass panel of the office door told him that they were about to have company. A tall man wearing the uniform of an officer entered without knocking.

"I'm Lieutenant Leonetti. This is my office. These accommodations may not be up to your usual standards, but they are the best we have under the circumstances. I'm sorry that we have kept you here for so long. Your information has been critical to the successful conclusion of our investigation. The details from your meeting several weeks ago about a young man with disheveled hair carrying a violin case led us to a rooming house on East 19th Street."

"Please tell me if you've uncovered any reason for this heinous crime. David . . . Mr. Phillips . . . did not know this man. I'm sure of it," said C.A.

"You are right about that, Sir. We found the assailant's diary. His name was Fitzhugh Coyle Goldsborough, an unemployed violist who worked last with the Pittsburgh Symphony. He was from a rich family. He attended Harvard and was an accomplished musician, played in Paris, Vienna, and throughout Europe. Then, something snapped. Apparently, he became obsessed with your friend because of a novel he had written."

"You are saying that he shot Phillips because of a book?"

"Exactly, it's all in here," said the Lieutenant opening a frayed volume that bore the title Diary in faded letters.

"He was enraged that Mr. Phillips wrote a book ridiculing and defaming his younger sister. Of course, Phillips did no such thing. Goldsborough confided to his diary that he decided to kill a man he had never met. However, Goldsborough claimed that Phillips insulted her in his latest novel, calling her a 'fashionable noodle-head' who was promiscuous. Because of these imagined slights, he claimed that Phillips 'is an enemy to society.' Goldsborough wrote. 'He is my enemy.' In his twisted mind, he decided to kill David Phillips. He has been stalking him since he came to New York about two months ago. Today was the day he finally worked up the rage to kill Mr. Phillips."

Lindbergh sat in stunned silence. He mourned the attack on a man of integrity, brilliance, and courage. He rubbed his eyes trying to expunge the scene on the sidewalk. Two lives, polar opposites, shattered by a fusillade of hot lead. It made no sense.

"Oh, one more thing. Your friend is at Bellevue Hospital. He survived the surgery. He is in critical condition. They don't know if he will live."

"May I leave now?" asked Lindbergh in a weak and weary voice, suddenly drained of all energy.

"Yes, of course. I'll have one of the men take you out the back to avoid the tabloid vultures. We will take you to your hotel."

Lindbergh woke up the next morning with the worst headache

ever. It felt like his head had been battered by one of the stamp hammers that Big Charley used to mark his logs. Blakey looked at him, his big brown eyes oozing sympathy. C.A. took a drink of water and some analgesic powder. He hurried to the lobby to check the newspaper. The headlines blared an account of the attack.

On page three he read the dreaded news. David Graham Phillips had died from his wounds. The words seared him. It was nothing compared to the glib, disrespectful account that appeared in the newsletter of the Princeton Club which recorded the incident as follows: *"David Graham Phillips, (class of) '87, editor, publicist and novelist, was shot six times today as he approached the Princeton Club, by Fitzhugh Coyle Goldsborough, a Harvard man...*[51]*"*

1911 Little Falls, MN

Admit nothing. Explain nothing.
~ Senator Nelson W. Aldrich

The dark winter clouds blocking the sky mirrored the Congressman's mood. He was lost in gloom. The Minnesota winter matched his life – cold and lonely. The view from his office in Little Falls did nothing to lift his spirits. His dull eyes stared at the pale apparition reflected back at him. A gust of frigid air penetrated the dried, window caulking. Outside, all was still; only the chimney smoke drifted across the tundra-like landscape. He thought dourly that even the smoke was in danger of freezing.

He was having trouble accepting the murder of David Graham Phillips. The affable writer had been minutes away from meeting with C.A. in their mutual quest to thwart the Money Trust when he was gunned down. Lindbergh's brief relationship with Phillips was a rare blessing. To witness the lunatic fire six bullets into Phillips was traumatic. The amount of blood on the sidewalk made him physically ill.

A few days after the murder, Lieutenant Leonetti called him with a follow up report. The police had uncovered evidence that Fitzhugh Goldsborough was prone to violence and suffered from delusions. Conjuring up a perceived insult based on a character in one of David's novels, the madman became obsessed with Phillips. After stalking him for months, the killer finally gunned him down in cold blood before taking his own life. What a waste.

In the aftermath of the tragedy, Lindbergh lost his desire to complete his manuscript. Rumors that the Money Trust was planning a massive educational program and media blitz, depressed him further. The frozen landscape reminded him of his friend Sam, who was somewhere in Russia trying to extricate Elisha from the clutches of the degenerate Felix Yusopov.

His attention was drawn to his desk. He picked up a photograph of Sam and him from one of their hunting trips. With their arms draped and their shotguns held in the crooks of their elbows, they were the picture of happiness. He offered up a prayer for Sam's safety.

"Sir, there's a gentleman visitor from Brainerd here to see you. He does not have an appointment. What shall I tell him?"

"Carrie, do you even have to ask? I'm sure this gentleman has made a difficult journey in this ghastly weather to see his congressman. We will not disappoint him. Please show him in."

Lindbergh tugged his vest and ran his fingers through his hair trying to look presentable. He walked past the desk across the room to greet an elderly constituent who Carrie was leading into the room.

"Congressman, may I present Commander Hyatt from Brainerd."

"C.A. Lindbergh, sir. Welcome," said C.A. offering his hand.

The old man recoiled. His eyes blazed as he turned toward Carrie.

"Madame, what sort of cruel trick are you playing on an old man?"

Pointing his cane menacingly at C.A., he shouted, "This is not C.A. Lindbergh. I met the man personally. This is an imposter. Where is Lindbergh?"

"I'm sure you are mistaken, Sir. This is most definitely Congressman Lindbergh. I've worked for him these last five years. This gentleman is C.A. Lindbergh," said Carrie, a bit flustered.

"Sir, please have a seat. Maybe you and I can untangle this situation," said C.A. to the irritated man.

"Please have a seat," he said motioning toward a comfortable armchair. Confused, the elderly man allowed himself to be guided to the chair.

"Carrie, please get Commander Hyatt a nice hot tea."

Hyatt's head swiveled as Carrie left the room. He grumbled something in Swedish.

"Now, Commander, you say that you met C.A. Lindbergh before. May I ask you to describe the circumstances of that meeting?"

The old gentleman sat ramrod straight with his arms crossed and looked at C.A. as if he were evaluating a battlefield. He withdrew his pocket watch, checking the time. There was an awkward silence that lasted until Carrie entered carrying a tray with tea service. He sipped from his teacup with his pinky rising in the air like an aristocrat.

"I met candidate Lindbergh in the summer 1906. We invited him to address our veteran group of Indian and Civil war veterans. It was at the schoolhouse and my wife, Victoria, God rest her soul, made cookies. Mr. Lindbergh was gracious enough to serve the cookies to our members," said Hyatt, with a look of disdain and the lack of cookies on the tea tray.

"That Mr. Lindbergh was several inches shorter than you, Sir. I had several private conversations with him; that's how I know that you are not the man I spoke with. Now, if Mr. Lindbergh is not here, please let me know. I have a long ride home."

Lindbergh sat back in his chair and rubbed his chin.

"Commander Hyatt, I think I can clear this up with one question. Did you give the candidate known to you as Lindbergh anything?"

"Yes, I did, but only Mr. Lindbergh would know what it is," said Mr. Hyatt.

"It was a Bible. The very Bible I use each time I am sworn to office," said C.A. triumphantly.

Commander Hyatt shot him a skeptical glance.

"You may have guessed correctly. However, I am sure that you are not the man that I gave a valuable Bible to."

Hyatt fidgeted in his seat and placed his hands on the armrests preparing to rise. Halfway up, his eyes narrowed. C.A. turned to see what the old man was staring at.

"There, there, that's Lindbergh," he said in an excited voice. "That's the fellow who took the Bible from me!"

In a flash of remembrance, C.A. slapped himself on the forehead. The picture of Sam and C.A. on the hunting trip was propped right in the center of his desk.

"Of course, now I remember. My campaign manager Sam Wurthels was with me that night. I had already given five different campaign speeches that day and my voice was kind of raw. Sam offered to give my speech and I let him," said Lindbergh. "It sounds quite juvenile all these years later. I am profoundly sorry, Commander Hyatt. We should not have played that trick on you and your veterans."

C.A. brought the photograph over to Commander Hyatt. Pointing to the hunter standing to the right, C.A. said, "Is this the man you gave the Bible to?"

Peering over his spectacles, Commander Hyatt said, "Yes, that's the man. That's Lindbergh!"

"Sir, that is Sam Wurthels my former campaign manager and one of my dearest friends."

"Where is he? I want to see him and ask him directly," said the old man.

"I'm afraid that's not possible," said C.A.

"Well, where is he? What have you done with him?"

"We have not done anything to him. He's traveling somewhere in Russia trying to liberate a lady friend who was abducted."

"This makes no sense. I must leave," said Mr. Hyatt.

Carrie entered the room. She was carrying a large framed photograph.

"Please don't leave Commander Hyatt," she said. "Here is a photograph of Congressman Lindbergh with President Roosevelt, signed 'To my friend, C.A. Lindbergh, Always Yours, Theodore Roosevelt.' When you look at this picture, there is no mistaking that this is the Congressman," said Carrie, holding the picture up next to C.A.'s face.

The elder gentleman collapsed back into his chair with a sigh of resignation. C.A. reached into his desk drawer and removed a tin. Opening it, he presented it to Mr. Hyatt.

"Would you like a Minnesota Monster cookie, Sir?"

$ $ $

While Warburg was in Chicago launching the education program under the auspices of the National Citizens' League for the Promotion of a Sound Banking System, Otto was in New York City with Senator Aldrich preparing the report of the National Monetary Commission that would come to be known as the Aldrich Plan. It identified the emergency issuance of currency as the top priority for monetary reform. The Panic of 1907 and other so-called panics were the result of banks being incapable of returning deposits to customers when demanded. Runs on banks threatened to collapse the entire financial system.

The Aldrich Plan addressed this problem by proposing the establishment of a Federal Reserve Association composed of regional groups of national banks that would have the power to issue currency when there was an emergency. To avoid the danger of banks issuing too much money, the Plan empowered only those banks with outstanding bank notes secured by government bonds would be given the privilege of issuing emergency currency. In essence, without saying it, the Aldrich Plan attempted to create a central bank by indirection.

Despite having spent years working on monetary reform, Senator Aldrich failed to appreciate the implications of establishing a central bank. Otto explained in layman's terms that the authority to issue currency increased the supply of money available and the power over the discount rate amounted to the power to set interest that could be charged. The combination of authority over the money supply and interest rates would give the Federal Reserve Association unprecedented power over the economy.

In accordance with the ultimate scheme, Otto suggested that the Report state directly that, " *"Such a power is not now possessed by any institution in the United States.*[52]"

$ $ $

"These are the best cookies I've ever eaten," said Commander Hyatt. "What's in them?"

"That, sir, is a family secret that will have to await disclosure when Mother Lindbergh publishes her cookbook."

They shared a laugh. The ice had been broken.

"So tell me, Commander, what brings you to Little Falls in the dead of winter?"

"It's a long story that starts in Sweden. My father served in Parliament with your father. When your father was accused of embezzlement, my father was the head of the committee assigned to run the investigation. He uncovered a ledger in your father's office detailing all of the financial irregularities. Your father protested that he was being framed, but the committee voted to sanction him and forward the case for prosecution. Rather than address the charges, your father fled to America."

"My father was innocent," said Lindbergh in a steely voice.

"Yes, I know. The ledger book was a forgery planted in your father's office by one of his enemies. Sadly, the damage had been done. Your father was already on a ship with you and your mother."

"My father made it his mission in life to clear your father's name. We came to America to find your father and exonerate him. Unfortunately, my father was stricken on the voyage and was gravely ill when we arrived in New York. I was twenty when we arrived in the United States. With father convalescing and my mother tending to him, I joined the Union Army."

Lindbergh stifled a yawn, glanced at Carrie and smiled to the Commander.

"I'm sorry for being so long-winded, but I'm getting to the point of my visit."

He took a cookie and ladled it into his tea with his spoon, then slurped it down.

"Where was I? Oh, yes, the Union Army. After officer training, I was assigned to an elite unit that functioned as couriers for the Treasury Department. Toward the end of the war, Treasury Secretary Chase sent us on a secret mission to deliver currency printing plates and gold certificates to a national bank in San Francisco.

"We took a northwestern route west through Fort Ripley, Minnesota. I was in the rear guard carrying the certificates. Then disaster hit.

"A rebel spy within our ranks, a fellow named Aloysius Gleeson, betrayed us and we were ambushed. There was a dreadful firefight with massive carnage. I raced up to the front to help my commanding officer. His horse had been shot out from under him. He was pinned down behind the carcass when he saw me ride up. He shouted to me to ride like hell to Fort Ripley for reinforcements. That was the last I saw of him or any of our detachment.

"It took three days to get back to the fort. I was hounded the entire way by rebel cavalry. When I finally made it to the fort, the Commanding Officer, a colonel from New Hampshire, told me that General Lee had surrendered at Appomattox. The war was over and he was heading home. I pleaded with him for help. He said that there were no troops. With the news of Lee's surrender, many soldiers just left. It was total chaos.

"I was trying to persuade some soldiers to join me for a rescue mission, when a messenger handed me a telegram. My father was on his deathbed and my mother needed me. I know that I was wrong to do what I did next, but I was young and surrounded by chaos. I rationalized that it was now five days since the ambush and no one from the mission had returned. Thinking about the dire situation I left, I concluded that they must all be dead. I left for home.

"When I arrived my father was barely holding on. He told me that the biggest regret of his life was his role in the injustice done to your father. He despaired that he would be unable to rectify the wrong and begged me to accomplish this for him."

Lindbergh regarded the elder gentleman with a skeptical look. He really had no idea where Hyatt's story was heading.

"That's quite a story. What does it have to do with me?"

"It has everything to do with you. My father died in my arms with me promising to rectify the injustice done to your father. While I was on bereavement leave, I received a telegram from Treasury Secretary Chase advising that they finally sent a unit to the ambush site and all they found was the burnt remnants of the convoy. I was ordered to report to New York City for immediate embarkation to Stockholm, Sweden.

"Due to my language skills, I was assigned to the American Embassy to assist the Swedish Ministry of Finance with a counterfeiting problem. I know that this is going to sound odd, but with all the confusion surrounding the ambush, my father's death, the end of the war and everything else, I left immediately. I completely forgot about my saddle and tack supplies, including a leather satchel that I thought contained instructions for installation of the currency printing plates. The Army told me to leave everything behind and they would come to retrieve it. Of course, after President Lincoln was assassinated there was more chaos. That equipment lay abandoned in my family barn for decades."

C.A. looked at his watch and stood. "This is all very interesting Commander Hyatt, but...."

"Please, sir, just a few minutes please. I'm almost finished," pleaded Commander Hyatt.

Giving the man a raised eyebrow look that he used to reserve for his children at bedtime, Lindbergh sat down.

"Years later, after a lengthy military career, I returned home when my mother passed away. While clearing out and selling off her possessions, I came across my old Army saddle and tack. It was buried in dust and grit, cracked and useless.

"Under the saddle I found the leather satchel. It, too, had deteriorated and broke when I lifted it. I nearly collapsed from shock when I saw the contents."

At this point, the Commander indulged in another cookie.

"Well, stop dawdling," cried an exasperated Carrie, "Tell us what was in it!"

"It contained one hundred gold certificates that were in $10,000 denominations. These bills entitle the bearer to redeem each of them for $10,000 in hard gold," said the old man matter-of-factly.

"What did you do?" asked Carrie.

"I contacted the Department of the Army. They referred me to the Department of the Treasury who sent me to the War Department who sent me back to the Army and on and on. After four years of communications going round and round in circles, they stopped answering my letters. Finally, one of my friends in the War Department, a general that I had worked with, told me, off the record, to give it away.

"One night, after praying for guidance, I had a dream about my father on his deathbed. Then, I knew that I could use the certificates to fulfill his final wish. I spent the next day rolling the gold certificates into small tubes and inserted them underneath the binding of a large family Bible. It so happened, that candidate Lindbergh was scheduled to appear before our veteran's group. That night, I took Mr. Lindbergh aside . . . well, the fake Mr. Lindbergh . . . and gave him the Bible, explaining my father's wish and the secret of the Bible binding. And, that's the whole truth."

28

December 4, 1911 Washington DC

The pending Aldrich measure by far is the most daring and dangerous scheme ever introduced into Congress.
~ Alfred Owen Crozier

Lindbergh settled into his seat on the train heading to Washington. He had to admit that Commander Hyatt had certainly weaved a spell-binding story. If C.A. had read his story in a book, he would have questioned the sanity of the author. And yet, the old man's story had a fair amount of verisimilitude. In a quirky way, it had a ring of truth.

After more than five years as a Congressman, he had definitely seen that the federal government was capable of mind-boggling ineptitude and dysfunction. However, to disregard one million dollars in gold certificates seemed improbable even for the federal government. On the other hand, perhaps, Commander Hyatt was delusional. Lindbergh would find out soon enough.

Since the burglary, the Bible had been locked in his office safe. It had seen the light of day only when used to swear in the Congressman. When C.A. and Blake arrived at the office, he closed the door behind him and went directly to the safe. The Bible was exactly where he had left it.

It appeared to be exactly what it was – a family Bible. Rotating it front to back, he shrugged; nothing seemed out of the ordinary. Carefully resting the pages on the desk, he lifted the cover up like eagles' wings. The binding along the spine remained flush. There was no separation. He could see nothing under it.

Reaching into his pocket, he withdrew a tweezers. C.A. squinted as he wedged the pointed tips under the leather binder. They caught something stiff. Squeezing tightly, he pulled gently. There was solid resistance, then a slight give. He tugged to no avail. Sitting back, he rubbed his eyes. Was it his imagination or did he see little circles in the darkness coiled up like larvae in the binding? Should he slit the binding with his pocketknife? Would that be sacrilegious? He was wasting precious time. He would wait until another time. Perhaps, he needed a steam kettle to release the glue. That would be his next attempt.

Right now he had more important matters to handle. Several months had passed since the Aldrich Plan had been disseminated. The actual Aldrich Plan was encompassed in legislation that was attached to the report of the National Monetary Commission. To Lindbergh, the so-called reform bill was a traitorous capitulation to the Money Trust. He vowed to fight it with every ounce of energy he could muster. He arrived in the Capital in early December to prepare for the opening of the 62nd Congress. C.A. spent the next few days crafting a resolution.

"Mr. Speaker, I rise to present Resolution 314."

"Congressman Lindbergh, please describe in short, non-adjectival English the nature of your resolution," said the Speaker.

"Yes, sir, Mr. Speaker, the purpose of Resolution 314 is to authorize a congressional investigation of the Money Trust."

The Speaker rolled his eyes and banged his gavel, "Resolution 314 is referred to the Rules Committee."

In the days of Uncle Joe Cannon's reign, referral to the Rules Committee meant an un-ceremonial death to the measure. Now, under the new leadership, the measure might actually progress to meaningful action. During his battles against Cannon with the Republican Insurgents, C.A. had developed relationships with his colleagues on the Democrat side of the aisle. There was a strong feeling of mutual respect that C.A. intended to utilize.

He spent the next weeks nurturing members of the Rules Committee with excellent result. The decision of the Committee exceeded his wildest dreams. On the basis of his resolution, two subcommittees were established. The first, under the chairmanship of Representative Arsène Pujo from Louisiana's 7th District, was charged with the task of investigating the Money Trust.

Pujo was a no-nonsense lawyer who had recently been appointed to chair the House Committee on Banking and Currency. He was a well-built man with dark hair and thick mustache. Although he was short, he had a powerful, domineering personality. Like most politicians he could be charming when the situation called for it. Lindbergh and Pujo had a common passion, both loved to hunt. On one occasion while hunting in the Louisiana canebrakes, Pujo impressed C.A. by carrying a shotgun with the stock sawed off and using it like a pistol. C.A. was comfortable working with Arsène to investigate the Money Trust.

The second subcommittee, under the chairmanship of Carter Glass from Virginia's 6th District, was charged with revision of the nation's monetary system. Representative Glass had been a prominent journalist and newspaper editor before entering politics.

At 5' 4" and barely one hundred pounds, he was headstrong, bigoted, and ambitious. He walked around on tiptoes to avoid jarring his sensitive stomach. One of few antebellum Southerners in Congress, Glass was a force among Democrats. Carter Glass never trusted the independent-thinking Lindbergh. Nevertheless, as 1911 ended, C.A.'s work was finally bearing fruit.

Today was the day that the committee was scheduled to vote on the fate of the Aldrich Plan. A positive vote would move the bill forward for consideration by the entire House. C.A. feared that the tentacles of the Money Trust were so pervasive that passage was a strong possibility. His best chance to defeat the monstrous bill was in the committee. C.A. was excited as he approached the committee room. After hours of debate, he succeeded.

"It's a miracle! The Aldrich Plan has been derailed. The Committee ruled that it will be delayed until the Money Trust investigation has been completed. Praise the Lord we have won!"

Rarely, if ever, had C.A. experienced such joy as a legislator. Joy, that was the only way to describe it. Years of effort against the Aldrich Plan had at long last produced victory. As C.A. walked down the halls of Congress, friendly colleagues slapped him on the back, or shouted their congratulations. An equal number gave him dour looks of disdain.

When he entered his office, his staff stood and applauded. Someone handed him a bottle of champagne which he opened and poured for all.

"A toast. Your unstinting efforts led to the defeat of an evil bill that would have given the Money Trust control over our currency and banking system. You are the best support any Congressman has ever had," said C.A., nearly overcome with emotion. "I thank you all from the bottom of my heart. Cheers."

Not one to miss the import of a well-deserved victory, Lindbergh thought of the future and how he would treasure this moment, recalling the smiling faces, clinking glasses and sense of satisfaction.

So swept up in the euphoria of victory, he contemplated sharing it with Anne; then, thought better of it.

29

June 1913, New York City, NY

The LORD doesn't see things the way you see them.
People judge by outward appearance,
But, the LORD looks at the heart.
~ 1 Samuel 16:7

The defeat of the Aldrich Plan was the crowning achievement of 1911. After the celebration, Lindbergh and his staff hastily packed for a well-deserved Christmas holiday. The office was so anxious to leave that all open matters were crammed into filing cabinets. There would be ample time in the New Year to address issues that seemed less important than they did the day before. One of the staffers placed the Hyatt bible back in the safe under some charts from the Office of the Controller.

Fresh off his defeat of the Aldrich Plan, C.A. was the darling of the speaking circuit. He spent every spare moment perfecting his manuscript. Before he knew it, he had to run for re-election. Except for one fleeting instant when he was being sworn in after another victory in 1912, the memory of Commander Hyatt's tale had faded to the far recesses of his mind.

Lindbergh had entered another phase of his career and lacked the time and the interest to put the tale to rest. The further from the telling, the more preposterous it seemed. By temperament Lindbergh preferred to move forward, not back. In any event, momentous opportunity was in the air.

The spring of 1913 had been relatively quiet as the new Congress found its pace. Now, after a remarkable week, he was back in New York City. Despite the fact that it was Friday the thirteenth, he felt buoyant.

He was much too grounded to be superstitious. His office called him at the Waldorf Astoria Hotel advising him that one of the causes that he advocated had passed a significant hurdle.

The U.S. Senate Committee on Woman Suffrage reported favorably on a proposed amendment to the U.S. Constitution providing women with the right to vote. Progress certainly came grudgingly. Who knew when the amendment would be adopted? All he knew was that the granting of voting rights to half the population was inevitable. A deep breath fed a feeling of satisfaction for his role in advocating for women's suffrage.

A brisk walk down Fifth Avenue on a sunny day with temperatures in the mid-seventies was a perfect complement to his mood. His briefcase contained several copies of his book, *Banking and Currency and the Money Trust*. His thoughts drifted to several days earlier when he had received the first box of books from the publisher.

After years of work, the sensations of looking, smelling and handling the fresh copies were indescribable. The blue cover with the light gold lettering set the proper tone. He felt a strange and bittersweet sensation that authors experience when their work finally appears in print.

The nervous tremor in his hands when he picked up the first book surprised him. A slight crack of the spine preceded the chemical smell of fresh ink. With his thumb and forefinger he shuffled through the pages of the book. The chapter headings and page breaks swept past like images on a nickelodeon machine. The black letters danced and swirled. His eyes rested on the Dedication. His work was dedicated to the Public. He hoped that the message of his book warning against the takeover of the American currency would capture the attention of his fellow citizens. Despite the defeat of the Aldrich Plan, the enemy was relentless.

With mixed feelings, he strode toward his rendezvous with Anne Tracy Morgan with a vague hope of repairing his broken relationship with her. He knew that in this endeavor also the odds were not in his favor. He had said some awful things to her when he learned after years of involvement, that she was the daughter of the personification of the Money Trust.

In Lindbergh's eyes, J. Pierpont Morgan was the epitome of

Mammon. At first, he was devastated by Anne's betrayal of trust. He berated himself mercilessly. To make matters worse, he had let her into his bed. They had been intimate for years and he believed that he loved her. Yet, it was all built on a lie – and not a lie about something inconsequential. It went to the essence of their relationship. He wondered how she had lived with the lie.

Even a granite mountain erodes over time. The effects of heat and cold, the incessant winds and glacial degradation will reduce the highest mountain. Despite the appellation, even the Zeus of Wall Street was not immortal. C.A. thought how remarkable it is that people like Morgan appear invincible. In life they seem to prosper. But, with one divine exception, the grim reaper collects every life. J. Pierpont Morgan was the latest icon to succumb to the reaper's scythe. On March 31, 1913 Anne's father died in his sleep of heart failure at the age of seventy five during a stay at the Grand Hotel in Rome, Italy.

When C. A. heard the news his heart went out to Anne. He had experienced the loss of his father and paradoxically shared in her loss. After wrestling with his emotions, C.A. cast aside his own hurt and drafted an empathetic condolence letter to his former paramour. In reply, he received a printed note card signed by Elsie de Wolfe of all people. Despite his disappointment, C.A. chalked it up to the masses of condolences Anne undoubtedly received.

As he read the eulogies for the man, Lindbergh's perception of Pierpont Morgan softened. By all accounts, he personally saved the Treasury of the United States from financial collapse in the Panic of 1893 by pledging his personal fortune to support the financial system of the United States when the government proved incapable.

Lindbergh read with interest about Morgan's extensive art collection and philanthropic donations. C.A. was amused by an interesting tidbit which appeared in one of the financial periodicals – the song "*Jingle Bells*" was written by Pierpont's uncle James. A smile came to Lindbergh's lips as he imagined a juvenile Morgan singing the famed carol at the top of his lungs while traversing the back roads of his native Connecticut in a one-horse open sleigh. Lindbergh fondly recalled his own youthful sleigh rides through the forests of Minnesota.

When C.A. read the accounts of the funeral in New York City, he studied images of the funeral cortege to get a glimpse of Anne. Blurred shadows in windows of the horse-drawn carriages precluded any identification. The funeral took place in St. George's Episcopal Church at Stuyvesant Square where Morgan was a senior warden and treasurer. Thousands of people, the curious and respectful, lined the streets around the church to pay their respects to the famous financier. The memorial service was remarkable in its simplicity.

After the funeral, a procession of hearses and carriages traveled past a closed New York Stock Exchange; an honor normally reserved for deceased Presidents. The family and Morgan's intimates traveled to the Cedar Hill Cemetery in his birthplace of Hartford, Connecticut where he was buried in the Morgan family mausoleum. After the funeral an expression of gratitude was issued by Elsie de Wolfe who was identified as a close personal friend of Anne Tracy Morgan and a prominent designer of interior spaces for the ultra-wealthy.

Walking out of Grand Central Station, Lindbergh turned south toward the Morgan Mansion on 36th and Madison Avenue. After a respectable period of time after her father's passing, C.A. had communicated with Anne and arranged a meeting at her home where they first met when he was a rookie Congressman. In his most circumspective moments he had to admit that he still harbored feelings toward her. She suited his temperament perfectly. Being introspective people, they both enjoyed the rigors of academic-type research and writing on complex issues. Anne was his intellectual equal and he savored their theoretical discussions.

He also felt that they were physically compatible. His body anticipated a return to their regular dalliances. C.A. was ready to resume where they left off. He hoped she would willingly return to their prior relationship. As far as he was concerned, once he accepted her failure to reveal her identity, there was no impediment to going back to the way they were. Time, extraneous events and the completion of the book, their cherished project, had given him a new and guardedly optimistic perspective. Unfortunately for C.A., he had no clue about what she had done over the last few years and how her interests had changed.

As he turned onto 36th street, a few blocks from her mansion, he spied a street vendor selling flowers. The floral fragrance helped to mask the acrid odor of mud, horse manure and urine that wafted from the street. C.A. selected Anne's favorite, a nosegay of lavender flowers. At the mansion's door, he was received by a severe-looking doorman who eyed the flowers disdainfully.

C.A. followed him into the study which was redolent with floral arrangements, some as tall as a baby elephant. Lindbergh regarded his bouquet sheepishly and thought, of course, the manse is no longer ruled by the cigar-puffing Pierpont; it had been transformed into a feminine domain under Anne's hand.

The afternoon light streamed through the study through gauzy sheers. The windows were framed with window scarves and valances in bright blues and yellows. Gone were the dark flocked coverings. In their stead was an oyster-with-blue-pinstripe paper, punctuated by lavender nosegays similar to the one he was holding. The feel of the room was dramatically recast by the change to bright, flowery wallpaper. The strong masculinity that suited J.P. Morgan was replaced by an atmosphere of ethereal femininity.

Left in the room alone, Lindbergh perused the artwork. He was drawn to a small watercolor bearing the title, *Sappho and Erinna in a Garden at Mytilene.* The image consisted of Sappho embracing her fellow poet Erinna in a garden at Mytilene on the island of Lesbos. Wearing a crown of laurel, a dark-complected Sappho adopts a masculine pose as she kisses the feminine Erinna who is painted in soft, flesh tones, and whose robe has slipped off her shoulder. A pair of turtle doves, symbolic of their love, sits on a wall the behind the two women poets, mimicking the kiss. The picture shocked Lindbergh who blushed.

"What do you think?" asked Anne, entering the room. "Hasn't Elsie just transformed Pierpont's stodgy, old study into a garden of delights? You know, after his death, it took us a month to expunge the smell of cigar smoke from this room."

"It's good to see you, Anne," he stammered. "Oh, . . . I almost forgot. These are for you."

"Thank you. They are lovely," she said with mild surprise. In their time together he had not exactly showered her with flowers. It was not in his nature. She placed them on a table next to a gigantic vase filled with a variety of aromatic lilies and birds-of-paradise.

"Anne, I've missed you. I want to tell you how sorry I am . . ."

"No need. I'm over it."

Before he could respond, she whirled and said, "We have new additions to our art collection for this room. This is Pierpont's last acquisition," she said pointing to a painting on the wall to the left of the desk.

Unsure, Lindbergh moved toward the two-foot high oil painting. It depicted a young woman in flowing robes in a supplicatory position before a massive, golden statue of a seated, youthful man. Her hands are clutching desperately at his knee. With an imploring look, her face is upturned toward his face which stares down impassively. He is seated on a pinnacle high above distant mountains and is framed by a night sky lit by stars. A bag of gold is in his right hand which is outstretched, unreachable, above her.

"It's called '*The Worship of Mammon*.' Pierpont adored the irony of the woman forsaking the bag of gold for the love of the deity Mammon. It was . . ."

"Anne, stop," C.A. interrupted with quiet insistence. "I came here to apologize and to give you this."

He handed her a copy of their book. She paused and accepted the gift almost reverently.

"Oh, Ridgy, you did it. It's finished, it's published. Why, it's beautiful," said Anne, her eyes beaming.

She sat on a bench and motioned for him to join her. As if she were handling one of Pierpont's rare illuminated manuscripts, she leafed through the book. She searched and found the dedication page.

"Dedicated to the Public. That's a nice touch. I like it."

"The most incredible thing happened when I got the galleys from the printer and the book was one step away from reality," said C.A., pausing for effect.

Anne smiled as if she already knew what he was about to say. He stammered, "You know, . . . you know that I was offered two million dollars to abandon publication of our book. Hully gee, that's a lot of money where I come from. But, you already know that I rejected that bribe, telling them, *'The point is, Banking and Currency no longer belongs to me. It is public property, and the public has a right to every copy it can use.*'³³"

Anne nodded, giving him the same look that his mother used to give him when he would rant about some juvenile injustice. Her eyes and posture said 'why does that attempted bribe surprise you?'

C.A. reached toward her and opened the book to a page bearing his inscription to her. As she read, Anne withdrew a handkerchief from her wristband and sniffled into it.

"You are much too generous, Ridge. You surely could have written it without my help. I was hardly instrumental in formulating your arguments..." she said.

"I mean every word. You made it possible and I am forever in your debt."

He reached for her hand. Anne looked at his hand and let him hold her's. She sighed deeply. Her eyes went to his and he saw confusion and fear. What was it?

"Anne, I know I behaved like an ass. Now, I understand. You sincerely believe that the Money Trust is destroying the average person. I reacted heinously when I learned that you were Morgan's daughter. I felt betrayed. But, now, I realize that none of us can select the family we are born to. You did not share his avaricious heart. Your heart is true."

Her hand touched his cheek with such tenderness that an ember of hope sparked in his chest. Yet, a hint of something, sadness, pity lingered in her gaze.

"Anne, I miss you. Please forgive me. I know that it may take time, but, I want you back. I want what we had. Please..."

C.A. had shifted partially off the bench and his knee touched the floor. He paused about to offer her his heart. Just then, a loud commotion in the hallway broke the spell.

"Olivia, if you don't let me in there, I will hurt you. Get out of my way!" screamed an incensed voice.

Anne muttered inaudibly as both the doors slammed open. A girl in a striped maid's uniform back-pedaled into the room. She was trying to prevent an older, smaller woman from entering the room. Anne and Ridge froze.

"Get out of my way, you stupid little strumpet!" snarled Elsie de Wolfe. She grabbed the girl's chestnut hair and whipped her aside like an enraged banshee. Without warning, Elsie raced across the room and kissed Anne flush on the lips. She took Anne's hand from C.A. and thrust it into the top of her low cut dress. Elsie pressed herself against

Anne with such passion that C.A. had to look away, embarrassed.

His gaze fell on the girl. It was Olivia, the girl with the apple basket in Grand Central Station from so long ago. Then, in a jolt of recognition, he realized that she was the same girl he had seen on that afternoon at the Clearinghouse building when he had been showered with broken plate glass. Confusion and shock showed on his face. Olivia mouthed 'I'm so sorry' to him.

Lindbergh straightened up and tried to get Anne's attention. Elsie and Anne were so engaged in a passionate kiss and embrace that he could have been one of the massive vases for all that they cared. Elsie began to moan loudly as she pulled Anne onto the couch. C.A. was struck motionless. Startled, shocked and enraged, he stood there watching the appalling scene. Then, he felt a tug on his arm. It was Olivia, trying to remove him from the room. Numb, he followed her lead.

In the foyer, he looked back wistfully at the doors to the study.

"What just happened?"

"Well, sir, you know how you should never get between a mama lion and her buck lion? You trespassed on the territory of one mean, jealous lioness. Miss Elsie is a *femme* who considers Anne hers. They have been a couple together for the last year. You can see from her behavior that she will fight tooth and nail to keep you away from Lady Anne."

"I've lost everything, haven't I?" said Lindbergh to no one in particular. He had no idea how prophetic these words were.

December 1913 Washington, D.C.

> History records that the money changers have
> used every form of abuse, intrigue, deceit, and violent
> means possible to maintain their control over governments by
> controlling money and it's issuance.
> ~ James Madison

A bright green fir wreath encircled the brass knocker of the tall black door to the mansion that stood in a row of similar buildings on a quiet side street within walking distance of the Capitol. Pine rope punctuated with red ribbons framed the door to the mansion that bore no signage. The Lakota Club was a private enclave for Washington's purveyors of influence and power. With an exclusive clientele who paid handsomely for the privilege of membership, it was a place where momentous events were orchestrated. The club had been established as a home away from home by the New York banking interests after the Panic of 1893.

J.P. Morgan initiated the project with the purchase of the mansion on 16th Street in the shadow of the Capitol. The mansion had been the home of "Wild Rose" Greenhow, the Washington socialite renowned for her exploits as a Confederate spy. She was an intimate of Dolly Madison and, in the days before and after the commencement of the Civil War, entertained most of the important personages in Washington regardless of their sympathies in the oft-divided capitol. There was never any doubt about Rose's politics; she was a daughter of the South and was never shy in pronouncing her loyalty.

When her husband died accidentally in 1858, she transformed her large mansion into a place where influential people could go to get away from the stresses of the day. Before long, Wild Rose employed a stable of attractive young women who were known euphemistically for their social charms. Her thriving new endeavor put her in position to learn sensitive information from leading government and military officials. She used this capability to great advantage once the war began.

She was eventually arrested as a Confederate spy and imprisoned. Even after she was locked away with her younger daughter, Greenhow continued to convey sensitive Union military information to visitors. Her jailers knew that she continued to transmit information from prison, but they never figured out how she was doing it.

Among her methods of communicating information like troop numbers and armaments was to use a cleverly-devised system of colored knots in her embroidery. The number, order and color of the knots conveyed critical military information to Confederate General Beauregard that was instrumental in the Confederate victory at the first Battle of Manassas. Otto Kahn was so fascinated by Wild Rose's methods that he adopted them in his communications of sensitive information, only he used the precious stones in jewelry.

The mansion's reputation as a place of illicit pleasures and espionage only enhanced its allure. Morgan made it his personal mission to return the somewhat dilapidated structure to its antebellum splendor. He reportedly directed the architects to, "Build a club fit for a gentleman and damn the cost." They took him at his word.

To say that the Lakota was opulent would be a disservice to the concept of opulence. The finest woods were meticulously matched and fitted to create paneled rooms in the "business" portions of the facility. No expense was spared in outfitting the Lakota with the latest electrical equipment; every conference room was equipped with the latest telephones, telegraphs, telexes, and wireless devices. When President McKinley visited the Lakota on the occasion of its grand opening, he remarked enviously that it was better equipped than the White House. To which Morgan reputedly quipped that it was because decisions of greater import were made there. The President did not laugh.

The "social" portion of the mansion was adorned with silk draperies, Persian rugs, Swarovsky crystal and fine Corinthian leather. The exquisite mahogany dining furniture was filled with Royal Doulton bone china, Petruzzi & Branca silver service and Baccarat crystal. The wine cellar boasted some four thousand bottles of vintage wine. The famed cigar room contained a humidor that was so well-stocked that the valet had to use a ladder to reach the upper shelves.

The "Dormitory" or, living quarters, was filled with four-posters and antique armoires. Each room had a scrapbook of famous figures who had had liaisons there. In order to guarantee the efficacy of the Lakota as a place for the discreet transaction of business, Morgan, ever the soul of discretion, realized that a 'private' entrance was necessary. The building behind the Lakota mansion that was situated on Independence Avenue, perpendicular to the Lakota's rear yard, was purchased. An underground corridor between the buildings was installed. This 'private' entrance was used by visitors wishing to enter and depart from the Lakota free from potential observation.

Since its inception the Lakota had served as the locus for the brokering of many deals favorable to the banks. But none was more important or far-reaching than the deal that was currently being brokered. The artfully-constructed election victories by the Democrat Party in 1912 gave them complete control over both houses of Congress and the White House, thereby presenting the Mammon Mob with a unique opportunity to ram their agenda down the country's throat.

Otto and his comrades had set up a command post in the Auric Conference room at the Lakota in order to coordinate the tactics that would bring them the ultimate prize – control over the currency of the United States of America. He and the members of the Mammon Mob firmly believed in the words of one of their esteemed predecessors, Mayer Amschel Rothschild, "Permit me to issue and control the money of a nation, and I care not who makes its laws."

They were on the verge of seeing the enactment of the Federal Reserve Act of 1913. This law would, at long last, give the bankers control over the currency of the United States. The irony of the party of Jefferson steamrolling into law the establishment of an all-powerful central bank was lost on the conspirators.

The key principle in the legislative battle had already been determined. Kuhn Loeb's investment in Woodrow Wilson, the obscure college president from New Jersey, was paying manifold dividends. The plan had been executed perfectly. Take over both houses of Congress and support the candidature of the eventual President and anything was possible.

The incumbent, President Taft, supported establishing a Federal

Reserve Association to implement monetary reform, while challenger, Woodrow Wilson supported the Federal Reserve Bank approach. Unbeknownst to the public, both approaches ceded public control over the currency to private banks - the Federal Reserve Association gave control to one central bank, while the Federal Reserve Bill gave control to twelve regional federal reserve banks. Six of one, half a dozen of the other.

Otto mused over the successful strategy that he had devised while on Jekyll Island three years earlier. Pursuant to this strategy, the National Monetary Commission would propose legislation dubbed the Aldrich Plan. This was a diversion designed to occupy the Congress, but which they all knew would never pass. The Aldrich Plan would propose a National Reserve Association comprised of national and regional banks that would allow for the rapid movement of money from one region to another. Ostensibly, this would address the elasticity problem that plagued the economy and caused the most recent bank panics. However, the Aldrich Plan was destined to be stillborn from the get-go and that was precisely what Mammon wanted.

According to Kahn's scheme, the legislation that the Money Trust craved was the Federal Reserve Act that was drafted at Jekyll Island. Their real goal was enactment of the legislation that they had written in secret, sequestered away like cockroaches avoiding the light. The twofold plan was that while the gadflies and do-gooder legislators were distracted attacking the Aldrich Plan, the Money Trust would establish an educational program to convince the banking community and the public of the merits of the Federal Reserve Act. The plan had worked to perfection.

Otto took special glee in deceiving Congressman Lindbergh into believing that he had defeated the Money Trust. The arrogance of the man, thought Kahn.

The Kuhn Loeb partners had spread their financial support to insure that they would be in position to cash in after the election. Jacob Schiff had funded and nurtured Woodrow Wilson's Democrat campaign. Paul Warburg backed Republican Howard Taft. When the Aldrich Plan was roundly denounced as a creature of Wall Street, the Mammon Mob concluded that Taft would not be able to get the Federal Reserve Act enacted if he were elected.

So, at Otto's instigation, they conjured up Plan B. And, in a stroke of brilliance, Otto appealed to Theodore Roosevelt's massive ego and funded his campaign for the Presidency under the Bull Moose Party. The charismatic former President was most likely to siphon votes away from the Republican incumbent, thereby paving the way for a Wilson victory.

When it looked like the popular and fiercely independent Roosevelt just might pull off the greatest upset in American politics, his campaign was interrupted by an assassin's bullet. Had Roosevelt's campaign not been derailed by an assassination attempt just weeks before the election, Roosevelt might have become the first third party candidate to be elected to the Presidency. But, a bullet that entered his chest, forced hospitalization and interrupted his campaign in the crucial final days doomed his candidacy. The Mammon Mob was relieved, but not surprised.

None of that mattered now, because Wilson had proven particularly compliant, much more so than Roosevelt would have been. To insure that the newly elected President would bend to their wishes, the Mammon Mob installed Colonel Edward Mandel House as Wilson's handler. The inexperienced scholar appreciated the expert guidance of Colonel House. In fact, Wilson had confided to author and Yale Professor Charles Seymour, Jr. that, *"Mr. House is my second personality. He is my independent self. His thoughts and mine are one.*[54]*"*

Immediately after the election, Colonel House had arranged a meeting with the President and Otto, Jacob, and Paul. Warburg explained to Wilson the importance of putting the full faith and credit of the country behind the fiat money issued by the proposed central bank. According to the bankers, the reserve notes would lack credibility and acceptance, unless the United States backed them. After the meeting, the Kuhn Loeb partners were gratified that the President had seen the wisdom of making the reserve notes of the Federal Reserve Bank obligations of the United States.

Wilson later characterized his full faith and credit position as a "compromise," but, ultimately, it was a blatant capitulation to the forces that had gotten him elected.

Colonel House had reported that shortly after the meeting with the bankers that Wilson had dutifully summoned his key legislative advocates for the bill to a meeting in the Oval Office. In House's presence, the President met with Senator J. Hamilton Lewis, the first

Democrat whip ever, and Senator Carter Glass and instructed them to support the principle that the Government would legally honor Federal Reserve notes.

Lewis, the Senator from Illinois, was a strong ally of the President and agreed without hesitation. Senator Glass balked, complaining that there was no government obligation warranting such a drastic measure and that the people expected their currency to be backed by specie.

The President calmly stated that it was not a matter for debate. He had made his decision to compromise on this point in order to save the bill. The public would be mollified by the education program that was going to be released when the bill was signed. The people would find out what was in the bill after it passed. The senators acquiesced to Wilson's mandate to require Federal Government backing of the Federal Reserve currency.

It was now a week before Christmas and time was running out for their carefully-nurtured plans to achieve their Holy Grail. The legislation was bogged down in the Conference Committee. The Republicans, insisting on strong Congressional oversight of any central bank, refused to make any more concessions. The conferees were at an impasse.

The Mammon Mob realized that unless the bill was passed before Congress recessed for the holidays it would lose momentum and possibly never pass. If Congress were allowed to recess, the legislators might be confronted at home by their constituents and pressured to revisit their support for the bill. There were too many variables that could prevent the bill from passing if Congress were allowed to recess without passage. Accordingly, the Mammon Mob resolved to pull out all the stops.

To break the deadlock, Otto had devised a plan that was brilliant in its simplicity. Unfortunately, it violated the rule of gentlemanly tradition that significant legislation would not be considered during the week before the Christmas recess. Otto and the Mammon Mob had no regard for political courtesy, quite the opposite. He instructed the Democrat whip, Senator "Ham" Lewis to suggest to Joseph L. Bristow, his Republican counterpart, that the Conference Committee take some time to reconsider their positions. Bristow, a former postmaster from Kansas, was a first-term Senator and inexperienced in the wiles of Washington.

If the Republicans bought the subterfuge, the Democrats could reconvene the Conference Committee and proceed to the final version of the bill. The plan worked. Otto's sources reported that several key Republicans on the Committee had departed Washington for the holidays. The opportunity for mischief was at hand.

Otto convened a secret meeting of the Democrat conferees at the Lakota to work on the differences between the House and Senate versions. The President had been alerted and had delayed his departure from the Capitol so he would be available to sign the bill passed through the Conference process.

The Lakota's private entrance was extremely busy that evening as Democrat conferees flooded in. A buffet of gourmet food was set out on the sideboards in the Auric Conference Room in anticipation of a lengthy working meeting. The pleasant aroma of coffee in huge urns filled the room, with the promise of copious quantities of caffeine to power the guests through the night.

The last to arrive was Senator Lewis. He had delayed leaving the Capitol until the last minute so that he could post notice of the Conference Committee meeting scheduled for Monday, December 22nd between 1:30 A.M. and 4:30 A.M. After a light repast, Ham Lewis called the meeting to order. Attendance was taken and the minutes noted that a quorum was present. There was no mention in the minutes that no Republicans were present at the meeting of the Conference Committee.

The clerk distributed copies of both the Senate and House versions of the bill along with a memorandum of the differences that had been prepared by the Mammon Mob. With exaggerated formality, Chairman Lewis called each discrepancy for discussion and debate. The minutes reflected a dizzying pace of deliberation, reconciliation and adoption of provisions to the final Act. When the long night ended, some forty differences had been reconciled in a remarkable four-and-a-half minutes per item. The final reconciled bill was sent to the printer at 5 A.M.

As Lewis prepared to leave for a quick shower before heading to the Senate, Otto asked him what he thought of the final product. Lewis smiled, "I think the bill is in excellent shape. It may not be perfect, but the key is to pass it. We can fill in any gaps with minor amendments to the law later."

$ $ $

When Republican Senator Bristow arrived at the floor of the

Senate the next morning, he expected a perfunctory 'get-away day.' He was horrified to see on his desk the final Federal Reserve Act ready for a vote. Vice President Thomas R. Marshall, the former Progressive governor of Indiana, called the assemblage to order from the imperious throne that was the seat of the President of the Senate. He entertained a motion from the 'gentleman from Illinois,' Democrat Senator Ham Lewis, to move the Federal Reserve Act to a vote.

Republican Senator Bristow rose to object. He was red-faced and sputtering as he decried the foul play of the Democrats, arguing that the Republican members of the Conference Committee had not been notified of any meeting, nor had they participated in the reconciliation of the differences between the Senate and House versions. His words echoed through the sparsely occupied chamber. His comments that neither he nor his colleagues had any knowledge of the contents of the bill were duly placed in the Congressional Record. The bill was passed by the Senate by a vote along strict party lines.

$ $ $

Meanwhile in the House, C.A. was in his office packing for the Christmas recess. He unlocked the safe and placed the Hyatt Bible in his briefcase which he rested against his suitcase. Before leaving Washington, he wanted to visit the commissary for a quick breakfast and to present a small token of his appreciation to the chief steward, Reginald Truxton, for his extraordinary service during the session. The young man worked the graveyard shift and was always available with nutritious food whenever C.A. requested a piece of fruit, a ham and cheese sandwich, or a bowl of oatmeal.

With C.A.'s long hours and unpredictable schedule, the Steward's ability to accommodate the Congressman was impressive. Invariably, C.A's late night/early morning orders were accompanied by a thoughtful treat for Blakey, a bone or leftover chop or, on too many occasions, a steak dinner that he been sent back to the kitchen because it did not suit a finicky Congressman. There was a mutual affection between Blakey and Reggie that Lindbergh found heart-warming.

"Let's go see Reggie, boy," Lindbergh said to Blake who wriggled with enthusiasm, tail thumping on the luggage. Needless to say, at 5 A.M. when Lindbergh arrived, the Commissary was virtually deserted. A minimal staff of mostly part-timers loitered near the kitchen waiting for the rush of Congressman that would never come. Most had either left town of were sleeping off the previous night's round of carousing disguised as Christmas celebrations. Leaving his luggage and Blakey in an alcove outside the Commissary, Lindbergh entered.

Reggie welcomed him with a big smile and a gesture that said, 'I'll be right back."

C.A. seated himself and Reggie greeted him with a large, piping hot bowl of his favorite oatmeal. As Reggie approached, Blakey started yelping and rearing up like a mustang in heat. The oatmeal would have to wait. Both men left the table and attended to the ecstatic dog. Reggie slipped a piece of breakfast sausage to his canine friend and was rewarded with copious licks and the ultimate - a rub-my-belly rollover. He obliged Blake with a vigorous petting.

"Sir, I'll take care of this rascal," said Reggie. "Don't let your oatmeal get cold. Go ahead, he's no trouble."

"You know that you spoil him to death. He expects me to rub his belly just like you."

They shared a laugh. As C.A. returned to his table, he heard Blakey growl. To Lindbergh, the sound registered as playful banter with Reggie, rather than the warning that it was.

When C.A. returned to his table, he noticed a man walking away. There was something about his gait that reminded C.A. of something he could not place. The man had close-cropped black hair and was wearing a waiter's uniform. When he turned into the kitchen, C.A. noticed that his right ear had a notch in it like it was missing a portion of the ear. Again, something nagged at him while he savored the oatmeal.

He was halfway through eating, when his thoughts and his breakfast were interrupted by George Norris.

"C.A., I'm sorry to disturb your breakfast, but we need you on the floor. You will not believe what is happening!"

Lindbergh had just placed a spoonful of oatmeal into his mouth. He looked up at his friend with a puzzled look. Certainly nothing important could be happening on the floor. Norris was red-faced, frantic at the situation. He grabbed C.A.'s arm and pulled him toward the door.

"Hold on, tell me what is going on," Lindbergh said,

"The Democrats are moving the Federal Reserve Act. They claim that the conference committee resolved all outstanding issues last night."

"What!?" exclaimed C.A.

Norris shrugged.

"I don't know how. All I know is that they are pushing for a vote as soon as possible. We have to get to the chamber immediately."

C.A. sprang into action. After all the work he put into investigating the Money Trust, writing *Banking, Currency and the Money Trust* and his defeat of the Aldrich Plan, he was incensed at this ploy. He strode over to Reggie.

"Listen, Reggie, I need a favor. Would you please take Blakey and my luggage to the office of the House Doorkeeper? Tell him that I've been called to emergency session and I'll pick them up later today. He knows Blake and he will take good care of him. Thanks."

He was racing after Norris before Reggie could respond 'Yessir.'

As Lindbergh entered the chamber, he realized that his napkin was still tucked under his chin. He ripped it away in disgust. The Speaker was entertaining a motion to adopt the report of the conference committee with respect to the Federal Reserve Act.

C.A. took his seat in the rear of the chamber. He nearly toppled the huge stack of paper on his desk. It was the conference report for the Federal Reserve Act. The phenol smell of the ink made him nauseous. Suddenly, he bent over and vomited into the wastepaper basket at his feet. No one in the chamber noticed; the seats of most of his Republican colleagues were unoccupied.

Flush with anger, he raised his hand and shouted, "Point of information."

C.A. was sweating and his knees buckled slightly when he rose. His tongue and lips tingled. There was an abnormal tightness in his chest. He rocked from side to side as Speaker Clark looked down over his half-spectacles.

"Who said that?"

"Sir, Charles A. Lindbergh, Sr., representing the 6th District of Minnesota. I wish to understand the procedural posture of the matter under consideration."

Clark's voice dripped with condescension as he explained that the conference committee had completed its work and the bill was ready for final consideration. He concluded by declaring, "We will vote on this bill before anyone is allowed to leave for Christmas recess."

Clark hammered his gavel to quell a rising tide of grumbling.

Lindbergh gulped down a glassful of water in an effort to cool the burning in his gut.

"Point of personal privilege, Mr. Speaker."

Clark glared, "The gentleman from Minnesota is trying the chair's patience. What is it?"

Lindbergh wavered in place and blinked furiously to drive the sweat from his eyes.

"I . . . I am not feeling well and may have to leave this session. While I am able, I wish to express my strongest opposition to this highly irregular procedure. This is nothing more than a *congressional Christmas present to the Money Trust.*55"

The chamber turned black for a second, C.A. grabbed his desk for support. He started shivering.

"Furthermore, I vote against any attempt to move the Federal Reserve Act forward. Failing that, I vote 'nay' on this heinous bill."

"You are out of order, Sir," said Clark, who was now standing.

"I will not be silenced," slurred Lindbergh. Inhaling deeply, with great effort, C.A. declared, *"This Act establishes the most gigantic trust on earth...When the President signs this act, the invisible government of the monetary power, proven to exist by the Money Trust investigation, will be legalized....the worst legislative crime of the ages is perpetrated by this banking and currency bill.*56 "

The Congressman from Minnesota collapsed on to his desk with such force that the massive pile of papers fell sending several sheets of paper floating upward.

"Get a doctor," shouted George Norris, "He is not breathing."

$ $ $

"Nurse, get the gastric lavage in here stat before we lose this patient!" shouted Dr. Whitley.

"Here it is, doctor," said nurse Grise, as she unraveled the tubing. Functioning expertly, the team had the tube inserted and suctioning before the cart came to a full stop. Nurse Cavanaugh was announcing the patient's vital signs, her eyebrows furrowed.

"The patient is not responding, doctor."

Dr. Whitley turned to his colleague with a gesture of resignation. The tube attached to the lavage pump was suctioning air.

"BP falling, sir," said the nurse with desperation in her voice.

"May I?" said the short muscular doctor standing adjacent to Dr. Whitley who signaled his assent.

He unbuckled the patient's trousers and probed gently.

"Uretic catheter, please," said the doctor, bowing slightly.

George Norris paced nervously. He could not shake the vision of a blue-faced Lindbergh on a gurney as they rushed him into the emergency room. He tried to reconstruct the events of the attack. One minute his friend was his vibrant self eating breakfast and the next, he was on his back on the House floor barely breathing. Norris bit his lower lip. Although they had been stedfast colleagues in the Insurgency, Norris did not know who to contact about Lindbergh precarious position. What if his friend died? He was the last one to have spoken to him. A deep, weary sadness engulfed him.

A nurse wearing a badge bearing the name Cavanaugh approached him. She looked bone-weary.

"Please follow me, sir."

Norris obeyed. She led him to an office bearing the stenciled name of Dr. Whitley. There were two men inside.

"Congressman Norris, I apologize for the long wait. We had our hands full with this case. This is Dr. Toshi, he said, pointing to the short Asian doctor.

"Normally, we only tell the next of kin, but since the patient is a Congressman we feel compelled to provide you with the information about the patient."

After a slight pause, apparently in expectation of some acknowledgement, receiving none, Dr. Whitley continued, "The patient arrived in extreme duress, presenting symptoms of poisoning."

"What? How could that be? He just left the House Commissary...." Norris was incredulous.

"We had to perform a stomach lavage on him in an attempt to purge the contents of his stomach. The procedure is rough on the esophagus, but we were able to achieve complete evacuation of the contents. Unfortunately, the patient continued to fail. His vitals were nearly undetectable." Whitely paused and took a deep breath.

"Then, divine providence intervened in the form of Dr. Toshi here," said Dr. Whitley.

When Lindbergh regained consciousness, he was in bed at the Casualty Hospital. He had a pounding headache. His neck and stomach were sore. His throat was scratchy as if it had been gouged by one of Big Charley's barkers that were used in the pulp mills to remove bark from logs. Dr. Whitley was standing over him when he opened his eyes.

December 1913: Washington, D.C.

Gradually the ceiling came into focus as Dr. Whitley explained, "We had to perform a stomach lavage on you in an attempt to purge the contents of your stomach. The procedure is rough on the esophagus, but, it will heal in a few days and your voice will return. We believe that you may have been poisoned. We caught it not a moment too soon. Given your overall excellent condition, we expect a complete recovery," said the doctor.

C.A. pantomimed that he wanted pencil and paper. A nurse handed him a pad and took a pencil from the bun behind her head. He wrote, "Poison?"

"Yes, we are not sure of what type; it appears to be Tetrodotoxin. How it got into your system is a mystery. But, you definitely had all the symptoms of TTX poisoning. You are fortunate to be here. One of our visiting professors from Japan recognized this type of poisoning and recommended immediate catheterization to remove urine from your system. One of the symptoms of this type of poison is urine retention. By removing your urine, Dr. Toshi probably saved your life."

Lindbergh scribbled, "Japan?"

"Yes, Dr. Toshi is an eminent physician and toxicologist who has studied the venom of the blue-ringed octopus extensively. He recognized your symptoms from his studies."

"How could I have eaten octopus poison?" wrote C.A., with a disbelieving look.

Dr. Whitley shrugged. "All we know is that you had the symptoms and now they are gone. You should recover fully. You will be discharged as soon as you feel up to traveling. Now, if you have no further questions, I must continue rounding."

Lindbergh nodded weakly.

As soon as the doctor left, a nurse entered and asked if he was ready for a visitor. He wrote, "Depends on who it is," managing a wan smile.

A scurry of nail scratches and whimpering signaled the entrance of Blakey. The dog rushed to his master, licking him furiously. C.A. grinned, thinking that this was the best visitor he could imagine.

The doctor's report to the Speaker stated that Lindbergh had suffered an 'acute attack of indigestion.' The episode was closed.

$ $ $

The Federal Reserve Act was presented to President Wilson for signature at 6 P.M. on December 23rd, 1913.

Within minutes after Woodrow Wilson signed into law the transfer of the country's sovereign power over its currency to a combine of private banks, a messenger delivered a note to Otto Kahn at the Lakota. He opened it and smiled at its contents. It was from Nitro and stated, "Mission accomplished: octopus delivered to St. Charles; Bible secured and delivered to Fire Rescue Station in New York."

Otto motioned for the group to join him. He opened the French doors leading to the balcony and beheld a wondrous scene. Before them was the Capitol Building, lit by a full moon hovering brightly on the horizon. Snowflakes drifted lazily toward the ground. The bells of the Washington Cathedral chimed in the distance and a choir sang Handel's *Messiah*. As if on cue, a butler appeared with a tray of champagne flutes filled with effervescent liquid that seemed to glow magically.

Kahn raised a glass to his comrades and said, "We lift our glasses to celebrate this memorable night. Unto us has been given a wondrous gift. The creature conceived at Jekyll Island has been born this day. His name shall be Wonderful, Counsellor, the mighty Mammon!"

"Here, here," the Mammon Mob intoned blasphemously.

The End of the Beginning

EPILOGUE

C.A. Lindbergh lived a life beset by many challenges and tragedies. From the elation of defeating the Aldrich Plan to the depths of defeat with the passage of the Federal Reserve Act, Lindbergh was buffeted in ways that few American political figures have endured.

Unfortunately for C.A., after the Federal Reserve Act was passed, the hits just kept coming. In the later stages of his life, Lindbergh exhibited the courage of his convictions and was treated brutally by political opponents in Minnesota and in the White House.

Before President Woodrow Wilson signed the Federal Reserve Act into law, Lindbergh could delude himself that both major political parties were not subservient to the Money Trust. Once the act was signed into law, it was no longer deniable.

Back in Little Falls during the autumn of 1915, Lindbergh was in Big Charley's hunting lodge where he commiserated with his loyal friend.

"You know, Big Charley, after five terms in Congress, I am thoroughly disenchanted with Washington. Both parties have sold their souls to Mammon. And, now, it looks certain that the Mammon Mob will use their financial might to drive us into the war in Europe so that they can make obscene profits."

With a disgusted shake of his head, he gulped his drink.

"This will be my last term. I've decided against running for Congress in 1916. Whenever I am in Washington I feel dirty, like I have to take a shower. The whole system has seared my soul," said the disconsolate Congressman.

"I know how you feel, Ridge. A tree can only take so many whacks before it falls." Big Charley sipped his whiskey and regarded his friend with a soulful look.

"However," the big man continued, "I know that the last few years have been tough on you, but President Wilson promised to keep America out of war. The slogan for his re-election campaign is 'He Kept Us Out of War.'"

"Don't you see it, Big Charley?" C.A. protested. "They ignore the best interests of the people and are propelling the country toward a European war that is none of our business. I fear that America will sacrifice many of her sons for no real reason. I despair for our future."

"Despite all this personal turmoil, you can't back away. The stakes are too high. You said it yourself; these fools are angling to involve America in the war in Europe. You need to expose the folly of this war for our country. You are the best one to articulate the case against this war."

"Are you suggesting that I write a book decrying the stupidity of American entry into this 'War to End All Wars,' as the politicians are calling it?" said C.A., pronouncing the label with biting sarcasm.

Big Charley paused, smiled and leaned forward in his chair. His friend was brilliant, but sometimes Charley thought that C.A. could be dense.

"Sure, Ridge, that would be a worthwhile project. However, I believe that what you need is a larger platform to promote your convictions."

Lindbergh scowled at his friend. He knew Big Charley too well. He had something up his sleeve.

"OK, you might as well just come out with it," C.A. chuckled. Weyerhaeuser grinned and raised the whiskey bottle. C.A. nodded and Big Charley poured a healthy dose of Ol' Hiram's medicine.

"So, here's the deal. We think you should run for Governor. " Big Charley knew not to oversell. He would let the idea marinate.

With an early October snow falling on his shoulders, Lindbergh stood on the steps of the capital in Minneapolis to announce his candidacy for Governor of Minnesota. Then a strange thing happened. Before Lindbergh could get his campaign off the ground, the incumbent Democrat Governor, Winfield Hammond died of a stroke on the day before 1915 ended. He was succeeded by the Republican Lieutenant Governor, J.A. Burnquist. Under the circumstances, Lindbergh abandoned his campaign for governor after receiving personal assurances from Burnquist that he would adopt Lindbergh's proposals.

Now, he faced a quandary. Lindbergh had quite vocally expressed his disdain for further service in Congress. Having withdrawn from the gubernatorial race in deference to Burnquist, Lindbergh had few options. Friends persuaded him that his work was more suited to the national approach of the United States Senate.

Somewhat impetuously, C.A. made an ill-fated decision to run in a primary against an incumbent Republican Senator. C.A. was not the only politician who decided to challenge the incumbent; two others joined the fray, splitting Lindbergh's base. In the first defeat of his political career, Lindbergh came in fourth in the primary. Electoral defeat was nothing compared to the tragedy that would soon befall him.

In November, 1916, his oldest daughter, Lilian succumbed to tuberculosis. Lindbergh had spent the last few weeks of her life caring for her. He drove her from Minnesota to the more hospitable climes of California, only to watch helplessly as she passed away.

Although his constituents would have understood it if he never returned to Washington, Lindbergh had one last task to perform in Congress. During the waning weeks of his term, Lindbergh drafted Articles of Impeachment against five members of the Federal Reserve Board. On February 12, 1917, Lindbergh stood in the House of Representatives and used the high privilege of his office to present Articles of Impeachment against Paul Warburg and four other members of the Federal Reserve Board. He accused them of high crimes and misdemeanors by conspiring to violate the Constitution and laws of the United States. C.A. read all fourteen Articles of Impeachment into the record. He identified the overall plan of the conspiracy was *"to force the masses of all mankind into absolute and abject industrial slavery."*

Lindbergh charged that the conspirators, specifically mentioning Warburg and J.P. Morgan, deceived the people of the United States by means of "secret connivance" and "general chicanery" regarding the nature of the Federal Reserve System and by "subterfuge, manipulation and false administration" implemented the law in contravention of the spirit and letter of the law for the special benefit and advantage of the conspirators. Their goal was the establishment of "one gigantic combination with an absolute and complete monopoly" over all National and State banks.

He accused them of holding secret meetings to establish the Citizens Leagues in 45 states and, by means of misrepresentation, secretly and ingeniously promoting their corrupt scheme. Further, by use of "secret, clandestine and underground means," the conspirators utilized news-disribution agencies to deceive the public into accepting their plan to reform the monetary system. The Articles of Impeachment also charged the conspirators of disbanding the Citizens Leagues after passage of the Federal Reserve Act and re-forming them as the United States Chamber of Commerce.

Lindbergh's Articles of Impeachment were sent to Judiciary Committee to die.

$ $ $

The drumbeats for entry into the war in Europe grew louder in the early months of 1917. Although a cynical Lindbergh might have believed otherwise, there were two factors that the Wilson administration used to generate support for a declaration of war against Germany in April 1917. Both were worrisome. At the end of January, German Ambassador Count Johann von Bernstorff notified the United States that Germany intended to implement unrestricted submarine warfare. Pursuant to this policy, all neutral vessels sailing within certain prescribed shipping zones were at risk to attack without warning. The German high command was gambling that they could defeat Britain before the United States could mobilize its forces and become a factor in the European war. In response, President Wilson severed diplomatic relations with Germany.

The second factor was the so-called Zimmerman affair which involved the interception of a telegram from German Foreign Minister Arthur Zimmerman to the German Ambassador in Mexico City. The telegram contained a startling proposal: in return for Mexico's assistance in a war against the United States, Germany promised to help Mexico recover territory that the United States had taken during the Mexican-American war nearly seventy years earlier.

C.A. shook his head as he read the newspaper reporting the President's announcement that the United States had withdrawn its Ambassador from Germany and expelled the German Ambassador to the United States. Lindbergh removed his spectacles and rubbed his eyes with a weary sigh. The inevitable involvement of America in the European war was approaching rapidly just as he had anticipated.

He recalled his conversation with his good friend Big Charley Weyerhaeuser the last time he was in Minnesota. C.A. predicted that Wilson's election slogan that 'He Kept Us Out of War' was an empty promise. The forces of the Money Trust had too much to gain if

America entered the war. Lindbergh felt that armed conflict was inevitable because the 'inner circle' of financiers would reap obscene profits from the impending agony of millions.

Consistent with his prior practice when he was passionate about an issue of major public concern, C.A. wrote a book. He called it, *Why Your Country Is at War and What Happens to You after the War, and Related Subjects.* Invoking his standing as a sovereign citizen, Lindbergh exposed the nefarious forces behind the war fever. Although he pledged his patriotic allegiance to his country despite its foolish choice to enter the war, Lindbergh was vilified by those caught up in the furor for war.

Shortly after the July 1917 release of the book, C.A. was back in Little Falls sitting in a spare office at his brother's law firm when the phone rang.

"Sir, the printer in Washington D.C. is on the phone. He would like to speak to you," said Carrie.

A look of worry creased her face. She had been with Lindbergh for more than a decade and was concerned about the recent threats to the Congressman after the release of his book. Just last week, there had been a story in the *Minnesota Gazette* that an effigy of C.A. Lindbergh had been hung and burned at a war bond rally in Minneapolis. As a safety precaution, she walked to the post office every day to sort through Lindbergh's incoming mail with Ezra the letter carrier to prevent any suspicious packages from reaching the Congressman.

"Hello, Jim, this is C.A. What can I do for you?"

"Sir, there is a gentleman here from the Department of Justice. He has made an unusual request regarding your books. I thought that you should speak to him directly."

"Sure, put him on," said C.A., gesturing to Carrie to shut his door.

"Good morning, Congressman. This is Agent Arthur Skelmo from the Department of Justice, Loyalty section. As I told Jim here, we have orders to impound all copies of the book entitled *Why Your Country Is at War* from this printing plant."

"Agent Skelmo, I am not familiar with the Loyalty section of the Justice Department. Exactly what is it? Is it a formal section of the Department?"

"Well, sir, as you should know, Attorney General Gregory helped draft the Espionage and Sedition Acts which are designed to stop the efforts of those who impair the war effort. The Loyalty section is a group of agents who have volunteered to work with Postmaster General Burleson in curtailing seditious writings. Your book has been designated as a seditious writing."

"By whom?" asked Lindbergh, trying to control the tone of his voice. His outrage over this assault on the First Amendment freedom of speech was approaching the boiling point.

"The President, sir," said Agent Skelmo. "Now, if you'll excuse me, sir, we have a lot of work to do."

C.A. sat holding the dead receiver for a few minutes as he tried to digest this decidedly un-American phone call. Had his country sunk so far into war-frenzy that the Bill of Rights no longer mattered?

"Carrie, get me Bernard Baruch, the chairman of the War Industries Board, on the phone."

After a few minutes, Carrie announced that she had Chairman Baruch on the the line.

"Barney, it's C.A. Lindbergh here. How are you, sir?"

"Fine, fine, busy, you know that coordinating the procurement of war supplies is like herding cats. What's up?"

C.A. reiterated his conversation with Agent Skelmo and asked Baruch whether the President had actually ordered confiscation of his book.

"You meet with him every day. How can this be true?"

"C.A., we are in difficult times. I was with Tommy, er, the President, yesterday and he told me that he had finished your book and was outraged. He ordered General Gregory to confiscate it. However, this morning he told me that, on reflection, he had concluded that it was a masterpiece of patriotic dissent. He mentioned your commitment to the war effort, specifically where you wrote, *'the thing has been done, and however foolish it has been, we must all be foolish and unwise together, and fight for our country.*[57]*'* That is when he suggested that we offer you a position on the W.I.B. Are you interested?"

It was not often that C.A. was speechless, but this sequence of events certainly rendered him unable to respond.

"C.A., are you there? Can you hear me?" said Baruch.

"Yes, I'm here. Yes, I'd be honored to serve my country on the Board," said C.A.

"Capital. Good, good. When can you get to Washington? Listen, I'm late for a meeting. Let my secretary know when you can be here.

She'll make arrangements for your accommodations. And, don't worry; after this nastiness is over, I'll make sure that your books are returned."

That day Agent Skelmo and his over-zealous crew not only confiscated all copies of *Why Your Country Is at War and What Happens to You after the War, and Related Subjects*, they took the printer's file copies. In a fit of autocratic enthusiasm, they also impounded all copies of Lindbergh's book on *Banking, Currency and the Money Trust*. Not content to destroy all copies of both books, they proceeded to throw the printing plates into the refiner's fire for good measure.

Lindbergh was sworn in as a member of the War Industries Board, but, was forced to withdraw two weeks later due to a storm of protests. His daughter Eva wrote, *"The whole thing was disgraceful and I know it hurt father keenly, tho' father would not admit it."*

He never held public office again.

$ $ $

Anne Tracy Morgan was the youngest child of J. P. Morgan and his second wife, Frances Louise Tracy. Although Anne was raised in luxury, she devoted her life to the under-priveleged and downtrodden, often attacking the business class. After the horrible Triangle Shirtwaist Factory fire in New York City, she supported strikes to improve working conditions, especially for women. Anne enlisted the support from other wealthy women and they became known as the mink brigade. To his credit, J. P. Morgan never interfered with his daughter's attacks on his natural allies in the business class.

Anne Tracy Morgan never married. She became intimate friends with decorator and socialite Elsie de Wolfe and theatrical/literary agent Elisabeth Marbury. The three women purchased the Villa Trianon near Versailles, France and were affectionately known as "The Versailles Triumvirate."

During World War I, Ms. Morgan started the American Fund for French Wounded (AFFW) to deliver humanitarian aid to wounded French soldiers and civilians. After the war, she purchased the estate at Blérancourt, and, with the assistance of Anne Murray Dike, converted it into a museum extolling the long history of friendship between

France and the United States.

$ $ $

Unfortunately, C.A. did not live to see his aviator son, Charles A. Lindbergh, Jr., achieve great fame and success by being the first man to fly solo across the Atlantic Ocean in 1927. C.A. Lindbergh died in 1924, but not before he ran for office one last time. In 1918, C.A. ran for Governor and demonstrated great courage under fire, literally.

Due to his strong anti-war stance, his campaign was met with bitter opposition, vitriol, and violence. On one occasion while campaigning in Rock County, the threat of violence was so great that rotten eggs, fire hoses, and yellow paint chased Lindbergh from the podium. At the insistence of the police chief, Lindbergh retreated calmly to his automobile. Irate villains fired shotguns at the departing car. As C.A.'s companions cowered down to the floor of the car, Lindbergh sat ramrod straight and, with characteristic aplomb, said,

"Don't drive so fast, Gunny, they will think we are scared. [58]*"*

Acknowledgements

During a lecture about the Federal Reserve Bank that I attended several years ago, I learned that my belief that the Fed was a government agency was incorrect. The revelation that, in actuality, the Fed was a cartel of privately owned, locally controlled banks so astounded me that I began researching this unusual and seemingly all-powerful entity. After much reading, particularly the *Creature from Jekyll Island* by G. Edward Griffin and *Lindbergh of Minnesota, A Political Biography* by Bruce Larson, I was inspired to write this historical novel to bring to life the genesis of America's central bank.

This book is a prequel to the *Behind Every Great Fortune®* series and fits into the themes of human striving for money, power, and love. The protagonist of *Dread the Fed* is Charles A. Lindbergh, Sr., who would have faded to obscurity, but for the accomplishments of his famous aviator son. However, the senior Lindbergh was an American hero in his own right. As a congressman, he was a champion of the working man and fought with all his might the establishment of a central bank controlled by the Money Trust, or, in today's parlance, the 1%.

Many people helped in the creation of *Dread the Fed,* including some former employees of the Fed who wish to remain anonymous. Unfortunately, time and space preclude me from mentioning all those who assisted me in this project. However, I would be remiss if I did not express special thanks to my editor, Robert Kuncio Raleigh and to my designer Christy King Meares. Both were instrumental in the production of this work. Of course, any mistakes are solely mine. Last, this book would never have been completed without the support and guidance of my devoted wife, Rhonda.

$ $ $

Be on the lookout for Mr. Amoroso's next book which is expected to be released in 2016. Entitled *The Wopper,* it tells the story of how a young Babe Ruth handled the crisis of his father's death on the eve of the 1918 World Series between the Boston Red Sox and the Chicago Cubs. Amid the maelstrom of anti-German war fever, on field violence and a players' strike, the emotionally devastated baseball star faces the most daunting challenge of his life.

We're on social media: Like us on Facebook - *Author Frank Amoroso*; follow us on Twitter-@Ottosmonocle, and please check out our website-www.BehindEveryGreatFortune.com, or, email to Frank@ Behindeverygreat fortune.com. We'd love to hear from you!

Endnotes

1 House Comm. On Currency and Banking, Report of the Committee Appointed Pursuant to House Resolutions 429 and 504 to Investigate the Concentration of Control of Money and Credit, H.R. Rep. No. 1593, 62d Cong., 3d Sess. 56 (1913).
2 *New York Times*, October 3, 1894.
3 Larson, Bruce, *Lindbergh of Minnesota: A Political Biography*, Harcourt Brace Jovanovich, New York, New York (1973) p.22.
4 Haines, Lynn & Dora, *The Lindberghs*, Vanguard Press, New York, New York (1931) p. 47.
5 Lindbergh, Charles A., Sr., *Banking and Currency and the Money Trust*, Omni Publications, Hawthorne, CA (1913) p.22.
6 *Ibid., p. 17.*
7 *Ibid.,* p. 19.
8 *Ibid.*
9 *Ibid.,* p.20.
10 Lawson, *Op. cit.,* p. 206.
11 *Ibid.*
12 *New York Journal-American,* (June 26, 1906) p.1.
13 Schiff, Jacob, Speech to New York Chamber of Commerce, January 4, 1907. Herrick, Myron T., "*The Panic of 1907 and Some of Its Lessons,*" Annals of the American Academy of Political and Social Science (March 1908) pp. 8–25.
14 Shakespeare, William, *Othello,* Act 3, scene 3, p. 8.
15 Baum, L. Frank, *The Lost Princess of Oz,* Books of Wonder, New York, New York (1917) *Dedication.*
16 Steffens, Lincoln, "*Rhode Island: A State For Sale, What Senator Aldrich Represents – A Business Man's Government Founded Upon the Corruption of the Peoples Themselves,*" McClure's Magazine, Vol. XXIV (February 1905) No. 4.
17 Morgan, J. Pierpont, *Art and Progress,* Vol. 4, No. 8 (June, 1913) p. 1005.
18 Gorky, Maxim, "*The City of Mammon: My Impressions of America,*" Appleton's Magazine, VIII, (July-December 1906).
19 *Ibid.*
20 *Ibid.*
21 *Ibid.*
22 Watson, James, E., *As I Knew Them – Memoirs of James E. Watson,* Bobbs-Merrill Company, New York, New York (1936) p. 274.
23 Bolles, Blair, *Tyrant from Illinois,* W. W. Norton & Co., New York, New York (1951) p. 119.
24 Beatty, Jack, *The Rascal King: The Life and Times*, Da Capo Press, Boston, Massachusetts (2007) p.115.
25 Pinchot, Gifford, *The Use of the National Forest Reserves*, U. S. Department of Agriculture, Forest Service (Washington, D.C., 1905) p. 8.
26 *Ibid.,* p. 33.
27 Roosevelt, Theodore, "*In the Louisiana Canebrakes,*" Scribner's Magazine, Vol. 43 (January 1908) p.47.
28 *Ibid.,* p.59.
29 *Ibid.,* pp. 56-58.
30 Rivkin, Steven, R., "*Words and Gestures in an Uncrowded Room: Debating Gives Undergraduates Opportunity To Transform Classroom Into*

Endnotes

Courtroom," Harvard Crimson, May 17, 1956.
31 Jones, V.C., *"Before The Colors Fade: Last Of The Rough Riders,"* American Heritage Magazine, Vol. 20 (August 1969) p. 26.
32 Lindbergh, *Op. cit.,* 10%
33 Lindbergh, *Op. cit.,* 8%
34 Lindbergh, *Op. cit.,* 14%
35 Lindbergh, *Op. cit.,* 8%
36 Lawson, *Op. cit.,* p. 96.
37 Busby, L. White, *Uncle Joe Cannon,* Henry Holt, New York, New York (1927) p. 269.
38 Lawson, *Op. cit.,* p. 114.
39 Lawson, *Op. cit.,* p. 97
40 *New York Times,* October 3, 1894.
41 Chantal, Allan, *Bomb Canada: And Other Unkind Remarks in the American Media,* Athabasca University Press, Edmonton,, Canada (2009) p. 18.
42 Williams, Samuel, M., *A Millionaires' Paradise,* Munsey's Magazine (February 1904) p. 642.
43 Mullins, Eustace, *The Secrets of the Federal Reserve,* Bankers Research Institute, Staunton, Virginia (1991) p. 3.
44 Alexander Hamilton on Banks, Hamilton's Argument On The Constitutionality Of A Bank Of The United States, February, 1791.
45 *Nation Magazine,* Jan. 19, 1911.
46 "Report of Delegates from the New York State Chamber of Commerce to the Monetary Conference in Washington, January 18, 1911," The Federal Reserve System, Vol. 1, 569. The name of the organization, "Business Men's Monetary Reform League," was later changed to the National Citizens' League for the Promotion of a Sound Banking System.
47 Haines, *Op. cit.,* p. 47.
48 Wheeler, Harry A., *The National Citizens' League: A Movement for a Sound Banking System.* The Annals of American Academy, p. 26-29.
49 Deuteronomy, 7:23.
50 Duffy, Peter, *The Deadliest Book Review, The New York Times,* January 16, 2011, p. BR23.
51 *Ibid.*
52 Crozier, Alfred Owen, *U.S. Money Vs. Corporation Currency. "Aldrich Plan.": Wall Street Confessions Great Bank Combine – Primary Source Edition,* The Magnet Company, Cinnintati, Ohio (1912) p. 8.
53 Larson, *Op. cit.,* p. 159.
54 Seymour, Charles, *The Intimate Papers of Colonel House,* vol. I, Houghton Miflin, New York, New York (1926) pp. 114-115.
55 Larson, *Op. cit.,* p. 166.
56 Larson, *Op. cit.,* pp.166-67.
57 Lindbergh, Charles, A. Sr., *Why Your Country Is at War and What Happens to You After the War and Related Subjects* (Washington, D.C., 1917).
58 Larson, *Op. cit.,* p. 237.